SECOND NATURE

SECOND NATURE

GORDON GLASCO

ST. MARTIN'S PRESS
NEW YORK

10 9 8 7 6 5 4 3 2 1
First Edition

Library of Congress Cataloging in Publication Data

Glasco, Gordon.
    Second nature.

    I. Title.
PS3557.L312S4   813'.54   81-8860
ISBN 0-312-70844-0   AACR2

For Pauline, Peri Winkler, and Wendy Smith:
thanks to Michael Denneny

We slept in the bed of flesh
and as flesh met, melting back
to the lost action, we kept
    forgiving, and for good: no questions asked.

"Domesticities"—*Richard Howard*

SECOND NATURE

I

Without turning her head on the pillow, she realized her husband was not lying next to her. Out of habit she slid her hand across the bed and felt the cold, unwrinkled sheet. She could see the curtains drawn together over the bedroom window. The lamp from the garden illuminated the room with a pale, blue-green, iridescent light. But Alan had come home that night, she remembered. An hour after she put the kids to bed, when it was time for them to retire, he had gone to his study to read medical reprints on a surgical procedure he had to perform.

Alexis looked at the digital clock on the bedside table: 2:43. Alarmed, she sat up and swung her legs from the bed. He had said "in a little while," not four and a half hours! With a familiar feeling of panic, she got up and took her bathrobe from the chair. In the past, his occasional absence from home at night had caused her terrible anxiety. But this—his presence in the house, but his absence from bed—felt worse. She turned on the lamp and hurried barefooted into the hallway, pausing at the open door to Chris's bedroom to look in at their eight-year-old son sleeping. In the spill of light down the hallway she could see that he had kicked the sheet to the floor and lay in a sprawl across the bed. She started to go in and draw the sheet over him, but realized it was his way of sleeping on warm summer nights. She moved on and glanced into Karen's bedroom to see their nine-year-old daughter curled up under the bedsheet with only her long black hair—Alan's hair—visible against the white pillow. At the end of the hallway the door to Alan's study was closed. A thin ribbon of light glowed through the crack at the base of the door.

"Alan?" she called softly and opened the door.

Seated in his wingback chair near the desk, Alan looked up, startled from his reading. The floor was littered with medical books and reprints. "I'm almost finished," he said.

"It's after two, honey."

"I know. But I have work to do." He gave her a wary look.

She hesitated, peering at his face, and recalled the tired, worried look she had observed when he came home from the hospital. He had made an effort to play with the children, had even joined them in the pool, but was clearly troubled and preoccupied. During dinner she had looked for an opening to ask him what was wrong, but he was so withdrawn she dared not intrude. The tired, worried look had now deepened to anxious exhaustion. "Alan." She crossed to him, "What's wrong? Is it Berrey again?" Arnold Berrey, the chief hospital administrator, had been on Alan's back for months now.

"No, not that." He sat back with a guarded look of relief. "It's a patient. I've got a difficult case of surgery on my hands."

She stopped a few feet from his chair and drew her bathrobe together, relieved to have an opening at last. "Do you want to talk about it?"

"There's not much to say. It's a patient of Jim Fowler's. I may have to assist him on a pelvic node dissection." A hint of fear flickered through his pale blue eyes.

She stared down at him. Sometimes, especially when he was tired, he looked surprisingly like his father, Max, at least around the eyes. He had inherited deep-set blue eyes from his father's side of the family, Austrian-born Jews. His curly black hair had come, he always said, from both sides. "You've done those before," she said.

"Not recently." He closed the medical reprint in his lap.

"If you're not comfortable with it, let Donald do it." Donald Lindquist, also a general surgeon, was Alan's partner in their new medical corporation. On several occasions he had stood in for Alan, who preferred not to handle what he called the more "morbid" diseases.

"I'm comfortable with it. Besides, the patient asked for me specifically and I agreed. I just have to brush up on the literature, that's all."

Again she stared at him, puzzled, for a moment. The black curls on the top of his head were yanked up and tangled, as if he had been pulling at them. "Do you know the patient?" she asked, then regretted the question, realizing she was back on that all-too-familiar ground of suspicion.

"Indirectly." He tossed the reprint to the nearby desk and shifted in his chair.

The reprint had fallen face-up on the blueprints of their new house, which were spread out across the desk. Under the light of the desklamp, she caught sight of the title: *Lymphatic Spread From Prostatic Cancer.* "Does he have cancer?" she asked, feeling ashamed of herself and curiously relieved to know the patient was not a woman.

Alan looked up, startled. "Probably. From the test results, it looks like a leiomyosarcoma of the prostate. That's very rare for his age group. We may have to do a radical pelvic lymphadenectomy to find out the whole story."

"When will you operate?"

"I don't know. Maybe a week. It's up to Fowler and Karlsberg, the radiologist."

"Sweetheart." She reached out and stroked the top of his head. "Why do you take on these cases? You know how they affect you." After fifteen years of surgery, Alan still had trouble dissociating himself from his patients' suffering, especially in cases of life or death. It was his only professional weakness.

"This time I have no choice in the matter." He sat back stiffly and reached up to smooth his hair.

She looked at the clock on the wall over the filing cabinets. "It's two fifty-five. Why don't you come to bed now?"

"In a few minutes. I've got one more reprint to read."

She noticed the look of withdrawal return to his face and knew it was time to go. "I'll leave the bathroom light on." As she turned towards the door, she caught sight of the turntable in the bookcase behind Alan's chair. A record was turning idly. "You've left the turntable on, honey," she said and crossed to the shelf.

"Oh. I forgot."

She pulled the control lever and stopped the record with the edge of her hand, absently glancing at its label. *Das Lied von der Erde— The Song of the Earth*—a record Alan frequently played when he was in what she called "one of his moods." Occasionally in the last few months she had found him alone in his study, listening to Mahler's melancholy *Song of the Earth.* Alan had once described it to her as music that "celebrates the darker side of life on this earth," words that had startled her, for they didn't sound like Alan. At the door she said, "Good night."

"Good night, honey."

She started down the hallway. *The darker side of life on this earth.* The words made her uneasy every time she saw the record. At Karen's bedroom she paused, remembering the appointment she had made that afternoon with Dr. Evans, her gynecologist. Two days ago, she was already sure she had missed her period. She had waited, though, until today to phone for an appointment, keeping even from Evans her suspicion that she was almost certainly pregnant. In these last two days she had debated with herself whether she should tell Alan. But if she was *not* pregnant, she would have raised his hopes for nothing.

If I go back and tell him now—she thought, but then hesitated, confused by vague feelings of uneasiness and dread.

No, she would not go to bed. She would go to the kitchen, make him a snack, and, between making and delivering it, decide if the time had come to tell him.

Alexis retraced her steps down the hallway. In the front foyer, she turned on a light to see her way through into the dining room. The black-and-white checkered tile felt cold against her bare feet. She remembered the night back in February when she had been awakened by the sound of his car turning down the driveway and Banjo's barking. He had phoned to say he would be delayed at the hospital until ten. She had gone to bed at midnight, feeling helpless and afraid, but had gotten up in anger to meet him as he came through the front door. It was well after one. For the first time—it had happened eight times before, beginning at the end of December—she confronted him and demanded, not asked, *demanded* to know where he had been. He was drunk, which doubled her fury. That night, for the first time in sixteen years of marriage, he had lied to her, saying he had been drinking with members of the hospital staff. It was his lying, not what he was hiding, that had silenced her that night. She remembered wondering where she had failed him, what kind of woman had replaced her, how many more lies it would take to reach the truth. At the kitchen door, she felt along the inside of the wall for the light switch. It was the repetitiousness of it all over the last six months that wearied and emptied her.

The overhead fluorescent lights flickered on. Alan had eaten very little dinner that night, using his diet as an excuse. She opened the refrigerator and began rummaging among the contents—the remains of the chicken that Claire had cooked; yesterday's lemon pie; the children's packaged luncheon meats; orange and grapefruit juice—she went on digging through the five laden shelves. A quart of vodka. Alan never drank on evenings prior to surgery. *She,* if anyone, needed a drink. She stood up, bewildered. Nothing was right, nothing was enough, nothing would hide the fact that she was trying to bribe him into closing the space between them. Absently, she took out the milk and carried it to the counter. She reached for a package of chocolate chip cookies from the overhead cabinet, took a glass from the dishwasher, and poured the milk.

If she told him tonight she had missed her period, if she used that to win him back, and tomorrow the tests proved negative—? The milk rolled up over the rim of the glass and splashed across the counter. Her hand was shaking. She went to the sink for a sponge.

If she *was* pregnant, it had been his idea, not hers. It had come about one night in March. He had come home late again, and she'd found him in the pantry, struggling to open a can of soup. Anticipating another lie, she had let out her frustration and rage in a fit of biting sarcasm. He had tried to embrace her. The feeble guilt in his stumbling effort had made her suddenly hate him. Then he told her he was the target of a nuisance malpractice suit, and from rage she had dissolved into tenderness, seeing him as a frightened man who needed her love and understanding. Later, after they spent themselves in an hour of frantic lovemaking, he had laid his face against hers and, in a voice dragged down by some still unspoken desperation, said, "Alexis, I want another child."

She began mopping the spilled milk from the counter.

After that night, Alan had seemed his old self, attentive, loving, playful with the children; he had even begun to talk of building a new house if they could find a suitable lot. But within ten days, it began again: canceled dinners, nights away from home, strange moody behavior around the house. She hid her anger. Tried to appease him. Then abruptly she came up against a new feeling: of his absence when she was alone with him. She tried to be sympathetic: he was setting up a medical corporation, the new offices were a mess, the new nurses disorganized. Arnold Berrey was on his back trying to force him to increase his days on staff call. One night, as they lay silently in bed together, she gave in to the urge to slide next to him and put her arms around his waist. His body felt sticky, damp with old sweat, and she detected the odor of cologne. Alan did not wear cologne. She moved back to her side of the bed and lay for a long time performing those elaborate mental gymnastics which, in the weeks to follow, would leave her drained. He was seeing another woman, she was sure now. It was then that she had turned into a detective, had used Alan's home directory and raced through the list of possible female patients, realizing as she flipped through the pages that her search was useless and hysterical; Alan had never shown the slightest sexual interest in any of his female patients. A woman among their circle of friends? Outside their circle? That seemed even more frightening.

From the counter, she tossed the sponge into the sink and began arranging cookies on a salad plate.

Where had she failed, what was it about her that repelled him? If she could find and identify the "other woman," she could possibly discover what the woman had that she did not. She could then adapt herself to fit his need. Finally, one night, she had asked him outright if there was another woman. He had denied seeing any other woman, and she had believed him for a while. She had gone back to an old excuse and tricked herself: work pressures at the hospital. The fact was, by now she was simply afraid.

Carrying the plate of cookies in one hand and the glass of milk in the other, she nudged the light switch off with her elbow and started through the dining room.

Then, the second week in May, Alan had phoned from his office to say he had booked rooms at a beach hotel in Laguna for the week-end. Friday afternoon, with the kids sprawled in the back of her station wagon, they had driven down. Once again for a night Alan had seemed himself. They had had sex again for the first time in over six weeks. On their bed, with the covers still up, he had devoured her body with his hands and mouth so roughly, and entered her so forcefully, that she'd found herself staring up at him with amazement rather than desire. It had seemed suddenly like a strenuous athletic event, with Alan racing to the finish line twenty yards ahead of his competitor.

At the door to Alan's study she paused to maneuver the glass of milk onto the cookie plate. Two cookies fell to the floor. She retrieved them. Both hands were shaking. She knew she would look foolish when she opened the door; she didn't dread what he would say so much as what he would think. She couldn't just walk in and say "I think I'm pregnant, Alan." She would have to orchestrate her announcement to win the response she wanted, lead him gently to her own *brighter* side of life on this earth.

"Alan," she said and opened the door at the same time.

He looked up from his reading, this time bewildered. "I thought you went to bed."

"I thought you might be hungry," she said, backing against the door to close it. "You didn't eat your dinner."

He sat back, gave a sigh of resignation, and waited for her un-wanted "care" package. Trying to appear oblivious of his reaction, she padded towards him and made a fuss of clearing a place on the corner of the desk.

"Thanks, honey, but I'm not hungry. I ate a big lunch at the hospital."

Another little lie, she was sure. He never ate big lunches anywhere. She set the milk on the desk and leaned over to rearrange the cookies on the plate. "They're fresh. I just opened the package." After sixteen years of marriage, she had all the little answers to all the *little* questions, from the color of his buttons to the flavor of his favorite cookies. She broke the momentary silence. "You don't have to eat them if you don't want, Alan," she said and realized that her advice was idiotic: of course he didn't and he wouldn't. She finished arranging the cookies, feeling like a fool, grateful that her long auburn hair had fallen over her cheek to conceal the flush in her face.

"I'll drink the milk, honey. You go back to bed."

She straightened up and looked down at him. "I only brought it because I'm concerned, Alan. You look so tired tonight."

"It's this bloody surgery. Fowler wants to wait a week. I don't agree with him."

She had always been able to read his face. It was like a familiar map. Behind the exhaustion, she saw something new: coiled around his intense blue eyes, an expression of fear that made him look older than his thirty-nine—almost forty—years. She hurried to change the subject. "Which reminds me. Next week is your birthday, remember?"

"Yes, I remember. Why does my surgery remind you of that?"

"The kids want to give you a party."

"You know I don't like big parties."

"I didn't say a big party. Just family. Your dad, my parents, maybe a couple of the kids' friends."

"Let's talk about it tomorrow."

"You know, for a man about to turn forty, you look like a tired thirty-two," she said and smiled, feeling suddenly protective. Even if it was a red herring, the news of her missed period would, at least tonight, brighten his mood. "Alan—" she reached over again to smooth his hair with her fingers.

"Please!" He jerked his head back and shouted, "Will you go back to bed and stop *mothering* me?!" For a brief moment, as the shock of the explosion registered, they stared at each other: he with bewilderment, she with astonishment. She started to back away from him, frightened. "Alexis—" He sat forward quickly, grabbed hold of her arms and drew her back. "I didn't mean that." She let him pull her down beside him. "I didn't mean it," he pleaded, embracing her. She folded against him like a limp doll. Until now, all the anger between them had been hers. She closed her eyes, feeling an ache roll up her body, and tentatively touched his sides with the palms of her hands. "Forgive me," he said with his face against her neck, and she knew by the sound of his voice that he was about to cry.

"Alan. What's wrong? Tell me what's happening to you."

After a moment he said, "Nothing's wrong. It's nothing to do with you. I'm just tired tonight. I had a bad day and I'm . . ." he left off and kissed her neck.

This time, she knew he no longer expected her to buy his tired excuse. "Tell me, Alan. Please."

He drew back, holding her by the shoulders, "There's nothing to tell. Go back to bed. Get some sleep. We'll talk in the morning."

With that, she heard the familiar clank of refusal, like a steel door closing. "All right, Alan." Obediently, she rose from her knees and felt his hands slide down her arms.

He kissed her hands. "I'll come in a minute, I promise."

She saw that it was three now. Before closing the door behind her,

7

she looked back and said, "When you finish, turn out the garden lights. I don't need them tonight."

In the bedroom, she lay down on her side of the bed and waited for her body to warm the cold sheet. *Get some sleep.* As if that were possible. In the bathroom there was the bottle of Librium, which Alan had reluctantly given her last month, but there wasn't enough of the night left for that either. Tomorrow morning she would carpool the children to school, do the grocery shopping, help Claire with the housework, lunch with Phoebe, visit her mother, and be back at school by three. She could do it with her eyes closed. After sixteen years, some five-thousand-plus days of marriage, she knew all there was to know about the domestic machinery of a family.

She closed her eyes and took a deep breath, trying to exert mind over matter. She was traveling in circles. Their marriage, their sex life, it was all grinding to a halt, and she couldn't find the cause. She opened her eyes. The ceiling above her glowed with the pale blue-green light from the garden. How often she had lain there, listening to the silence, looking at the . . .

She closed her eyes again, wanting to cry, but even that had become a repetitive pattern. She forced her thoughts back to the beginning: those first eight years of marriage. Sixteen years ago, she had wholeheartedly chosen to be a housewife and a mother; she had openly prided herself on being that. Being Alan's wife and the mother of his children had felt adequate. Until recently, she had not even missed her piano! She had willingly given up her musical ambitions when she married Alan. For the first six years of marriage, until he finished his residency, she had postponed the second half of her life as well: motherhood. She had divided her time between housekeeping and part-time secretarial work to supplement their income. In those first six years, she had gotten used to thinking of herself as a supplement, used to talking of *his* need and *his* love in the same breath. Then came Karen. And a year later, Chris. She was finally a mother and a complete woman. Until the old dream of a third child had awakened, and she'd found she would have to wait, limited once again by their economic realities. But gradually, even that need seemed to dissipate itself in monotony. In the last few years, they had settled into being a two-child family. Until six months ago, when for the first time, she had woken up and found herself having to *fight* for her validation in sex and motherhood.

Alexis opened her eyes. The blue-green light was brighter now.

I am thirty-seven, she thought. I have no business having a child at thirty-seven. It was Alan who had postponed their third child, and it was Alan who had now decided it was time for one. Of course, without question, she *would* have it: she would do anything to bask again in his love.

Suddenly, she sat up on her elbows and thought of something new and frightening: Yes! That's it!

She lay back down and pursued the thought. Perhaps, if there was a cause, it lay in the fact that she had become little more than a mirror. When he looked at her, he saw nothing more exciting, more challenging, than a perfect reflection of himself. Saw himself in everything about her except her moods. Of late, those violent shifts of mood. So far, both she and Alan had written them off as part of her womanly makeup, and therefore forgivable. But were they?

The lights in the garden went out. For a moment she lay quite still in the darkness, listening to the perfect silence. Then she rolled onto her right side away from the center of the bed, closed her eyes, and waited for the bedroom door to open.

At the stainless-steel scrub sink in the corridor outside the operating room, Dr. Alan Stegman brushed the sterilizing Betadine solution into the skin of his left hand. Under the surgical mask, his lips were tense as he concentrated on the vigorous movement of the small, bristled brush. Minutes before, in the doctors' locker room, he had caught sight of his face in the mirror and seen the tension. Dressed now in the green operating room gown, his head covered by the paper OR cap, his mouth and nose hidden behind the mask, only his eyes would be visible during the procedure. But in an operating room, under the glare of lights, the eyes revealed everything.

Alan looked through the window above the scrub sink into the operating room. The patient, Bradford Hollis, was on the operating table in the center of the room. Next to him, George Bass, the anesthesiologist, was preparing to inject his solutions of sodium pentothal and succinyl choline into the plastic diaphragm on Brad's i.v. drip. Jim Fowler, the surgeon, was at the view box across the room, studying the illuminated series of lymphangiograms. Betty Carlin, the scrub nurse, and Angela Hopkins, the circulating nurse, were going about their routine preparations. It was four minutes after seven. The procedure had been scheduled for seven. For once, Alan thought, the orderlies and OR tech staff of West Hollywood General were on time.

He moved the brush to his right hand and thought back two weeks, to the morning when Brad, an X-ray technician employed at West Hollywood General, had taken the X-rays during a surgical procedure Alan was performing. He appeared to be in the prime of health at twenty-nine, but the following day, alarmed by symptoms he had observed weeks before but ignored, Brad had gone to Jim Fowler, one of the top urologists in Los Angeles. Two days later, after initial tests, Fowler had diagnosed sarcoma of the prostate—a rare form of cancer for a man Brad's age. Alan himself only learned of the diagnosis three days later, the afternoon

Brad came to his office on Wilshire Boulevard and informed him of Fowler's findings. By then, as Alan had learned in a phone call to Fowler, the lymphangiogram results had come through; they were inconclusive but suspicious: a filling defect in one of the lymph nodes of the left external iliac chain. That afternoon, Brad had spoken plainly about his own prognosis. He had done X-rays on similar cases and had received limited training as a therapy tech. He knew what lay ahead. Fowler had ordered a complete X-ray survey, a CAT scan, anterio-posterior and lateral chest X-rays, radioactive isotope studies, liver function tests, other blood studies, an acid phosphatase—everything possible to discover the fact or the extent of metastasis. The biopsy of the prostate itself was positive. The question now was whether the primary cancer had spread to the lymph nodes or even beyond. Alan had listened to Brad's self-diagnosis without interruption, knowing before he spoke what the forecast could be. He stared at Brad across the desk. They were both ashen-faced. Brad had tried to sound dispassionately objective, even clinical, but his fear was obvious. He had come, he said, to ask Alan to assist Fowler on the surgery, if the operation took place. At first, Alan had declined and suggested another surgeon. Brad had pleaded, saying there was only one surgeon in Los Angeles he wanted to assist Fowler, one surgeon who could help ease his fear. Reluctantly, Alan had agreed to assist. Fowler, he learned, had already approved of Brad's choice.

Alan released the pressure of his knee on the lever controlling the flow of water into the scrub sink. With both hands raised, he moved to the south door of the operating room and pushed his way in with his shoulder. Betty Carlin, the scrub nurse, came towards him with a sterile towel. "Good morning, doctor." Alan nodded, took the towel, and glanced towards the operating table where Bass was inserting the laryngoscope into Brad's open mouth. The silver-haired anesthesiologist was the best in town, Alan thought to himself with a sense of reassurance. From Bass, he glanced down to Brad's half-draped body under the bright overhead lights. His athletic build, the leanness in the abdominal region, would make entry into the lower pelvic area relatively easy. Betty came towards him again, this time with a sterile surgical gown. He extended his arms and she drew the gown up to his neck. Angela Hopkins, the circulating nurse, was behind him, ready to tie the laces. He glanced quickly around the room, checking the layout of the surgical equipment. Betty had laid the instruments out with her usual exactness. At the head of the table, Bass's anesthesia ventilator was in position, ready to pump the necessary mixture of halothane and oxygen into Brad's lungs. Betty handed him the damp sterile towel to remove the powder from his gloves. "Got it?" he said to Angela over his shoulder as she tied the last lace on the back of his gown.

"Got it."

Alan crossed to the laundry bin, tossed the towel inside, and turned towards Fowler at the illuminated view box. For a moment, in the polished stainless-steel door of a cabinet, he caught sight of his face again. As always, his eyes revealed exactly what he felt. They looked tired and a little frightened. A week ago, the night he sat up late reading medical reprints on leiomyosarcomas of the prostate, Alexis had remarked that at forty he looked like a tired thirty-two. This morning, the strain of the last week had clearly surfaced to his eyes. "What do you think?" Alan joined Fowler before the illuminated photo.

Jim extended his hand and, without touching the surface of the lymphangiogram, pointed to the tiny white dot. "The filling defect is too blurred to be conclusive."

"The other nodes seem to be in good shape," Alan said hopefully, "but Christ, who knows." His breath, he realized, was audible through the mask over his nose and mouth.

"I still find it hard to believe a guy this young could have a metastasized sarcoma of the prostate," Fowler said and looked at Alan. Over the mask, his large brown eyes widened. In his early fifties, Fowler had bushy salt-and-pepper hair that protruded haphazardly from under his surgical cap, giving him a deceptively careless look.

"The percentages for his age are less than one."

"I take it you know him," Fowler said.

"Indirectly. He's done X-rays for me in surgery."

"I see. That explains why he wanted you to assist. He's *seen* how good you are," Fowler smiled behind his mask.

"Maybe." Alan felt his face color.

"He says he has no relatives here in Los Angeles."

"No. I think both parents are dead."

"A shame. I hope he's got friends."

"I'm sure he does. At least here in the hospital." Alan stepped closer to the view box. For probably the twentieth time, his eye traveled up the network of hazy white dots, the negative of Brad's lymphatic system in the pelvis and lower abdomen. On the left external iliac chain his eye stopped on a faintly irregular dot about the size of a pencil eraser. The upper side showed a faint, punched-out mark. To the experienced eye, the pinpoint breakage in the circumference of the node was a clear filling defect. He had seen these defects a hundred times. At best, they were evidence of former lymphatic infections; at worst, the telltale sign of metastasized cancer.

"Ben Greeley is going to make the iodine implant," Fowler said, "he'll scrub in and join us about eight-fifteen." He turned towards the nurses. "Is everything ready?"

"Yes, doctor," Betty Carlin replied, "we're ready when you are."

Fowler and Alan turned from the view box and moved to the operating table. Bass was seated at the head of the table beside the anesthesia ventilator and the electrocardiograph machine. The ventilating tube in Brad's trachea was correctly inserted, Alan noted. He could hear the automatic ventilator pumping gas and oxygen into the lungs. He took his place on Brad's left and Fowler approached on the right. Brad was fixed to the lower end of the table, his legs raised and supported in the low lithotomy position, his body naked down to the protective padding on his legs. The lower end of his pelvis, from the navel to the pubis, had been shaved clean of the black body hair. The youthful, suntanned skin, darkened by the iodine-colored Betadine prepping solution, reflected the intense white lights overhead with an amber sheen.

"Let's go," Fowler said and nodded to Alan. Holding the blade end of the scalpel, Betty slapped the handle into the palm of Fowler's gloved hand. With a single, automatic movement of the arm, he brought the blade over quickly in an arc and touched the razor-sharp point to the center of the body just below the navel. At the instant of contact, as the blade pierced the skin and released a tiny spurt of blood that welled up vermillion around the sparkling stainless-steel blade, a picture flashed before Alan's mind: *Bradford Hollis in surgical greens coming towards him down a hospital corridor, smiling.*

Alan instantly thrust the picture from his mind as Fowler drew the scalpel blade down the center of Brad's lower pelvis, parting the skin, leaving a scarlet ribbon of blood in its wake. The movement took less than five seconds and penetrated the skin and outer tissue one eighth of an inch.

Following at once behind Fowler's incision, Alan applied sponges to absorb the initial flow of blood. Fowler handed Betty the scalpel and received the metal cautering rod. Alan followed the point of Fowler's cautery down the bleeding edge of the incision with his fingers. The cautery point touched the tiny ends of the vessels, searing off the flow of blood from the small bleeders. The smell of burning blood and flesh filtered through Alan's mask. He felt himself flinch, realizing where the odor came from. He glanced up, wondering if his reaction had been noticed. Working behind Fowler, he began applying clamps to the larger bleeders. As he reached the lower end of the incision, he realized his hand was trembling slightly.

Before them lay the lower midline incision, cauterized, clamped, and sponged clean of blood. Now their task was to separate the surface tissue which, in Brad's case, involved minimal adipose tissue. Working together with Fowler in blunt dissection, Alan placed his fingers on the edge of the tissue and started down.

"Don't worry, Alan, I won't call your office or your home," Brad had said that afternoon in the Golden Dragon, where they had gone to

*have a drink. "Which means you'll have to contact me." He had tilted
back the upholstered restaurant chair, grinning, and put his hand on the
lower part of his stomach to keep from belching.* Alan realized his fingers were resting, at that moment, in the soft tissue at the exact spot
where Brad had touched his stomach.

*"You know the conditions: no demands." His own voice, he remem-
bered, had been strained and edgy.*

With Fowler leading, they had begun dividing the rectus sheath in
the infraumbilical area at the midline. Alan's mind raced over the sta-
tistics he had reviewed the day before. Though prostate tumors were
rare in men Brad's age, the survival rate was good after radical pelvic
lymphadenectomy, followed by radiation therapy. Provided there was no
extensive metastasis. No clear metastasis had showed up in Brad's tests
during the last week. But, of course . . .

· In a reflex bucking spasm, Brad arched his back in a quick jerk.

"Let's give more relaxation," Fowler said, easing up with his fingers.

The spasm in Brad's body had shot through Alan's arm.

"I'll take him down more," Bass said, turning to the ventilator to
introduce the appropriate amount of gas flow into the lungs.

When they finished dividing the rectus sheath with sharp dissection,
Fowler called for the spade-shaped retractors and they began dividing
the tough fibers of the rectus muscles laterally.

*A week ago Alexis had found him preparing for this procedure in
the middle of the night. He had wanted to tell her everything then, but
hadn't been able to find the right words. She had seemed so fragile and
vulnerable that night. Besides, he still hoped that it was a passing thing,
that he would break free.*

The entire incision was initially complete, lined with clamps, hemo-
stats, and sponges. They had reached the crucial threshold: the thin
pinkish-grey peritoneal membrane surrounding the abdominal contents.

Alan glanced at the clock on the opposite wall as the minute hand
reached 7:54. They were moving at a good speed, without complica-
tions. Fowler extended his right hand. The scrub nurse slapped the
handle end of the scalpel firmly into his glove. They would now begin
entrance into the retroperitoneal space.

*Whatever muddle he had made of his personal life in the last six
months, in surgery he was beyond reproach. The best. The long years of
study, his exacting determination to school his mind, eyes, and hands in
faultless coordination, had paid off. This morning, more than most mornings, he felt rewarded.*

"We'll ligate the vas, Betty," Fowler returned the scalpel he was
using and was, in turn, presented with the necessary suture.

His father, Max, until he retired after the death of Sarah, had run

13

*his small jewelry shop in Detroit with that same meticulous and method-
ical attention to detail. Like Max, he had often thought of himself as a
kind of watch repairman for the human body.*

To give better exposure and retraction of the spermatic cord,
Fowler looped the suture around the vas and carefully drew it back.
Alan held the cord in place while Fowler completed the ligation.

*At the end of February, Alan had taken his new BMW to the dealer
on Olympic Boulevard to have a faulty turn signal repaired. The shop
manager said it would be a three-hour wait, so he had taken the afternoon off and now had three hours to kill. It was raining, one of those
dull gray midwinter rains. Against his better judgment, he'd phoned
Brad at the hospital. Up to then their meetings had been accidental en-
counters at the hospital. As a staff surgeon he had at first found it awkward and conspicuous to socialize with a young OR tech. But occasionally they had lunched together in the hospital cafeteria.*

Again, Fowler called for a scalpel, this time to begin the alternating
sharp and blunt dissection to expose the retroperitoneal and pelvic vessels.

*It was Brad's open, easy-going personality, his combination of hu-
mor and intelligence, that had first attracted Alan. Later, when Brad's
interest in him had begun to look and feel like affection, he had reasoned
away his discomfort by telling himself it was merely the experience, new
for him, of male friendship. Brad in turn had opened himself even further, had begun assuming interests that were not there. His affection began to look very much like need, a need that was frightening in its
implications. By accident he had discovered that Brad was gay—in a
conversation he overheard between two OR techs. After that, he had
refused to associate with him. He withdrew, investing Brad with moral
threats and sexual dangers that he soon learned belonged only to himself.
In Brad's absence, he awakened to a new, but not entirely unfamiliar
need. He spoke to Brad and they met again, but still only as "friends."
It was then, torn in opposing directions, that he had begun his secret
life: an occasional drink in a restaurant after work, two hours stolen
from Alexis for dinner with Brad. On several occasions, drinks and dinners. And finally that afternoon visit to Brad's apartment. To cover his
tracks he had been forced to lie: to the world, to Alexis, even to himself.*

"So far, he looks clean," Fowler said, working in blunt dissection
near the iliac.

"So far," Alan said, softly.

From here on, of course, there was the possibility, slim as it was,
that the primary tumor would have already metastasized into the vessels
and organs of the lower pelvic area, or even further up. They were approaching the suspicious node on the left external iliac chain.

Alan spoke silently to the figure lying open before him, "You're okay, Brad. You're going to be just fine." He felt a trickle of sweat run down along his hairline at the side of his face. Angela Hopkins reached up to pat it dry with a cloth.

That afternoon in February he had stood in the rain on Olympic Boulevard waiting for Brad's green MG to appear, feeling successively nervous, guilty, confused, and afraid. But he had also felt a kind of defiance. For the first time he had taken the initiative. When Brad arrived he tried to sound like the innocent victim of a mechanical failure, but neither of them was fooled. His heart was beating too fast, he was hyperventilating. In their drive up San Vicente Boulevard to a hardware store, between complaining about shopping in the rain and accepting Brad's offer to dry off in his apartment, he had felt like a man teetering on the edge of a cliff.

"Sure. Why not," had been his reply to Brad's offer. And with those words, he realized they had both crossed over. The idiotic, self-effacing game of pretending he was nothing more than tolerantly comfortable with Brad's homosexuality ended. He was no longer the inaccessible, invulnerable surgeon with a wife and two children; he was open game, and anything could happen.

They had passed the external iliac artery without evidence of metastatic disease. The filling defect in the lymphangiogram had been merely the residue of a former infection. They were now at the iliac and hypogastric arteries and nerves. "Alan," Fowler said, running his finger over the lymph nodes along one of the branches of the internal iliac artery, "feel this."

Alan saw the evidence with his eyes before he felt it with his fingers: small, disfigured gray lymph nodes clinging to the artery. For a moment, staring at the nodes, he felt his blood go hot. He touched the chain of nodes, rolled it gently between his fingers. It was hard.

"Christ," Fowler said.

"It could be just lymphoid hyperplasia," Alan said shakily. Fowler moved the artery to the side. It was there, matted to the branches of the internal iliac artery, a cluster of distorted lymph nodes resembling the surface of a cauliflower, with the mottling clearly visible. Alan saw it was densely fixed to the pelvic wall. "It's all the way down, Jim," he said with a quiver in his voice, "into the pelvic bone."

"I'll take a node and send it to pathology for a frozen section." Fowler turned to the scrub nurse for a scalpel.

The thing was, of course, that Brad had taken things too far, had formed an attachment over the months that Alan could never reciprocate. He had made it clear to Brad from the beginning: he would never go beyond a casual sexual involvement. By then, he had accepted the fact that he was bisexual. But as far as love and emotional involvement were concerned, those belonged exclusively to Alexis. He was clear about that. When time and the responsibilities of his other life permitted, he could indulge in sex with Brad. About that he had never lied. True, the frontier between sex and emotion had blurred off and on, and his hours with Brad had crowded into those he owed to Alexis, but always the horizons had cleared afterwards. If he had kept anything from Brad in their mutual agreement, it was his conviction, indeed his hope, that sooner or later even this period of bisexuality would pass.

As the circulating nurse left the operating table with the container holding the dissected node, Fowler turned back and said, "Since we're dealing now with the pelvic bone wall, Alan, I'm going to wait for the biopsy before going on."

Alan glanced at the clock. It was 8:16. The biopsy would take fifteen minutes. If it came back positive, the metastasis would have reached an unresectable area of the body. He felt the sweat break from his forehead. They would now wait.

He had seen them die before. He had done this massive, desperate surgery to sweep the abdomen clean of every affected lymph node, only to discover in the process that the disease had spread beyond control. Then the long suturing of organs and tissues, knowing that the malignancy was still inside, growing. Then the months, sometimes just weeks, of radiation and chemotherapy, a battle against hopeless odds, as the body wasted away, corrupted beyond recognition. The days of drugged agony and finally the blessing of death.

Before the verdict came back from pathology, he knew Bradford Hollis would die.

Alan glanced at the clock. Seven minutes had passed. The room, he noticed, was silent. Normally the doctors and nurses engaged in casual conversation while they waited for results from pathology. He looked down at Brad's handsome young face with the plastic tube running from his nose. Today, no one felt like speaking. He stood by the table and felt the blood drain from his face.

He remembered standing beside Brad's bed that afternoon in April, pulling on his trousers, dressing to leave.

"You're playing games, Alan." Brad lay on the bed, naked. They had just made another faltering attempt at sex. "You want the best of both possible worlds. You take what you want from both Alexis and me, but you end up giving only half to either."

"I told you not to expect an emotional relationship with me," he replied angrily, "you're pushing now, and I can't go that far!"

"You forget, you came to me after you and Alexis returned from Laguna."

"You forget there's one difference between us. I'm bisexual, I'm married, and I intend to stay that way." The defensive ring in his voice had sounded hollow.

"Miss Hopkins," Fowler broke the silence, "while we're waiting you might as well phone down and have them start the pre-op on my next patient. I don't think we'll be here much longer."

"Yes, doctor." Angela turned towards the phone on the wall.

Alan closed his eyes and tried to think of something hopeful.

"Well, look! What do you think?" he put his hand on Alexis's shoulder and drew her close to him. They were standing on the edge of the lot he had bought that day, in Coldwater Canyon, in the hills overlooking the city. He knew it was the lot she wanted. Spread out below them were the lights of West Hollywood, just beginning to twinkle in the early evening. Further west, clearly visible, was the island of Catalina, rising out of a pink and gold sea, silhouetted against the setting sun.

What had he hoped to gain that afternoon?

"Alan." She had turned and pressed her body against his, "I love it." She kissed his chest through his shirt. "And I love you." He held her close, thinking how different the feeling of her embrace was from Brad's, comforting in a way that his could never be, reassuring and somehow right.

He would give her anything to hold back the avalanche of guilt and fear, the sinking sense of defeat threatening the life they had built together for sixteen years. The important thing, then and now, was to build permanently, to hold.

Over the sound of the anesthesia ventilator came the soft ring of the telephone attached to the operating room wall. Angela Hopkins hurried to answer it. Fowler looked up at Alan. In the tense brown eyes, Alan read the verdict before it was given.

"Doctor Fowler, it's Doctor Kern in pathology."

From his place next to the operating table, Fowler addressed the microphone box on the wall. "This is Jim Fowler in surgery, Walt."

"I have our findings on the Hollis frozen section specimen you sent down, Jim." Walt Kern's rasping voice filled the room.

"Right," Fowler called.

"The node I have here is largely displaced by sheets of cells with bizarre nuclei, frequent abnormal mitoses . . ." Kern went on monotonously with his list of technical findings.

"I didn't plan on it being this way, Alan," Brad had said not a month ago. "What are we going to do?"

"Stop seeing each other. That's the fair thing, for both of us."

"Yeah. That's the fair thing."

"I'm sorry."

As he had opened the passenger door to get out, Brad had turned and said, "I'm sorry for you, Alan. The truth is, you're gay. You know it, I know it, and one day Alexis will know it. You'll both have to face it. I hope you have somebody around for you then."

"That's right, Jim," Kern concluded over the loudspeaker, "this tumor is identical to the biopsy from the prostate. A very aggressive looking leiomyosarcoma."

Alan stared down at the sheath of malignant lymph nodes matted to the wall of Brad's pelvis, felt his own insides sink with guilt and helplessness.

"Thanks, Walt," Fowler said, looking across the table at Alan. "In that case, there's no point in continuing on with the lymphadenectomy, Alan. He's unresectable."

Alan nodded. "Yes." His voice caught in his throat. "I agree."

"Miss Hopkins, we're not going to proceed with the iodine implantation, either. Phone Doctor Greeley and inform him that we're closing up. He won't have to scrub in."

"Yes, doctor."

"Let's begin, Alan." He turned to Betty Carlin for the necessary needle and suture.

It would come slowly. He had seen it many times. Weeks of relentless disintegration, drugged delirium followed by unbearable periods of lucidity, corrupting from the inside out. The sight of a young body like Brad's lying on a hospital bed, mauled by the slow, silent collapse of its cells. As always, death alters the way one looks back on life. His own inability to love Brad now felt like an irretrievable failure.

As they closed the surgical wound, Alan's mind emptied of everything but the slow, meticulous movements of the procedure, which now seemed mechanical.

"Sponge and needle count," Fowler said, drawing the retention suture of number two nylon through the fascia tissue.

"Twelve sponges, six needles," Betty counted off the line of sponges and needles on the Mayo stand.

"Correct," Alan replied.

"We'll close the fascia with interrupted figure-of-eight sutures of number zero closure," Fowler said.

They continued on, packing and then irrigating the wound with sterile water, closing it with a number one Prolene running stitch to the fascia.

The clock read 8:55. They had been in surgery almost two hours.

"We've lost less than three hundred cc's," Fowler said, referring to Brad's blood. He pressed closed the last inch of the incision. Alan centered the stapling gun and sent the metal clip into the skin.

It was finished.

Alan turned from the table in silence, moved towards the north door to the operating room, and paused to remove his gloves. They were flecked with blood. He pulled them off, threw them into the plastic-lined waste barrel, and pushed his way out into the corridor. Ignoring the nurses preparing surgical instruments in the anteroom outside, he walked hurriedly towards the door leading to the outside corridor.

Back in February, he had awakened to find himself in a labyrinth. He had wandered into it blindly. Now (and the thought that suddenly crossed his mind horrified him), there was no way out. He had first seen it as a small, narrow sexual labyrinth, one that he could wander in and out of alone; but he was wrong. In the darkness, he had come up against both a man's body and a man's emotions, and somehow they had become inseparable.

At the far end of the eighth-floor corridor, Alan pushed open the door into the men's public toilet and went inside. It was empty. In the metal-walled stall he slid the latch closed and turned, leaning his weight against the tiled wall above the toilet. The tiles were cold against his open palms.

He had failed Brad, first as another human being, then as a doctor.

Against all his instincts, he began to cry, watching the drops stir the water in the bowl below.

II

Alexis Stegman edged her Buick station wagon into the slot in the crowded hospital parking lot, turned off the ignition, and got out quickly. Her watch said 12:26. Alan had said to meet him on the eighth floor at 12:30. He would take an hour and a half off (the half hour she had pleaded for), and they would have lunch a few blocks away at Ma Maison on Melrose Avenue. He had agreed to that much of a celebration on his fortieth birthday.

As she dashed across the parking lot she smiled to herself. She had argued in favor of a small barbecue in the backyard with family present, the children, Alan's father, Max, who lived in retirement in Santa Monica, and her own parents, Helen and Chris senior, the Bateses, as Alan called them. Alan had refused, saying he preferred an evening at home with her and the kids, a preference which secretly pleased her.

But the real reason for her smile was inside her. Moving with a swift, exuberant stride towards the tinted doors, Alexis caught sight of her reflection in the glass. Her hair needed combing, but she looked good. Alan liked her hair that way: long, swept back from her face, a little wild. She pushed open the doors and started across the hospital lobby towards the elevators.

Well, she did feel wonderful, and if you feel wonderful, you often look wonderful. For the first time in six months, she was *sure* she looked wonderful. Alan would be upstairs at the reception desk. She would take his arm in the elevator on the way down, and he would look at her, suspecting something. She would tell him in the middle of lunch—that was her plan—warmed by the slow, cool rush from a very good, very dry bottle of Montrachet: "I'm pregnant again."

Reaching the elevators, she gave the button a decisive jab with her finger. That's the way the scenario *should* read: the two of them caught up together in a moment of shared realization, a moment of completeness like the one ten years ago when she had met him at the door and announced that she was pregnant with their first child.

In the elevator, Alexis looked down at the blank square of gray industrial carpet. Sometimes, she wondered if she'd ever really grown up.

With a ting from the bell overhead, the doors opened, and she stepped briskly into the corridor, heading for the nurse's station midway down.

Six days before, she had gone to Dr. Evans, her gynecologist, convinced. "It's in the oven, Joe," she said, walking through his office door. The test results were positive. She was glad she had refrained from telling Alan the night before, glad she decided to wait a week and tell him on his fortieth birthday.

Alexis approached a nurse bending over paper at the reception desk. The nurse looked up, assessing her, "Can I help you?" She was middle-aged, with thick-lensed silver-framed glasses. Alexis saw her worry register in the softly powdered face set under the gray, primly curled hair. Alan was nowhere in sight.

"Will you page Doctor Stegman for me, please?"

"Are you a patient?" the nurse smiled, but her voice was patronizing.

"No. I'm Mrs. Stegman," she replied with a pleasant feeling of sudden power. She detested the hierarchical game of status. It had infected every hospital Alan had worked in.

"Oh," the face relaxed into an expression of cozy camaraderie, "I'm Mrs. Klaus. How nice to meet you," she smiled broadly now, revealing a gleaming gold bridge.

"Thanks," Alexis glanced at the clock above Mrs. Klaus. It was 12:36. Alan had said 12:30. He was precise about time and, as usual, she was a few minutes late. "Would you page my husband for me?"

"Certainly. But I haven't seen him all morning, not since he went into surgery at seven. He usually makes rounds after surgery, but today he didn't."

"He said he'd meet me here at twelve-thirty."

"Well now, you just relax, Mrs. Stegman, and I'll track him down for you." Klaus turned to the microphone on her desk. She was being treated like a silly distraught child, an overanxious housewife. Alexis's jaw tightened.

"Paging Doctor Stegman," he voice floated cheerfully through the corridor, "Doctor Stegman to reception, please." It was soft, disconcertingly female, considering the face it came from, even seductive.

Alexis looked down the corridor in both directions. From the left end, two orderlies in green were wheeling a gurney towards them. On it lay a figure draped in a white sheet.

I must compose myself, she thought. Look cheerful. It's his birthday. I want this child and he wants it, too. She suddenly found herself about to say a prayer. She had not prayed for years, not since she was twenty-one. Not since she had cut herself off from the Catholic Church. The Church belonged to her childhood: restricting, crushing, suffocating with its notions of sin and guilt. When she had finally broken its hold over her, she left behind a childhood weighed down by a morbid preoccupation with punishment.

"Mrs. Stegman," the nurse asked from behind the counter, "are you all right?"

"What?" she turned quickly. Despite her attempt to check it, a note of shrillness crept into her voice, "Oh, yes. I'm fine." She turned her gaze towards the gurney approaching down the corridor. Lying on it, covered to the neck by a sheet, was a young man. He was startlingly handsome, she noticed, in his late twenties, with short dark hair, a finely boned nose, and long dark lashes that hovered, partly raised, over heavily drugged eyes. His face was ashen. As he passed, Alexis was suddenly moved by the shocking convergence of beauty and death.

"Mrs. Stegman?"

"Yes?" She turned to see Klaus staring at her curiously.

"I'll page him one more time. If that fails, we'll have him beeped."

"Thank you."

"Are you all right?"

She crossed to the opposite wall and pretended to stare at a Picasso lithograph. "I'm perfectly fine."

"Doctor Stegman to reception, please." The voice was now testy and flat, "Doctor Stegman to reception."

Reflected in the glass over the lithograph Alexis saw the nurse staring at her. Feeling suddenly foolish, she moved away towards the next picture, a rather second-rate Buffet print.

He had promised to meet her at 12:30 sharp. She had booked a table for 12:45. Alan was never late for appointments he intended to keep. Her heart sank at the thought that it was beginning all over again: the forgotten appointments, the excuses, and the lies.

"That's a very pretty scarf," said Mrs. Klaus from the counter.

Alexis lowered her hand, aware that she had been fidgeting with the scarf around her neck. "Thank you." She forced a smile and crossed the corridor to a Miro lithograph.

Damn him, she thought. She saw the top half of her body in the glass covering the picture. Like a ridiculous schoolgirl, she had debated all morning what she would wear. What would please Alan? She had decided on the gray pantsuit and the white blouse with the St. Laurent scarf he had given her on the way to Laguna. Alan liked that combination. And, of course, she dressed for Alan. *No, honey, I disagree.* She suddenly recalled Phoebe Amherst's words two weeks ago. *Your opinion of yourself is controlled entirely by Alan's good favor.*

"Now, you just relax, Mrs. Stegman," Klaus's voice was patronizing again. Alexis turned to see her staring over the top of her glasses, as if Alexis had become a patient in the interval. "I'm sure we can track him down for you. I'll have him beeped, is what I'll do."

On a sudden angry impulse, Alexis started away towards the elevators, "No," she called back, "don't bother. Just say I was here at twelve-thirty."

"Certainly! I'd be glad to!" The mocking note of triumph in the woman's voice propelled Alexis faster down the corridor.

She was back to square one again.

Her eyes blurred and began to burn.

She reached the elevator, pressed the "down" button, and stepped back as her eyes flooded.

She had conceived this child, she realized, to win back Alan's loyalty. She was not young enough to have a child. If she had a child at thirty-seven, she would be fifty-five before she could begin doing any of the things she wanted to do for herself! Angrily, she opened her purse and dug down to the bottom for the half-empty pack of Dorals she had kept there for the last month. She had given up cigarettes at the beginning of May. Another gesture to please Alan, who hated her smoking habit. Fishing out a damp, stale cigarette, she put it into her mouth and returned to her purse for a match.

At breakfast, she had teased him about his record for keeping appointments with her. *That's all in the past,* he had said with a look of genuine repentance, *so let's forget it, okay?* Sometimes it only took a word from him to change her entire climate.

She struck the match and put it to the end of the cigarette. Her eye caught a sign screwed to the corridor wall: "No Smoking. Violators will be Prosecuted." She drew in deep and felt the dizzying rush of nicotine and defiance in her blood. At least she had not surrendered *all* of her power to choose! She took a second drag and then felt suddenly nauseated.

No. She wouldn't lunch alone. She'd drive over to her mother's in Beverly Hills and have lunch with *her.* But Helen would read her mood, question her again about Alan, and there would be a scene. Her mother sometimes made her feel like a sixteen-year-old. No, she'd go pick up Phoebe, hit the Rodeo Drive shops, and spend some of Alan's goddamn money. Buy something for herself—something outrageously, uselessly, flagrantly sexy.

She took a third drag and listened to the faint rush of air up the elevator shaft.

"Alexis." Alan's voice came towards her down the corridor.

Startled, she turned to see him walking hurriedly towards her. He carried his blue blazer slung over his shoulder. His pale blue shirt was unbuttoned at the collar, his tie hanging unknotted over his chest. "Where were you?" Her voice was an octave too high for detachment.

"With a patient. I'm sorry." He came up beside her as the elevator door glided open. "Come on." He took her elbow to guide her into the elevator. "Let's get out of here." Then he noticed the cigarette in her hand. "You're smoking again." His left arm went out to stop the elevator door from closing.

"Just one." She looked around quickly for an ashtray, but there was none.

"You'll have to carry it." He guided her into the elevator. The young nurse inside fixed her with a disapproving stare. Guiltily she turned to face the doors, holding the cigarette upright between her thumb and index finger. As they started down, a thick gray streamer of smoke rose into the air. *Why do cigarettes always give off the most smoke in situations like this?* she thought. They went down in silence. Beside her, Alan stood staring down at the floor. The withdrawn expression on his face had nothing to do with her cigarette, she realized. The doors opened on the ground floor. Without waiting for her, Alan stepped off the elevator. She followed, dropping the cigarette on the polished terrazzo floor.

At the head of the steps leading down the landscaped quadrangle outside the front entrance, Alan stopped. "Let's take your car."

She caught up with him. "Alan—" She took his arm, "What's wrong? Are you all right?"

"I'm fine," he said in the same voice she had just used for Mrs. Klaus's question. He reached up and ran his fingers through his unkempt hair. The tension in his face relaxed a bit. He took her shoulder and drew her close to him. "Why do you ask?"

"Well, to begin with—" She could think of only one all-inclusive answer to his question. "I love you."

With his hand on her shoulder, pressing her close to his side, they started down the steps. "I thought you were going to tell me I look forty today."

He would have preferred a table in the corner of the garden area. Michel, the restaurant's maître d', seated them at a prominent center table instead, surrounded on all sides by people from the film and TV industry. By 1:15, the restaurant's little outdoor garden was alive with the brittle, effervescent chatter of actors, actresses, producers, and agents.

"I guess I should have chosen someplace quieter," Alexis said, glancing at him across the table. The waiter brought the salads they had ordered.

"This is fine, sweetheart. I'm having a good time, really." He forced a smile. Brad's—he went on with the thought running through his head at that moment—radiation therapy would begin as soon as the wound would tolerate it.

"You're not. You're hating every minute of this."

"I had a rough morning. I'll be all right by the main course."

"Do you want to tell me about it?"

"Not particularly. We're supposed to be celebrating my entry into middle age."

"*Middle* age?" Her mouth turned suddenly in a graceful, teasing smile. "How many eighty-year-old men do you know?"

Despite himself, Alan chuckled. "Not many. My dad."

"Max is only seventy-six." Behind the smile, her hazel eyes looked worried and puzzled.

He looked down, toying with a piece of watercress.

"You've been crying, haven't you, Alan?"

He tensed but kept his eyes averted. "Why do you say that?"

"Your eyes. I can tell. What happened?"

His face reddened. "I assisted on a case this morning. It turned out to be unresectable. I got upset. The guy's going to die, and it could have been prevented—" He left off as his throat tightened.

"Excuse me, sir." The waiter was beside their table with the bottle of Montrachet Alan had ordered. He poured a little into Alan's glass.

"Not for me, thank you," Alan moved the glass towards Alexis, "Here. You taste."

"It's your birthday, Alan." She looked at him, bewildered, "Can't you have one glass?"

He recalled the nights he had come home to her, drunk. "Sure. But just one. I have patients this afternoon." He lifted the glass and tasted the chilled wine. "It's very good," he nodded to the waiter.

"Your father phoned this morning," she said when the waiter had filled their glasses and gone.

"How is he?"

"Fine. He called to wish you happy birthday."

"He remembered?"

"Yes. I think he was disappointed you weren't coming out to see him."

"I'll drive out on the weekend."

"We'll both go. I haven't seen Max for weeks. We'll take the kids. He loves playing with them."

"Yes. We'll do that," he said, fidgeting with his fork. Again, silence descended between them.

Max. As always, the picture of his aging father brought a sense of pain. Max had spent the last seven years in a retirement home in Santa Monica. After Sarah's death nine years before, he had hung onto the small house in Detroit, trying to keep up the pretense that life would go on as it had for over forty-five years of marriage. Two years later, when they visited him, Alan had been appalled by his father's life and surroundings. He was a sad, confused old man who hid his grief by withdrawing from the world completely. He ate his meager supper out of cans and sat for hours, absently watching television. That September, Alan moved Max to California, placing him in a comfortable rest home on the coast and augmenting his monthly pension. He paid the bills for his father's retirement but otherwise avoided him. Except for the monthly visit.

"I should have invited him for dinner tonight," he said finally.

"I don't think he would have been comfortable."

"Meaning?" He looked up at Alexis, piqued.

"I would have had to invite mother and daddy. You remember how uncomfortable he was at my parents' house last Christmas."

"How could I forget?" Alexis's Catholic parents, particularly her mother, were arch but silent anti-Semites. Always had been.

"Aside from his visits to my parents, your father's visits to our home have never been altogether successful, either," she retorted with sudden and surprising vehemence.

They both sat in silence as the busboy began removing their salad plates. The anger he saw in Alexis's face as she pretended to watch the surrounding tables had nothing to do with Max or her parents, he knew. Since they had met at the hospital, everything both of them wanted to say had remained coiled up and lost in small talk. In the delicate features of her face he saw hurt and frustration, and behind that, an aborted expectation. "Alexis." He said her name like an apology.

Quickly, almost automatically, she turned, and their eyes locked. He sent out a silent look of appeal through his eyes.

"Alan," she smiled tentatively, "I have a birthday present for you."

"Oh?" he returned her smile.

She leaned forward, stretched her arm across the table, and put her hand over his. "It's something you asked for some months ago."

He tried to think of what he had asked for in the last few months. "I don't know. What?"

"Think back."

He felt silly. "What? Season tickets to the bowl?"

Her fingers dug into the top of his hand. "No. A child. I'm pregnant."

He heard and understood, but could not comprehend her words at first. There was a sudden feeling of stillness around him. He went on looking at her face, watching the changes in it as she waited for him to respond.

Back in March, or was it April? The night he had come home late from Brad's apartment, the second time he had gotten drunk enough to have sex with Brad. The chronology of his fall was confused. He remembered the kitchen pantry, the can of soup, the feeling of panic and guilt as the liquor began to wear off, remembered her voice from the kitchen: "If you spent more time at home, you might learn how to run a fucking electric can opener!" That night, driving home, he had wondered if he was really inflicting all this pain on Alexis for the mere pleasure of sex, or was his investment larger than he wanted to admit? Was he kidding himself? That night, realizing he could very well destroy their whole world if he went on like this with Brad, he asked Alexis to give them another child.

Alan opened his mouth to speak, but nothing came out. He closed it, swallowed, then opened it again. All that came out was air.

Alexis gave him an understanding grin.

"You're sure?" His voice cracked in mid-word.

"Yes. Positive." She relaxed her grip on his hand.

"When?"

"At the end of next February."

"How long have you known?"

"A week, ten days."

"Did you go to Evans?"

"Of course."

"You had tests?"

"Of course I had tests."

"And they came out positive?"

"*Alan*," she laughed.

"I'll be damned." He felt light-headed. A tingle of foolish pleasure ran through his body. "Why didn't you tell me before?"

"I thought it would make a nice birthday present."

"Oh."

"Does it?"

"Yes." He slipped his hand from hers and encircled her fingers tightly. "Sure!"

"Do you mean that?"

"I mean it." He sat up, breathed in the sweet air of the outdoor garden, and was aware suddenly of sunlight and vivid color. "I mean it more than you know."

She knit her brow, puzzled and amused.

"Let's get the check and go," he said.

"Go where?"

"Anywhere. Driving. They've started the foundation on the house."

"Don't you have patients to see?"

"They can wait. Donald can see them." He raised his hand and signaled the waiter for the check.

Twenty minutes later they were heading west on Sunset Boulevard through Beverly Hills, Alan at the wheel of Alexis's car. At Coldwater Canyon Boulevard, he made a right turn and started up the winding drive into the hills. Alexis slid across the seat and leaned against Alan's shoulder, giving in to her feeling of romance, childish though it seemed. "I'll bet you a Spanish tiled bathroom with a sunken tub that this one's a boy." She reached down to stroke Alan's leg.

"You're on. Of course, if you lose, it's an old-fashioned tub on rusty legs, and a noisy toilet with a pull chain."

She looked up at him, realizing that, inadvertently or not, he had described the bathroom of his childhood home in Detroit. "You know what?"

"What?"

"I think you'd rather have a girl."

"What makes you say that?"

"Oh, a hunch, that's all."

"Boys have more troubles than girls."

"Bullshit."

"But they do," he laughed, "just look at me."

At the top of the canyon, they turned off the main road onto the narrow lane leading to the new lot. It circled the eastern side of the canyon, making a series of winding, hairpin turns along the bluff of the hillside. From her passenger window, Alexis looked down into the green basin of the canyon. Here and there, nestled among tall eucalyptus trees, palms, and California oaks, she could see the shingled roofs of large, rambling houses. She moved closer to the door and rolled down the window, letting a cool gust of canyon air fill the car, relishing the momentary sensation of security and peace. It was a good sign when she and Alan were comfortable with silence. Perhaps now, with the prospect of another child, Alan would come back full circle to his former self. Their first two children, born scarcely a year apart, had had a galvanizing effect on their marriage, she remembered with pleasure. Until Karen's birth, Alan had seemed as much wedded to his work as to her. Then abruptly, with a tiny, screaming infant crying and sleeping in the same room with them at night, he had turned into a proud father. More than that, a warm and protective lover and husband. The birth of Karen one year, and of Chris the next, had profoundly affected Alan. A confidence in himself suddenly surfaced that had not been there before. He had taken to playing his roles of father and husband with such pride that he sometimes went to excess, spoiling the children with lavish presents one day, disciplining them rigidly the next; and with her, he became so protective and solicitous that, at times, she felt possessed. A feeling she admittedly enjoyed, for with it came the comfort of blissful security. Back then, she had liked him being the tall, dark, quiet, sensuous, and responsible man who made the decisions and reprimanded her when she failed in one of her duties. Perhaps now, with the birth of another child, they could be as they had been at the beginning, together at the center of a single life.

"By the way." Alan drew up against the curb in front of the vacant lot. "You'd better talk to Cagle about adding a nursery to the plans." He turned off the ignition, winked at her, and got out.

Strange, she thought, how the patterns repeat themselves. Ten years ago, it was a question of where they were going to put Karen's crib at night, in the bedroom with them or in the living room.

Alexis got out and hurried across the dry, rocky sandstone clearing to catch up with Alan. Already, she knew where the nursery would go: there, down at the southeastern corner of the lot, extending out from their own bedroom. She caught up with Alan in the center of the lot, at the place where they had stood on the day he bought it, and took hold of his hand. His grip was firm around her fingers.

"Look," he said and pointed towards the southwest side of the lot. Some thirty feet away, amid a network of honeycombed dirt mounds, a small, diligent gopher was at work, burrowing into the soil. "I'd hoped we'd be leaving those destructive little fuckers behind."

Alexis smiled. "Do you think he followed us here from Benedict Canyon?"

"If he has, rest assured he brought his wife and three children."

"Well," she said, "we can't leave everything behind."

Alan entered the elevator and pressed the basement button, which would take him down to the oncology ward. He would have thirty minutes with Brad before his meeting with Arnold Berrey and the administrative staff.

He opened the manila folder containing Brad's medical report, which he had requested from the intensive care unit, where Brad had been for the last eight days. The X-ray results indicated extensive metastasis in the lungs which, combined with the findings from his liver and kidney tests, clearly indicated that the end was near. Sixteen days ago, after two months of outpatient radiation and chemotherapy, he had been admitted to the hospital for an intense, last-ditch dosage of both

therapies. Neither had worked. In a matter of days, the metastasis had
spread with vicious speed through his liver and kidneys, and then into
the lungs. Eight days ago, Jeff Marks, his oncologist, had terminated
therapy and moved him into the ICU. In a matter of days, it would be
over.

At the basement level, Alan turned down the corridor towards
the oncology ward.

In the two months Brad had been an outpatient, Alan had seen
him during each of his visits to the hospital and occasionally outside.
With each visit, the prognosis worsened. Brad demanded to know the
truth, being alone responsible for himself, and Marks concealed nothing: at this rate, three, maybe four months. Even then, Brad knew that
Marks was stretching it. Knew it, finally, with his own eyes, when the
side effects of the disease reached the surface of his handsome body.
Then, Alan observed a remarkable change in Brad: the sight of his
disease burned away what vanity he had left, leaving him with a frank,
unalloyed sense of humor that gave no room for self-pity. What life
there was left for him had to be lived in the present, he once said, and
for itself: career, future ambitions of what he could become, the motherlode of happiness he might one day discover if he lived long enough, no
longer meant "jack shit," in his words. With raw clarity, he saw that
love, if only this one-sided kind, was the only thing worth living for,
if only for two months. Knowing that it could not be returned in kind,
that he now had nothing to lose, he allowed himself to let go and love.
There was, of course, no question any longer of sex; he no longer had
the physical strength to desire. For both of them, the knowledge that it
was coming to an end had a strangely freeing effect on their relationship.
For Alan, it meant he could give all that he had to give: compassion,
affection, and his own kind of love, which was closer to intimate friendship than to Brad's limitless commitment. For the first time, there was
no need for demands.

Scotty Oates was behind the counter at the nurse's station, bent
over a stack of papers on the desk, her plump rear end outlined tightly
under the white uniform skirt. "Napping?" Alan asked with forced humor. It was 4:46.

"Doctor Stegman!" she turned quickly, "I was beginning to wonder
if you were going to show today!"

"Did I ever fail you, Scotty?" He winked at her. It was part of his
camouflage to play this flirtatious game with Scotty and the other oncology nurses, hopefully confirming in their minds that he was entirely
straight. He had been at the game now for two months. In the last two
weeks it had begun to disgust him, like a cheap lie. But it was a habit
he could not break. "Where's Cathy?"

"Down in the ICU, I imagine. If I had known you were coming,

I'd have—" She left off abruptly, observing the grave look on his face.

"I'll catch you later, Scotty." He tapped the manila folder on the counter top and moved off.

"Sure."

In the last two weeks, he had found himself praying that the end would come soon, that he would walk into the ICU and be told that Brad's suffering was over. In the last eight days, he had prayed openly to himself for a mercifully swift end.

Cathy Riddel, the trim young blonde in charge of the ICU, was in the monitoring station adjoining the ward. She looked up from one of the screens as Alan came in. "Doctor Stegman." She acknowledged him with a nod.

"Thanks for sending this up, Cathy." He handed her the manila folder. "How is he?"

"Bad. He's been going in and out of coma since last night. I don't think he can hang on much longer."

Alan looked through the glass partition separating the monitoring station from the ICU. Across the small ward, separated from the patients on either side by partially drawn curtains, Brad lay on a bed with the sheet drawn up to his chest. An i.v. was connected to his left arm, an oxygen mask over his nose and mouth. "Is he awake now?"

"He's conscious, but that's about all."

Alan turned from the monitoring station into the corridor, followed by Cathy. "Has Doctor Marks been in?"

"About an hour ago."

"Does Brad know where it's at now?"

"I think so." She looked at him meaningfully. "In fact, I think he asked Doctor Marks to go ahead and pull the plug."

"I see." Alan turned away towards the ICU with a sinking feeling. He had wanted the end to come; but now faced with the fact, his instincts rebelled at this senseless loss of young life. He moved down the line of six beds and stopped at the foot of the fourth. The curtains had been drawn forward from the wall to conceal Brad from the patients around him. Besides the i.v. drip and the oxygen mask, there was an EKG machine connected to his heart through wires taped to his chest. Under the oxygen mask, his face was deeply bronzed from the excess of bile following the failure of his liver functions. Alan moved alongside the bed. The dehydrated skin lay on his face and skull like a thin, translucent parchment, dry and necrotic. A noticeable odor hung around him, the sweet odor of death.

For an instant, Alan recalled the nightmarish pictures of Nazi war camp victims he had seen in books in his parents' house. His uncle Aaron had died in Auschwitz. The pictures had haunted him as a boy.

It was astonishing how suffering could so rapidly alter a face. The last two weeks of excruciating pain had carved Brad's face into a permanent expression of agony, even in sleep.

"Brad," Alan said softly. At the sound of his voice, Brad stirred and forced his eyes to open slightly. They were deeply jaundiced and glazed, thinly laced with bright red broken blood vessels. His left eye had formed a cataract. Alan knew he could see him now only faintly, as a blurred image.

Brad made a sound under his mask, broken by catarrh in the trachea.

"I'm right here," Alan settled his hand on Brad's arm, "just lie still." His gaze quickly covered the fresh evidence of decay that had appeared since yesterday. More hair had fallen away, leaving the top of the skull virtually bald. The sores at the corners of his mouth had enlarged. The eyebrows were gone now, the face strangely unreal in its nakedness. The eyes were further engorged in their sockets from the fluid pressure.

Again, under the mask, Brad tried to speak.

"You don't have to talk." Alan touched his shoulder. "I'm with you. Just rest now."

Brad's eyes opened further, staring up at him with urgent appeal. He murmured something under his mask.

"Wait." He squeezed Brad's arm and leaned down to his ear, "I'll remove the mask, Brad." Aware that Cathy was in the adjoining monitoring station and could observe them through the glass partition, he stepped quickly to the foot of the bed and drew the curtain closed. He returned to the head of the bed and gently removed the oxygen mask. "Take your time," he said shakily, "I'm not going anywhere."

The tension in Brad's body relaxed. The mouth remained open. His tongue moved, trying to form a word. His gaze, fixed on the ceiling, seemed to be focused on something far away.

Alan leaned down, "What is it? Tell me." He spoke slowly, enunciating his words clearly.

Slowly, Brad's mouth shaped the words. "Stop it," he whispered.

"Stop what?" Alan's voice stuck in his throat. He knew the answer before he asked the question.

Brad's face visibly altered. For an instant, an expression of intense concentration drew his features together, as though a thought of immense importance was forming in his mind. His lips came together. "Pain," he said, quite clearly.

"It's bad, isn't it?" Alan said. A shock ran through his body. He felt suddenly inane.

Motionless, riveting him with glazed eyes, Brad continued to stare at him, questioning.

"I'll ask them to give you something more for it," Alan stumbled on, dreading what he saw forming in Brad's eyes.

The tip of his tongue found its way to the roof of his mouth. "No," he said hoarsely. His teeth closed, and the muscles of his neck strained as he lifted his chin to form another word. "Stop it," he blurted out, a streak of awful pain running through his eyes. "Finish," he said faintly, then his head fell back against the pillow. He continued to stare up at him, the question burning in his eyes.

For a moment, as he hurriedly weighed the consequences of his answer, Alan said nothing. Under the law, removing a patient's support systems while he still had possession of his brain functions or, worse, administering a lethal dose of morphine into the i.v. drip, was euthanasia: murder. Brad could sign a court order to have his supports turned off, but that would take time. If he himself did either . . . Then he thought of the recent malpractice suit in which he had been blamelessly named. "I'll do what I can," he said, touching Brad's arm, and tried to give an encouraging smile as his face went scarlet.

Brad, though, read the look in his face. His eyes, Alan saw, altered suddenly with a look of shock and realization, then suddenly narrowed with helpless acceptance. The air spilled out of his lungs with a rush. He lay in silence, the look of acceptance flickering away like a lamp in a dense, rolling fog. Quickly, Alan replaced the oxygen mask over his mouth and nose.

The lids of Brad's eyes, he saw, remained partly open, fixed. For an instant, he thought that death had come. He took Brad's wrist and felt the slow, feeble pulse. Counting the pulse beat, he fought to grab hold of a single thought, but thoughts seemed to fly at him from all directions, crazily, without coherence: thoughts and mental pictures of moments spent together in the last eight months, which now seemed unreal, thoughts coiled up with feelings of guilt, grief and, as they drained away inside him, finally of loss.

He released Brad's wrist and looked down at his face. The eyes under the lids remained fixed.

"Here! Catch!" Brad ran along the sloping beach at Santa Monica. He ran down along the water's edge, his head turned back and his right arm crooked along his side with the bright yellow Frisbee in his hand. He had spent an hour trying to teach him how to throw the plastic disk; he had refused to give up trying. A broad smile broke over his face as he sent the disk sailing gracefully through the air. The water on his body reflected the sunlight. The tide was running in and a wave broke over his legs, sending up white spray. His laughter was lost over the rush of surf up the beach . . .

Alan went on staring at the death mask on the pillow, the face now of a ninety-year-old man. If he had now lapsed into a coma, and if the coma was deep enough, he would not return. If he had lapsed into coma, it was likely that he had simply given up.

Alan closed his eyes. If he were in coma, and the coma were deep enough, there would be brain death. With brain death, they would be free to turn off the oxygen and the i.v. Death would come quickly, painlessly after that.

He opened his eyes. From the pillow, Brad went on looking up under half-closed lids. The last expression of his conscious life was fixed in his eyes, in his whole face: the bewildered acceptance of Alan's refusal.

"I—" He broke off and made an inane gesture with his hand, realizing it was pointless now. Except for the mechanics of permissions and procedures, it was over. He turned away towards the foot of the bed and drew the curtains back. He felt numb, knowing nonetheless that the numbness was a temporary bandage over a deep sense of shame. Behind the glass partition, Cathy glanced up at him from a monitoring machine. He motioned for her to join him in the corridor.

"I want an electroencephalogram run on Mr. Hollis, Cathy," he said outside the ICU. "I want it done now. He's gone into coma. This time, I suspect he's suffered brain death."

"Yes, doctor." She looked at him with relief. "I'll have it done right now."

"I'll wait."

It took fourteen minutes for the nurses and techs to assemble the equipment in the ICU and complete the test. Alan spent the time pacing the corridor outside the ward, planning his next move. If the encephalograph showed no brain pulse, Brad was legally dead. He was a short distance down the corridor when Cathy came out of the ICU. He knew the results before she spoke. "The graph is negative," she said. "Nothing. No brain waves whatsoever."

"There's no point, then, in going on with this."

"No, doctor. None."

"In that case, I'm going to phone Dr. Marks and ask him to turn off Brad's machinery." He started towards the phone located in the nurses' station.

After two transfers, the in-house operator located Marks in the radiology unit on the far side of the basement level. "Doctor Marks here," his brittle voice came on the line.

"Hello, Jeff. This is Alan Stegman."

"Yes, Alan."

"I'm over in the ICU. I just left Mr. Hollis. While I was with him, he lapsed back into coma. I took the liberty of running an EEG on him. This time, there's definite brain death," he left off, waiting for Marks to draw the obvious conclusion.

There was a long pause at the other end. Alan could sense the irritation building. For the last two months, Marks had resented his presence in the oncology section, seeing it as meddling interference. "I take it you're suggesting that we pull the plug," Marks said, finally.

"Yes, Jeff, I am."

There was a short pause. Alan could hear Jeff's breath through the receiver, slow and thoughtful. "You and Hollis are pretty close, aren't you?"

Alan leaned forward against the desk. "How so?"

"The other day, when I was with him, he thought I was you. You know how they sometimes hallucinate."

"So?" Alan tensed.

"He asked me to hold him, Alan." The voice was suddenly icy. "Asked *you,* that is."

In the silence that followed, Alan realized that his hands were shaking. "People in his situation are scared," he said, knowing that his sudden panic was audible, that Marks had intentionally led him around this detour. "They need a lot of care sometimes."

"And sometimes, as you know, they have periods of delirium, when they talk."

Alan reached up and touched the beads of sweat forming on his forehead. "So?"

"All I'm saying is, I can understand why you might want to step in, order an EEG, and pull the plug."

The sarcasm in Marks's voice left Alan momentarily breathless. Then, repressing a rush of anger, he said, "He was conscious when I went in. He asked me to do it, stop the pain. *He* wanted it done, not me."

"You, of course, know what Mr. Hollis wants more than I do."

The pettiness of the remark, the maliciousness of it, pushed Alan's anger to the flash point. He checked himself and said in a level voice, "He's beyond wanting anything at this point. He's had brain death. At this point, it's the humane thing to do. It's also perfectly legal and within the bounds of hospital policy."

"I know the law, Alan, and I also know hospital policy regarding physicians and patients."

"Will you, or will you not?"

"I'll come over and read the EEG and make my decision on the basis of that." There was an impatient sigh through the receiver. "I'm sorry, Alan. I think I understand your feelings in this matter. I'm very sorry for you. And for Brad, of course."

Slowly, Alan lowered the receiver to the hook. For a moment he stood at the desk watching the red second hand sweep around the face of the clock on the wall in front of him, paralyzed, turning the professional, ethical, and human pieces of Marks's puzzle in his mind. They did not fit together. Quickly, he left the nurse's station and started towards the ICU. Halfway down the corridor, he stopped.

Why was he going back? There was nothing more he could do. Marks, he knew, would turn off the oxygen and remove the i.v. In a matter of hours, overnight at worst, Brad would be free. He had done what Brad asked. It was over.

He turned back down the corridor in the direction of the elevators. He saw nothing of the corridor around him, though, only the picture of Brad's face and its expression of defeated acceptance. The numbness, he realized, had lifted. He walked slowly, feeling a terrific pull backwards, trying to grasp the full meaning of what he had not done.

III

"Of course, Phoebe! Bring him, we'd be delighted!" Alexis balanced the telephone receiver on her shoulder and went back to folding the dripping lettuce leaves in layers of paper towels on the kitchen counter.

"You're sure it won't throw your seating arrangement?"

"*Seating* arrangement?" She glanced over her shoulder and rolled her eyes in mock despair at Claire, busy shaping meat patties on the butcher-block table, "*Phoebe*, this is an outdoor, do-it-yourself hamburger barbecue birthday party for kids. There is no seating arrangement and one more mouth won't make a damn bit of difference."

Claire's wrinkled, thin face tightened into a dour smile. After four years of working for them as housekeeper, cook, and nanny, Claire no longer hid her opinions about people who frequented the Stegman house. Her verdicts, often delivered with a single word, were unfailingly accurate and afterwards quoted by both Alexis and Alan with a great deal of laughter. Phoebe Amherst, four times married and three times divorced, and Alexis's best friend, had been judged "fast and loose" by Claire. The judgment had become Alan's nickname for her.

Phoebe went on, "He's actually quite intelligent and, I might add, attractive. Charles says he's brilliant. He's a psychiatrist and Alan ought to meet him; he's attached to West Hollywood General."

"Sounds like you're the one who's attached, Phoebe."

"Don't be silly, he's a friend. Charles and I both adore him. You're so fucking suspicious of me, Alex."

"Well, I've known you for what, ten years? You go through men like water through a colander."

"Bitch," she laughed, then cleared her throat, "I'll have you know Charles and I are madly happy. Dr. Milner is a friend. *Only.* And besides—" She broke off, chuckling.

"Besides what?"

"Nothing."

Alexis glanced up at the clock over the sink, "Listen sweetheart, it's twelve forty-five and you're due here at one. Now you and Charles bring this Dr. Miller along. I have twelve adults, and one more won't matter."

"Thirteen? You're not superstitious, are you?"

"Plus fourteen kids."

"Oh, Jesus."

"You can bring Miller or not, I don't care. But I've got to get off the phone! I've got six heads of lettuce to dry!"

"Milner. His name is *Milner.*"

"Milner, whatever."

"*Hamburgers,* Alex? God, honey, you're slipping."

"Buzz off, Phoebe. This is a kid's party. Alan planned it, and Alan's doing the cooking."

"*Alan?!*" she exclaimed, laughing.

"That's right. It was Alan's idea, and he told Karen she could have anything to eat she wanted for her birthday. He's done the whole thing himself, and if you make any jokes about the menu, I'll kill you."

"The big master surgeon *cooking*?! My my, wonders never cease."

"Neither do you," Alexis said, now exasperated. "We'll talk when you get here. Good-bye." She hung up without waiting. "That woman." She dropped a handful of wet lettuce leaves on the layer of paper towel and covered it with a second layer. "We're now up to thirteen adults, Claire. How's the meat holding out?"

"We've got enough meat here for General Patton's Fifth Army. All I can say is, when Doctor Stegman shops, he *shops.*"

Alexis smiled to herself. The day before, Alan had sat down with Claire and worked out a menu. Hamburgers, potato salad, french fries, and coleslaw. Everything Karen had ordered. "Just like McDonald's," Claire had remarked dryly, referring to the countless Saturdays she had driven the kids down to their favorite McDonald's in West Hollywood for lunch. And of course there would be ice cream, three different flavors, and the eight-pound chocolate cake Alan had ordered from Delights by David.

From behind her came the sound of Claire's high, brittle voice, humming the tune of her favorite song, "Happy Days Are Here Again." When Claire sang, Alexis always knew that all was well with the Stegmans. Alexis smiled. The stern, rather prim housekeeper had been with them for four years. A widow without children, she had become like a surrogate mother to the kids, strict in her discipline and unbounded in her affection. Since moving into the rooms above the garage, she had tacitly become a member of the family. Aware of the strain that had pulled Alan and Alexis apart since the previous February, Claire had often prevented Alexis from acting rashly by giving quiet, commonsense advice.

"By the way," Claire interrupted her reverie, "while you were on the phone with Mrs. Amherst, I heard the doctor arrive with his father. They're out in back by the pool."

"Good God, forty minutes to Santa Monica and back," Alexis grabbed a dish towel to dry her hands. "He must have broken every traffic law in the book." She threw the towel on the counter and started towards the dining room door. "I'll go out and see if Max wants something to drink."

In the dining room at the long table she paused to shift the bowl of carnations an inch towards the center and saw her face reflected in the polished surface. Over the past month, certainly in the last two weeks, she had been conscious of a wonderful rightness of things. The euphoria, she realized, was reflected in her face.

In the last month, Alan had not missed a single meal with the family. Last night, they had sat with the children until well after eight. Last night, for the second time in two weeks, they had made love, falling asleep well after midnight. She had awakened before dawn with a need to stretch, but relishing the pleasure of Alan's arms wrapped snugly around her stomach, she chose not to wake him and went back to sleep.

Alexis hurried down the corridor into the black-and-white-tiled foyer, made a mental note to shift the ailing schefflera onto the back terrace, and continued into the living room. Instinctively, her eye scanned the surfaces of the glass-topped coffee table and the end tables at either side of the sofa. Her mother, of course, would note their dustless readiness. Alexis smiled to herself, recalling the housewife she had seen in a TV ad for furniture polish. Of course, her mother would also cast a cold eye on the new painting above the Regency chest that she and Alan had bought the week before, a large canvas of bright crimson, ultramarine blue, and pale cadmium yellow pools.

She stopped momentarily at the mirror to run her fingers through her hair and flatten the collar of her blouse. Before he had left to pick Max up at the retirement home in Santa Monica, Alan had passed her in the corridor outside their bedroom and turned to embrace her from behind, pressing his hands against her stomach. "You look great; how do you manage it?"

"Manage what?" She had turned her face and kissed his chin.

"To get into these slacks." He moved his hands over the faint bulge.

She chuckled softly, "I moved the buttons, you prick. It shows, doesn't it?"

"A little." He bit the nape of her neck, "Are you comfortable?"

"Very," she squirmed, goosefleshed from his nibble.

Alexis leaned closer to the mirror to look down at her stomach. She grimaced. In two or three months she would be too big for slacks or jeans. A fortune in Weight Watchers down the drain. Back to muu-muus or loose shifts; but no maternity dresses, not this time. With both Karen and Chris she had blown up overnight like a Flemish housewife in a Breughel painting. All stomach and no hips. Another one of nature's little female cruelties.

Passing the big black Steinway grand, she paused to close the key-board cover. She had given up the piano sixteen years before. The only exercise the keys ever got was the kids' banging, and they never bothered to close the cover. The ivories on both the G and A above middle C were chipped. She had once played rather well—not brilliantly, but well. She would never have been a Gina Bachauer, but she had once dreamed of playing professionally. The piano had been hers since high school, and when they moved into the present house six years be-fore, she had brought it from her parents' house in Beverly Hills, hoping that having it in the house would get her playing again. She never did. Somehow, her talents for Chopin and Mozart had been redirected in those first years of marriage. She had quite willfully put aside the dream of a music career in favor of being a wife and mother. Never mind. Now, in the coming months of pregnancy when she would have to cut down on her work around the house, she might once again take up where she had left off long ago. Not professionally this time, but for Alan, herself, and their friends. Odd how one is prepared to settle for smaller pleasures as the years go by.

Alexis grasped the handle of the sliding glass door and pulled it open. On the far side of the pool, sunk in a deep canvas chair, was Max, the top of his bald head crowned by his black yarmulke, visible above the back of the chair. Chris was perched on his knee.

Stepping into the bright sunlight, Alexis closed the door behind her and started towards the buffet table, where Karen was arranging the silverware. In her kelly green dress and with her dark hair tied back with a pale yellow silk ribbon, she looked like a diligent little leprechaun.

"I hope you remember how to do that tomorrow when I ask you to set the dinner table," she chided her as she passed the table.

"Oh, mom," Karen groaned. The thought of tomorrow and mun-dane dinners obviously had no enchantment.

"It looks lovely, sweetheart." Alexis laughed and continued across the terrace towards Alan, who glanced up as he poured charcoal from a sack into the barbecue pit. A smile broke across his face. He looked like a swinging single from Marina del Rey in his red Lacoste shirt and faded jeans.

"God, that was fast!" she called to him.

"That's what the cop said to me," he grimaced.

"Oh, Alan! You didn't!"

"Just a little one. Ten miles over the speed limit." He dropped the charcoal on the ground.

"But your car insurance will go up!"

"Well," he spread his arms, smiling, "the malpractice went up with the lawsuit, so we might as well be consistent."

Somehow it didn't matter. Not today. She walked towards him, struck suddenly by the thought of how complete they seemed. Max, Alan, herself, and the children. Three generations. A family.

"Do you think it's too early to start the fire?" Alan asked, as she came towards him briskly, smiling, her hair caught up in a gust of wind off the hillside.

"It's almost one. We should serve the kids by two, don't you think?"

"If we don't, we'll have fourteen screaming cannibals on our hands." He turned his own charcoal-blackened hands to meet her.

"God, honey," she kissed him on the chin, chuckling, "you look like a Yorkshire coal miner."

He made as though to draw his arms around her, "You've been reading *Lady Chatterley's Lover* again, haven't you."

"Alan, don't." She flattened her hands against his chest. "This is the only clean blouse I've got."

"Then don't flirt with coal miners," he smiled.

"Listen, we've got one extra guest coming."

"Who?"

"Some friend of Phoebe's and Charles's." She started off towards Max seated on the far side of the pool with Chris.

"Adult or child?" he called.

"Adult," she smiled back at him, "but with Phoebe's male friends, you never know." She continued on across the grass towards Max and Chris.

Alan turned back to the barbecue, took a deep, satisfied breath of air, and uncapped the charcoal lighter. From the side of the pool came the excited garble of Alexis's, Max's, and Chris's voices. "Oh, Max, keep your seat!" he heard Alexis cry.

"Ach!" he heard Max sink back into the canvas chair, "I think I have no choice." There was a round of commiserating laughter.

Alan squeezed the fire-lighter can and sent a jet of liquid evenly around the coals. Maybe, after all, he should have gone up in the elevator to Max's room at the Georgian and helped him down instead of phoning up. He had balked at the idea of giving in to Max's senile dependence. Max used his infirmities to control him, to level him with feelings of guilt. He hadn't visited Max for over three weeks, and then it was to take him down to the corner grill for a sandwich. But still, when they were alone together, it was Max who always started the arguments. They were invariably over petty things, whether he should use a cane for his afternoon walks along the Palisade, or whether his Santa Monica GP was prescribing the right blood pressure medicine. But it wasn't Max's senile petulance that kept him away. It was the old man's rigid refusal to accept the fact that he had given up his Judaism.

"It makes you look ten years younger, Alexis, being a mother again," Max said with his faint German accent, more pronounced now that he was older.

Always strictly orthodox, after Sarah's death he seemed to have turned back the clock into another century. He gave up his jewelry business in Detroit and retired, sitting in his dark study at the back of the house for hours on end, poring over the Talmud, Midrash, and Mishnah. He had brought six crates of books with him to California, which was fine, but he had also brought an obsession for religious observance and a closed mind. In his old age, his father was turning into a nitpicking rabbinical, Middle European old Jew, scratching around in the past for answers to the present, giving endless advice from his store of paternal Jewish wisdom, a crazy hodgepodge of learning, half rational orthodoxy, half mystical Cabala.

Alan knew what a blow his mother's death had been. In a sense, the old man had died with her. After forty-one years of living in this New World, he had moved mentally back into some kind of pre–Second-World-War Austrian ghetto; Alan could remember his father's gloomy, repellent childhood stories. It was those stories of his grandparents, of uncles and aunts and cousins, particularly the ones who had died in the death camps, that had made him vow, even before the age of ten, that he would grow up to be a different kind of man.

"Oh, Max!" Alexis's laughter rippled through the garden, "Don't be silly! Aaron is a beautiful boy's name!" Strange, for all his rigid orthodoxy, Max had always been warm and affectionate with Alexis, had always seemed to overlook the fact that she was both a goy and a Catholic.

Again, Alan squeezed the can of fire lighter, sending a jet of liquid over the charcoals.

Of course, Alexis had always defended the old man's madness, even in the face of her parents' tacit but obvious anti-Semitism.

Realizing he had no matches, Alan started across the lawn towards Alexis. On the way, inadvertently, he ran his hands over his pockets. He stopped, feeling something like the square bulge of a matchbook in the right pocket. He had not worn these jeans for months. Occasionally, he picked up matchbooks from restaurants. He reached into the pocket, to his surprise drew out a bright red book, and started back towards the pit. Opening the cover, his eye caught the name of the restaurant written in gold letters. Golden Dragon.

"Don't worry, I won't call your office or your home. Which means, you'll have to contact me." Brad's voice came back, clear and alive, from the restaurant where they had eaten back in April.

"You know the conditions: No demands." His own voice with its familiar edgy strain.

Quickly, he pulled a match from the book, struck it, and threw it into the coals. A small golden flame edged up around the center coal, then spread, igniting the others.

Would that memory ever stop following him? It was like some kind of mental carcinoma, always just below the surface, eating its way up, always always always . . .

Alan reached over and dropped the matchbook into the center of the coals. The cardboard cover ignited, then the matches followed, a bright hiss of yellow flame. He stared down, bewildered, watching the red paper cover curl, darken, and dissolve away into ash.

"Chris! I said don't pester your granddad!" Alexis leaned forward in her chair and took hold of Chris's hand.

"Nonsense, he can pester me all he wants." Max beamed up from the depths of the wing-shaped lounge chair, sunlight reflecting off the thick lenses of his glasses. "That's why I came, to be pestered." He drew the squirming boy down against his big stomach and squeezed him affectionately. "Right, little man?"

"Did Alan show you the plans for the new house?" she asked.

"House plans?" he shrugged, "Now when does that boy show me anything before it's finished?" His face suddenly lit up with an impish smile, "But now more important than house plans, how does it go with my new grandson?"

"So far, great. Except, one of you is going to be disappointed. Alan is counting on another girl."

"After so long, who am I to complain?"

"Grandpa!" Chris broke in, "Can I wear your beanie?!" he rolled over, reaching for Max's yarmulke.

"Chris! Now stop it! Leave him alone!"

"I want to wear his beanie!"

"That is not a beanie, it's a yarmulke, and you know it. Now get down and stop being disrespectful to your granddad."

Laughing, Max reached for the yarmulke on Chris's head, "If you say it's a beanie, it's a beanie." He set it straight on Chris's head, "Now look at you. Who would believe it? A little blond Jew."

Chris looked up at Max, beaming sheepishly. "My daddy's Jewish."

A moment later, both Alexis and Max burst out laughing. She glanced towards Alan, who had turned to watch them from the barbecue pit with a look of half-amused, half-surprised embarrassment on his face.

"Now get down." She took Chris's hand to lift him from Max's lap, "and go help Karen fix the table." For a moment, she avoided Max's eyes, realizing he had observed the exchange.

Chris bounded from Max's lap and started around the edge of the pool towards Karen.

Alexis met Max's eyes with an awkward smile, and for a moment, they looked at each other in silence. Behind the smile on Max's face, behind the eyes staring at her through the thick-lensed spectacles, she saw a flicker of pain rise and then fall.

"Hello!" her mother's voice called musically.

"Nana!" Karen cried.

Alan turned off the spigot to the garden hose and stood up, drying his hands on the dish towel as Christopher and Helen Bates, Alexis's parents, came through the sliding glass doors onto the terrace. Alan smiled to himself. Elegant as usual, Helen wore a long, caftan-style dress of soft, pastel-colored material. Her hair was artfully swept back from her face in a matronly looking wave.

Informal, he had told Alexis to tell her.

Christopher, the hulking, sixty-two-year-old executive still playing the college quarterback, had conceded to informality with a white shirt, yellow V-necked sweater, and grey trousers. He waved to Alan from the terrace. Under his other arm was a long flat box wrapped in silver paper and pink ribbon.

"Coco!" Chris ran towards Christopher senior. Alan returned the wave, smiling, and saw Helen turn to look at the yarmulke on Chris's head. He started towards them.

"Alan, my boy!" Christopher boomed jovially and held out his hand.

"Hello! Welcome!" Alan quickened his pace and took the big hand. "You're looking sporty today, Christopher," he said, trying to sound convivial.

"I've been jogging in the mornings before work. I feel great! Say," he nudged Alan on the shoulder, "how about laying a little money on that Packers' game this afternoon?"

"I'll lay you ten on the Lions. They're going to trounce the Packers."

"It's a deal," Christopher laughed and reached down to pat Chris junior, who was pulling at his sweater, calling up "Coco! The box! What's in the box?!"

"Cool it, Chris." Alan turned to Helen and bent forward to kiss her on the cheek, "As usual, Helen, you look terrific."

"Why thank you, Alan. I know I'm overdressed, but it's a *very* special day."

"Nana!" Karen shouted excitedly, "Is that for *me*?!" she pointed to the box under Christopher's arm.

"Well, Sister Anne Marie at Saint Catherine's tells me she has the sweetest little nine-year-old in the third grade. Now who could that be I wonder?"

"Me," Karen giggled.

"Then," Helen took the box from Christopher and held it out to Karen, "this must belong to you. Happy birthday, sweetheart."

Feeling little Chris's arm around his leg, Alan glanced down and saw a look of crestfallen resignation on his face. He grasped the boy's soft neck with his fingers and gently stroked it, "Now come say hello to my dad," he interrupted brightly.

Alexis stepped forward to kiss her mother, who was coming towards her around the pool, "Mother, you look beautiful!"

"Hello, darling." Helen hugged her. "You said informal, I know, but I look ridiculous in pants."

"How's my little chickadee?" Her father came up and put his arm around her shoulder.

"Great. I haven't done a lick of work for this party."

Max stepped forward to greet Helen. "Mrs. Bates, how good to see you again."

"Mr. Stegman." Helen took his hand with her fingers. "What a nice surprise."

"Max, you look as healthy as an old bear." Christopher shook Max's hand vigorously.

The last time they had met had been Christmas, at her parents' eggnog party. Always politely gracious, the meetings were still stiff after sixteen years of resignation to a marriage they never, either of them, had wanted or approved of.

"Nana! Coco!" Chris came running around the pool with Karen and Banjo, their wire-haired terrier.

"Now settle down, you two!" Alan scolded.

Alexis saw Alan glance towards Helen who was looking at the yarmulke on Chris's head. "Give granddad back his cap," he said. Alexis realized he had consciously dodged the word *yarmulke*.

Alan took the yarmulke and handed it to Max. "Here, dad," he said, "if you don't hold onto this, it's going to end up in the pool."

In the sudden silence, Alexis checked an impulse to reproach Alan with a look. "Now if everybody will sit down," she said, "I'll bring out the punch."

For the second time, Alan found himself avoiding the young psychiatrist's eyes. "Rare, medium or well done?" he asked, turning one of the sizzling hamburgers on the grill.

"If you've got a medium, Alan, I'll take that." Dr. Stephen Milner held out the paper plate.

"Coming up." Alan lifted the patty and guided it towards the plate. "There's coleslaw and french fries over on the table." From the lawn at the shallow end of the pool there was laughter and chatter as their other adult guests settled into a circle of chairs with their plates. Alexis was distributing french fries to the children seated on the ground in a circle at the far side of the pool.

"Thanks, I'll help myself to some slaw," Milner said. He made no move, however, to go. "You've got a beautiful place here, Alan."

"Thanks," Alan looked up and smiled through the smoke rising from the pit. "We're getting ready to put it up for sale, though."

"I see." A smile played over Milner's face as he lifted the hamburger and bit into it.

"Don't you want some mayonnaise or mustard?"

"No," Milner said, "just plain." The eyes—they had fixed on him like that, with frank, open humor, when he came up an hour ago with Phoebe and Charles to introduce himself—the eyes were pale, startlingly pale blue. Alan wondered whether the young psychiatrist was somehow playing with him. "That guy over there in the white shirt," Milner indicated Jim Cagle seated among the others, "what's his name?"

"Cagle." Alan glanced in the direction of the silver-haired senior partner of Buchman, Cagle, and Prouse seated next to Alexis's mother.

"Cagle, that's right. Cagle says you're building a new place."

"Right. We are. We bought a lot up in Coldwater Canyon. Cagle's the architect." He flipped one of the patties on the grill. It sizzled and flamed for a moment. Out of the corner of his eye, Alan watched Milner bite again into his hamburger. He was in his mid-thirties, Alan judged. Despite the fair hair, blue eyes, a sharply angular jaw, and cropped curly hair, there was something Semitic about his face.

"I just moved, myself," Milner was saying, "I rented a place on Fountain Avenue just below the Strip."

"There're some great old buildings on Fountain," Alan said, then heard himself ask, "do you live alone?"

"At the moment I do," he replied, grinning at Alexis coming towards them with the basket of french fries. For the second time since Milner had arrived, Alan caught that same open, unguarded, confident expression of humor in his profile. Earlier, he had seen Sharon Berrey, Arnold's wife, hovering helplessly over the man. Milner, he concluded, was one of those men who, with their natural, unstudied, unprotected masculinity, attract women as flowers attract bees. Alan fanned the smoke billowing from the pit and smiled at himself, realizing he was actually jealous!

"Dr. Milner!" Alexis called. "How about some fries?"

"No, thanks, Alexis," he chuckled. "Vanity forbids, I'm afraid."

Alexis came up, laughing. Alan glanced at Milner's trim waistline under his denim shirt.

"You're crazy!" Alexis looked down and pressed her stomach. "Look at this!"

They looked at each other and laughed. "Phoebe tells me you're expecting another child," Milner said.

"Right. Our third."

"Congratulations."

"Thanks." Alexis caught his eye and smiled.

Alexis *too*, Alan thought, and looked down at the sizzling patties.

"How long have you and Alexis been married?" Milner asked him. The candor of it felt oddly satisfying.

"Sixteen years."

"Almost seventeen," Alexis added, glancing from Alan to Stephen.

"Your kids are beautiful," Milner said to both of them.

"Sometimes," Alexis said.

"And your wife, too." Milner grinned at him.

"Sometimes." Alan winked at Alexis. In the momentary silence that followed, he felt suddenly at the center of a triangular tension. Except that Alexis and Stephen were smiling quite comfortably.

"Phoebe tells me you're also with West Hollywood General," Alexis said.

"Right. I'm on the psychiatric staff."

"Alan's in general surgery."

"That's across the street." Stephen glanced at him. "They keep us shrinks in a separate wing." The smile spilled into his blue eyes.

"Amazing that you two have never met!"

"Not really. It's a big place. I've heard Alan's name a lot, but never had the pleasure." Stephen pointed to the patties on the grill. "I hope you don't mind the diagnosis of an uninvited guest, Alan, but your patties are burning."

Alan looked down quickly at the grill. "Oh, shit. They're cinderized." He reached for a platter on the table beside the grill.

Alexis stepped forward to help, laughing. "Never mind, darling, the kids like 'em charred."

Alan began scooping the patties from the grill onto the platter. "How about a cinderburger, Stephen?"

"Thanks, Alan. I'm full." He took hold of the other side of the platter and held it steady. Alan glanced at his fourth finger. There was no wedding ring, he observed.

"In that case," Alexis was saying, "Doctor Uninvited Guest, I'll grab the buns from the table and you can help me serve up seconds." She turned briskly towards the buffet table across the lawn.

"Sure thing. I'll be with you in a second."

Alan went on forking the last of the patties onto the platter. His left hand was at one end of the platter, Stephen's right hand on the other. In the moment before Stephen took the platter from him, Alan felt a curious sensation of affinity—an oddly pleasant sensation of having come to rest.

"Great. I'll pass these around with Alexis." Stephen put his empty paper plate on the rim of the grill's brick ledge. "Now if you want me to take over here while you eat, just give a shout." He took the platter in both hands and smiled.

Through the faint haze of smoke from the burning grease on the grill, Alan watched Milner cross the grass towards Alexis. He moved easily, confidently, carrying his body with the poise of a man sure of himself.

"Seconds?" Alexis moved around the circle with her basket of hamburger buns towards Sharon Berrey.

"Oh, my! I really shouldn't, dear!" Sharon caught sight of Dr. Milner approaching with the meat platter and her expression suddenly brightened. "On second thought—" she reached for a bun in the basket and opened it delicately with the nails of both hands.

Alexis's eyes rested on Sharon's salt-and-pepper hair pulled back tightly against her head into a chignon. It gave her face a hard, determined look.

Alexis moved on with the bread basket towards her mother. "Oh, come on, Arnie!" she heard Alan's voice across the lawn from the barbecue pit where Arnold Berrey had joined him moments before. "The fact remains! We got a no-fault decision!"

"Fault or no fault, it should have been prevented from the beginning!"

Helen looked up at her as she offered the bread, "No, dear. Nothing." She glanced with embarrassment towards the barbecue pit.

Alexis moved on with the bread basket.

"That's not true!" Alan exclaimed. "The damn wound dehisced on us!"

Around Alexis, the conversation died away as the adult guests turned to look at Alan and Arnold arguing at the barbecue pit. She held out the basket towards her father.

"No, thanks, honey," he said with a commiserating smile.

"Okay, Alan, okay," Berrey said, "let's eat. Business tomorrow."

Alexis left the circle of silent guests and headed towards the buffet table. Berrey had started the argument. Alan, as usual, had refused to concede. He was one of the few doctors on the West Hollywood General staff who dared openly oppose the administrator's cutbacks in staff and equipment. Alan's outspoken opposition had turned both Arnold and his career-promoting wife, social intimates on the one hand, into professional adversaries on the other. Arnold, as usual, had had one too many daiquiris. She set the basketful of bread between the salad and the cheese. So far, fourteen children and thirteen adults had scarcely put a dent into Alan's spread. Only she, Alan, and Milner remained to be served.

"Looks like you've got leftovers, Alexis," Milner came up beside her and put the platter of meat on the table.

"How many patties did you unload?" she asked.

"Two."

She shook her head and chuckled. "Even kids draw the line somewhere."

"There's still you, me, and the good doctor."

"I'll pass, thanks." She took two buns from the basket. "Here. I'll fix Alan's plate, and you two guys can eat the rest together."

"Photographs!" Alan exclaimed, "Oh, Christ, I forgot. Is this the only roll we've got?" He took the camera from Alexis.

"I'm afraid so, but never mind. Take four or five of the adults and use the rest for the kids."

Alan turned the camera around and looked at the frame number. Three. He stared at the number through the tiny window and felt a chill run through his body, remembering when he'd last used the camera. May. The first three pictures on the roll were of Brad. He had taken the camera to his apartment one afternoon and photographed Brad on the balcony outside his living room holding a can of beer, shirtless, leaning against the railing in a jokingly seductive pose. Afterwards, he had forgotten about the film in the camera.

"Now relax, darling." Alexis squeezed his arm encouragingly, "Everyone's having a wonderful time."

He put his arm around her shoulder and drew her close to him.

"Fuck the others," he kissed her on the nose, "I'm taking care of Karen today." They both looked towards the fenced area beyond the far end of the pool where the children were clambering noisily over the swings and slide with shrill screams of delight. Karen was leading three other kids up the steps of the slide.

"Who does she think she is," Alexis laughed, "queen of the ball?"

"Queen for the day, at least."

"If you go on spoiling her like this, we won't have a queen, but we will have a nine-year-old Jewish princess on our hands."

"You mean *half* a princess, don't you?"

"Listen," she pulled away, "don't you think it's time we got down to Princess Karen's presents? I'll go in and set everything up in the living room. Except the bicycle. You bring that out yourself."

"I hope to hell she likes it." He had bought the bike for her on Friday after work, the most expensive kid's bike he could find. Foolish maybe, but like with the party, he needed to give her something unexpectedly wonderful.

"She'll faint when she sees it." Alexis brushed his chin with her hand, "Now you go take pictures and I'll play Santa." She moved off towards the house.

On his way to the circle of adults seated near the pool, Alan advanced the film to number four. If Alexis had used up the rest of the roll and taken it to be developed? he thought to himself. He hurried ahead, feeling the edge of a slight panic, and reached the grownups as they broke into a loud laugh. "All right, you guys! All right!" Alan called over the laughter, waving his camera, "I'm here to take some pictures!"

"I object!" Donald, his partner, groaned, "this is blackmail!"

"Just pretend I'm not here," Alan started around the back of the circle, "and keep smiling!" He stopped behind Donald's chair and aimed his camera towards Jimmy Cagle and Stephen Milner.

"Actually, Phoebe," Jimmy had turned towards Phoebe with a look of strained dignity, "my only objection to the ERA is that it's constitutionally redundant." Alan caught the glint of a gold chain between the open panels of his white shirt. On several occasions Alexis had joked about Jimmy's penchant for discreet gold jewelry, amused by the tacit but, in fact, public knowledge that their architect was a "homosexual from the Beverly Hills jewelry set," which was strange to learn, since he had been recommended to them by her mother. Next to Cagle, Stephen Milner was giving him a broad, playful smile. Interesting contrast, Alan thought, these two men in the same picture.

Alan moved on, directing his lens now at Donald and Pat Lindquist. "If you want special legislation for one special interest group,"

Donald was saying, "then what about all the others?"

Alan let Pat arrange herself in a dignified pose, then pressed the shutter button.

"Here we go again," Christopher chuckled.

Alan smiled to himself. Patricia, always the proper wife of the proper surgeon.

"Donald's right," Sharon Berrey said, "you've got blacks, Puerto Ricans, Chinese, Indians, Mexicans—"

"And don't forget the gays," Arnold added, laughing, "you've got something like ten million gays to think about!"

There were spotted chuckles around the circle as Alan froze with the camera aimed at Christopher and Helen. His finger dropped on the shutter button, catching their faces in a moment of mild shock.

Alan moved on again, pretending to concentrate on advancing the film to the next exposure.

"Talk about privileged minorities," Arnold went on, "the neighborhood around our hospital is so gay, they're changing its name officially to Boys Town."

As Alan stopped behind Christopher's chair, there was a wave of mild laughter.

"You know what they call the Hollywood Hills, don't you," he heard Cagle quickly add, "the Swish Alps!"

On a reflex, Alan glanced at Stephen, next to Cagle, and their eyes met. At Cagle's cooperative, self-deprecating remark, the laughter relaxed. In Stephen's face, he saw a look of embarrassment, dismay, and anger. He looked away, realizing Stephen had read the expression on his own as well.

He lifted the camera again and saw Phoebe glance towards Stephen, embarrassed. He tried to steady the camera with Arnold, his father, and Sharon in the single picture.

"You know what they say about the Safeway on Santa Monica, don't you?" Sharon leaned forward. "It's the only supermarket in LA where you find *fruit* in the detergent section!"

Disregarding the camera, Arnold leaned back and joined the laughter. Max, unaware of the camera, looked down uncomfortably.

Alan squeezed the shutter button.

The laughter died away as Alan, paralyzed by the incriminating blush on his face, stared into the little window on the back of the camera. Eight. Three of Brad. Five of the group.

To cover the silence, he aimed the camera at Phoebe and Charles, and called "Smile!" in a voice noticeably too loud.

Through the viewfinder, he saw Phoebe level a look of embarrassment and disgust at him. "Oh, fuck off, Alan," she said flatly.

Alan felt the camera tremble against his face. Trapped, he went on and pressed the shutter button, then lowered the camera. To his right, he saw Stephen Milner's empty chair, then caught sight of the young psychiatrist already halfway across the lawn, heading towards the house, walking in a steady, unhurried pace.

"Well, *that's* a surprise," Sharon said, "They certainly come in all flavors, don't they."

"By the way, dear, I think for a children's party, Alan could have chosen his guests a little better."

Taken back, Alexis paused as her mother looked at her with disapproval, then turned away. Puzzled, she let her gaze sweep around the living room, resting for an instant on Max seated near Karen in an easy chair.

Surely not—perplexed, she reached for two glasses of lemonade on Claire's tray—then caught sight of Dr. Milner standing apart at the far end of the sofa. He looked withdrawn, though smiling, as he watched Karen unwrapping her present. Alexis handed the lemonade to two of the children. At that moment, something clicked in her mind. A short while before, she had been aware of an odd kind of tension among the adults as they gathered in the living room for the presents. An unpleasant feeling of strain. Something had happened in the garden while she was away, the liveliness had suddenly evaporated. Before that, while she was in the living room arranging the presents, Dr. Milner had come in and asked for the bathroom. He seemed angry, though he tried to cover it with a joke.

Alexis reached for the two remaining glasses of champagne on the tray. Later, when the chance came, she would ask Alan. Alan would know.

"Doctor Milner." She headed towards him, taking a sip from one of the glasses. "Join me in some very dry and very cold champagne."

Alan maneuvered the bicycle down the corridor towards the archway leading into the living room. For the last ten minutes he had stood in the bedroom, listening to the screams and squeals from the kids, hoping Karen would not notice his absence. He had planned it this way. The timing had to be good, just when she opened the last of her boxes. Then he would wheel it in and watch her face as she registered the surprise.

A few feet from the archway, he paused and smiled, anticipating the excitement to come, feeling proud of himself. For the first time in months, he realized, he was immensely proud of himself as a father.

He rounded the archway and stopped just inside the living room.

At first he did not see her. Only the other kids clustered around the heap of wrapping paper and ribbons. A few kids turned with looks of astonishment. Then he saw her. Across the room. Cuddled in Max's arms.

Alexis, standing beside Stephen Milner, looked up to see him with the bike. A grin broke across her face. "Look, Karen!" she called.

Turning in Max's arms, Karen's face went blank. Then she sat up, her mouth opening in a silent O. "Daddy," she said breathlessly. She got down and came towards him, oblivious of the amused looks around her. She stopped a few feet away, and the surprise on her face gave way to awe. Around her, the other kids looked on, caught up in the thrill of her moment.

"Happy birthday, sweetheart," he said.

There was a ripple of laughter from the adults.

Mesmerized, she moved towards the bike and touched it, tentatively.

"Take it." He leaned the gleaming blue bike towards her. "It's yours."

Spellbound, she took hold of it by the seat.

He moved around to her side and squatted beside her. "What do you think?"

"Oh, daddy." She let go of the bike and reached for his neck. He caught the machine with one hand and drew her close with the other.

"Do you like it?" Her cheek was cool and soft against his face.

"Oh, daddy, I love it."

He closed his eyes and pressed the small of her back, drawing her small, warm body close to his own. "And I love you," he said softly in her ear for her alone to hear. More than ever, he thought, now more than ever.

"I love you, too," she said.

He opened his eyes, aware that the room had gone silent around them, and drew back, resting his hand on her waist.

In the big oak-framed mirror on the opposite wall he saw the reflection of some twenty smiling faces turned in their direction. His gaze rested on one particular face, though. Stephen Milner's. Framed by a muted square of afternoon sunlight slanting through the sliding glass doors. Milner stood behind the others, apart now, holding a glass of champagne, with a pained look of sadness momentarily caught on his admiring face.

Taken by surprise, Alan colored with embarrassment.

At the moment, with an ominous feeling of dread for himself and a recognition of their tacit affinity, he realized he had unwittingly eavesdropped on that other, different world, the world where a man like

Stephen lives out his life knowing he will never hold in his arms a child of his own.

"Tired?" Alexis adjusted the pillow under her head. She lay on her side of the bed, looking at Alan's naked body with the sheet drawn up carelessly over his waist. His shoulders and arms were still damp from the shower he had taken. The black hair on his chest, flattened against the skin, was sensuous and inviting. He was on his side of the bed, his arms folded behind his head.

"A little. Just a little." He squirmed, nestling his head into the pillow.

"You amaze me sometimes."

"How so?"

"The party. You really pulled it off."

"Do you think she liked it?"

"It knocked her sideways."

"Arnold, you know, is an obnoxious bastard sometimes."

"It's the daiquiris."

"Sometimes I get the feeling he'd rather not have me on his staff."

The lower end of the bed felt cold. She drew her feet up under her nightdress. Alan lowered his arm and ran his hand over the damp hair on his chest. Under the languid detachment, she detected a guarded stir of desire.

"Never mind. It was fun watching Sharon make a fool of herself. She made a pass at Phoebe's friend, Stephen. Did you see that?"

"Yeah." Alan looked away towards the window. "I saw it." He lay still, his hand rising and falling to the breathing rhythm of his stomach. She felt an impulse to move across to his side and lie close to him, but checked herself, remembering her past failures.

"Something happened, didn't it?" she said. "I meant to ask you."

"What do you mean?"

"While I was in the house with the presents Milner came in. He was very upset. What happened?"

"Oh, nothing."

"Nothing?"

"They were all a little drunk. Some remarks were made. Milner got upset." He suddenly rolled over onto his side to face her. "Tell me about Karen, did she like the bike really?"

"I had to threaten her to make her go to bed after dinner. She hasn't been off it since she got it."

He looked at her for a moment, smiled, and sighed. In turning on his side, the sheet had fallen halfway down his thigh, exposing the dark scruff of his black pubic hair under the shelter of his hip. She lifted her eyes and swallowed awkwardly, knowing that her desire was clearly written on her face.

He lowered his arm to the bed, hesitated, then moved his hand towards her across the sheet. She felt her pulse quicken, reached out, and met his hand halfway, letting his fingers close over hers.

"Come closer," he said.

She wriggled across the bed, sliding her hand over his arm, then up the cool skin of his shoulder and down his side. The familiar ache vibrated through her body. "Your side is always warmer than mine," she murmured.

He reached around and drew her closer, his hand caressing the small of her back through her nightdress. Her face met the moist hair on his chest and she kissed him in the cleavage of his pectoral muscles, smelling the fragrance of soap. She felt his mouth in her hair, nibbling. He continued down her neck, his tongue leaving a cool wet ribbon in its wake.

"You feel so good," she whispered, feeling the warmth of his stomach, groin, and legs against her own.

"You'd feel better without this," he reached down and slid her nightdress up her legs.

As she raised her hips to pull the gown over her head, he leaned back to turn off the bed lamp. She lay down against the warm sheet and opened her arms. The weight of his body came down and closed around her. She responded, running her hands luxuriously down his back, feeling grateful and complete again.

IV

The books balanced. Alan closed the ledger and sat back. The clock at the head of his desk read 5:56. Beyond the door to his office the muffled noise of voices had stopped. Donald and the staff—Margaret, the receptionist, and their two nurses—had gone for the day. He leaned back in the swivel chair, let his head fall back against the soft leather, and looked towards the long, rectangular window of his fourth-floor office.

At this rate, after ten months, their two-man corporation would gross perhaps half a million by the end of the year, with a probable net for each of them of some hundred thousand, the result of combining their two established private practices.

He stared out at the dark skyline. December 3. The days were growing shorter now.

With payments on their loan for office space, staff, equipment and supplies, and malpractice insurance, they might finally see an unencumbered gross by the end of their second year.

Alan swung his chair around to face the desk again, sat forward and rested an elbow on the ledger.

It was back again, for the second time that day, the gnawing ache of desire. It had started earlier in the corridor of the hospital, when he passed a young lab technician. He had seen the guy turn the corner by the reception desk some twenty feet away and, from that distance, the resemblance to Brad was startling—the head of short black hair, the trimmed moustache, the sharp jawline, the solid body under the loose lab coat. They almost passed one another before he realized he was staring. In a quick, knowing glance, the guy had read Alan's expression. Periodically, all through the afternoon, the face had come back to him, smiling. Not Brad's face, but the technician's. And each time, it had hung there in his mind, firing his body with sudden desire.

Alan shifted in his chair, uneasy again.

Of course, a good quarter of their profits on paper were still in outstanding bills. You cure a patient of their disease and you sometimes cure them of the need to pay. You can't, like the Pacific Telephone Company, turn around and threaten to turn off the cure. And the Medicare patients: there were small profits in them.

In the corner of his eye, Alan caught the blinking button of an incoming call on his phone. Alexis, he thought. She would be calling at this hour if he wasn't home. Saved by the bell, he reached over, lifted the receiver, and pressed the button.

"Doctor's—" He cleared his throat. "Doctor's office."

"Alan?"

"Hello, sweetheart." He tried to sound relaxed.

"Everyone gone home?"

"Yeah. I was going over the books."

"Are you all right?"

"I'm fine." The technician's face flashed before his mind.

"Honey, I hope you're not going to be there till all hours. I've got a great dinner going."

"I've almost finished."

"Listen, could you pick up something at the market on the way home?"

"Okay." He closed his eyes, relieved for the first time to be sent on one of her between-office-and-home errands.

"Don't be cross."

"I'm not!"

She hesitated, then said, "I'm making something terrific. Your favorite."

"Gigot de pré-salé farci, with pommes de terre dauphinoise?"

She chuckled, "Pink's hotdogs à la Chris, with grease-fried potatoes à la Karen."

"And tapioca pudding à la Alan?"

"Better. Your favorite."

Apple pie. Homemade apple pie. "You forgot the brown sugar again," he said.

"How did you know?"

"You always do. It's that little voice in the back of your head saying 'I shouldn't feed him sugar, he's trying to stay on his diet.'"

"You can go back on it tomorrow."

"You said that last Thursday," he chuckled. "I'll stop by the Safeway on Santa Monica. Anything else?"

"And milk. A half gallon."

"Brown sugar and milk."

"Right," she sighed, "and cigarettes. I've got a little vice to support. A carton of Dorals."

"At least you're smoking yourself into a low-tar grave." A picture of the lab technician flashed before his mind. A little vice to support, he thought.

"Now try not to be late," she was saying, "I've got a roast in the oven. And Karen wants you to help her with her school project."

"I'll be there within the hour," he said.

"Drive carefully. It rained a little while ago."

"Yes, mother," he said, annoyed now by that streak of motherliness he had lately seen in her again.

"Bye," she said in a musical voice and hung up.

Alan sat back. There was one other errand he had intended to do before going home. Pick up the roll of film he had used at Karen's birthday party. The roll with the three pictures of Brad. He remembered looking through the lens that afternoon. Brad's face. Gentle, affectionate, sometimes childish and impetuous, even foolish, often haggard-looking after work, but then suddenly glowing with energy after a run on the Santa Monica beach. When he got the photos back, it would be there—the big silver cowboy buckle on the belt around his jeans, the grinning face, the shirtless torso, the can of Budweiser in his right hand. All of it would still be there as it was seven months ago.

Alan leaned his head back against the chair. When had it all begun? Not with Brad. Brad was not the first man he had desired. The first he had desired openly, true, but not the first. Gerald Dorn, his Ohio friend in med school. Outside school, they had hung around each other like nails around a magnet. He had told himself at the time that it was friendship, close friendship, but in retrospect there was something more, a deep, unspoken need for his physical presence. He had once embraced Gerald after a three-week separation and held him just a moment longer than simple friendship allowed. Observing Gerald with women, he had sometimes wondered whether it was country-boy awkwardness that kept him at a distance, or something more. A lack of desire? Was he a repressed homosexual? Even if he was, the affinity between them was there. Not sexual desire so much as a feeling of affinity, belonging, a need for closeness with him, a peculiar pleasure when they went off to a movie alone together. It was that same feeling he had had in Stephen Milner's presence at Karen's birthday party. Not sexual desire, but something larger and more telling—that feeling of having come to rest.

Stephen, however "straight" he looked and behaved, was a homosexual. Alan lifted his head. Odd how awkward the word was for him still. Even now, in his liberated forties. Almost a lifetime had passed since he revolted against the suffocating sexlessness of his parents' home and applied to med school a thousand miles away. Now he wondered if his father had seen something many years ago. Max had once blistered him with a belt when his mother found a muscle-building magazine in his room. At the time, his father's rage had seemed extreme, unjust. Like the other boys in school, he was lifting weights to improve his body for the girls.

With Brad, though, he knew he had come to the end of that murky childhood labyrinth. After forty years, he had gone stumbling into bed with a man, telling himself on the way that he was merely passing through.

His cousin Lenny had once jokingly referred to that act as "making the beast." He had made the beast with Brad and had come to enjoy every guilty, unnatural minute of it—at least in retrospect, *after* his death. And of course in retrospect he was wont to forget that he had forced Brad to play the needy role to keep at bay the possibility that his own needs for Brad might run deeper than the bed. Even now, though, it was difficult to know his feelings back then. Death has a way of sweetening the memory. He still did not know whether he could have really loved the man.

Alan closed his eyes, sick now of the old need to cry when he was alone with the memory, sick of the self-pity that it brought with it.

And because he did not yet know where his needs were taking him, because there was still the chance that it would all go away, he was still torturing Alexis with his silent charade. One day she could know. But not now, not until he had passed through the fire and they were safe again on the leeward side of danger.

Alexis turned the pie shell, fluting the upper end of the dough with the fork. She shook her head, smiling at her housewife self. The lamb roast was plain, seasoned with rosemary and garlic, surrounded by small new potatoes. Gigot de pré-salé farci. Alan would be pleased with plain roast lamb cooked just to the point of pink, with golden potatoes. She could smell the rosemary and garlic in the kitchen air. Claire had put it in the oven before she retired to her rooms to bathe for her night off.

The apples were sliced, the orange and lemon rinds grated, and if the recipe for dough was as foolproof as Claire had promised, the pie would turn out butter-rich and flaky, the way Alan liked it. Complain all he wants about my behaving like a middle-class housewife of late, he *won't* complain about tonight's dinner. Besides, being the woman she was, how many weapons did she have against the lingering threat of infidelity?

"Mom!" Chris bounded into the kitchen. "Can I have a cookie?!"

"Not before dinner. We're eating in forty-five minutes," she looked down at the tousled blond head and wondered if he would stay blond or go dark like Alan.

"Aw, mom! Forty-five minutes!"

"Dad will be home then."

"Are you making pie?" He craned his neck to see the counter top.

"Yep. A big American apple pie." She rubbed the top of his head with the back of her floured hand. "Especially for you."

"For me?"

"For you."

"It's not for Karen and dad?"

"Don't be silly. Of course it's for them, too!"

He was silent for a moment. "I don't want it to be for them."

"Why?"

" 'Cause you always make it for dad."

She looked at him, puzzled. "What makes you say that?"

"The last time when you made it, dad didn't come home, and you cried."

Alexis put the fork down. "That wasn't why I cried," she said, surprised and uneasy now.

"Yes, it was." The tone of his voice was teasing.

"Don't be silly."

"It was! It was fucking so!" he called loudly.

"Chris!" She turned to him, stunned, "You must never use that word."

"Karen says it."

She stared at him, struck by the realization that they were already on the point of stumbling into the world. "That is an ugly word, and I don't want to hear you use it again, is that clear?"

He looked down in silence for a moment, then nodded.

She went back to fluting the pie shell, troubled vaguely by a mental image of Alan with some naked woman, fucking. "I always bake pie for our whole family," she said firmly, pushing the image from her mind, "and if dad doesn't come home or doesn't eat any, it's fine by me."

"I hope he's on a diet tonight."

Alexis smiled to herself. "Here," she took a slice of apple from the bowl, "you can have a preview of the pie, but just one."

He took the apple slice and put it into his mouth. "I love you better than anyone in the whole world," he said, trying to chew and talk at the same time.

Sugar, milk, and cigarettes; Alan finished placing his purchases on the cashier's stand and reached for his wallet.

"Seven eighty-five," the cashier announced to the customer ahead of him.

The young man in the faded, straight-legged jeans and plaid shirt he had seen earlier by the cheese counter wheeled his basket up to the next cashier and began unloading his purchases. As Alan glanced at him across the rack of *TV Guides*, he looked up and smiled. Alan looked down quickly, pretending to count the bills in his wallet. Out of the corner of his eye, he caught the key ring hooked to the belt loop over the side pocket of the jeans as the young man leaned towards the stand, setting a large package of dog food on the conveyor belt. The firm, rounded shape of his rear end pressed against the cloth of his jeans.

"Sir?" He heard the cashier's voice and looked towards the young girl, wondering whether she had caught his interest in the guy's rear end.

"Is this yours?" She indicated the three items on the belt.

"Right. That's it." He moved along the counter and stopped with his back against the railing. The young man followed along the opposite aisle and stood half turned towards his cashier, half towards him.

The cashier quoted the price of a box of brown sugar.

The young man was an inch or so taller than Alan, six foot one, maybe two. In the stark neon light, his short-cropped, sandy-colored hair looked almost blond. As he reached into his back pocket for his wallet, he looked towards Alan and caught him staring. For a moment, their eyes locked. The meaning in the dark brown eyes was unmistakable. Once again, he smiled.

Flushing, Alan forced himself to return the smile.

The cashier rang up the half gallon of milk. "It's gone up three cents this week." She smiled at him.

Alan shifted uncomfortably, aware that she had seen the exchange of smiles. He glanced towards the customer behind him, a man his father's age in a blue leisure suit. Glances. He seemed to be trapped in a four-way confession of glances.

"Tom!" a voice called from the far end of the opposite checkout stand.

"Hey, man!" the sandy-haired young man looked back over his shoulder and grinned at a short, black-haired man unloading a basket heaped with food. "Jesus, are you shopping for the whole street?"

"Seven sixty-one." The cashier reached for a brown paper bag under her counter.

Alan put a ten-dollar bill on the ledge above the counter.

"Larry and I are having some guys over for dinner," the black-haired man announced clearly, "You wanna join us?"

"Thanks, but I've got plans already. I'm meeting someone at the Motherlode in a few minutes." The sandy-haired young man gave Alan a frank, unabashed smile.

The Motherlode. Alan knew the bar. Brad had pointed it out to him: "the busiest gay bar in West Hollywood." On the corner of Robertson and Santa Monica Boulevards, less than half a block away. Flustered, Alan started to open his wallet again, then saw the bill lying in front of him on the ledge. He hurriedly pushed it towards the waiting cashier, feeling suddenly like a prim, prudish, middle-aged surgeon who had lost touch with the younger world.

The cashier finished counting off the change into his palm. "Eight, nine, ten." She looked up and smiled disinterestedly. "Have a nice night, sir."

"Thanks. You, too." Alan took his package. At the supermarket door, he turned to look back at the handsome face watching him from the checkout stand and aimed his shoulder towards the glass door. The electric eye of the door clicked and unexpectedly he found himself catapulted through an open hole onto the sidewalk outside.

It was true, he *was* a stuffy middle-aged surgeon, and a clumsy one at that: running in one direction after the things he had wanted, a career, a wife and family, security and achievement; meanwhile, the world had passed him by, going in the opposite direction. Embarrassed as *he* was by the young man's open acknowledgment of his homosexuality, no one else in the supermarket seemed to care. But then, no one else in the supermarket was fighting his battle.

Alan placed his package in the passenger seat, closed the door behind him, and sat at the wheel with the motor runing. In the opposite row of cars, the young man's yellow VW pulled out of the parking slot and headed towards the west exit of the lot.

The Motherlode. He had always wondered what it would be like in a gay bar, surrounded entirely by men. What kind of men went to bars? Brad had not. Stephen Milner? And if he did go, and if Stephen *was* there—what then?

Alan turned off the motor and sat for a moment looking towards the west side of the parking lot where the yellow VW had pulled into a slot close to the corner of Robertson and Santa Monica. The sandy-haired young man was locking his car door.

If he went in and found Stephen in the bar, there would be one other person in the world who would know of his dilemma. One gay man, a psychiatrist, to talk to. Look in for five minutes, then leave and be home in ample time for dinner.

Alan opened his car door and got out. The December night air was chilly, but it quickened his blood and it felt good. He would have to look more casual than this, he thought. He took off his suit jacket and tossed it onto the seat. Then removed his tie. He felt nervous, jittery, a little frightened. He thought of Alexis in the kitchen preparing dinner, then felt an immediate rush of anger. He had been on time for thousands of dinners. He had sat down to them like a man falling into a trap. He was a squirrel running around inside a wheel. There was no freedom left for either of them to simply *be*, to have an unplanned moment of surprise—like Karen turning to find a bright new bike.

Alan turned the key in his car door.

He had wanted to see Stephen since the day they met. He had wanted to look inside the Motherlode since the day Brad pointed it out—and Christ! he was a forty-year-old man!

He started across the parking lot towards the corner of Robertson and Santa Monica. He could see the facade of the bar on the opposite corner, an open, darkened door.

Alexis finished lighting the cluster of white candles on the living-room coffee table, dropped the match in the ashtray, and crossed to the piano. From the kitchen she could smell the fragrance of rosemary and lamb. She sat down and opened the keyboard cover, feeling that wonderful kind of peace she always looked forward to at the end of the day when the meal was ready, everything arranged, and she was alone with herself just before Alan arrived.

Funny, after all these years she could still remember the notes of the polonaise. Yesterday and today she had practiced it for three hours, working out the fingering again, trying to recover a mere fraction of the limber strength she had once had in her fingers and wrists. Of course, it was all but gone now, gone with those adolescent illusions of concert fame (she smiled to herself), gone with all the fire and quick brilliance of easy youth. But she could still get through the polonaise if she played it slowly. Her teacher had once told her that the important thing was tempo: play it slowly for accuracy, but above all keep the tempo! Strange how the fingers remember, even after they have lost the power and facility.

After dinner, she would simply sit down at the keyboard, open the cover, and play for him, however poorly. His surprise would be reward enough. The kids knew she had practiced, but they had promised to say nothing.

Alexis looked down at her undistinguished hands. Despite the creams, they were housewife hands now, trophies from the diaper derby. She spread her fingers, closed them. They were stiff and a little cold. She would limber up after she cleared the dinner table and stacked the plates in the dishwasher. Then play.

She glanced through the floor-length window next to the piano. She would be able to see Alan's headlights in the trees over the pool when he turned into the drive. With her fingers positioned over the keys, she struck.

The four opening chords of the polonaise set the tone—brilliant, arrogant, accomplished. They also brought back the silly, youthful fantasies she had had twenty years before—imperial Polish fireworks, laughter, jewels, palaces. Strange how the imagination alters the pleasure of things with its associations. The polonaise had not changed. She had. It was still beautiful, but she had lost touch with its luster.

She began fingering her way up the keyboard with her right hand.

She was at the age, now, for Chopin's études. The defiant pain in the études was somehow closer to the center of things.

She faltered in the glittering run of the right hand, but countered with the broad, open fifths of the left. She smiled at herself trying after sixteen years. Chopin would have laughed, of course. Hopefully, though, Alan would join with her in the small pleasure of her little comeback.

He reached the doorway, stopped to transfer his beeper from his belt to his trouser pocket, then went in. The muffled throb he had heard from the street exploded into a snappy disco beat. Six or seven men near the door turned to appraise him, then went back to their conversations. Indirectly lit from the ceiling by low pink and amber spots, the room was paneled in wood painted pale green. Between him and the bar running the length of one wall, some twenty young men in jeans, dungarees, plaid shirts, T-shirts, and a variety of windbreakers stood drinking and talking. Alan made his way awkwardly through the crowd, feeling scrutinized and evaluated, and squeezed in at the bar between two older men. Three young men in jeans and printed T-shirts were busily making drinks behind the long oak bar. The tall black-bearded one came towards him.

"Tequila and tonic, please," Alan answered the inquiring look.

The bartender gestured to his ear, indicating the noise.

"Gin and tonic!" Alan called over the confusion of voices and music, simplifying matters. He reached for his wallet and took out a five-dollar bill. In the mirror extending the length of the bar he caught his own worried expression. A curl on top of his head stuck up crazily. He had not combed his hair since morning. As casually as he could make it appear, he reached up and flattened the curl with his hand.

The man on his right looked at him and smiled.

"Here you go," the bartender placed the drink on the bar and took the bill.

Alan took a long swallow of the cold, bittersweet liquid and turned to face the room. The liquor ran down his throat, sharp but warming. He lowered the glass and noticed that no one seemed aware of his presence. He let his gaze wander over the crowd. Most had mustaches or beards and close-cropped hair. Many had handsome rugged-looking faces. With the exception of a dozen, they were all a good ten years younger than he. His eye stopped. Across the room, beyond a chest-high partition runing down the center, the sandy-haired young man from the supermarket stood against the wall talking cheerfully with a young blond in white carpenter's overalls. Alan sipped his drink. The liquor felt icy now as it sank to his stomach.

Another snappy disco song blared from the sound system.

So what had he expected? A dark hole in the wall with a dozen men standing around eyeing each other to the sound of an old Judy Garland song? A hand on his leg under the bar? A murmured invitation? It looked more like a fraternity house beer-bust!

He glanced the length of the room, searching the faces for Stephen Milner's.

"Why don't you and Frank join us?" he heard a snatch of conversation to his left. "We're driving down to Palm Springs for the weekend."

"We can't, John, I've got to work on Saturday."

Milner was not in the bar. Somehow, looking around, it did not surprise him. His gaze ran along a line of eight young men standing against the low wooden partition dividing the room. Their eyes, he noticed, were moving cautiously over the faces of the young men opposite them leaning against the bar. Brad had called the Motherlode a cruise bar, explaining how "it worked for some guys who need a quick, easy roll in the hay, but it's too impersonal for me. At least, the cruising side of it." Milner would not be the cruising kind either, he thought.

He looked down at the dark, chocolate-colored carpet and suddenly felt the stinging hurt of loneliness. There was really no reason to stay now; he had stopped in on the chance of finding Stephen. Alexis and the kids would soon start missing him.

When he glanced up, it was into a dark-bearded, sharply chiseled face with large, deep-set eyes that riveted him with frank sexual interest. The resemblance was there. But only faintly. In his coloring and in the trim of his black beard. Brad had once grown a beard, then shaved it after three weeks. The features were sharper than Brad's, rougher looking. Sensuous. His blue denim shirt, half unbuttoned, showed a well-developed chest with smooth black hair. He thought back to the morning and his chance encounter with the lab technician. Quickly he glanced away, feeling the disconcerting, unwanted signals of desire flood his body. He darted a look at two young men nearby talking cheerfully and wondered if they had noticed.

"Well, we sure as hell can't go to *my* place. I've got a lover at home," one of them was saying.

"We can't go to mine, either. *I've* got a lover."

Alan stared down into the hole of his half-empty glass. He had not planned on this. He really couldn't handle this. Besides, he shouldn't be here in the first place! His whole life lay elsewhere! Alexis was *waiting*.

When he looked up, the dark beard was leaning confidently against the partition with his gaze directed off to his right. A few feet away, Alan saw the object of his gaze—not unlike himself, with curly black hair, clean shaven, a few inches shorter. And younger. A good ten years younger. They were staring, faintly smiling at each other. His younger duplicate moved forward towards the black beard and stopped. He lifted his can of beer to his mouth, still smiling.

The black beard averted his gaze from Alan's younger, more handsome duplicate and looked at *him*, evaluatingly.

He recognized the game. Instantly. He had himself played it in singles bars.

Inside his pocket, against his thigh, Alan felt the soft vibration of his beeper.

Again, the black beard turned his gaze. Towards his smiling duplicate.

Suddenly, unaccountably, Alan realized he wanted to win.

Once again, the black beard looked at him. At first, impassively. Then he must have read something in his eyes, for a faint smile appeared at the corners of his mouth.

At one-second intervals, the beeper pulsed against his leg.

His younger version now looked at him, challenged.

As the dark-eyed black beard lifted his weight from the partition and came towards him, Alan felt his beeper go still.

Nervously, he smiled.

Alexis returned the receiver to the hook. She had phoned his office, the hospital, and then as a last resort, his service, to have him beeped. It was 7:23.

Angrily, she went to the oven and opened the door. In the last thirty minutes she had opened and closed it four times, trying to keep the roast from overcooking. The apples on the counter were starting to turn brown. She turned off the oven and left the door open. Maybe— she stared at the dark golden crust of fat—maybe something had happened, an accident. The streets were wet. She felt her anger dissolve.

"Mom! When are we going to eat? I'm starved!" Karen came through the kitchen door, still wearing her green and white school uniform.

"I told you to change out of your uniform," Alexis said sharply.

"I will, but when are we going to *eat?!*"

"Do it *now*, Karen!" Her voice, she realized, had risen to a point of rage.

Startled, Karen backed away. "I was doing my homework."

"Change, and then we'll eat." Alexis brushed by her into the dining room. She saw the two candles burning in their silver holders and blew them out.

"Is dad coming home?" Karen appeared at the door.

"He's delayed." She went around the table, stacking the dinner plates. "There was an emergency."

"You said he was on his way home."

"Well, obviously he's *not*."

Karen was silent for a moment. "He promised to help me with my project."

"I told you to change, little lady, now do it!"

She moved off in the direction of her room. "He promised. And now he won't. I know it. Just like the last time." She reached the opposite door. "And I hate him."

Alexis put the plates down, the breath momentarily knocked out of her. "What did you say?"

"I said I hate him," her voice went off through the foyer.

"Karen Stegman! You come back here!" Alexis shouted.

She caught up with her in the corridor outside her bedroom. In the spill of light from the room, she could read the look of cold hatred in the child's upturned face. "You will apologize for what you just said," her voice trembled.

Karen lowered her face and her dark hair fell forward, concealing it.

"Karen! Did you hear me?!"

"I apologize." She kept her head lowered.

"Why did you say that?"

"Because I felt it. He told me to say what I feel." She sniffled, then the tears came running down her cheeks. "He promised. He promised to help me with my project," she caught her breath.

Alexis lowered herself to her knees and took hold of Karen's hands. "I'll help you, how's that?"

"You can't. It's about nursing."

"I know something about nursing."

"I'm supposed to do it with dad," she broke into a sob.

"I promise you, when he gets home, he'll help you."

"No, he won't, he's going to come home too late. And I hate him."

"Listen to me, Karen." She took hold of her shoulders firmly. "Hate is a terrible thing. You must never say you *hate anyone*."

"I can't help it."

"Now go and change and tell Chris to come to the table." She rose to her feet. "We're going to eat now."

Karen turned away into her room, leaving Alexis standing and wondering if, just minutes before in the kitchen, she herself had not scratched the surface of a similar hatred.

"You work around here?" Bernie rested his arms against the bar, turning his beer can between his fingers.

"Yeah, not far."

"What do you do for a living?"

Caught off guard, Alan hesitated. "I'm a—I'm in real estate."

"I'm a cinematographer, presently unemployed."

"That must be rough."

"Rough? It's murder." Bernie looked up and raised the can to his lips. "I've been up for six camera jobs in the last month. I didn't get a one." Under the thick, close-cropped beard and mustache, his chiseled face broke into a wry grin. The playful movement of his large dark eyes implied that his thoughts were elsewhere.

The blast of disco drums over the sound system rose to a crescendo. Jostled from behind in the now closely packed crowd, Alan lurched forward a few inches. His hand came to rest on the bar close to Bernie's arm. He started to draw it back, then refrained.

"You an agent or a broker?"

"Agent," Alan felt suddenly trapped by his lie.

"Where do you live?"

"In—uh—Long Beach," he realized if he went on, it would begin to unravel, "And you?"

"Over on Larabee. About four blocks from here," Bernie tilted his head, smiled again, and jiggled the empty can. "That's probably more convenient than Long Beach."

The crowd in the area between the bar and the partition pressed in, sealing them against the edge of the bar. "Yeah. Much." To hide his blush, Alan lowered his face and caught sight of their left and right arms hanging side-by-side over the edge of the bar, less than an inch apart. The illuminated numbers of his digital watch read 7:43.

By now, they would be eating, Alexis at her end of the table, angry but silent. He should have left forty-five minutes before, should not have come here at all. *Should* have brought Alexis the sugar for her pie, her milk and cigarettes. But the pleasure of this stranger's company outweighed obligations at the moment. The loneliness, the aching need to connect with just one man for even a moment had gone. A new feeling rested in its place, a feeling unlike that he had had for Stephen Milner. Something purely physical that had nothing to do with friendship or future closeness.

"You want another drink?" Bernie raised his beer can. His sensuously sleepy eyes looked directly into Alan's with a much larger invitation than a drink.

"No, thanks." But on an impulse, Alan stared down at his chest, naked between the panels of his shirt. "I'll buy you one, though. I'm presently employed."

"I'm not much of a drinker."

"Neither am I."

Over the blare of disco horns, the female singer held her final note, half song, half cry, then broke off. In the momentary silence, Bernie reached out and touched Alan's hand with his fingertips, gently, tentatively. "You hungry?"

"Not particularly," Alan drew his hand back but then immediately regretted it. It was affection, he realized, not rape. The picture of Alexis's drawn, suspicious face as she carved the leg of lamb came to mind. It filled him suddenly with resentment. Of late, she had imposed on them both a schedule of breakfast, home by seven, dinner, and sleep. A little sex now and then. He knew *why* she had resorted to that dull Catholic boarding school routine they had begun marriage with. She was fighting for survival, using the old ax of housewife-and-mother that had worked so well when they were younger and new at love. Now, it only made him want to rebel.

"You want to have a drink at my place?" Bernie looked at him, wary but hopeful.

"Why not," Alan heard himself reply.

"Where'd you park?"

"In the Safeway parking lot."

"Me too."

Bernie reached back and put his beer can on the bar, "Ready?"

Alan hesitated. It was suddenly going too fast. A drink at his house. That odd euphemism. He looked again at Bernie's dark, hopeful eyes.

"It's up to you, man," Bernie smiled.

"Okay," Alan nodded, "sure." He felt the familiar edge of panic.

"Don't forget your change." Bernie pointed at the bar behind him.

Alan turned, gathered up the four dollars and change, remembered he had promised Karen fifty cents if she finished her school project, put the coins in his pocket, overtipped the bartender with a dollar, and began working his way through the crowd behind Bernie to the door.

The slice of lamb on her plate was lukewarm. Alexis sliced off a bite, pierced it with her fork, and forced it to her mouth. Across the silence in the dining room, she could hear the grandfather clock ticking in the foyer.

"Anyone for more lamb?" She tried to sound cheerful.

"Not for me, thanks," Chris said, moving the end of his potato around the plate.

"Karen?"

"No."

"No, thank you," she corrected.

"No, thank you."

At the end of the table, Alan's chair was empty. She had left his setting though, except for the plate. The mat, the silverware, the wine glass lay there. Reminders of past months.

"Is there any pie?" Chris asked.

"No. If your dad gets home with the sugar in time, I'll make it. If not, we'll have it tomorrow," Alexis said with finality to end the subject.

"He won't," Karen said.

Alexis caught sight of the glance exchanged across the table. "What do you mean by that?"

"He's not at the hospital and he's not at his office," Karen said in a categorical tone.

"So?"

"It's just like all those times before."

Alexis caught her breath. "And what does that mean, please?"

"I don't know." Karen shot a glance at Chris across the table, "Nothing." Chris looked down at his plate and sniggered.

"You know as well as I that your father has obligations outside the hospital and his office." She realized her voice was stridently defensive. "A doctor has all kinds of emergencies, Karen."

The clock in the foyer began striking the hour.

"If it's an emergency, why do you get mad at him?" Karen speared her meat with her fork.

"I only—" she faltered, looking from one impassive face to the other. "I get mad at him when he forgets to call, only because it ruins our dinner together," her voice trailed away lamely. Karen and Chris turned together and looked at her. In their faces she read the reflection of her own thought: the voice of the helplessly betrayed pathetic little wife.

The clock went on chiming, six, seven, eight, and then was silent.

"Hello, cat." Alan reached down to stroke the belly of the big grey Siamese cat curled up in a basket on the living room coffee table.

"That one's Smoke." Bernie turned on a floor lamp at the far end of the mustard-colored sofa. "The other one's Smog." He pointed to a second Siamese on the bookcase by the wall.

The living room of the one-story, one-bedroom cottage was small but neatly furnished, with still photographs of Bernie's camera work on the walls.

"What can I get you?" Bernie began pulling his shirttail from his trousers.

A taxi, Alan thought, but said, shrugging nonchalantly, "Oh, anything—a gin and tonic. With a lime."

The single closed button on the shirt opened on a slim waist and a line of dark stomach hair running from his chest down to his belt line.

"Make yourself at home." Bernie gave him a mirthful, puzzled look and turned towards an archway into a darkened corridor. "I'll see what I've got."

"Anything," Alan called after him. He glanced at his watch. It was now 8:21. Dinner would be over. Alexis could be almost anywhere—reading in bed, putting the kids to sleep, pacing the kitchen with the telephone.

A light in Bernie's kitchen went on. "If you don't have gin, forget it," Alan called. There was a rattle of bottles and the sound of the refrigerator door closing.

Alan turned towards the front door. He could be through it, across the small patch of front lawn, and into his car before the guy returned; he could end the whole insane thing *now*. Before the shirt came off entirely. Half of him was saying no, the other half yes. He was two people. If he let the old responsible side win, nothing in his life need change. There would be so little, then, to forgive. He would go into the kitchen and explain his problem, that he had a wife and children at home waiting. Thanks, anyway, but I'm really not ready.

Alan headed for the kitchen.

"Wine okay?" Bernie turned at the sink in his meticulously clean kitchen with a glass of white wine in his hand. His mouth widened in a frankly sexy smile. Under the overhead fluorescent light, the skin of his face was starkly fair against the jet black beard.

The flesh is willing, but the spirit is weak, Alan said to himself, suddenly feeling twelve instead of forty. "Wine's fine," his other half said nervously.

Bernie scrutinized his face. His smile became a grin. "Actually, this is your first time, isn't it?"

"My—?" Alan felt his face go crimson. "Not exactly. Almost."

Bernie came forward and handed him the glass, "Relax, man. It's only sex, it's not an execution." He looked him in the eye, smiling, and placed his hands lightly on Alan's hips. The wine sloshed from the glass over Alan's fingers.

Alan's heartbeat doubled.

"You either want to or you don't." Bernie stroked his waist gently. "And if you don't, then say so. The front door's open. On the other hand," he said as he pulled gently on his waist, "if you want, we can pretend I'm seducing you. If you like those games."

"No." Alan looked at the naked, dark-haired chest between the open panels of the shirt. "No games," he swallowed hard.

Bernie drew their bellies together until they touched. Alan listened to the rapid, alternating sound of their breathing. He wanted to touch Bernie's shoulder with his free hand but, for the moment, could not. Bernie's face came forward, the long black lashes sheltering his eyes. Alan closed his own and felt lips touch his neck. A warm jet of breath ran down his neck under his collar to his shoulder. He lifted his chin, felt the skin all over his body prickle. The wine sloshed again over his fingers. The breath moved up his neck, but before he could turn his face, he felt Bernie's lips graze his own. He winced. The clipped mustache and beard felt familiar. Brad had kissed him with a beard. Bernie's tongue now grazed his lips, wet and warm. Their breath mingled. As Bernie's arms closed around him, he felt a sudden luxurious impulse to yield. Without opening his eyes, he tilted his head forward and ventured a kiss on Bernie's mouth.

Bernie drew his head back, "Let's get comfortable, h-m-m?" he said softly.

Alan opened his eyes, stiffened at the sudden sound of a human voice, and nodded.

Moments later, facing each other beside the king-sized bed, Bernie dropped his shirt on the floor and reached for his belt buckle. Alan unbuttoned his own shirt. Bernie's jeans slid easily down his thighs. He wore no underwear. Alan dropped his shirt to the floor, unhitched the narrow belt around his grey trousers, pulled open his zipper, and looked down

at his blue boxer shorts. They were baggy and loose. He had always
worn baggy, loose shorts, he thought with bewilderment. He had never
thought how middle-aged they looked. Quickly, he pushed them over his
hips and let them fall to his ankles with his trousers. Bernie stepped out
of his jeans and came forward, naked. Lifting his leg to free his foot
from his trousers, Alan realized he had forgotten to remove his shoes.
Bernie saw his dilemma and, instead of embracing him as he obviously
intended, busied himself with the patchwork quilt on the bed.

Using the shoe of his right foot, Alan fumbled through the fabric
of his collapsed trousers and freed his left foot from the shoe. He shifted
his weight to his right foot and tried to repeat the same process, using
his left toe to hold down the lip of his shoe sole as he pulled his heel free.
The fabric of his long black socks was too slippery to hold.

Behind him, he heard the click of the digital clock on the bedside
table.

He bent over hurriedly and pulled his right shoe off, leaving it
somewhere in his trouser leg. With his index finger, he slid the tight black
stretch-sock down his left leg, pulled his foot out, and left the sock where
it fell. He did the same with his right sock. It had all taken, it seemed, an
eternity! He stood upright, naked now, and caught sight of the soft roll
around his lower abdomen. The erection he had, had gone. In comparison to Bernie's, it looked quite modest.

Lying stretched out on the yellow sheet, Bernie reached up and
took his hand. He was, Alan saw, slender but muscular against the sheet.
A white bathing suit line circled his groin and hips. He was erect, too.
Gently but firmly, Bernie drew him down beside him on the bed. In the
dim light of the bedside lamp, Alan blinked once. Bernie's arms circled
his shoulders and drew their bodies together. The hair of the chests
touched, made a soft scratching noise. Bernie's face came forward.
Alan opened his mouth to kiss and tasted, in the meeting of their tongues,
the bittersweet sourness of wine dissolve in their saliva.

"Alan Stegman! Alan W. Stegman!" Alexis glanced towards the
closed kitchen door, wondering if her shout had carried to the back of
the house, "He's a surgeon with West Hollywood General," she lowered
her voice, "Forgive me for shouting, sergeant. I'm worried, that's all."

"I understand, Mrs. Stegman," the desk sergeant sighed patiently
into the phone. "Do you know what time he left work?"

"Yes. About five forty-five."

"Did you talk with him then?"

"Yes. At his office on Wilshire Boulevard."

"In other words, he's about two hours and a half overdue."

"To say the least."

"About all we can do at this point, ma'am, is check our accident report files."

"That's what I asked you to do to begin with!" She jabbed her cigarette into the stainless steel sink.

"Now lady," he sounded suddenly threatening, "get ahold of yourself."

"For all I know, he could be slumped over his wheel dead somewhere with his head through the windshield!" There was a pause at the other end. She choked back a burst of tears.

The sergeant's voice came back, level, businesslike. "A new beige BMW, you said, license plate KVJ 648."

"Yes."

"Hold on, ma'am, I'll check the files." She heard the click of a hold button. Alexis shifted the receiver to her other ear and leaned against the counter, wiping her nose with a paper napkin. The streets *were* wet. Alan *was* a terrible driver. Her Aunt Margaret had died that way, in a car crash on a wet freeway. Uncle Lewis didn't find out for hours afterward! Alan drove that damn German toy like a movie stuntman!

"Mrs. Stegman," the sergeant's voice came back on the line.

"Yes?" her heart leapt.

"I've checked our accident files and there's no record of your husband's car being involved in any mishap."

Alexis sighed.

"If you want, we can put out a missing person report with his car license number, but you'd have to come down and file it personally."

The memory of Alan standing in the pantry, drunk, trying to open a can of soup came to mind. "I think I'd better wait, thank you."

"Give me your number and I'll notify you if something turns up."

"Five five O, four seven three two."

"Now if he doesn't turn up in the next few hours, phone us and we'll do what we can."

"Yes, I'll do that. Thank you." Alexis returned the receiver to the wall bracket and looked vacantly at the pie dish of uncooked dough drying on the counter. In the mixing bowl beside it, the apples had gone brown.

He was moving too fast, he knew, and if it happened again, he could not stop himself. At the other end of his body he felt Bernie's mouth. If he did that again, it would be over. He felt Bernie's body against his face, but kept his eyes closed, as if that somehow excused him from reciprocating. He had always refused to do this with Brad. It came again, this time crossing the point of no return. At that moment, Bernie moved away. Alan shook his head and made a sound, half groan, half cry. He reached down and took hold of himself, opened his eyes, but saw only the ceiling.

"Jesus," Bernie said.

Half a finish, but he couldn't help it. He closed his eyes again, caught between embarrassment and ecstasy, and went on spilling himself.

"You okay, swifty?"

Alan opened his eyes. Below, supporting himself on his elbow, Bernie smiled. Alan nodded and sighed.

"Are you sure this isn't your first time?"

He sat up on both elbows and tried to smile. "Yeah. I'm sure."

"Well—I guess, like anything, it takes practice."

Alan shrugged.

"If you want to use the john, it's in there." He pointed to the door.

"Thanks." Alan sat up and swung his legs off the bed. The digital clock beside his wine glass on the table clicked to 9:07. He rose, a little shaky, breathless still, and padded over the green shag carpet into the bathroom. He pulled out the plastic, fluted faucet head, turned it to the right, to the left, to the right, and then again to the left. The water went warm, then hot, splashing up in the yellow, oval-shaped sink. Alexis and he had had crazy faucets like these, but they had put normal ones in. He adjusted the temperature, took a cake of soap from the brass dish on the sink, and made a lather. In the heavy Victorian mirror he looked at his chest and waist, confirming his earlier comparison. He was a mess. Love handles on the sides, sagging pectoral muscles. If he had not passed over into homosexuality, he had certainly passed into middle age.

With Alexis, he had never really worried much about his physique. He looked down at his cock dangling over the basin with the spittle running up into his pubic hair. *Post coitum omne animal triste est.* After sex, every animal is sad. He had read that somewhere years before in college, and it had stuck.

He leaned forward to soap himself. On the shelf of the toilet tank, amid a cluster of *chachkes*, he saw a small bronze statue of the discus thrower, a chunk of uncut quartz, a small crystal frog, and a framed photo of a man in a turtleneck sweater and dungarees, caught in mid-laugh. Behind him was an early 1960s Ford. On the photo, scrawled in faded ink, was the inscription "Love always, Bob."

It was working. She could feel the languid euphoria through her body. One Valium would not have done it. Thank God she had taken two. Alexis moved her leg under the sheet towards Alan's side of the bed. It was cold.

The garden lights were on, throwing a pale blue-green light over the dark ceiling. Alan would wonder why she had turned out all the lights

in the house except for the porch and garden. He would see the pie shell
and apples on the kitchen counter. It was childish, she knew, but she was
limited in her weapons.

The outer edges of her anxiety and anger were crumbling away
now. She would sleep. Tomorrow, in the clear light of day, she would
cope with the bitter facts. This time realistically.

Her lids drooped.

Somewhere far off in the canyon came the sound of a wailing siren.
She listened to it with indifference, then drifted off.

"You're turning it the wrong way." Bernie came up beside him at
the door and twisted the nob. "Counterclockwise, this one." He opened
the door, obviously enjoying Alan's clumsiness. "Like a lot of things, it
turns the opposite way you expect." He stood back to let him pass.

"Thanks." Alan edged around the door and stepped out onto the
porch. The cold night air was welcome on his face. He took a deep
breath and turned. In the yellow porch light, Bernie's naked body was
boldly framed in the open front door.

"Good night." Alan looked down self-consciously.

"Good night."

He hesitated, wondering what he could add for the sake of polite-
ness.

"By the way, that wedding ring on your finger, is it for real?"

Alan nodded, ashamed.

"Well, listen man, I don't know what you're planning to tell her,
but it might make things easier if you zipped up your pants."

Alan dropped his eyes to his fly. It was open, with the tip of his
shirttail sticking out. Quickly, he stuffed it in, zipped up the fly, and
blushed. "Thanks," he said lamely, "I didn't notice."

"Forget it." The smile on Bernie's face widened into a mischievous
grin. "As Winston Churchill once said in a similar situation, 'Don't
worry, dead birds never fall from their nests.'" He chuckled and closed
the door.

For a moment Alan stared at the door, puzzled.

Startled by a noise, she rose up from her drugged sleep, lingered
momentarily on the edge of consciousness, then slipped back and
dreamed:

*She wore a wonderful blue silk dress as she sat at a concert Steinway,
fingering the notes. She was young, ten or eleven. She positioned her
fingers over the notes. She struck. No sounds came from the piano. From
the darkened cavern of the auditorium, there were titters.*

*She struck again. Nothing. Out of the corner of her eye, she saw
her parents in the first row, dressed in formal clothes, rise from their*

seats and start out of the hall. Deep inside the wonderful blue dress, she felt the sensation of warm liquid spreading through her underclothes. It felt good, made her feel strangely secure. As though she had suddenly grown up.

She smiled and began to play the waltz from Gounod's Faust. *She played the notes perfectly, even expressively, but they were silent. She looked down at the dress. Instead of urine seeping through, there was bright red blood.*

She got up, smiled apologetically, curtsied, and left the stage.

He turned off the kitchen light, leaving the pie shell and apples on the counter, and headed through the darkened house towards their bedroom. Leaving obvious clues to express her feelings—she had not resorted to that kind of childishness for years! It made him angry.

He felt his way along the dark corridor wall to the bedroom door. It was closed. She never closed the door, for the children's sake. He was suddenly frightened.

He stood still, just inside the bedroom door, listening to the faint rise and fall of her breath. In the glow of the garden lights through the window he could make out her shape on the bed.

Everything was forgivable, she had once said, except *in*deliberate cruelty.

Quietly, he closed the door and began to undress, dropping his clothes on the floor where he stood. If she woke now, he would break. Challenged, he would tell her everything. He would beg her, first, to hold him.

Naked, he crossed to his side of the bed. She was beautiful with her hair spread out across the pillow. She did not move. He opened his mouth to say her name, swallowed, then formed it silently on his lips. Still, she did not move. Slowly, he lifted the sheet and bedspread and carefully lowered his weight onto the bed. He lay with his body outside the covers and waited for her to stir. The sheet against his back was cold. He closed his eyes, mentally signaling her across the bed, begging her to wake up. He opened his eyes and looked up at the ceiling. It looked blue-green. It was really off-white.

Like a lot of things, the opposite way you expect.

After sixteen years, at the age of forty, he was running backwards. They both were. But he was the one destroying, not making, life.

This time—he closed his eyes, stung suddenly and deeply in his gut—for a moment's satisfaction, he had pushed her so far that she had simply stopped caring.

Under the descending weight of dread, he closed his eyes. The tears began, welling up between his closed lids, and then spilled, running past his temples into his sideburns.

V

"**B**ut mom!" Karen jerked at her pajama top. "You said this year we could get it two weeks before!"

"She promised!" Chris exclaimed to Alan next to him at the breakfast table.

"If Karen has decided there isn't any Santa Claus, then I don't see why we should even bother about a tree this year." At the stove in the kitchen, Alexis forked the last strip of bacon from the skillet.

"*She* said there wasn't, not *me!*"

"Finish your pancakes, Chris," Alan said.

"Phoebe and I are doing some Christmas shopping this morning," Alexis said. "Where are you having lunch?"

"At the hospital with old Driscoll from the accreditation committee. And you?"

"I don't know, I may drop by mother's." She felt vaguely relieved. Instead of his usual bathrobe, he had come down this morning in that same blue suit and maroon tie he had worn two days before, the day she phoned his office at noon to find that, contrary to what he had said that morning, he had gone out to lunch. Margaret, his receptionist, had not known with whom.

"These two are yours, Mrs. Stegman." Claire started into the breakfast area with a plate of pancakes.

"Thank you, Claire." She looked down at the slight bulge under her terry-cloth robe. Alan was on a diet now, getting thinner by the day, and she—blowing up like a Guernsey cow.

"Look! You used it *all!*" Chris shouted, "That was *mom's* butter!"

"She doesn't *use* butter, dummy!"

"That's enough!" Alan suddenly slapped the folded newspaper against the table. "You two are behaving like spoiled brats! Now finish and go get dressed for school!"

In the dead silence, Alexis transferred the bacon from the paper towel onto a platter. Passing her on the way to the sink, Claire shot her a troubled glance. It had been like this for the last nine days, since the morning of the fourth. The poisonous tension between them had spread to the children, and even to Claire. That morning, with her one question "Where were you?" and his one reply "Tied up," she had reached her decision. She would say nothing until he decided to come forward himself with the truth.

Alexis carried the platter of bacon to the table and sat down across from Alan. In the last nine days, they had been like boxers in opposite corners, waiting for the bell. Alan glanced at her, then went back to his paper.

"Well, Karen," she said, pouring herself a cup of coffee, "is there or isn't there a Santa Claus?"

"Do you believe in him, daddy?" she asked.

"Of course," he glanced at Alexis, "you can't expect *anything* from Santa unless you believe in him."

"If daddy believes in him, then I do too," Karen announced.

Sides, Alexis thought, and now the kids, without knowing why, are in their corners choosing sides.

"Then that settles it." Allan smiled, "If mom's agreeable, she'll get the tree today and decorate it tonight."

"She?" Alexis looked at him. In the past, Alan had been the one to buy the tree.

"I've got meetings with the committee all afternoon. Do you mind?"

"Since it's for the children, no, I don't mind."

"Mom!" Karen exclaimed, "Can we have a *white* one this year?"

"They've got pink ones, too!" Chris added.

Alan's eyes were on her, bewildered. "This year," she said, "I think we need a big traditional green one." She could not repress the note of pain in her voice.

"All the way to the ceiling!" Chris shouted.

"With the angel on top!" Karen squealed.

"Settled. A big green spruce." Alan kept his eyes on her and reached for the bacon.

"Sounds like we're getting some Christmas spirit around here!" Claire said from the kitchen. "Now if you want, Mrs. Stegman, I'll go ahead and roll the piano into the other corner this morning."

"Speaking of the piano." Alan broke the bacon on his plate with his fork. "If mom practices, we could all sing Christmas carols tonight."

"Practice!" Claire called, "if she keeps on running up and down those keys like she's *been* doing, I'm gonna have to buy earplugs!"

Alexis spooned sugar into her coffee. Damn Claire, she thought, I could kill her.

Alan stared at her, baffled.

Karen and Chris exchanged glances and giggled.

"You didn't tell me," Alan said.

"Rather than tell you, I was going to surprise you and play." She stirred her spoon in the coffee. "But that was ten days ago."

Alan lowered his eyes, silent.

"I'm full, mom," Chris said.

"I am, too," Karen said.

"In that case, go get dressed for school. And remember, Karen, Mrs. Winchel is picking you up after school; and Chris, Mrs. Salters is bringing you home. So both of you be out in front and don't keep them waiting."

Karen turned at the door. "Will the tree be here when we get home?" she ventured.

"It will if I can find one for a decent price," she replied tightly.

There was a naked silence when the kids had gone, broken only by the sound of Claire's pots and pans. Alexis concentrated on her pancakes. Twice yesterday she had come close to breaking her rule of silence. Far back in her mind was the old conviction that somehow Alan was different from other men regarding women. Over and over, she had tried to picture the kind of woman he might want. Nothing fit. She knew that instinctively. Always, she came back to the same conclusion: whatever he was looking for in another woman, *she* was the reason. And if the reason was to come out, *he* would be the one to announce it. Besides, for the moment, unfounded suspicion was still less wounding than the truth.

"I've got a rough day ahead," he said.

"*You?*" She detected the self-pity and asked, "Will Berrey be at the meeting?"

Alan nodded. "This time, they're going to serve the poor guy's head on a platter."

"Why?"

Alan folded the newspaper. "There was an incident at the hospital yesterday. Two cases of disseminated intravascular coagulation in patients who had undergone surgery that morning. They traced the cause back to a batch of i.v. solution of contaminated *E. coli* bacteria. Berrey and the administration are in serious trouble. Both patients died."

Alexis sat back. "Oh my God."

"It was an accident, but the FDA and the Communicable Disease Center are both calling for investigations, as well as the accreditation committee. They're going to open up a hornets' nest when they find out Berrey's reasons for contracting the lab that supplied the solution."

"The patients, they weren't—"

"No, they weren't mine. But the committee called me in to testify."

"You're going to testify against the administration, aren't you?"

"I'll answer questions. Berrey's there to see that the hospital makes money, I'm there to see that it provides health care. One has to make choices."

Alexis reached for the coffeepot. "Yes. One does." Stubborn and determined, as usual. The same virtues that made him a dedicated surgeon made him also at times an impossible human being and a husband who could not face being wrong.

He folded his napkin. "Will you do me a favor today?"

"Of course."

"Buy something for me to give dad for Christmas. I'm no good at shopping."

"What?"

"Something nice. I don't get out to see him much."

"Bullock's doesn't sell any substitutes for love," she heard herself say. She caught the wince in his face. "I'm sorry. That was unfair."

"*Alex.*" Surprised by the ominous color of his voice, she looked up. "Tonight, after we've decorated the tree, I want to talk to you about something."

The air ran out of her body. "All right."

He got up, leaned forward, and kissed her forehead. "I'll be home tonight by six-thirty."

"This morning, you know, I realized that Karen's growing up." She touched his hand on the table. "This is her last Christmas with Santa Claus. She's beginning to ask questions about a lot of things. Yes, I want you to talk. If only for their sake."

She listened to the sound of his feet heading towards the back door.

Funny, she thought, I'm actually glad you're going to be stuck all day in the hospital with meetings.

"You're aware, of course, you may have just cost this hospital its accreditation." Berrey kept pace with him down the corridor.

"Alexander and Driscoll asked questions and demanded examples. I gave them." Alan turned right and started counting off the numbers of the patients' rooms.

"You made me look like the director of a death camp," Berrey said.

A picture of his Uncle Aaron crossed Alan's mind. "One way or other, Arnie, we all have to die. My job here is simply to postpone that event."

Berrey dropped behind a pace. "You failed to mention the fact that your scrub nurse Carlin *requested* her promotion to a desk job."

Alan looked at the card with the number of Mrs. Vernon's room on it. He said, "The point was, she should have been replaced by a qualified RN, not an OR technician."

"In that, we were entirely within the law," said Berrey.

"Within the law or not, I will not continue to operate with inexperienced OR technicians acting as scrub nurses." He read the room number on the door: 432. Vernon was 859, at the far end of the corridor. "The technician on the Webber retrograde pyelogram case used xylocaine as a diluent for the radio-opaque dye instead of normal saline. The patient reacted under anesthesia with hemorrhagic cystitis."

"Oh, *come on.* Any RN could have made that mistake."

"Not Betty Carlin or any other competent scrub nurse. Except when they're so rushed and overworked by cutbacks in the nursing staff that they haven't got time to think."

Berry gained on him. His lean, colorless face was splotched with red. "Do you know what it costs to staff ten operating rooms with around-the-clock full-time registered scrub nurses?!"

"I do, Arnie. And I also know what it costs in human life and health when you close two out of ten operating rooms and staff the other eight with part-time truck mechanics. Yesterday, in the confusion, someone left an emergency case waiting unattended on a gurney in the hall outside an operating room."

"There was an alert! The entire staff was on the run!"

"Exactly. That's my point."

A nurse came towards them down the hall, carrying a medication tray.

Berrey fell back, his breath punctuating the air. Alan nodded and smiled at the nurse as she passed. "How long has it been since you had a cardiogram, Arnie?"

Berrey was silent. Their feet moved in rhythm on the industrial carpeting. "You don't seem to realize, Stegman," his voice was low, ominous, "if we ran this hospital your way, we'd be bankrupt in a month."

Alan looked at his watch, "I have nineteen minutes before I'm supposed to meet Driscoll for lunch. I have to see a patient, Arnie."

With two quick steps, Berrey was face-to-face with him. "I'm not going to let you and your partner Lindquist bring down this entire hospital, Stegman," he said, choking on his anger.

"Donald and I are working to bring it *up,* Arnie," Alan smiled. "If it fails, you may have your local pharmaceutical company who supplied your hospital operating rooms with a batch of quarter-normal saline contaminated with *E. coli* to thank."

Berrey's face whitened. "We have proof that the fault was entirely theirs."

"Yes, but someone's bound to ask why, when the bids were made for contracts to supply i.v. solutions, you settled for an outfit like Sunset Labs." He turned toward the door.

"By the way, Stegman—" the tone of voice behind him was deadly.

Alan turned back to see a menacing smile on Berrey's face. "The accreditation committee had a look at the operation reports."

"So?"

"It happened that one of the first ones they saw was for an operation you assisted on last June. On a certain Bradford Hollis, a radical pelvic lymphadenectomy."

Alan stared rigidly ahead. "So?"

"I checked with Jeff Marks, the patient's oncologist," Berrey's eyes narrowed, "and he raised the question of your relationship with the patient subsequent to the operation. During the two and a half months while he was undergoing therapy here at the hospital with Dr. Marks."

For a moment, in silent astonishment, Alan stared at Berrey. "Mr. Hollis was a friend of mine. Marks knows that."

"We have very strict codes here at West Hollywood General about physician-patient relationships."

"Are you trying to tell me something, Arnie?"

"No, I just want to point out that we're not all saints in this business." Without waiting, he moved off down the corridor.

Minutes later, Alan closed the door behind himself in one of the first-floor public telephone booths and fumbled in his pocket for a dime. After four conversations on the phone and two visits, he knew the number. He dropped the coin in the slot and quickly dialed.

"Psychiatric clinic," the switchboard operator two buildings away answered.

"I'd like to speak to Dr. Stephen Milner, please."

"Just a moment." The switchboard rang Milner's line.

"Doctor Milner's office," a woman answered.

"This is Doctor Stegman, I'd like to speak to Doctor Milner, please."

"I'm afraid he's not in, sir. Today's his day off."

"Would he be at home, do you know?"

"He phoned a short while ago, doctor. He said he was on his way to play tennis. He's got his beeper. Shall I have him beeped for you?"

"No." Alan steadied his voice. "Do you happen to know *where* he's playing?"

"I'm not sure, but I think he plays over on that court south of Wilshire on La Cienega."

"Thanks. I'll try there." He hung up, pushed the door open, and hurried across the vast lobby towards the door leading to the basement parking garage.

Downstairs, in the cavernous third level, he was halfway to his car at the far end when the realization came to him that Berrey's threat was, in point of fact, idle. True, sexual relations between a physician and a patient were grounds for revoking a doctor's hospital privileges, but in this case he had only the opinion of one biased, resentful man. And Marks's opinion, as evidence, was nothing more than slanderous hearsay. Useless.

Alan slowed his pace, relieved. Why this panic? He was being paranoid.

He glanced towards an empty parking slot on his left and read the sign stenciled in paint across the concrete tire buffer: *Reserved.* After almost a month, Rutledge's slot was still empty. Back at the end of summer, the rumor had started circulating around the hospital that Pete Rutledge had a drinking problem. No formal charges were made, it was just a rumor. Then one day, Pete's black Cadillac was no longer there. He had simply and quietly withdrawn.

Alan inserted the key into the lock on the driver's door of his BMW. In a hospital like this, rumor had been enough to force Rutledge out. Among nurses and staff, dropping a rumor was like throwing a burning cigarette out of a car window into the dry brush of Malibu Canyon. He opened the door and got in. And now, before the day was over, he would have to share with Alexis not only the truth of his relationship with Brad, but the possible effects of it on their future lives.

"For God's sake, Alexis, wait up!" Phoebe called.

Alexis maneuvered her way through the crowd of women around Bullock's first-floor bag counter and drew up beside a glass case displaying perfumes. She shifted the clutch of four small sacks from her right to her left arm.

"Jesus!" Phoebe came towards her, "Are you Christmas-shopping, honey, or running the decathlon?!"

Alexis ran down her mental list of purchases. The blue wool cardigan for Claire (to replace the old brown one she wore from November to April), the greenhouse plant thermometer for her mother, the wallet for her father (he had carried the same old ratty black one for the last two years), and the plaid wool skirt for Karen.

"Now just what the hell is going on?" Phoebe blocked her way down the aisle.

"I'm sorry, this Christmas crowd is getting to me." She sidestepped Phoebe and continued through the oncoming flow of shoppers.

"Damn it, Alexis," Phoebe shouted over the noise of the department store, "you're behaving like a madwoman!"

"I don't feel well!" Alexis called back over her shoulder. "I want to finish and get home!" It was noon now. Alan would be on his way to lunch with Driscoll.

"I don't believe you! Something bothering you and I want to know what it is!"

Alexis bore down on three young men in jeans and lumberjack shirts coming towards her down the main aisle. They parted as she passed and turned left between two counters. After buying Max's backgammon set and Chris's skateboard (she had finally given in to his pleas), she would stop at a pay phone and call the hospital. She could use the backgammon set as a pretext.

"Listen, Alex." Phoebe zigzagged up and kept pace a foot behind her. "You might as well tell me because I'm going to find out one way or the other."

"There's nothing to say."

"It's written all over your face, sweetheart. I know a Christmas breakdown when I see one."

"I don't want to talk about it," she said, at the same time admitting to herself that she did. She had wanted to tell her best friend for the last nine days. She halted suddenly alongside the jewelry counter and saw herself reflected in the display-case mirror. "I look ridiculous, don't I?" she stared at her face, then at her distended stomach.

"Hysterical is more like it," Phoebe drew up beside her.

"This dress," the larger despair was momentarily funneled into the outdated, bloused silk print dress she had chosen earlier for comfort, "I look like a pregnant Napa Valley grape picker."

"Alexis, look at me!"

"I do." She pulled at the skirt. "You heard what that saleswoman said up in the sportswear department."

"Turn around and answer me, Alex!"

Without waiting, she started off again down the aisle and rounded another counter.

"It's Alan, isn't it?" Phoebe caught up with her, breathless now, and reached out for her arm.

"Yes!" she spun around, exploding, "I could kill him!" she jerked her arm back, "It's happened! Just like with you and Roy!"

"Oh, for God's sake," Phoebe's face fell. She reached up to the lapel of her tailored, grey pantsuit. "Another woman?"

"No! A two-hundred-pound talking parakeet. Phoebe, for Christ's sake, what else?"

They stared at each other for a moment.

"You, of all people."

"Yes. Me of all people."

"The rotten bastard. I would never have thought."

"Well, that makes two of us."

"Do you know who the craven bitch is?"

"No. If I did, I'd kill her too."

Nearby, the young male clerk behind the counter looked in their direction, worried.

"Are you absolutely *sure*?"

"Of course I'm sure! Where did you think Roy had been those nights when he came home drunk?!"

"Now don't go by *Roy*. Roy is not Alan. Roy was a *compulsive* fucker."

"Compulsive or not, he's been fucking another woman!" Alexis glared defiantly at two passing women who turned abruptly to stare at her, shocked. "I may be *slow*, but I'm not *blind*!" she went on vehemently, feeling a sudden exhilaration in publicly letting herself go.

Phoebe came forward with a look of alarm, "Now control yourself, Alex. Let's go have a coffee somewhere."

"I don't want coffee, I want a little justice!" She stepped back a foot, "This has been going on for months! I've had enough!"

From the direction of the jewelry counter she heard the sound of a suppressed chuckle. She turned to see the young salesman smiling at them with what looked like ridicule. Further down the counter, a middle-aged couple exchanged glances and smiled. She looked away, vacantly staring at a twinkling silver collage suspended from the ceiling by a transparent wire. The store decorations, sprays of fake spruce with trailing ribbons, suddenly struck her as empty, cheerless, and sad.

With a sudden feeling of shame for her outburst, Alexis moved off towards the luggage display. She had lost her eleven-month battle, and it was now only a matter of time.

"Alexis." Once again Phoebe caught up with her, "Let's get out of here and go have a drink somewhere."

"I'm going to buy a backgammon set," she said, keeping her eyes fixed on the flow of shoppers shuffling towards her down the aisle.

"I've been through this kind of mess three times. I want to help, but I'm not going to chase you down the labyrinthine ways of Bullock's!"

"If I don't keep shopping," her voice trembled uncontrollably, "if I don't find a backgammon set, a skateboard, and a nine-foot spruce by three this afternoon, if I don't hold onto some plan for the rest of this day, I am going to *crack*."

"Nietzsche once said, 'If they do not love at first, pass on.' "

"After sixteen years, you do not just *pass on*."

Phoebe, she noticed, was keeping five paces behind her. "The thing is, my sweet, have you got positive proof?"

"I have lived with the man for a decade and a half, I don't need a signed affidavit. I can read his mind."

"Jesus!" Phoebe jumped aside to avoid a child darting suddenly from behind a clothes rack, "If you don't slow down, you're going to kill some *innocent* person!"

"Just stay behind me." Alexis kept her stride, bearing down on a cluster of men milling around a rack of sport coats. "No man, except a husband, would run down a six-months-pregnant woman."

"No, Stephen, I've changed my mind," Alan said, watching Stephen's tennis partner head off towards a blue Mustang parked at the curb, "I'm going to tell her everything. About the guy ten days ago, about Brad—everything. I've got to now."

"You said you had several choices on Tuesday when we talked. What happened?" Stephen wiped his face with a towel.

Alan sighed, "It's a long story. Have you got time to talk?"

"Sure. It's my day off. I'll get my stuff together, and we'll walk." He squatted on the ground, and began gathering the loose tennis balls and dropping them in his gym bag. The sweat on his back had soaked through his white T-shirt.

"If you're tired, we can sit on that park bench over there," Alan indicated an empty bench under a tree beside the tennis court.

"It'll be easier for you if we walk."

Stephen's partner opened the trunk of his car and threw his tennis bag inside. Alan had arrived at the La Cienega courts just as the two men were finishing. He had waited out of sight and watched them. Richard, the partner, had played well. They had obviously played together before. They were evenly matched—in age, as well. The easy, good-humored way they played together, the affection Stephen had shown his handsome, dark-haired opponent when they said good-bye (absently holding his arm while they talked) had given Alan a feeling of jealousy—surprisingly, considering what he had come there for.

Stephen stood up with his racket and bag in his right hand and looked at him. His tanned face darkened with worry. "You look like you've seen a ghost, Alan."

"I have," he turned away.

Together, they started down the long tree-lined sidewalk along La Cienega Boulevard, heading south towards Pico. Alan wondered if he could say what he wanted to, walking on a crowded street in the open, midday sunshine with the oncoming pedestrians staring at them. Stephen was conspicuous in his white tennis shirt and shorts. Alan took a deep breath. "I need your help, Stephen."

"Up to now, you've only wanted to talk. What happened?"

"I've got to get to the psychological cause of this thing and reverse it," he replied in the words he had prepared, "before it's too late."

Stephen was silent for a moment, then said, "I see. You mean, you want me to help you return to where you were before, to the Alan of last year?"

"Yes."

"Do you think it's possible?"

"People have found themselves before," Alan said a little lamely.

"People have adjusted their *behavior*, yes."

"Until the other night, I was okay with the behavior—at least for these last three months. I'm not talking about behavior."

"*Alan*—" Stephen slowed his pace and looked at him. "Come on, now, use your head. You're a doctor. You've read enough psychology to know that no medical science, mine included, can alter the simple *direction* of your sexual desires."

"I'm not talking about sexual desire, either." His voice wavered. "I can take a cold shower or jerk off for *that*."

Stephen reached up and rested his free hand on Alan's shoulder. "What's happened, Alan, have you fallen in love with some guy?"

"*No*." He looked down at the cracks in the cement passing under their feet. "Not yet. I've looked ahead, though. I know where this is *heading*. It's one thing to want to *ball* a man now and then, it's another to want to *be* with them—all the time. I've"—he momentarily lost his breath—"I've got a family. A wife and two kids and a third on the way. I love them. I love her. I've got a profession, I'm forty years old, I've got a wife and three kids—" He stopped and turned away from the street. "And I'm going to lose them."

"I'll help you all I can, Alan."

"I'll be damned if I'm going to become a goddamn fucking *faggot!*" The rage barreled up out of his gut. A hundred feet away, an elderly couple sitting under the trees turned to stare.

Behind him, Stephen said quietly, "If you mean by that a tormented little girl trapped in a man's body, I hope not."

"I'm sorry—that was unfair."

"The guy you were seeing all those months, was he a faggot?"

"No," the word was inaudible and he shook his head.

"He's still around, isn't he? You're still seeing him."

Alan felt his eyes fill. He closed them.

"Bradford—is that his name?"

He nodded.

"You told me he'd gone for good."

Alan opened his eyes and turned slowly. "He's dead."

Stephen's face registered the expression in his own. For a moment, there was only the noise of the street traffic. That, and the leaves of the tree overhead shaking. "This is no place to talk," Stephen said. "Get your car. Follow me. We'll go to my place." He reached out and gripped his arm reassuringly.

"I'm sorry to run, mother, but I've got shopping to do before the kids get home." She entered the Tudor-style living room and crossed to the green velvet armchair. "Thank Rosa for me; as usual, her shrimp salad was wonderful!"

"If you don't slow down and stop chain-smoking, dear, you're going to ruin your health," Helen followed her into the living room. "And the baby's."

"Stop harping, mother," she said as she scooped up the backgammon set in the seat of the chair. "I'm as healthy as an all-star quarterback!" She tried to sound brisk and cheerful.

"*Alexis*," her mother said, following her towards the foyer.

"Please, mother, I have to *go*!"

The sound of Helen's heels came toward her on the marble floor of the foyer where she was trying to turn the heavy brass doorknob, "Don't you think a hundred and forty-two dollars is a bit steep for a backgammon set?"

"Actually, there was one for four hundred." She gave the knob a frustrated yank.

"To the left, or have you forgotten?"

"Alan specifically said something *nice*." She turned the knob to the left and swung the heavy oak door open. "And besides, Max is seventy-six years old, and how many Christmases has he got left?!"

"At that price, dear, I hope he can take it with him—wherever they go."

Alexis stepped out onto the wide, blue-slate front steps and glanced back at her mother. "For someone who goes to mass and communion six times a week, how do you account to yourself for your anti-Semitism?" In the bright sunlight she squinted to see her watch. It was 1:25. She had phoned Alan at the hospital at 1:10, but he had not answered the page.

"Just a moment, young lady."

Alexis continued down the steps towards her station wagon parked in the gravel turnabout. He was still in the cafeteria with Driscoll, she had decided. Later, after she had hung up, she had felt ridiculous for trying to chase him down again.

"*Alexis*."

She turned to see her mother scrutinizing her from the top step, worried.

"Are you all right?"

"All right?" She thrust the backgammon box under her arm and opened her purse to dig for her sunglasses and car keys, "Of course I'm all right. I'm fine! Why?"

Helen came down the steps towards her, "You're not yourself today. You're a nervous wreck, you spent the entire time chattering about nothing, and you look dreadful."

"I told Phoebe this dress looked awful." Flustered, she let the keys drop to the gravel.

"I meant you, not the dress."

As she stooped for the keys, she covered her eyes with the sunglasses, "I have a million things to do before the holidays and this Christmas shopping is driving me bats."

"You needn't hide behind sunglasses."

She rose, adjusting the glasses on her nose, "What *are* you talking about, mother?" She should have followed her instincts and grabbed a sandwich with Phoebe at Hamburger Hamlet. If she could read Alan's mind, her mother was no worse at reading hers.

"Don't be evasive, Alexis, I'm your mother."

"I have a skateboard and a Christmas tree to buy before three o'clock." She turned towards the car door. "I wish you'd say what you mean."

"I will. You're having problems with Alan, aren't you?"

She opened the door quickly, "Don't be ridiculous," she said, and got in.

Helen continued across the gravel, "The other night when you and Alan brought the children over, you hardly spoke to each other. I noticed it, your father noticed it, and even Rosa noticed it."

Alexis pretended to hunt for her ignition key on the ring. She had dreaded this moment for months, knowing that when the truth came out, her parents would instantly unload seventeen years of stored-up artillery against Alan.

"Alan is under terrific pressure at the hospital, mother." She thrust the key into the ignition, "He's waging an all-out war with the administration and Arnold Berrey is gunning for him. Tuesday night, he came home exhausted." She turned the key and started the motor. "We were both tired that night."

"He seemed quite cheerful at lunch," she heard her mother say.

Alexis stared at the steering wheel, feeling her face go white. "At lunch?"

She heard Helen's feet on the gravel, coming towards the car. "Yes, at lunch. I was having lunch with friends at the Bistro and I happened to see Alan."

"Oh?" Suddenly dizzy, she concentrated on the emblem in the center of the wheel.

"You seem surprised by that." The voice came through the open window, toying playfully it seemed.

"Why should I be surprised," she blurted out, "he eats lunch there all the time!"

Her mother's hands came to rest on the door above the window opening. She could see the glint of her big diamond wedding ring in the sun. "I merely mentioned it because he looked quite cheerful and rested that afternoon."

"Really?" Alexis paused, then heard herself say "Who was he with?"

She could feel her mother's eyes on her, interpreting the expression on her face.

"I didn't recognize the person. We came in late. They were on the far side of the room. His guest was behind a potted ficus tree."

"Then you didn't speak?"

"No. I assumed they were talking business." The motor idled in the stillness. Alexis turned her head and met her mother's narrow, reproachful gaze. "He was with a man, Alexis. Did you think I was speaking of a woman?"

For a moment, they locked eyes. Alexis felt her face go hot, realizing she had been outmaneuvered, as always, by her mother.

"If you say anything to dad, I'll kill you." She put the gear into drive and shot ahead, leaving an empty furrow in the gravel turnabout. Halfway around, she saw her mother lurch backwards to the narrow lip of grass between the gravel and the steps, her hand pressed to the midline of her innocuous-looking beige wool dress, a look of injured shock on her face.

Damn you, she thought.

Moments later, she skidded to a halt between the stone gate posts at the far end of the drive. She sat back, gripping the wheel, and with an almost giddy sense of relief drew in a deep breath.

"And Alexis has said nothing?" Stephen came towards him across the polished hardwood floor with a steaming mug of coffee.

"Not directly, no. She wouldn't. She's too scared to ask." Alan took the mug and turned towards the sliding glass doors leading out into the patio. "She thinks I've been seeing a woman."

"You and Brad never told anyone?"

"No." He looked out into the small, tropically planted patio. Through the open door he could hear a dribble of water falling from the stone face of a gargoyle into the Spanish fish pond against the far wall. "At the end of March, she asked me, and I denied seeing another woman. I preferrred that to the truth."

"Even while he was dying?"

"Even then. Even after."

"And nobody in the hospital suspected?"

Alan turned back towards Stephen, who was standing between the glass-topped coffee table and the sofa. In his white tennis clothes, against the opposite white wall, his face, arms, and half-naked legs looked even darker than they were. "Yes. Jeff Marks, his oncologist. Brad mistook him for me one day. And after him, Scotty Oates and Cathy Riddel, the floor nurses. You know how gossip flies in hospitals." His voice sounded small and distant in the huge, vaulted living room. Considering the man looking at him across the room, the surroundings were puzzlingly austere. A comfortable modern sofa and two armchairs, a few oriental carpets, a big bookcase over the work table at the far end of the room, and plants, lots of plants. But it was all curiously austere, almost monastic.

After a moment, Stephen said, "It was slow in coming, wasn't it?"

Alan nodded. The dribble from the patio went on monotonously. "I operated with Fowler on June sixteenth. He died on September fourteenth."

"But you stuck by him."

Again, Alan sensed something inside him give way. The steaming coffee sloshed in his mug. A long trickle of it splattered on the shiny floor. He held the mug out and looked down.

"Never mind, Alan. Forget it."

He turned again towards the patio, set the mug on the old copy of *Time* lying on a nearby table. At the open door, he looked out at a huge banana tree sheltering a corner of the patio. "No, I didn't. Not really." His voice carried outside and sounded lost. "In all the months I knew him, even when he was dying—even that last day—I never once let him think I needed him." He took a deep breath, then went on, "A few hours before he died, I went to the ICU where they had him. He was"— Alan closed his eyes. The picture was still clear in his mind—"he was very small then, weighed almost nothing. For a moment, he was conscious. He recognized me. He asked me . . . he asked me to stop the pain. I knew what he meant. I knew I could do it; once he lapsed back into coma, I could do it, even though he wasn't legally gone. It's done all the time. They simply turn everything off, pull the plug. Nothing is said. I could have said yes. He was conscious, and I could have let him know that I loved him enough to do that much for him. But I didn't. I was afraid. He was Marks's patient, not mine. And I was afraid. I said nothing. Which was the same as refusing. Brad understood, I saw it in his eyes, he knew I wouldn't stop the pain. I could have given him that"— he opened his eyes and caught the blinding sunlight from the patio— "but I didn't."

Behind him, there was the sound of Stephen's feet coming towards him.

"I know it sounds like a little thing, my refusal. But it isn't," his voice broke. "You know what I mean? Just acknowledging his love for me would have meant everything to him, and it would have cost me nothing."

Stephen's hand came to rest on his shoulder.

"I loved him, but not in the way he loved me. I couldn't. Not then. Still"—he could no longer control the shaking in his voice—"I could have said I did. That lie would have been closer to the truth."

In the stillness, for what seemed minutes Stephen's fingers went on gripping his shoulder.

Alexis smiled to herself. Through the rearview mirror of her station wagon she could see the huge blue spruce protruding out five feet through the open tailgate. Uncertain about California laws for hauling ten-foot Christmas trees in the five-foot rear of a station wagon, she had tied her grey and blue Hermès scarf to the end of the tree, the branch where Karen's angel would sit.

Through the thick foliage she could see the scarf flapping crazily in the wind. The woman at the wheel of the car behind her was smiling, too.

She had haggled the man down from an absurd forty dollars to an outrageous thirty-six, pointing out a gaping hole in the side of the tree, exhorting him about the Christmas spirit, even reminding him of Scrooge's fate. That argument obviously had had more effect on him than the hard-nosed-salesman approach. She had driven away from the lot on West Pico, however, with a gigantic fulfillment of her promise to the kids and, even better, the first tingle that year of Christmas spirit.

Momentarily breaking free in the northbound traffic on La Cienega Boulevard, she let up on the accelerator for the Melrose streetlight to turn green, then speeded up again. She would swing into West Hollywood, stop by the store where Phoebe had remembered a sale on skateboards, then double back down Fountain and Sunset for home. The kids would already be there, waiting for her return with the tree. She looked forward to gliding down the drive to the front door, honking the horn, and watching them charge out of the house, squealing with excitement.

She took a deep breath, inhaling the sweet foresty odor of the tree. Alan would be pleased with her choice.

"Did you think it was a woman?"

Grasping for straws or not, she had been wrong again, at least about Tuesday's lunch. Maybe tonight, after decorating the tree and putting the kids to bed, they could sit down under the lights and face each other with honesty.

Alexis reached over and turned on the radio, feeling relieved and strengthened. The sound of a piano filled the car. She frowned, unable to identify the dissonant, angular melody. Keeping her eye on the bumper of the car ahead, she began to play a familiar game with herself, narrowing the piece down from century, to country, to possible composers.

"Marks, I think, has told Berrey everything." Alan lifted his mug from the magazine and sipped the lukewarm coffee.

"Even so, what can he do?"

"Nothing directly." He turned towards Stephen, who was leaning against the back of the armchair with his thumbs hooked in the pockets of his tennis shorts. "We both know he'd like to get me off his staff. I'm a thorn in his side. But his hands are tied. He can't accuse me of anything publicly."

"You mean, accuse you of seducing a patient."

"I didn't. And besides, if he makes a charge like that and can't prove it, he opens himself up to libel. Berrey's a businessman first—only a fool second."

"Then you have nothing to fear." The tension in Stephen's face relaxed.

"What he can't do publicly, he can do privately. With rumors. We move in the same social and professional circles. His wife talks regularly with mine."

Stephen's eyes widened with surprise.

"That's real paranoid of me, isn't it?" he smiled.

"I don't know. I find it hard to believe he could be that malicious."

"That depends on how much of a threat I am to his ambitions. In our business, Stephen, rumors alone can be very effective."

"Jesus."

"But more important than that, I don't want Alexis to find out about me through an ugly rumor. I'll tell her myself—everything. Tonight."

Stephen looked at him thoughtfully for a moment. "I've met her only once, Alan. She loves you. If you tell her everything—and tell it honestly—she'll understand."

Alan nodded, then sighed, "Nonetheless—I'm still scared. It's going to change everything for us. She's not a sophisticated woman."

"You'll manage," Stephen smiled. There was confidence in the smile.

"I'll need help."

For a moment, in silence, they looked at each other. "There are psychiatrists who believe they can change the direction of someone's sexual desires," Stephen said, "but I'm not of that school. You know that."

"Right or wrong, I've got to try. I love her."

Stephen's gaze wandered, and for a moment he seemed caught up in his own thoughts.

"You've met her," Alan continued, "she's worth fighting for."

The alert blue eyes turned back to fix on him. "Yes, she is. And so are you. You for your*self*."

Alan moved towards his suit coat draped over the back of the sofa, thoughtful for a moment. "I understand what you're saying, but if you can't help me professionally, maybe you could help me as a friend. I—" He hesitated. "I don't really know any gay men I can talk this way with."

"It may come as a surprise to you, Alan, but that afternoon at the party, before I knew anything about you, I knew I wanted you for a friend. Gay or straight."

Alan looked back at Stephen, who had turned towards him. He recalled the brief moment at the party with the platter between them, and later, his foolish, lonely excuse for going into the Motherlode. Now, he felt suddenly the tug of mutual affinity. "Thanks." He threw his jacket over his shoulder, "I'll be needing friends."

Zindler. She had never heard of him. Alexis reached over and switched off the radio as the announcer came on to serve the next classical treat, the second movement of Brahms's First Piano Concerto, another old chestnut made popular by the movies. Annoying, she thought, how the two FM stations in Los Angeles usually fed you a diet of hit tunes.

But Zindler. Some new sun rising on the musical horizon; but not so new, obviously, that his rays hadn't hit the shores of Southern California.

She turned off the steep grade of North La Cienega and started eastward on Fountain. It annoyed her not to have kept up with composers these last six years.

A half block ahead, an ancient black pickup truck turned from a sidestreet and lumbered into the lane directly ahead of her.

She applied her brakes, dropped her speed to ten miles an hour, then glimpsed something, the tail end of a tan BMW parked in the sloping drive of a huge, Spanish-style apartment building on the far side of the street. The front half of the car was concealed behind the wide trunk of a sycamore on the lawn. The car looked familiar, even from a hundred feet away. She pressed down quickly on the brakes, edged to the curb, and looked again towards the driveway. He was standing by the half-open door on the driver's side, his blue suit almost black in the shade of the tree, talking to someone screened from her view by the tree. As he swung the door open, the figure stepped from behind the sycamore and moved toward Alan. She recognized the man at once, Stephen Milner, the young psychiatrist Phoebe had brought to Karen's birthday party. He was dressed in a white T-shirt and tennis shorts. For no apparent reason, the sight of him moving towards Alan struck a chord of dread in her. Without thinking, she raised her hand from the steering wheel. As he moved towards Alan, she knew by the way he held his arms that he would not stop. By the way Alan moved his arm from the open door and held it forward, she knew that he did not want the man to stop. Milner reached Alan and, without hesitation from either, they embraced. In the instant their arms closed around each other, she told herself it was an ordinary embrace—an embrace of simple affection —nothing. The embrace held. It held and then still held—for a moment too long—held on as her body recoiled, struck from the front, stomach level, dead on, by an unseen hand. She opened her mouth, unable to speak, scream, or breathe.

They pulled apart, smiling.

Her free hand hit the steering wheel with a thud. She arched backwards, her arms and hands rigid on the wheel, and forced herself to breathe in.

They stood talking, face-to-face, smiling. Alan nodded.

The deep, sudden air in her lungs made her dizzy. She exhaled, made a low, unbroken sound through her open mouth. Her mind emptied, then seemed to fill, holding only one thought: to get away, to leave without being seen.

Mechanically, her eyes now fixed on the yellow stripe in the center of the street, she pressed down on the accelerator. She drove, it seemed, as though she were going on a leisurely holiday—slowly, a little mindlessly—and approached the next corner. Through the rearview mirror, she watched with indifference as a fast-moving Porsche drew up behind her. The driver had a look of disgust on his face. Calmly, disregarding a car approaching in the opposite lane, she made a slow, curving left into the sidestreet with all the serenity of a little old lady in an old Plymouth. With an utter lack of concern, she listened to the angry blare of a car horn passing behind her.

A hundred yards up the steep grade towards Sunset Boulevard, she stopped in the center of the deserted, residential street. For a moment, she sat staring through the windshield at the black asphalt strip tapering off towards the crest of the hill. Far down inside herself something fell away, like the center of her body. With that, like the inpouring of a terrific light, she let the understanding of it break on her. The light of it bleached the landscape around the car.

She lowered her face and, stoop-shouldered, gripping the upper rim of the wheel, felt her tears wash down and fall from the center of her open eyes onto the fabric of her cumbersome, hideous dress.

I promise you, you're the only woman I want.

She raised her head. The long, unbroken sound that came from her mouth filled the car. The street outside wavered and blurred before her eyes, then came into focus, starkly black and hard.

Did you think it was a woman?

She took her foot from the brake and shoved down on the accelerator. Behind her, the bottom of the Christmas tree rose up and struck the ceiling of the car. It held there as she raced up the hill and braked at the crest, then lurched downward, coming to rest with the naked trunk thrust forward over the seat a foot from her head.

And all along, fucking her, he was fucking men.

Gunning the motor, she shot forward through the eastbound Sunset traffic, whipped left, then cut between two westbound cars. There was a screech of brakes and a blare of horns on both sides. On her right, in the next lane, an elderly couple inched up beside her and stared, alarmed and outraged, through the window. Creeping forward in the stalled Sunset Strip traffic, she reached up and wiped her eyes, leaving a black streak of eyeshadow on her palm. The tears came again, this time with an uncontrollable trembling of her entire body. Disregarding the cars around her, blinded by the yellow blister of the sun ahead, she gave in and wept.

With a woman, with another woman, at least he could have gone with a woman!

In her slow, interminably winding drive down the Strip towards Beverly Hills, the thought kept breaking in on her. With a woman, at least, she would have had some fighting chance! With a man, against that she had no defense. Turning from Sunset onto Benedict Canyon Drive, she reached for her purse and fumbled inside for the crumpled wad of Kleenex at the bottom.

She herself had done something wrong. She had, without knowing it, failed him. In the last years, she had somehow stopped being a woman for him, had driven him to it. She drew the wad of Kleenex over one eye, then the other, feeling suddenly the emptiness of complete failure. A back draft through the open tailgate sent the sweet, sickening odor of spruce through the car. She looked out at the rapidly passing avenue of tall, manicured palms lining the drive.

Stephen Milner. How long had it been going on? Had he come to Karen's birthday party, pretending to meet Alan for the first time? Had Alan—the thought of it sickened her further—slept with him in their bed? And before Milner? Gerald Dorn, his friend from Ohio? Bill Spalding, him too? And Walter, his sometime racquet ball partner? Hurriedly, she raced back through the men he had introduced her to in the last few years, picturing each of them naked with Alan, kissing and embracing. Fucking. She felt her stomach go loose, like pudding. How could she have lived with him for sixteen years and not known?

She accelerated, starting up the winding grade into the canyon. On one of the spacious lawns fronting the line of sedate, two-story mansions, a middle-aged man adjusting the sprinkling system in front of his house turned to look at her and smiled.

It was not true! Not after two children! Absently, she let her hand drop to her stomach. Not with a child! Men just do not—! She swung off the road into the driveway leading down to the house and stopped just inside the entrance posts. Nervously she twisted the rearview mirror to see her face and dabbed away the dark blotches under her eyes. The children would notice. They would ask questions. She would say that she was not feeling well.

She released the brake, glided down the slope of the driveway, crossed the broad asphalt turnabout before the porch, and turned off the ignition before the car had come to a stop under the carport.

The children. The child. She sat back for a moment, rigid with dread, then reached out mechanically, honked the horn, and got out of the car.

"Mom!" Chris was the first through the front door and came racing towards the car.

"She got the tree!" Karen followed, shouting. "She got one!"

"Look how big it is!" Chris pulled at the scarf tied to the end.

"It's a spruce, too!"

Ignoring them, Alexis gave the tree a final tug and let it fall to the pavement behind the car.

"It's a monster!" screamed Chris.

She took her purse from the pavement next to the rear wheel and turned towards the house. "I'll get Claire to come help you. You can pull the tree into the living room." She walked stiffly towards the front door. "And take the decorations out of the boxes. We'll wait for your dad to set it in the stand."

"Oh, mom!" Karen called after her, deflated, "aren't you going to help?"

"I don't feel well. I'm going to lie down and take a nap." Without waiting for questions or comments, she went in.

Claire stood holding a freshly ironed shirt, her wrinkled face pale with concern. "We'll take care of the tree, you go back and rest."

"Yes, I'll just take a nap." Alexis started out of the laundry room.

"Can I make you some tea, Mrs. Stegman?"

"No, thank you. Nothing." She started towards the corridor leading to the bedrooms. "Just tell Dr. Stegman when he comes in that I'm in the bedroom." She closed the bedroom door behind her, crossed to the window, and drew the curtains.

Three hours to think, compose herself, and choose her words. It would be enough; after eleven months, it would be enough.

Carefully, out of the force of habit, as though it still mattered, she drew back the crocheted bedspread and folded it in neat layers to the foot of the bed. Her grandmother had given it to them. Strange, she thought, how systematic she had been in the last half hour. In the cool, silent semi-darkness she lay down, face forward on the bed. Nothing came to her. She listened to the faint purr of the heating system through the ventilator overhead, closed her eyes for a moment, tried to make a logical list of her grievances, then opened them. She thought how nice it would feel to cry now, to unleash the rage she knew was there. In the dim light, her eyes focused on the cascade of tiny wildflowers printed on the pillow case under her head. She stared on, realizing she was frozen.

VI

Alan looked at his watch again and took a deep breath. It was 6:24. Still, he was ahead of his self-imposed deadline. He pulled into the carport next to Alexis's station wagon and turned off the motor. He had left the office at 5:25, a good half hour earlier than usual, stopped by a florist in Beverly Hills to buy a dozen long-stemmed white roses, but then found himself trapped in a rush-hour line of bumper-to-bumper cars inching around an old Pontiac stalled in the winding narrows of Benedict Canyon. That morning he had told Alexis he would be home by 6:30.

He turned off the lights and sat in the darkness for a moment, staring at the yellow bug light over the back door leading into the kitchen, relieved that he had made it under the line by six minutes.

In two, maybe three hours, it would be over. She would know everything. They would finish decorating the tree by 9:30 and Alexis would put the kids to bed. He would tell her then. But how? All day he had racked his brain for a sentence, a phrase to open with, something gentle and painless. But how do you tell the woman you have loved and lived with for sixteen years that you still love her but you *want* men?

On the cement porch under the yellow bug light he could see Banjo standing on the top step outside the screen door, waiting with his stub of a tail anxiously wagging. He had dreaded this event for eleven months now. And yet, there was a sense of approaching relief, too. Relief in knowing the games, the lies, the hiding, the double life would soon be over. But now that the moment had come, he was afraid of her. Not afraid of the telling, afraid of *her*. What she would say and do to him. After sixteen years of sharing their most intimate secrets, he felt like a criminal about to face a sentencing judge. He had never hesitated to lay his failures, his fears, his most secret fantasies before her—save that one —and now he was flailing about in his mind to find soft ways of indirection to tell her that he had stumbled on and finally opened a sexual Pandora's box at forty. Had he been having an affair with a woman, like a lot of doctors he knew, it would have been painful but relatively simple to confess. But this, this sliced through every bond between them like a scalpel through an artery. More than that, knowing her attitude towards "fags," liberal towards them in general, contemptuous towards the particular, the prospect of facing her with the truth about himself threatened to wipe him out totally as a man in her eyes.

Alan pulled the ignition key from the lock and reached for his briefcase. On top of all this, he felt like a small child. He knew he would stammer out his confession. He, the surgeon who faced hospital accreditation committees and vindictive administrators without flinching, was about to shrink into a guilty, squirming adolescent before his wife.

And now it had to be done, before time ran out and she found out by accident or through an insinuation from Jeff Marks or Arnold Berrey. Alan gathered up his briefcase and the box of roses and got out. As he crossed the asphalt pavement to the back door, he took a deep breath of the cool, damp canyon air. Beyond the spill of yellow light under the carport, the surrounding woods looked impenetrably dark and still. Next July they would be alive with crickets. But by then they would no longer be here. They would be in their newly planted, sparser landscape high atop Coldwater Canyon. A home with a view this time.

Banjo looked up at him eagerly as he fumbled with his key. On the top step, Alan noticed the dry, empty plastic dog bowl. Alexis always fed the dog early in the evening while she prepared dinner. For some reason, tonight she had forgotten. "What's wrong, boy?" He turned the key and opened the door. "Did mom forget to feed you?" Banjo looked up at him imploringly, wagged his stubby tail, and whimpered. "Relax, man. I'll go in and have a talk with her."

On the linoleum laundry-room floor Alan noticed sprigs of spruce needles, a faint trail of them leading into the kitchen. He smiled to himself as he heard Chris and Karen break into excited chatter from the kitchen area.

"Daddy!" Karen shouted from the breakfast table as he stood looking at them from the door between the kitchen and the laundry room. "She got the tree!"

"It's a giant!" Chris cried.

To his surprise, Alan noticed they were both halfway through hamburgers and french fries. Claire came towards them from the kitchen area with a bottle of ketchup.

"So why are you two having dinner now?" he asked. From the look on Claire's face he knew that something was wrong.

"Mom's sick," Karen said.

"Mrs. Stegman came home this afternoon with the tree, doctor." Claire uncapped the ketchup bottle. "And she didn't feel so well. She's been lying down in the bedroom since." Her voice sounded stiff and uneasy.

"Sick? What's wrong?"

"She wouldn't say." Claire set the ketchup on the table beside Chris. "She just went in and lay down and wouldn't say what's wrong. I tried to take her some tea about an hour ago, but she wouldn't drink it. I knocked, but I didn't go in to see."

"Why the hell didn't she call the hospital?" He started around the table towards the kitchen. The thought that she had chosen this night to get sick, that he had steeled himself for nothing, made him suddenly angry.

"I was going to do that myself, doctor, but when I brought the tea she told me most emphatically not to."

"Dad!" Karen called, "when are you going to put the tree in the stand?"

Alan looked back across the kitchen. "Later. You finish your dinner."

"She asked me specifically to say she wanted you to come back to the bedroom when you got in, doctor," Claire said.

Alan turned again when he reached the dining-room door. "Where did she think I would go if she's sick in bed? To the TV room?" He left the kitchen and headed through the dining room to the foyer. It was unlike Alexis not to phone if she or one of the kids was sick. A headache, anything was enough to send her to the phone, and her calls to his office over the years had become a running joke between them. He always teased her about being a hypochondriac when it came to minor ailments.

Alan crossed the foyer and started down the corridor leading to their bedroom. The door was closed, but he could see from the crack beneath that the bedroom lights were out. He set his briefcase on the floor outside his study, then continued on, suddenly uneasy. Outside the door he hesitated, listening for sounds. It was silent on the other side. He turned the handle, opened the door, and stood, backlit from the corridor, staring into the darkened room.

"Alex?" He shifted the box of roses from one arm to the other. In the faint spill of light from behind he could see her figure on the bed with the sheet drawn up to her waist. He had the feeling that she was lying there awake, staring back at him.

She did not respond.

"What's wrong?" He felt the knot in his stomach tighten and stepped into the room.

She moved on the bed slightly but still did not respond.

"Claire said you were sick."

In the darkness he saw her raise herself up against the pillows.

He moved two steps towards the bed. "What is it, honey?"

"Close the door, Alan," she said finally. In the weight of her falling voice there was a leaden sound of cold anger.

Paralyzed for a moment, he stared at her. She was sitting up now against the pillows, fully dressed.

"I asked you to close the door," she said, clearing her throat.

The tone of voice sent a chill through him. He stepped back without taking his eyes from her and closed the door with his shoulder. In the now totally blackened room, the anger rolled at him in a palpable shock wave. "Alexis," he said, then broke off, utterly bewildered.

She moved on the bed, reaching, he suspected, towards the bedside lamp. When it came on, she was leaning out of the bed with her arm outstretched. She was wearing a dress that she hated. The silk print one with the full skirt she had worn years before when she was pregnant with Chris. She lowered her arm, settled back against the pillows, and looked at him. Her face was cold and drawn. From where he was standing, he could see that her eyes were puffy. Sometime back, maybe even hours before, she had been crying. She took hold of the sheet over her lap and drew it closer, clutching it in her fingers, studying him intently. "A question," she finally said.

He stood four feet from the foot of the bed, holding the box of roses under his arm, resisting the feeling that he was a small boy facing an accusing parent. He said nothing. Waited.

She reached for the pack of cigarettes on the bedside table, took one, lit it, and blew out a jet of smoke across the bed in his direction. The gesture was a challenge calculated to provoke.

Alan reached up and fanned the cloud of smoke drifting towards his face.

"Where were you this afternoon?" He knew by the sound of her voice that she already had her answer.

"What do you mean, where was I?"

"Exactly that. Where were you?"

"At the hospital until noon. Then I went to see Stephen Milner, Phoebe's psychiatrist friend."

"I know who he is, thank you."

He went on, "And from there back to the hospital until four-thirty, and then to the office." Like a child, he was being drilled.

"I see." She looked down thoughtfully, waiting for him to say what he knew, at that moment, he could not conceivably say—what, he realized, she already knew.

"Claire said you were sick. What's wrong?" he heard himself say after a moment.

"Forget what Claire said, we're talking about you." The sharpness of her voice took his breath away.

"I brought you these," he said and put the box of roses on the foot of the bed.

"I don't want flowers now, thank you. I want facts."

He swallowed to free the knot that had now risen to his throat. She was unleashing eleven months of suffering. His face went hot with the flush rising in his blood. The lid of the flower box would not come off. He pulled at it roughly, it came off, and he dropped it on the coverlet folded to the end of the bed. Though the sheets were in a turmoil, he noticed she had taken time to fold her grandmother's hand-crocheted coverlet neatly. He spread the green florist tissue, lifted the box to show her the long, perfect white roses, then looked up feeling absurd. Her eyes were riveted on his face, expressionless and cold. He let the box fall back on the bed.

"Do you want to tell me or do you want me to pry it out of you?"

"Pry what out of me?" His insides went to jelly.

She lifted the cigarette to her mouth without taking her eyes from him. The glow at the tip rose to a hot gold point, then died away. She let the smoke curl from her mouth around her lips. He was seeing a side of Alexis he had never known was there, and it frightened him. She was toying with him like a cat with a mouse. "The story of you and Dr. Milner."

He opened his mouth and the air flowed out of his lungs. He started to speak, made a meaningless sound, then closed his mouth. He saw the glow of a suppressed rage rise in her face like the glow of her cigarette ember, then die. "I had a problem I wanted to talk about. I went to see him.

"A *problem*?" She feigned a look of amazement which struck him as mocking and cruel. If the quality of revenge is an index to the depth of the hurt, then hers must be bottomless, he thought.

"Yes, a problem." He cast about for all those opening phrases he had tested earlier in his mind. *I have something to tell you. Something strange has been happening to me, honey. For a long time I've been keeping something from you.* They sounded pathetic now. "What are you trying to say?" he asked, fighting for time.

"I don't think it's my turn to say anything at all," her voice rose to the challenge.

For an instant, he had an intimation that, until he came out with the facts, they would go on and on and on like this, circling each other. For the rest of their lives. "If I have anything to say, it's not about Stephen Milner," he said.

Her face hardened. He could see the question rising in her eyes. "Tell me, then, do you make a habit of embracing men when you ask them for advice?"

The question swept by him. He blinked.

"This afternoon, Alan. I was on Fountain Avenue"—his heart rose in his chest—"on my way home with the tree. I passed you and Milner in the driveway."

"Alexis—" He made an inane gesture with his hand.

"You embraced."

"Let me explain—" he said before he could reflect how he would explain.

"I saw you embracing him, Alan."

"You don't understand. We weren't—"

"I saw it, Alan!"

"Yes, we embraced! But it was not that kind of embrace!"

"Not that kind of embrace? I saw it! In broad daylight!"

Rattled, Alan shook his head, "You've got it *wrong!*"

Her arm shot forward with her finger pointing rigidly at him, "You put your arms around him! And you weren't just saying good-bye!"

"Yes!" he exclaimed, "that's exactly what I'm telling you! You've got it wrong!"

"Don't lie to me, Alan!" She suddenly catapulted forward with both hands landing on the bed. "You've been sleeping with him, haven't you? With Stephen Milner!"

"No! With other men, yes! But not Milner!"

She hung there for a moment, open-mouthed, gaping, shock and outrage scrawled across her face.

He hurried on before she could speak, "The fact is, I have been to bed with other men, but not Milner. Others, yes. But not him." His voice died as he felt the familiar weight of guilt descend over him. "I was going to tell you tonight. Everything."

She sank forward, face down, for a moment. He reached towards her, but before he could touch her shoulder she raised herself and slumped backwards against the pillows, raising her hands to press them against her face.

"It started almost a year ago, less than that. Eleven months." He felt an ache to go to her, hold her in his arms.

She shook her head, holding it between her hands.

"I met a guy a year ago." He forced himself to go on, "That's when this started. Before that I never touched a man. You must believe me."

"No." She moved her head from side to side, mechanically. "No."

"His name was Bradford. I went to bed with him eight weeks after we met."

"No."

"There was one other guy. Ten days ago. That's all."

She dropped her hands and fixed him vacantly. A glimmer of recognition flickered in her eyes, then faded. "I don't believe you."

He moved around the edge of the bed towards her. "I didn't want this. Believe me. It just happened." He started to sit beside her on the bed.

"Don't!" Like a frightened wild animal she drew her legs away from him, hesitated, then quickly threw the sheet back and swung her bare feet to the floor, "You are not telling me the truth!"

"If I wanted to lie, would I invent one like this?"

With a wild, agonized expression on her face, she lunged from the bed, pushed him aside, momentarily lost her balance, and stumbled against the bedside table. "All right! So you've been to bed with men!! What does that prove?!" She swung around, jabbing her cigarette out in the ashtray on the table. "People do not just change! Not like that!" She shoved past him towards the end of the bed. "You are forty years old! You do not change your sex at forty!"

"I haven't changed my sex."

"You know what I mean!" She whirled around to face him. "People are that way from the beginning!"

"That's debatable. In any case, it happened to me at forty."

"Happened? What the hell does that mean, *happened?* Happened to you like coming down with a case of arthritis!! Are you telling me you've caught an overnight case of homosexuality! That overnight at the age of forty you've up and turned into a *faggot?"*

"Bisexual is the word."

"Oh!" She threw her head back, sending her long hair flying back from her face. "You mean you've decided that now, at forty, you want *everything!"*

"No, I do not mean that."

From the far side of the house came the muffled shouts of the children. Alan glanced towards the door and tensed.

"Look at me, god dammit!"

Suddenly on the offensive, Alan turned and said quietly but forcefully, "Lower your voice."

"Bisexual?" she went on stridently, ignoring him, "Are you saying you've reached your damn midlife crisis? *Bisexual?* What the hell does that mean?!"

"Alexis!"

"Does it mean you're trying to make a Custer's last stand at sex by screwing everything that walks? Don't tell me that's your way of swimming upstream against male menopause!"

Always, faced in arguments with an irrefutable but untenable fact, Alexis had the habit of retreating behind rhetoric. In these moments, she always sounded literary to him. Out of self-defense, because he knew she could outdistance him there, he retreated to his corner behind the literal. "I mean, I am a bisexual," he said, trying to rein her in.

"Horseshit!" she shrieked.

From the direction of the living room now came Claire's voice, muffled by the walls but calling loudly, "One at a time, Christopher!" followed by squeals and garbled, excited shouts from the children. They were now less than thirty feet away, he realized, pulling the Christmas decorations from the boxes stacked on the living-room floor. The thought of them there and he and Alexis here, squared off against each other, filled him suddenly with an overwhelming sense of sadness.

"If you want to punish me, do. But leave them out of this," he said.

Arrested by the children's voices, Alexis stared at him with anguish. "How?" Her face fell. "How are we going to leave them out of *this* ugly little picture?" Absently, she took hold of the folds of her skirt and clutched them close to her body. Then abruptly she seemed to cave in. "Why?" she asked softly but hoarsely.

He realized it was a blanket question, covering everything. "It happened. I don't know why. Not yet, at least. That's why I went to Milner, to begin to find out why."

"You said nothing. All this time you said nothing to me."

"I couldn't." He saw the inevitable question forming in her eyes. "Eleven months, I know." He hurried on to give her the answer he had given himself a thousand times before. "But the need would come and go. I kept telling myself, wait, keep it to yourself, it's just a passing thing."

For a moment, she drifted away, letting her gaze rest on something behind him. He knew she was battling privately with her own doubts. Again from the living room came the children's delighted squeals. How lucky kids are, he thought, to move so fast and easily from anger to joy, from tears to laughter.

"Is it something I did?" She broke the silence and fixed him dead center in the eye.

"No."

"Or *didn't* do?"

"No, it has nothing to do with you."

"Nothing to—?" She caught her breath. "I'm your *wife*, Alan."

"Believe me, you are not responsible."

"*And* the mother of your children. *This* child!" she jabbed her finger into her stomach.

He winced, feeling the pain in his own. From the beginning he had known that she would heap the blame on herself. Worse than finding that she had failed him was the realization that what she had or had not done in the final tally did not matter. If he could have found in her some failure to point to, she could at least feel involved and plan for the future. What hurt most was finding that she stood wholly outside, isolated. On impulse, he moved towards her to take her in his arms. "The reasons, whatever they are, lie entirely within me."

She stepped back, lifting her hand to stop him, "Don't be so fucking pompous. Either you wanted it all along or you didn't, and if you didn't, then it can only mean there was something missing between *us*."

"I never felt that," he made a lame gesture of appeal.

"No!?" she lifted her chin, suddenly outraged, "Well, obviously there was *one* thing missing!"

"I have always loved your body."

"Then what are you, Jekyll and Hyde?"

"I still do."

"Did it occur to you while you were out doing whatever you do with them that you were living with a woman? Where was I when you were out till all hours balling with some *guy!?* Where am *I* in this, tell me!"

"Alexis, I—" He broke off, hearing an angry shout from Karen in the living room.

"Did you stop to think that I love you, but faced with a *man* I'm not even in the running! Do you care or even know where this puts me as a *woman?*"

He nodded.

"Do you know where this dumps the last sixteen years of *my life?*"

He nodded again. She had let go. It would all pour out now, everything he had dreaded hearing for the last eleven months.

"Answer me!"

"The desires came! They—" He made an angry, idiotic gesture to his head. "They were there! I didn't *want* them!"

Claire's voice suddenly broke through from the living room, her angry nanny's voice, voluble and commanding, "All right, little Miss Karen! That's enough! If you don't share—"

"But it's mine!" Karen shouted back.

Alexis went rigid.

"You're going to spoil everyone's Christmas, you two!" Claire had raised her voice, they both knew, to cover their own. In the interval of silence between them, the frozen expression of rage on Alexis's face thawed and fell. Her shoulders sank. She looked down at the floor, defeated. "Then I take it, it's always been there," she said softly.

He swallowed back the gummy saliva caught in his throat. "If it was, it was far off in the wings."

"In the wings?" she looked up, amazed. Then her face hardened.

"In the wings. That's cute," her voice wavered. He could see she was beating down the need to cry. "But I'll tell you this—now that it's on-stage, now that *he's* on stage, I'm not playing understudy to any *man.*"

"There is no man."

"Bradford, you called him? I'd say that eleven months pretty well qualifies you two for an affair. In *anybody's* book."

He shook his head and reached to his face before his eyes could spill. "Ten months. He died ten months after I met him. Three months ago." He lowered his hand.

In her moment of hesitation he detected the relief in her eyes. How could he blame her?

"Having spared me the introduction and let me go on thinking he was a woman for ten months, don't ask me now to come up with feelings for him."

"I'm not. Believe me—" The old familiar image rose up in his mind, Brad on the hospital bed that afternoon, sleeping through his death. He reached up again quickly and flattened his palm over his eyes as the tears spilled out. Across the five feet separating them, he heard the long, deep sigh that flowed from her body. The silence was broken only by the small, choked sounds that he caught and held in his throat.

"It wasn't only sex, was it," he heard her say quietly, "you loved him. Didn't you?"

In the distance, she heard Chris shout "That one's mine, Mrs. Saunders!"

She held her breath, paralyzed, waiting. After a moment, he took hold of himself and lowered his hand. His face was splotched red, his cheeks wet. He looked directly into her eyes for a moment. She saw his determination.

"I operated on him for cancer in June. He died in September." He always announced things simply, clinically. She did not move, only stared back at him, feeling hollow, vacant. "We had an affair, but I was never in love with him. Not like that. I was incapable of loving him in the way that he loved me. Believe me."

Chris's high-pitched little voice cut through the silence, "I'm gonna tell dad!"

"Dummy!" Karen yelled.

She remembered the evening in June—yes, it had been mid-June —when he had come home from the hospital looking deathly pale and troubled. When she'd asked what was wrong, he'd said, "Problems at the hospital." After a nearly wordless dinner, he'd gone to the study and sat for hours, pretending to work, listening over and over again to his recording of Mahler's *The Song of Earth*. She recalled, too, how relieved she had felt to know he was in there stewing over a hospital problem rather than plotting his affair with the Other Woman.

"He was dying. He asked me to stop the pain." His words sounded almost apologetic. "Legally, at that moment, my hands were tied. Humanly speaking, I could have done something. I could have given him my consent and then done something about it—an injection of morphine into his i.v. But I didn't. I was afraid."

She shook her head, "Alan, don't."

"In the end, I think he realized I wouldn't do it. So he did the next best thing himself. He gave up. He went back into coma. Before I left his side, he went into coma again. That time for good."

The feelings flooded in on her too fast for her to grasp or hold onto any one of them: horror and disgust, fear, longing and separation, panic, even compassion, and finally emptiness. She raised her hand and gestured for him to stop.

"I ran an EEG on him. By then, he had suffered brain death. Legally, he was dead. I phoned Jeff Marks, his oncologist, and asked him to pull the plug. In our conversation, he let it be known that he was aware of my relationship with Brad." He looked away for a moment, then said, "Do you understand what I'm saying?"

She nodded, but had not really been listening. She had been searching his face as though recognizing the man for the first time.

"Marks turned off the machines. Brad died early the next morning. When it was over, I realized I felt glad. I did not want to be gay or bisexual or anything I had not been before. I thought with him gone— dead—it would all go away. I blamed him for everything, at first. Afterwards, I told myself I was lucky the way things turned out. For the first time, cancer seemed to be on *my* side. Now that an accident of nature had cut off the source, I thought the well would run dry." He paused, looking absently surprised by his own words. "But it didn't. And he wasn't the source." His voice faded, he withdrew and fixed his gaze on some distant inner point.

"Alan," she said after a moment to call him back.

He did not seem to hear her.

"Mrs. Saunders, look!" Karen cried gleefully. "The angel!"

A familiar sensation returned. Of absence. Like the evening they'd spent at her parents' house decorating their Christmas tree; like the Saturday he sat on the floor in the living room and took apart the stereo receiver. For him, she was not in the room, not even in the same universe. "Alan, look at me!" she said.

"For a month, almost six weeks, I felt safe," he went on determinedly. He had not even heard her. "Then it started all over again. The needs, I mean—" His attention seemed to flow back into the room, and he glanced down at the floor.

Eleven months of lonely isolation flushed out of her suddenly. It felt like sludge through a sewer. "But then, of course, you found another man."

"One. For one night. You remember ten days ago when I came home late?"

For a moment, crazily, she wanted to scream. The bitter irony was, he understood nothing of *her* pain! Nothing whatever of *her* loss! It was all *his* loss, *his* grief, *his* failure, *his* guilt! The look on his face of dumb, guilty innocence made her want to slap him.

"I get to hang all the tinsel!" Chris shouted.

Alexis quickly checked herself. "Remember?" she said tightly, "how could I forget?"

"It was after that I knew I needed to find help. I went to Milner two days later."

"Of course, a one-night stand isn't quite grounds for marriage." She let the luxury of her bitchiness roll over and blanket her pain. "Unless maybe for homosexuals."

"Alexis," his voice splintered and he gaped at her.

"The question is, after that one will there be another?" Despite the pull towards him, she could not relent.

"Not if I can help it."

"Can you?"

"I want to, I've got to try."

"Try what?"

To go back to—" He lost control again and his voice skittered off. "—where we were before!"

She wanted to say "Where were we before?" but realized she had run aground against a deeper feeling. Hope. "Do you think that's possible?"

"I think it's worth the try."

Always the scientist, the prognosis never as strong as the hope. "What can you do about it?"

"Find help. That's why I went to Milner. But he's not the right one for me, we both agree on that," he glanced off distracted for a moment, then came back, "I'd be more comfortable with a straight one. If I can find the cause, then maybe I can find the cure."

"People often want and try to do one thing but desire quite another. You know that as well as I do."

"You forget one thing—I love you."

"I know that," she felt a wall breaking apart inside her, "at least I've kept telling myself so for the last eleven months. But there are different kinds of love. I know that and you know that. My mother and father have nothing more now than a comfortable habit."

He nodded. "The evidence is against me, I know. But believe me,

I not only love you, but I still want—desire you. All that's still alive."

"I don't know what to believe anymore." The wall gave way, and the reservoir behind it rushed through her body and poured from her eyes.

He came towards her and encircled her waist with his arms. She folded easily into him, submissively, out of habit. She was tired now. She realized he was merely holding a limp, lifeless doll.

He reached up and pressed her head against his chest. She could feel the bulge of her stomach against his groin. "Help me," he said in a voice she had never before heard—high, thin, and broken.

She raised her face and kissed him gently on his neck above the stiff, white collar.

VII

Alexis reached a level clearing in the broken, rutted earth, caught her breath, and felt a thrill of accomplishment run through her. They had done it. The square and rectangular wooden molding frames were now filled with concrete. She looked back at Alan coming towards her with the ice chest. "What about here?!" she called, "it's level!"

"That's perfect!" Balancing the ice chest, he jumped a pile of steel reinforcement rods. Behind him came Karen and Chris with the thermos of lemonade swinging between them. And behind them, Max with his walking stick, trying to keep up with the kids over the wheel-scarred ground.

Alexis set the wicker hamper on the ground. "If we can find a plank or something, we can make a table."

"Good idea." Alan came up and put down the chest filled with ice and soft drinks and beer. "I'll grab a couple of Gruber's saw horses. The kids can hunt for a plank. We'll make a proper dining-room table."

"Terrific." She moved next to him and they stood for a moment surveying the foundation.

"What do you think?"

"It looks like Karnak *before* excavation, but it's wonderful," she said as she scanned the complex maze of low, concrete walls. There, nearest them, would be Alan's study, and to the east of that the entrance hall opening into the living room, and still further east the three bedrooms and the nursery.

"It looks smaller than I thought," Alan said.

"Foundations always do," she looked up at him, "are you *sure* we can afford this?"

"No," he smiled, "but don't *worry*. Beverly Hills is founded on credit. You forget, we're upwardly mobile now. We're *supposed* to invest in the future."

"Six hundred and seventy-five thousand dollars. It's utter madness."

"Dad!" Chris shouted as he and Karen came up with the thermos. "What's *that* thing?!"

"A cement mixer."

"Look at that big pile of sand!" Karen pointed to the huge mound of builder's sand next to the mixer.

"Come on," Chris said. They set the thermos down and started off down the slope towards the sand.

"Before you start playing," Alexis called after them, "find a plank for our table and something for your granddad to sit on!"

"And listen, you guys, if you wreck Mr. Gruber's sand pile, he'll skin you alive!" Alan warned.

"Now, Alexis." Max came up behind them. "If you're going to treat me like an invalid, I'll make your life miserable. I will sit like everybody else on the *ground.*"

"What do you think, dad?" Alan pointed proudly to the foundation.

"I'm impressed. Very impressed." Max balanced himself on his cane. "It's a far cry from the cracker box you grew up in, I'll say that."

For a moment, in the softening haze of the midwinter sunset, the three of them stood looking out across the darkening ravines of Coldwater Canyon towards the flats of Beverly Hills and West Hollywood. South, in the direction of the Palos Verdes peninsula and the sea, across the expanse of flatlands, checkerboard lines of tiny, ice-blue streetlamps were coming on. Alexis leaned closer to Alan, chilled suddenly by the January breeze blowing up through the canyon.

"You cold?" Alan squeezed her shoulder.

"A little," she smiled, watching Karen and Chris struggling up the sand mound. "I'll zip up my jacket and be fine." In the darkening light, the kids looked like phosphorescent june bugs in their yellow windbreakers. She felt a sudden sense of peace.

Max lowered himself to the ground with a grunt.

"What say we build a fire?" Alan said.

"Why not? Who's to stop us? It's our land, we're home."

Alan let go of her. "I'll take the kids and hunt up a board, get some saw horses and some firewood."

"Do. But you'd better hurry, it's getting dark." Alexis turned to the hamper on the ground.

"You realize, don't you," Alan said over his shoulder as he started towards the kids, "this is our first meal in the new house."

"So it is." Alexis uncovered the hamper and chuckled, "Of course, our neighbors may think we've moved in a little *prematurely.*" She glanced towards a lighted window in the house on the eastern side of their lot, "They must think we're crazy!"

"Fuck the neighbors," Alan said, then looked back again. "Sorry, dad." He hurried off down the slope.

"Oi," Max sighed, "What does he think I am, an old prude?"

Alexis laughed, "How about something to drink? There's lemonade and soft drinks."

"You too? What *is* this, a picnic or one of those geriatric outings we get once a month? Tonight, I'm on vacation. No boiled fish and no tapioca pudding. I take beer, thank you."

"One beer coming up." Alexis opened the lid on the ice chest. She took out two Heinekens, one for Max and one for herself.

"All right!" Alan called from the mound of sand, "Whoever finds me a wooden plank gets a nickel!"

"I will!" Chris tumbled down the sand, followed by Karen.

"Claire worried that I was taking you off your diet," Alexis said to Max, "so she made you an egg-salad sandwich on pumpernickel with tomato and lettuce."

"This is a conspiracy." Max sipped his beer. "I'm going to eat fried chicken and, after that, a chocolate donut."

"If I weren't turning into a blimp, I'd join you on the donut."

"Don't be foolish. It becomes you. How many months to go?"

"Three."

"Good. Your timing is very good."

Alexis glanced at him, puzzled. "Why do you say that?"

"Because." He took another sip of beer and looked off towards Alan and the kids at the lower end of the property.

"Because what?"

"Because I see things in Alan. Little changes over the last year or so. Something has been troubling him. What, I don't know. He tells me nothing and I don't ask. But I see, I look at him when he comes to visit me, and I see."

Silent for a moment, Alexis began removing the plastic bags of food from the hamper and setting them carefully on the ground. "See what? I'm not sure I know what you mean, Max." She kept her eyes averted.

"I think you do, but it's not my business to meddle, is it? I see— until recently, I saw signs of a man running from something. Avoiding something. Every time he was with me, I saw fear behind his eyes. And sadness. Before Christmas, he seemed so sad."

"I know. And I understand." She went on arranging the food.

"He's a sensitive man, Alan is. As a boy he used to try to hide his sensitivity. He pretended to be tough, like the other boys. He grew up in a rough area of Detroit. His mother understood him better than I did. I wanted him to grow up with a thick skin. I guess that comes from the years in Vienna before the war. So much trouble then. My brother was a sensitive man, like Alan. He wanted to play the cello all the time, I remember. In the end, he was too sensitive for his own good. He tried to please everyone. Thank God we left Austria before the war, before Alan was born. As a boy, he would never have survived the war, I'm sure of that."

"I know all about Alan's sensitivities, believe me." She watched him crossing the lower end of the lot with the kids, only their yellow windbreakers visible now in the darkness under the trees. "And I know how uncertain of himself he can be in some things. But whatever failings he has, he's a *good* man. A loving husband despite himself, a wonderful father, and a dedicated surgeon."

"You are like a daughter to me, Alexis," Max said in a low, gentle voice edged with anxiety, "I love you as a daughter of my own flesh and blood."

"I know that, Max."

"Promise me something. Promise me one thing."

Alexis lowered the folded tablecloth against her stomach and looked at him. "What?"

"He is a happier man now, that I can see. In the last month, I can see that."

"*What*, Max?"

"Don't misunderstand me. I do not want to meddle in your lives." Alexis kept silent, waiting. "Everyone has marriage problems. You marry someone and, over a period of years, they change. You change. The match is never as perfect as it was in the beginning. On the bad side, marriage is like rheumatism. No sooner does one ache go, then another one comes. On the good side, though—"

"Promise you what, Max?" she broke in. She could hear Alan coming up the slope with the kids.

"I think you are having trouble with Alan. He's changing on you. But he also needs you, he needs *you* more than you need *him*. He needs this new baby now, maybe more than he needed the others. Promise me this—that you will be patient with his changes, and that you will try to love the new man that comes out of them."

Alexis reached into the hamper for the napkins. "I promise you, Max, I will."

"How's this?" Alan called, laughing. Followed by Karen and Chris, he came towards them balancing a huge piece of plywood against his shoulder.

"Perfect!" she called and, at the same time, caught the look of doubt in Max's face. "Who got the nickel?" she asked cheerfully.

"I did! We both did!" Karen and Chris exclaimed.

"I'll grab those saw horses." He lowered the plywood to the ground and glanced from Alexis to Max, then back again. "What's going on?" he asked, puzzled, "You two hatching plots?"

Alan dropped his empty paper plate in the garbage bag and sat down next to Alexis on the log in front of the fire. "That was the best fried chicken you've done in ages."

"I didn't. Claire cooked everything. I spent the afternoon collecting brick samples."

He looked at her. The firelight played with the wry smile in the corners of her mouth. "On second thought, it was only average." He bent towards the ice chest for a second beer.

"And after brick sampling, I played tennis with Phoebe."

He thought he detected a pointed note in her voice, and glanced at her again. She was staring off blissfully towards the twinkling lights of the city below. He had played tennis with Stephen on Sunday afternoon while she was at the Huntington Museum with the kids. At Stephen's suggestion, they had met at the La Cienega courts to talk about Schaeffer, Alan's new psychiatrist, and play one set. He had not played tennis in years. For a moment, he joined Alexis in contemplating the view. Beyond the tops of the eucalyptus trees below their lot, the glitter of city lights spread southwards for miles towards the sea and tossed skyward a pale incandescent halo that fused with the light of a rising three-quarter moon. At the lower end of the lot, where Max had taken the kids to look at the area where the pool would be dug, he could see the beam of his flashlight and the yellow glow of two small windbreakers. "What are you thinking?" he asked.

"I'm thinking how peaceful the silence is up here."

"Yes. Very. If everything goes on schedule, we'll be ready to move in the first part of August."

"Summer will be wonderful up here with the pool."

For a while, he poked the embers with a piece of kindling in silence. Fifty yards away, Max's deep, throaty laughter broke the quiet, followed by surprised, gleeful shouts from the kids. They had obviously trapped him into one of their games of hide-and-seek. "Max should get out more often," he pushed a bright ember with his stick. It gashed open, throwing a soft gold light on Alexis's face.

"I'm glad you said that." She rested her hand on his knee, "He's well cared for at the Georgian, but it's lonely for him. He loves you very much, you know."

"I know that." He felt the irritation of his old resistance. "But it's like I've never changed. I'm still nine years old to him."

Out of the corner of his eye, he saw a smile come and go on her face. She said, "Maybe that's the only way left for him to hold you in his mind, as you were. He's not the only one like that at the Georgian. Last week, when I took the kids to see him, they were all together out on the verandah after supper, watching the sunset over the ocean. Sitting together—alone. He made a joke out of it, said there are only two times in life when you really need family, at the beginning and at the end."

"More wisdom." He stabbed the embers again and they crackled, sending up sparks into the air. "I disagree. Some people have a rougher time in the middle."

Her fingers closed around his knee.

He said, "Have you ever thought what it would be like to be homosexual and wake up, say at fifty, and find that you're alone, that you've got no family, that you've got twenty-five years ahead of you *alone*?"

Alexis turned to him, surprised.

"Don't be shocked." He smiled, "Schaeffer says I should be open with you about my feelings. Besides, I'd like for you to know what's going on inside me. Now and then, I have thoughts, fears—feelings I'd like you to know about. Up to now, I've kept everything to myself. Somehow, if I could feel free to tell you my feelings, even if they're— well, homosexual—I think I could stay ahead of the game."

"Okay. It's a deal," she moved her hand along his leg, feeling both relieved and apprehensive. Until now, they had kept silent about those kinds of feelings. She had left everything up to Schaeffer and Alan. She had not really wanted to know. "When you feel the need," she said purposefully, "I want you to tell me *anything*." She hesitated, then went on. "I know there'll be times when you may feel like being with a man. That's bound to be." She stared into the reddening heart of the embers, "There are no overnight changes. I know you're afraid of that—and embarrassed, even afraid to admit it when it happens," she looked down. The hot glow of the embers stung her eyes. "This may all be new to me, but I'm not a child. Months ago, I remember telling you—if you can't trust me, who can you trust? I meant it then, and I mean it now," she drew a breath, feeling a sudden dead kind of weight descend on her. "Even if one day it happens. I mean—because of chance events, you end up sleeping with a man . . . I want you to feel safe in telling me."

For a moment, neither of them spoke. The dying embers at their feet made soft, sputtering noises. Then he leaned forward and dropped the stick of kindling into the fire.

"Look at me, granddad!" Chris shouted from the direction of the sand mound, "I'm king of the mountain!"

Alan reached up and turned her to face him. She yielded easily. Against her ear, as he embraced her, his breath told her what he was thinking. For a while, they held each other.

"I think we've got company," he said softly and drew back, smiling at her. He glanced back over her shoulder. She turned. On the western edge of their property, silhouetted against the patio lights of the neighbor's house, a man stood staring in their direction with his hands on his hips.

"I think we may have to talk to Jimmy about putting a wall up on that side of the property," he said.

"I think you're right," she said.

"Forty-five, fifteen! Your serve!" Stephen lobbed another ball towards him across the net.

"This is a massacre!" Alan called as he caught the ball with his left hand. It was six to one in their third and final set. The best he had done was a deuce in the fifth game of their second set which, lousy as it was, was still better than the first time they had played two weeks before.

"This time, think of your racket as an extension of your arm," Stephen called to him as he started towards the back of the court. "Like you're *throwing* the ball with the racquet! And *relax*!"

After twenty years away from the game, try as he might to relax, the old body was stiff. At the diagonal corner across from Stephen, Alan turned and balanced himself to serve. Stephen smiled at him and stationed himself to receive. "Relax," Alan called, "I always blow the first one!"

"Not if you let your body do the thinking!" He grinned.

"What is this, tennis or therapy?!"

"Serve!"

"My back hurts, my feet are killing me; I must be crazy!" Alan tossed the ball into the air and swung. It hit the net, a couple of inches below the top. "Shit." He bounced the next ball once and positioned himself for his second serve. Think with your body, Stephen had said early in the game, your body knows where to place the ball; your brain only tells you what you *can't* do. Alan looked up to see a broad grin on Stephen's face. "Okay, what's so funny?"

"You look like you're getting ready to tackle the net!"

Alan saw that he had spread his legs and bent forward in a ludicrously aggressive-looking posture. "I'm nervous," he said more to himself, "you make me nervous."

"You what?!"

"I'm nervous!"

"Relax!"

"Stop telling me to relax, you make me nervous! If I blow this one, it's game, set and match!"

"If you *have* to ace it, you'll blow it for sure! This is a *tennis* game, baby, not *life*!"

Alan bounced the ball again, "Some analogy."

"What?!"

"Skip it!"

"Serve!"

"You shrinks never let up." Alan tossed the ball up and swung, laughing at that moment to himself. The ball zeroed in an inch above the net and hit low in the far right-hand corner of the service space.

"Great!" Stephen lunged and barely caught it, lobbing a high, slow ball into his left-hand court.

So what did he have to lose, Alan thought as he ventured a backhand. With a professional-sounding *thwop* the ball sailed fast, hard, and low into Stephen's left-hand court.

"Jesus!" On the run now, Stephen crossed the court and caught it with a backhand. Again, the ball did a slow arc and hit center-court.

This was what Stephen meant! His body *did* know. As he met the ball and returned it center-court, he realized he had momentarily achieved a feeling of grace and freedom. His mind had let go. He was playing now.

Stephen, positioned for his shot, sent the ball like a bullet into the far left-hand corner of his court.

"Motherfucker," Alan watched it hit the wire mesh and bounce back.

"I couldn't resist," Stephen said catching his breath, laughing.

"Game, set, and *match*."

"That was fantastic," Stephen came towards him at the net, "You see what I mean?"

"Brief as it was"—Alan caught his breath and smiled—"I think I do."

Stephen returned his smile, reached across the net, and playfully jostled him on the shoulder, "The brain sometimes only tells you what you *have* to do."

Alan caught a twinkle of affection in the pale blue eyes. "Like get to my office and go to work," he laughed and turned away as an awkward but pleasant warmth came and went in his face. "What time have you got?"

"Two-twenty."

"Jesus. I've got a patient with bleeding ulcers at two-thirty."

"Good. That'll be two of you." He started towards the back of his court. "I'll get the balls on this side, you get them on yours. Meet you on the grass outside."

Alan headed towards the four balls lying at the far end of his court. He had phoned Margaret at the office before lunch to tell her he would be away from the hospital until his 2:30 appointment. He had taken his beeper but left it in the car. Stephen had phoned him earlier in the morning after surgery and invited him to meet at noon on the La Cienega courts for a quick game. The courts were near the hospital, his racquet and clothes were in the trunk of his car, where he had left them after their previous game. "Sure! A quick game? I'd love to," he had said, using the added pretext of discussing with Stephen his last two weeks with Schaeffer.

Alan gathered the last ball, dropped it in the can, and started towards the exit gate from the court. He had been waiting for an invitation from Stephen to play again. It was a perfectly innocent way of spending time with his friend. Of course, he should have told Alexis about the first game; only something had prevented him. A vague realization that, despite their mutual pact, an innocent tennis game with Stephen Milner would alarm her more than any admission of passing sexual desire. It was all so confusing. He had even failed to mention his first tennis game to Schaeffer.

"Did you bring a towel?" Stephen looked up from where he squatted on the ground over his plastic carry bag.

"Only the one in my trunk. It's mildewed."

"Here." He tossed him his own towel, "Use mine, it's clean."

"Do you want to use it first? I'm drenched."

"Go ahead," Stephen smiled, "I don't mind."

Alan looked away toward the cars passing in the street. With a tense, uneasy kind of pleasure, he began mopping his face and neck.

"How's it going with Schaeffer?" Stephen asked after a moment.

"Okay, I guess. He doesn't say much, I do all the talking."

"He's not supposed to say much in the beginning."

"Last time, we got into my childhood and adolescence. That woke him up for a change."

Stephen chuckled, "That's where everything begins."

"I suppose so. Only it's hard to remember much. I did jerk off with a school friend a few times when I was thirteen. I guess most guys did that."

"Some." Stephen zipped up his bag.

An image of Gerald Dorn in the college shower that afternoon when they played soccer with the other med students came to mind. "There was a guy in med school, but I never considered—" He fell silent.

Stephen stood up and took the towel Alan was holding idly. "I'm your friend, Alan, not your shrink." A hint of reticent pain crossed his face as he drew the towel across it.

"Some things are easier to tell a friend than a shrink," he heard himself say.

The towel paused on his neck. "Funny, I was hoping you'd say that."

"Until now, I've never had the luxury of a close male friend."

"Gay or straight?"

"Neither."

"Even Brad?"

"I hated myself for needing him in any way."

Stephen nodded. "Like you hated yourself for the feelings you had in med school?"

"Like that, yes. It's all connected." He shrugged. "I was a religious kid."

"I understand." Stephen smiled again, encouragingly this time. "I was, too. My parents were Reform."

"Mine were Orthodox Jewish. It was a big influence."

"And, of course, being gay was the worst thing that could happen to a guy."

"I never stopped long enough to think. It was always the joke that nature played on someone else."

"And now, you're worried that the joke's on you."

"I don't know." Alan bent down to pick up his gym bag from the ground. "If it is, it's a little late at forty. I've got a wife, two kids, a third on the way."

"And one of those complex Jewish brains like mine that keeps adding up the score," he said and, as Alan stood up, rested his hand on his shoulder. For an instant, a foot apart, they looked at each other. In Stephen's eyes, startlingly blue in the open sunlight, he saw a gentle look of resigned longing come and go. The look sank into him and held, pulling at him, and for one moment he wanted to—thought he might—embrace Stephen. "I've really got to go now." Alan looked off towards his car parked at the curb. Stephen bent down and grabbed his carry bag.

As they walked side by side across the grass, Stephen's fingers closed around his arm, affectionately. Without yielding to his first impulse to pull away, Alan paused and looked at him. "Friends?" he smiled.

"Friends."

"Gay or straight?" he added.

"Gay or straight." Stephen chuckled. Alan relaxed his arm in Stephen's hand for a moment, gave in at that moment to the magnetic pull of something stronger than simple affinity, then nodded and turned towards his car.

"Right. Good," he pressed gently on the lower part of her stomach, just above her pubic hair. "Very good." His hands were warm, sensitive to the contours of her body. "We're in excellent shape."

Alexis smiled to herself. It always amused her the way Dr. Evans carried on a running monologue with himself during his obstetric exams.

"Fine, Alexis. I think it's going to be just fine." He pressed higher now, just below her navel. She stared up at the pink ceiling of the examination room. Baby pink. Why did he think baby pink was a good color for his examination room? Cozy? Comforting, maybe, for his pregnant women? Actually, it wasn't baby pink at all. It was cotton-candy pink. Thirty-dollar-hooker pink. . . . From the lower corner of her eye she could see his head and shoulders bent over her stomach, an expression of total absorption on his handsome face. Not more than thirty-seven or -eight, he looked more like a Mammoth ski instructor than an ob-gyn. Curly brown hair, a clipped mustache; and that rough, athletically angular face that always, no matter what season, sported a California tan. Even now, at the end of January!

"Nice. Everything feels just fine." His hands moved down the sides of her lower stomach.

She glanced away at his medical plaques on the wall above the examination table, feeling a flush come over her face. She could make out the words "award to Joseph M. Evans, M.D., for excellence . . ." *Nice.* She realized she wanted him to mean her body instead of the fetus inside.

"Just as long as it's not twins," she said.

"Wouldn't you like a pair of Alans?" he chuckled.

"One's enough, thanks."

He moved on, pressing the center of her belly. The night before, Alan had palpated her abdomen as they lay together in bed. He had put his ear to her stomach and teased her about hearing "five fetal heart tones." His hands felt different from Evans's, though he had been stroking her sexily. The hands now touching her stomach, she realized, were the hands of a *completely* straight man.

"Relax, Alexis, I'm not going to hurt you."

She took a breath and let the air flow slowly from her lungs. In the twenty minutes since he had started the exam, she had waited for him to bring up the subject of the tests he had made last week, the third week of January. She had phoned him last Monday and, in passing, asked if she could drop by for a VD exam. "Nothing special," she had said, "just routine. I have no symptoms." She had had a test after New Year's, and it had been negative. But the incubation period for syphilis was two to six weeks. Paranoid or not, in spite of Alan's assurances since Christmas, she was still not convinced he had not had sex with some man, some stranger. And after all, she was the one carrying the baby.

"Try to relax your stomach, Alexis."

"I'm sorry. I'm a little tense." She concentrated on her stomach muscles. Joe was an excellent ob-gyn man. If something was wrong, surely he would have told her at the beginning. She closed her eyes and found herself relishing the feeling of his strong hands against her skin. Curious, that for all the times she had lain here on his table, she had never until now felt the slightest bit aroused, never thought of him as anything but a doctor at work. Pat Lindquist, Alan's partner's wife, had lain here too. Pat—prim and straight-laced as they come—had she also felt this way towards Evans?

Alan and she had had sex last night, and it was good. She had needed it. Since that awful afternoon two weeks before Christmas, she had needed sex with Alan more than ever before. The periods of doubt had come and gone, true. As Max had said they would. But the need for sex remained. And when it came (and, oddly, it came with more regularity now than it had for years!), it felt like the proof of the pudding. For both of them, she suspected. But then, of course, if sex was only *that.* . . .

"So far," Evans said as he patted her stomach, "it looks as though we're on schedule."

She opened her eyes, startled. "When?"

"About the first week of March." He smiled and left the side of the table, crossing to his report sheet lying open on the table. "Now I want you to get dressed and come into my office for a chat. I'll fill you in on what we've got to do in the coming weeks."

"Doctor Evans, I hope you're not saving the worst till last," she said.

"The worst?" he looked back at her, surprised, "Oh. I see." There was a rattle of papers as he flipped through the pages of her chart. "I see what all this tension is about."

"I'm not tense," she said irritably, "I'm concerned about the baby."

"Relax. Both your cultures and your blood test are negative."

She checked a sigh of relief. "I just wanted to be sure." The saliva welled up in her throat. She sat up and swung her legs from the table.

"Your routine tests back in December and January were negative, and you're still negative. Now, unless you've noticed symptoms in the last week—"

"No, nothing." She detected a faint smile in his profile.

"Syphilis has an incubation period of from two to six weeks. We'll check again in a few weeks, if you're worried."

"Whatever's routine."

He glanced at her, smiling. "As I said the last time, if Alan's been playing around, then he ought to have a test himself. Of course, being a doctor, he'd know that, wouldn't he?"

"He tested himself. It was negative." She started to get down from the table.

"In that case, unless you've had outside sex yourself in the last few weeks, there shouldn't be any problem."

"No." She reached quickly for the open flaps of her gown. "I haven't."

128

"Well, if you do, or if you think Alan has—we'll check again at your next visit. Okay?"

Under the scrutiny of his knowing eyes, she felt suddenly challenged. Pat Lindquist had once told her that Evans was unmarried and played around a lot—"a lot of lots" had been her words, when pressed to say how much. Alexis looked away and asked, "Would it surprise you if I did?"

Evans closed the manila folder around her chart, "Well," he chuckled, "I don't know. I suppose it would. I assumed last week you were talking about Alan."

"The goody-two-shoes Catholic boarding school girl—" she smiled wryly, "It shows, doesn't it?"

"To tell you the truth, I haven't given it much thought, Alexis. I always thought you enjoyed being the motherly type." He grinned and started towards the door. "Now if you'll get dressed and come into the office, we'll go over your chart together."

The motherly type. As the door closed behind him, she looked down at her naked belly between the panels of the examination gown. With both Karen and Chris, she had gone through pregnancy feeling gloriously motherly, proud and secure in her bigness for what it meant both to Alan and to her.

She pulled the gown from her shoulders, tossed it on the table, and reached for her bra on the hook where her clothes hung.

The last month, over Christmas and New Year's, Alan had been himself again, more or less. Somehow, though, it was hard to believe it would last. There was always the memory of those past defeats. She lifted the ivory silk panties from the hook and spread the elastic between her fingers. Until this, the beginning of their seventeenth year together, she had never thought to consider what it would be like to live without Alan: had never had that threat before her. She bent down and inserted one leg into the panty.

Odd that Joe Evans's hands should suddenly arouse her like that. She inserted the other leg and drew the panties up.

In this period of adjustment, which was more important, being a mother to his child or a partner in his love life? After what had happened, could she ever really be both again? Besides, how could a man like Alan find her body, huge in its female exaggerations, desirable? He who had occasionally fancied slim-hipped, lean, muscular young men.

She reached for her slip on the hook. The motherly type. Lately, there had been that other rather nagging question: considering herself alone, as a woman, had she ever really wanted or needed a third child to begin with?

VIII

Again, Alan pressed down on the brake pedal to slow for the approaching streetlight, and again he saw Max's foot jump forward on the imaginary brake pedal on the passenger side.

"Before Christmas I was worried," Max went on, "when you came to see me on Hannukah, I could tell you were unhappy."

Always the same old Max, always fighting to hold onto the driver's seat. Even when Sarah was alive and did most of the driving, he was over there giving directions, kvetching the whole way. He had been on this homily now for the last twenty minutes, since they pulled out of the parking lot of the Westwood Theater. Alexis was wise to have stayed home and let him take Max to the movies alone.

"I will be truthful with you, I've known there's been trouble for almost a year now, but you seem better now. Since Christmas, you seem like a different man and I'm glad for that, son."

Alan counted the streetlights between them and the avenue running alongside the palisades fronting the ocean. Four. With luck, he could make all four without another stop and be at the door of the Georgian in minutes.

"Alexis is a good woman. You're lucky to have her, believe me."

The observation sounded fatalistically Jewish to Alan. "I'd say she was a saint, dad, wouldn't you? I mean, considering whom she's strapped with for life." He glanced at Max as he reached for the armrest on the door. The sarcasm had registered, he saw. *She was a saint.* Since Sarah's death, Max had used that Christian expression when he wanted to lament all the troubles he had put Sarah through during their years of marriage. She was a saint. A kind of self-deprecation with a proud admission of failure underneath it.

Max looked down in silence.

"Dad," Alan sighed, "getting a new medical corporation like ours on its feet isn't easy." He came to a halt at the intersection fronting the palisade. "I've had a lot of fights with the hospital administration in the last year, a lot of trouble. The new house, the baby, bills—I'm under a lot of strain." He set his gaze on the palm trees lining the mall across the avenue, hoping his bypass of the truth would satisfy.

"Did I ask you what the trouble was? I only said you look like yourself again. I don't stick my nose into your business, I never did." The light went green. Alan pressed on the accelerator and made a quick right. "You still drive too fast." Max braced his hand against the dashboard. "Slow down. I have a backgammon game tomorrow with Alice Orloff and I want to beat the old *goniff* before I die."

"*Dad!*" Alan eased up on the accelerator.

"This impatience of yours. I wonder you don't have an ulcer. You must have gotten that from your mother."

"Not mother. She never gave me an ulcer."

"I meant your impatience." He released one of his long-suffering sighs. "All right, I will shut up for the rest of the way."

Please do, Alan thought, please do. God knows, in the last three weeks since the picnic, he had gone out of his way to include the old man in their family outings. Dinner last Thursday, the drive up the coast to Santa Barbara on Sunday, and now tonight, dinner and a movie. Already he regretted his earlier enthusiasm when Alexis invited him on the telephone to the beach with them on Saturday.

On his right, there was another sigh, presaging another homilitic paternal observation. He really *was* like old Rabbi Horowitz, Alan thought, cut from the same old-world Jewish cloth. Rabbi Horowitz had directed the Hebrew school he had attended as a boy at their local synagogue in Detroit. A hundred years ago, it seemed.

"I will say this, though. You should thank God for Alexis. You have a steadfast woman for a wife. She's like your mother in that. Nowadays, most women of her age and background are busy competing with men at the office. They lose patience with men who give them trouble at home. Divorce is very easy now."

Alan pressed down on the clutch and let the car coast on its own momentum. The solemn, worried looks he had gotten from both Max and Alexis when he came up the hill with the plywood the night of the picnic came to mind. He glanced again at Max beside him. His profile was illuminated by the neon lights from the passing shops and restaurants on the street. His expression was impassive, but guarded. Alexis would never willfully betray him to Max. If Max knew about him, he had maneuvered it, wheedled it out of her. "What did you get her to tell you?" he asked.

"Who? What do you mean?"

"You know what I mean." Max had always done it, maneuvered him at second hand, through the ones closest to him. Like the time he forced his mother to beg him to apply to a med school close to home.

"No, I don't know what you mean."

"Alexis, dad. You've been questioning her, haven't you?"

"When do I ask questions? I never ask questions! I merely see with my own eyes!"

Alan swerved the car towards the curb before the Georgian and stopped abruptly. He drew a breath. His heartbeat raced. "In the future, dad, if you've got any questions about my personal life, I'd appreciate it if you directed them to me." He snapped off the ignition. "Do I make myself clear?"

"I know nothing, nothing whatever about your personal life."

Alan felt the blood explode in his face. "My personal life has nothing to do with you! I don't want to hear any paternal Jewish breast-beating anymore! I don't want advice, I don't want any Talmudic homilies, and I don't want you engineering me through Alexis!" The headlights of a car turning into the driveway of the Georgian swept across the windshield, blinding him. The old man beside him caught his breath. "You're a con man, dad!" The fury pounded out of him before he knew what he was saying. "Alexis thinks you're a fountain of eternal wisdom, but you're a con man! You've always been one!" He caught himself, reached at once for the door handle, and got out. He was half-way around the front of the car when he saw the expression of shock on the old man's parchment-white face through the windshield. As he started around the passenger side of the car, his eye caught sight of a discarded half-pint liquor bottle in the gutter. A sudden gust of wind whipped over the top of the car, sending a chill through his body. He felt his anger drain away under the downward pull of guilt. At the passenger door, he bent down and opened it. "Dad, I'm sorry. I didn't mean that. Any of it." He looked down at the face turned up to him from the dark interior of the car. It looked old and frightened.

"Never mind." Max took hold of his hand. "Just give me a hand to the door, son, and then you go on." Alan felt the shaky pull of Max's arm as the old man worked his legs through the door and got to his feet in the gutter.

"Watch the curb, dad."

"My stick." Max turned for his cane, propped against the front seat.

Alan reached behind him, retrieved the stick, and handed it to him. "Come on, I'll take you up to your room." Their feet were silent on the rubber skid pad as they started up the steps onto the verandah. Through the beveled glass of the front door, the refurbished Edwardian lobby, with its gilt-framed portraits, cut-glass reading lamps, and leather arm-chairs, looked like a museum. "I kept you out too late, didn't I?" Alan said as they reached the front door. "Everyone else is in bed." He looked at his watch. It was seven minutes to ten.

Max shifted his cane from his right to his left hand. "Never mind. They've gone to bed because they're bored talking to each other." He reached for the door handle, "Most of these old geezers don't have families anymore."

Alan took the handle from him and opened the door, "Dad, we'll be here at noon on Saturday, me, Alexis, and the kids," his eye rested on the newly installed blue wall-to-wall carpet. "We want you to come with us to the beach." It was the same deep sea blue as the industrial carpet in the corridor of the ward where Brad had died. It was as though the ocean behind them had washed in through the door and covered the floor.

"Sure," Max forced a smile. "I promised the kids I'd build them a sand castle."

"What I said in the car was unfair." Alan felt a pain in his tightening stomach, "I was wrong, I know. I'm sorry."

"Forget it. Go home to Alexis now, she's waiting for you." He patted his arm and moved forward.

Alan reached out. On an impulse, he wanted at that moment to hold Max.

The old man passed by him into the lobby.

Alan followed him inside a few feet. "Bring a coat, dad, it gets cold on the beach in February."

"I will, son."

"Noon Saturday."

"Noon. I'll be here." He shuffled off towards the elevator at the far end of the lobby. Jimmy, the night security guard behind the desk, lifted his head and murmured to Max, who nodded, waved, and continued on. He looked suddenly like a very old man.

I should have done it, Alan thought, gone ahead and acted on the impulse. While the moment was there. Before he passed by.

He pushed through the door and stepped out onto the long verandah with its empty wrought-iron tables and chairs. For one brief moment, he could have done it—bridged everything, closed the gap of thirty years between them. With one simple gesture. Connected.

It was a gesture as simple as opening and closing a door. And he could not make it.

As he started down the steps, he felt an aching knot form in his stomach. It had happened before, this moment of missed connection. The sense of something left undone, incomplete, unfinished was familiar.

Alan opened the driver's door, then closed it and stood for a moment in the street. Above the dark grassy park running along the palisade overlooking the ocean, the fronds of the giant royal palms were making a soft rattling noise in the wind blowing off the ocean. The last time he had visited Max, he had found him sitting alone on one of the wooden park benches while the other residents of the nearby retirement homes strolled slowly up and down the walks overlooking the sea.

Pulling the collar of his shirt over his sweater, Alan left the car and headed towards the crosswalk at the end of the block. In the last five weeks, he had noticed changes in his feelings towards Max. A new kind of sharpness in his perceptions of the old man. Now and then, an aching awareness that Max was out here on the palisade sitting out the last inning alone.

Schaeffer had constantly asked him questions about his childhood feelings towards Max. He had felt like a Freudian guinea pig.

Without waiting for the pedestrian signal to change to "Walk," he crossed the avenue and turned south down the sidewalk under the palms. The meandering sidewalks, lit by old-fashioned lamps, were deserted. Over the low railing running along the cliff edge, he could see the silver perimeter of the Pacific Ocean; and above, through the dark fronds of a palm tree, the pointed end of a winter half-moon.

Schaeffer had said the letting go of his feelings would be slow and painful. In the last three weeks since the night of their picnic in Coldwater Canyon, he had felt a warm joy in his father's company. Then tonight, for no justifiable reason, feelings of rage the likes of which he had never felt before. Then at the door, the need to hold the man. There was no logic to feelings; in that, Schaeffer was right.

Beyond the sculptured Japanese trees south of the Senior Citizens' Recreation Center, the glittering lights of the Santa Monica pier came into view. Alexis was waiting, but he would tell her he had needed to walk, to be alone and think. In the last three weeks, he had felt wonderfully free about telling her everything. She would understand.

He quickened his pace towards the concrete ramp running down the palisade towards the pier.

Up to now, his strategy for keeping peace with Max had been to outflank him from a distance. It was an old technique. He had used it at eighteen when he chose Johns Hopkins on the East Coast rather than a Detroit medical school. Tonight, he had found himself circling Max like a wrestler searching for a split-second opening, except that his opponent was now an old man with a bad heart and arthritis, puttering out his last years in a seaside retirement home. A man whose thoughts of his own death were sobered by the catastrophe of another, more awesome final solution. Tonight, years of conflicting feelings seemed to have converged on Alan. Come to a head, like an abscess ready to drain. Old angers and old joys from adolescence. Shame, dilatory as it was, for years of neglect. And even older than all those feelings, feelings of yearning and loss.

In dredging up the childhood bottoms of his homosexual needs, Schaeffer had told him a lot of other hidden feelings would come up, too. In a panic, a week before Christmas, he had begun therapy with the sole purpose of facing directly his year-long drift into—funny, he still found the word difficult to say—homosexuality. The assumption, at first, had been that he could treat it like a surgical procedure, isolate the affected organ and cut, without disturbing the healthy ones around it. The fact was, he had been drilling down into other reservoirs of his past and had tapped streams that seemed to pour out through every corner of his life, streams that crossed and connected and fed each other. Everything in the darkness down there was still confused, though. Max, his mother, Alexis, the kids, his friends and medical colleagues, Brad, Stephen, and somewhere at the center of the maze, himself.

At the top of the sloping, concrete causeway connecting the palisade with the pier below, Alan paused to look down. Built a half century ago, the two-lane causeway ran down a couple of hundred yards from the cliff side to the huge pier jutting several hundred yards into the ocean.

He and Brad had walked up it from the beach one evening after they had spent an hour in the shooting galleries and taken a ride on the merry-go-round. That night, streams of cars and pedestrians were moving up and down the ramp between the pier and the palisade. Tonight, with the playground closed for the winter, the lamplit causeway was empty.

Alan started down the sidewalk running along the causeway railing. Off in the darkness on either side of the pier, a heavy surf was breaking on the beach. The cold, salty wind felt bracing against his face. He drew in a long, freeing breath. There was space here.

Alexis. In the last seven weeks, almost two months now, he had daily grown more and more aware of how essential she was. In even those smallest, housewife things. Like yesterday, when he came home to find she had reorganized his clothes closet. In the months before Christmas, he had resented her motherly return to housewifery, told himself it was a disguised form of possessiveness. Now, it was a reassuring form of need. Like her reawakened need for frequent sex. When they made love—and they made love now at odd times during the day, as on last Sunday afternoon when the kids were outside playing—they both knew that it was, in part, the proof that nothing between them had been lost. The tacit suspicion that something *had* been lost only made them cling closer to each other.

A few yards ahead, Alan's eye caught something drawn on the sidewalk between two lamp posts. As he reached the spot, he looked down at a hurriedly drawn scrawl of spray-painted graffiti: *Kill faggots.* The sudden intrusion of the message startled and embarrassed him. A few yards on, the embarrassment gave way to a sense of uneasiness and dread, as though he had just come into contact with some malevolent and dangerous presence. Alan quickened his steps. At the end of the causeway, the esplanade extended out over the beach and ocean. Ahead, a few couples moved slowly in the eerie light of the old-fashioned lamp posts. He rounded the automobile barrier across the pier and reached an open section of railing overlooking the beach. Above the dark cliffs on his right, the lights of hotels, apartments, and restaurants ran off along the palisade towards the north, tapering to a single glittering strand of highway lights curving out towards Malibu. Thousands of lights. And each one, he thought to himself, marked the place of one human being. Odd he had never thought of that before. One light per person, each person going through the separate routine of their separate lives. Never connecting except to pass and go on. And he, alone here on a darkened pier above the white ocean breakers rolling up the beach. Until now, he had never really thought that the world had any other business but to revolve around himself; around himself, Alexis, and the kids.

On the beach below the pier, a movement caught his eye. In the sand twenty feet below, figures were moving. First one, then two and three. He watched the first, a man, as he ambled along the sand towards the ocean. He moved slowly, crossing a bright square of light falling from a lamp on the pier. He was young, dark-haired, bearded, and wore what looked like jeans and a denim jacket. The buckle of his belt glinted in the light as he moved on into the shadows again. Then a figure standing near the surf strolled in the direction of the first. To the north, further up the beach, a third figure stood watching the other two as they moved cautiously towards each other. Twenty feet apart, they veered off, keeping a distance between each other. They passed directly below Alan, each staring at the other. The pier lights shimmered off a black leather jacket. The second man wore jeans and a dark T-shirt. They both stopped, turned, and stood looking at each other for a moment. The black leather jacket then turned in the direction of the pier, moved into the deeper shadows below. As though on signal, the other followed.

Alan stepped back from the railing out of view. A curious sensation ran through his body, as though he had been suddenly drawn into the dangerous proximity of a high-voltage generator. He was aware of a profound silence, magnified by the sound of the wind in his ears.

He took two steps to the railing and looked below. Below him, sheltered from view by the pier's shadow, the two men came together. For a moment, they faced each other, then each reached out to touch the other's chest. The space around Alan felt suddenly and electrically charged. His heartbeat raced. He wanted to turn away and yet wanted to stay. Again, he looked down. They had moved deeper into the darkness below and now stood directly under him. The whites of their hands moved slowly over each other's bodies. As they vanished under the pier, he saw the whites of their faces come together in a kiss.

The spray-painted graffiti flashed before his mind, and with the image came a stab of anguish. A familiar ache began in his groin and spread through his arms and legs. It rose into his face with a fierce burning heat. In his mind, he saw the bearded man's face closing against his own. He could feel the soft, warm sensation of the man's lips on his own. His mind recoiled with a silent but strident *No*! But the desire pulling at his body, his blood, had the easy, natural, and commanding force of a physical law.

It was unthinkable.

He turned, leaving the railing, and hurried across the pier towards the causeway.

Impossible. He was four million light-years from that. Married, a husband and a father, a surgeon with a respectable practice. A man with a loving wife; with two, soon three children. A man who loved his wife. A desire like that one under the pier was out of character. With long, deliberate strides, he started up, keeping his eyes fixed on the huge green neon Holiday Inn sign towering above the palisade.

In all these weeks, he had been free from that kind of white-hot burn. That afternoon on the tennis court, he had *wanted* Stephen, true. But *that* was not *this*! That was only the body's natural warmth from natural emotional affection! A few yards up the ramp, he started to jog, taking deep breaths to keep up the supply of oxygen to his heart.

He was past forty. Alexis would be waiting for him. He would tell her about the men below. Max would be reading in his room. He must call Donald in the morning about assisting on the Goddard surgery. Their architect, Jimmy Cagle, wouldn't be caught dead under the pier like that at night.

So many different ways of *being* in this crazy world!

Stephen Milner. A psychiatrist with a sense of humor. So different from Marvin Schaeffer, who was too busy looking for reasons to see the crazy capriciousness of things and laugh. Stephen with pale blue eyes. A Jew with bluer eyes than his own. That afternoon on the court, they had looked at him with desire. Contained, yes; but it was there. Straight or gay, he had said. Friends, they had both said. That was the brain talking logically. But even he, the psychiatrist, could be caught in stronger tides. Brad's face on the pillow that afternoon flashed painfully before his eyes.

At the midway point, he stopped and breathed heavily, deeply, then leaned against the concrete wall. His eyes rested on the graffiti a few feet ahead. *Kill faggots.* The shock and embarrassment he felt had gone. Now, he sensed only the malevolence of the mind that had passed there with its can of spray paint. Behind the hurry and scrawl of the command, he now read something of the rage and self-punishment that had driven the person to put it there. He felt the tension in his body suddenly give way; reflected in the painted screed, he could now read something of his own.

Raus mit den Juden—Out with the Jews.

In the picture book of the Second World War in his parent's attic— yes, he had seen the photograph of the graffiti painted on a Berlin wall.

Alan looked up towards the crest of the palisade, let his gaze sweep along the miles of coastline holiday glitter, then began the remaining climb. But slowly now, for he was moving against the heavy, downward pull of a boundless sadness.

He had spent half his life protecting life. Perhaps that joy he felt every time he succeeded with his scalpel in saving human life was a feeling that connected with other feelings. The sad horror of his parents', his uncle's, wartime hell. Perhaps as a child he had dreamed the dream of medicine looking for some way to prevent that abyss of human suffering and death from ever opening again. The abyss that had once opened and threatened to swallow everyone he loved. The intolerance was still there, as blind and brutal as ever. The same stupid self-defeating human failure to bridge and connect.

At the top of the causeway, Alan turned left and retraced his path through the park, past the Senior Citizens' Recreation Center, where the teenagers on skateboards had laughed one afternoon at the old people at play, past the anomalous Japanese bonsai trees, past the empty park benches and the empty trash bins.

He thought back to the men under the pier. Impossible. He was four million light-years from that kind of connection. But nonetheless, intolerable as it seemed, he had felt the desires again, and the backlash on himself had been fear, panic, and anger. That afternoon at the courts, he had felt a charge of pleasure when Stephen touched and held his arm. An affinity again, a rightness—a need to reciprocate.

At the crosswalk, Alan waited for the light to change. Across the avenue, dwarfed by the tall, modern condominium next door, the Georgian, restored, looked somehow necessary and right on its tiny, truncated lot.

He would tell Alexis everything. Of his outburst with Max in the car, his impulse to hold the old man after all these years, his walk on the pier, and his sudden, unexpected desire for the men under it. And of his feelings that day for Stephen when they played tennis. Those feelings, though, not his sexual desire for the men under the pier, would be hardest for her to accept. He knew that. Until now, he had not even dared to tell her he had played tennis with Stephen. But if their pact meant anything, she should know it all.

His eye went up the darkened facade of the Georgian to the solitary light in the fifth-floor window. Through the old-fashioned lace curtain, there was the faint glow of Max's bedside lamp. Now, as always and as long as he could remember, Max would be up until one, reading until he fell asleep bolt upright against his pillows with the book in his hand. A man of old, eccentric habits.

Years before, in Rome, when he and Alexis had taken a midnight walk through St. Peter's Square, they had looked up at the dark facade of a building and seen a light still burning in the window of the Pope's apartment. Another old man of eccentric habits. Alan smiled. So many different ways of being.

The streetlight opposite turned yellow.

Max and Sarah, Alexis and he, Donald and Pat, the Berreys, Jimmy Cagle, Brad and he . . . Stephen.

So many ways of loving.

As Alan stepped into the street and started towards his car, the sign under the streetlight went from "Wait" to "Walk."

"I was above, Alexis, on the pier; they were down on the beach—below." He reached across the bed and took hold of her arm. "I did not go down."

"I understand." She rested her left hand on the book she had been reading. It lay open on the coverlet over her stomach.

"Even if I'd wanted to, I couldn't. You know the Santa Monica pier."

"Did you want to?" she tried to unload the accusation in her voice before she said it. She understood the literal meaning of his words, yes; but the meaning was incomprehensible to her.

"I'm saying I wanted sex, yes. But not like that."

Like that. Men embracing in the sand under a public pier at night, kissing, having sex. The image of it sickened and frightened her. "I understand, Alan, and I'm glad you've told me."

"I wanted you to know; that was our pact."

She nodded. He moved a few inches closer to her and lay on his side, staring at her. His fingers pressed her arm lightly. She lay quite still for a moment. She wanted to look at his eyes now, but his naked shoulder above her had blocked the light from the bedside lamp. His face was shadowed. It was crazy—the two of them lying here in bed discussing his sex as if it were a case of indigestion. When he had failed to come home by eleven-thirty, she had suspected him of stopping at some gay bar on the way. That—the willful weakness of giving into temptation—

she could have dealt with easier. In her mind, she had imagined it would happen that way. She had planned her understanding, compassionate response for the last few weeks, since the night of the picnic. "How long did you stay—and watch?" she heard herself say.

"Alexis—" He pressed her arm again, "Only a few minutes. I guess I was curious, I don't know. I left and went to my car."

"Did it turn you on, what you saw?"

"Yes. For a moment."

She felt suddenly naive, inept. The sexuality of men, straight men, had always confounded her; the sexuality of gay men confounded and revolted her. She had always pictured them in the act of sodomy—male into male—always with sexual violence. An act of animal gratification.

"I wanted the sex, nothing more."

"What stopped you? The danger of it?"

"Do you think I'm capable of having sex like that?"

"Obviously, some men are."

"There are as many different ways and needs as there are people, you know that."

"Oh, please, Alan. I'm not that stupid."

"No, but you're not the kind of woman who thinks of sex for the sake of sex, without any emotional ties."

"Oh?" She thought back to the feeling of Joe Evans's hands on her stomach that afternoon on the examination table.

"They were strangers, those men under the pier. That's one thing—it's another to want someone you know."

"I understand. You don't have to explain."

"I want to. There's something more I want to—"

"You wanted sex." She turned onto her side and faced him. "I told you I knew it would happen. I do understand, believe me."

"I wanted the sex tonight, yes; but there was—"

"Please, Alan," she touched his mouth with her fingers, "no apology is necessary. It was something that happened in passing. It would be something quite different if you needed something more from someone."

"I—" He lay his head against her arm on the pillow.

"Forget it. They were passing strangers. If you had other feelings, it would be different."

He said nothing, merely looked at her.

"You're tired. Let's sleep."

"Alexis." He drew his hand around her neck and pressed her against him. She lifted her face and kissed him on the mouth. For a moment, they held each other in an embrace that was gentle and comforting to them both.

IX

"Three stockbrokers got together and opened it about ten days ago. It's packed for lunch." Stephen lay his fork and knife down and sat back, spreading the sides of his blue blazer.

Alan scanned the small crowded room with its hanging baskets of ferns against the white latticework walls. He caught sight of Ellis Seligmann staring at him from his table across the room. He was sitting with three other doctors from the hospital staff. "Looks like a medical convention, though."

"It's convenient for the hospital." Stephen leaned forward and refilled his wine glass.

"Do you eat like this every day?"

"Good god, no. Only on special occasions." He glanced at Alan and chuckled, "I eat in the hospital cafeteria."

"What's the occasion? You still haven't told me." Alan sipped his wine. It was his fourth glass now. The nervousness he had felt when he walked in with Stephen and found the restaurant full of familiar hospital faces had gone.

"You mean, you *still* don't know?" Stephen sat back with his glass and smiled incredulously. He looked relaxed and easy in his beautifully cut blazer, white shirt, and black knit tie. Alan realized he had never seen Stephen in a tie before.

"No. You said this morning when you called that we were celebrating an *occasion*. What is it, your birthday?"

"Nope. That's two weeks off."

"Some kind of anniversary?" Alan went on, enjoying the game.

"Do you have a lover hidden somewhere that I don't know about?"

Stephen laughed. "If I did, would I be sitting here with you?"

"You were in San Francisco last week."

"I don't believe this!" He sat forward and rested his arms on the table. "Now either you're amnesic or you're disgustingly humble."

"Oh." Alan saw the knowing look in his eyes. "You mean that Dorothy Beck thing?"

"That Dorothy Beck thing—of course I mean that! How many times have you had a patient give a hospital a half-million dollars in your name?"

"Never," Alan grinned. Last night, Arnold Berrey had phoned him at home to say that his patient, Dorothy Beck, had notified the hospital board that she was giving the hospital half a million dollars in his name, "in acknowledgment of her gratitude for the successful outcome of the surgery you performed on her last fall," as Berrey had pompously put it.

"Well, I thought it called for a celebration."

"How'd you find out? She only made the gift late yesterday afternoon."

"It was all over the hospital this morning, even in my wing. What's wrong, you don't look very happy about it."

"Berrey phoned me last night and said he'd met with Conners, Darmstadt, and Bouvard. The board of directors all think it should go into the parking garage fund."

"And you?"

"I think it should go into equipment. Berrey says Mrs. Beck wants her name on something. I guess she'd feel kind of silly with her name on a brass plaque under an operating table."

"I'm sorry. I know how you feel." Stephen reached again for the wine bottle and topped his glass for him. "Still, it won't hurt your reputation around the place."

Alan glanced again towards Seligmann's table and caught the young doctor's eye. Seligmann smiled and went back to his conversation. "No." He sipped his wine. "I guess I can use all the good reputation I can get." He kept his eyes lowered for a moment, realizing that Stephen had divined his meaning.

"I was going to ask you to lunch last Friday when I got back from my APA meeting in San Francisco. But I decided I needed a pretext."

Alan glanced up, surprised. "That's funny, I started to call you on Friday, too. I thought I was the one who needed a pretext."

"If we're only friends, Alan, do we need pretexts?"

Alan pulled at the leaf of the single white rose in its thin vase between them. "I was going to use Schaeffer again as a pretext."

144

"How's it going?"

"Slow. He still doesn't say much. Just sits there in his armchair looking at me like Dr. Freud."

"Therapy is a slow process, you know that."

"The patient is moving a little faster than the cure, though. I went back to that bar aagin."

"The Motherlode?"

Alan looked into Stephen's eyes. They were genuinely startled. "Last week, I got to the point where I thought I'd go crazy if I didn't make some kind of contact with a man. I told myself I could have sex with some stranger, get it over with, and go back to being my normal self. I got there and stayed only ten minutes."

"And left alone?"

Alan nodded.

"Why?"

"Three reasons." He ran through the mental list he had made. "I was intimidated, I was scared, and I was depressed."

"That's a lot for ten minutes."

"It took a little longer than ten. The next evening, I left work early and went to another bar. I lasted thirty in that one."

"How does this tie in with your calling me?"

"I was intimidated in the first bar because ninety percent of the men were a good fifteen years younger and much better-looking than me. Nobody seemed particularly interested in balling a forty-year-old square. I wasn't even in the running." He glanced at the opposite table, then lowered his voice. "I was scared because there was the chance someone might recognize me, and I was depressed because I realized all those men, even the ones who were scoring, were looking for a fantasy man who wasn't there. I realized they're there every night, looking for Mr. Perfect. I told myself I was just looking for a quick lay, but it wasn't so. I stood there picturing myself cruising bars night after night for the rest of my life, looking for someone"—he hesitated, averting his eyes—"for someone who wasn't going to show, and I knew I had something better at home. Even if things aren't so hot at the moment with Alexis, at least there's some affection. Something real."

"Not all gay people spend their lives in bars, Alan."

"Do you go to bars?"

"Occasionally. With friends." He ran his finger around the rim of his glass. "When I moved here from New York, I had a lover. Living with one person that long spoiled the bar scene for me, I guess." He looked down, reticent now.

Alan sat back, momentarily silenced, while the busboy removed their plates. Only once, in passing, had Stephen hinted at his own past involvements. And that was to say that he knew what it was to love someone who "either won't or can't give you the center space." He had said that out of sympathy for Alexis.

"Have you talked about this with Schaeffer?" Stephen looked up when the busboy had gone. Alan realized he wanted to change the subject.

"The bar? Yes, I told him. Only—" He hesitated. The two of them stared at each other. Alan felt something brim up inside him, reach the spilling point, then subside. The truth was, for almost two weeks he had waited for a call from Stephen. When he learned he had gone to San Francisco for an APA meeting, he had spent four days feeling abandoned and jealous. There were a lot of available men in San Francisco.

"Only what?"

"Only I didn't tell Schaeffer why I really went to the bars. I went to those bars on the chance that I would see you there. Crazy, but that seemed less obvious than phoning."

Stephen shifted in his chair, surprised and nonplussed for a moment, then said, "Did you tell Alexis the reason?"

"No. I told her I dropped into two bars, had a drink, and left. She can handle that, believe it or not, but the idea of anything more—" He felt his face redden.

"Alan." Stephen's voice sank. "How many gay men do you know?"

"Two." He felt the same feeling brim up inside him, the need to let go of what he had kept hidden for weeks. "Maybe three."

"It's understandable you'd be infatuated with the first gay man you met."

"You're not the first. You're only the second," the feeling spilled out of him.

Stephen looked at him in silence. The sound of the voices around them seemed strangely distant at that moment. "I thought of sending you a postcard from San Francisco," he said finally.

"Why didn't you?"

"Where would I have sent it? To your home? And I make no secret of being gay at the hospital."

"I understand."

"We're supposed to be friends. Only friends."

"I know." He stared at Stephen's hand on the table. "But as you say, why have we both been looking for pretexts? If that's all we both need . . ."

"We're both nuts, you know that? Two grown men, a shrink and a surgeon, we should know better."

"Only you're the one who suggested letting the body do the thinking." On an impulse, Alan moved his right hand across the table and let the ends of his fingers come to rest against Stephen's fingers. The feeling brimmed up again, flowed down his arm, and spilled into his fingers. He breathed, realizing that something undeniably right for him, but also something huge and ominous for the future had finally come to rest.

"I said that to improve your tennis. This isn't a tennis game, Alan."

As Alan looked up, he caught sight of Arnold Berrey who, at that moment, was seating himself with a group of people at a nearby table. Arnold looked at the two of them, then smiled.

"There was a meeting at the hospital, and then I—"

"Honey, the point *was*"—she silenced him with a gesture—"all six samples we chose have to be *ordered. Specially*. It takes months. We promised Atlas we'd order them *today*. We're not building a two-room tract house in the Valley, you know."

He lay his suit jacket over his briefcase on the armchair and crossed to her arrangement of brick samples on the carpet. "I had an errand to run," he said.

An errand to run. The excuse he had used months ago when, in fact, he was with his friend Brad. "Of the six samples, Cagle prefers this one." She indicated the pinker of the two terra cottas with the toe of her shoe, "but it looks *pink* to me in this light. What do you think?"

"I think you're right."

"Do you now."

"Except that the light you've got them in distorts everything."

She kept her eyes on the bricks at her feet. She was right. She could hear the familiar tone of defense in his voice.

"We can look at them in the morning," he said.

"Choices have to be made, Alan." She checked an impulse to confront him there and then. "The point is, building a house takes a little organization. Things have to be ordered, choices made in advance. If you leave all the choices up to me, and I choose something you don't like, then we're both stuck with it. Once choices are made, they can't be reversed." Her voice wavered, "We're supposed to be building this house *together*."

"I trust your taste implicitly."

"You hated the color of wood I chose for the floors."

"I was wrong."

"You didn't think you were wrong, you simply gave in rather than deal with having to make a choice."

"I have lousy taste. I admit to having lousy taste! Every time I choose something, either you or Cagle tell me I'm wrong!"

They were at an impasse. Neither of them was going to say what was really on their minds. She lowered herself to her knees and began moving the bricks further into the spill of light from the lamp on the end table. It was beyond silliness now. After seventeen years, they were like a couple arguing over a toothpaste cap. The distance she had seen widening between them in the last two weeks was now unbridgeable. It was not the same kind of distance as last winter. No, this time Alan seemed quite comfortable with it. "Here." She separated two of the bricks from the others. "These are the two you liked best. Which do you prefer?"

"Sweetheart," he said from above, "I really can't tell them apart in this light."

"Do you have a preference, or don't you?" she pressed him. Until ten or so days ago, he had been frank about telling her where his feelings lay. Of late, when they talked, he had been editing something out.

"My preference is that *you* choose."

She sat back, tucking the loose folds of her skirt under her belly. She looked grotesque, squatting on the floor. Her choice was and *had* been simple: she wanted him to show her some kind of desire. Of late, even when they did have sex, she knew that his heart was not in it, even if his body was. "Alan!" Her voice broke. "I can't make all the choices!" She stared down at her belly. It almost concealed her legs. In a matter of a few weeks, it would be over, but she wanted it over *now*. Between wanting the baby and wanting him to desire her as a woman, there was only one choice now. But how could any man, let alone Alan, find a seven-and-a-half-month-pregnant woman desirable. "For God's sake, will you make a choice? I can't go on like this!"

"Honey, I'm trying." He knelt down beside her. "Believe me, I am *trying*." He grasped her shoulders.

"I'm not talking about the goddamn bricks!" she covered her eyes with her hand.

"I know you're not."

"I waited for two hours this afternoon at that brick company! I had to crawl around those fucking brick piles alone! You could have phoned me there!"

"I tried phoning twice. The line was busy."

"Phoned from where? Some gay bar in West Hollywood?"

"No." He let go of her shoulders. "Not this time."

"Then where were you?! At some man's *house?* Do you have a lover again?"

Next to her, she heard him get to his feet. The suddenness of the movement startled her. She opened her eyes, suddenly frightened, and saw him heading to the armchair. The thought crossed her mind that she had gone raving mad. That he was getting some medication from his briefcase for her.

"I went down to the Lamaze offices on Olympic Boulevard." He turned with a large manila envelope in his hand. His face, she saw, had gone white. "I picked up some material and brochures on the natural childbirth method. That's where I was."

She looked down, bewildered.

"I was going to suggest the Lamaze method this time. You know about it, don't you?"

The diamond on her finger glinted in the lamplight from above. She had not really stopped to look at that tiny prism of changing colors for years, had almost forgotten that the ring was there.

"It's done without anesthetics. The father is present during the labor. If you're into it, I'd like to be with you this time."

She went on vacuously staring at her stomach.

"The point is, I had to go there this afternoon; you have to start the exercises right away, if you decide to do it. It's up to you, honey."

"How many cylinders?"

"Four, but it's enough. It's got good torque." Stephen shifted down to second on the last curve up Laurel Canyon. Alan looked up at the sunlight through the trees overhead and felt the smooth, level swing of the open sportscar around the curve.

"Do you think I'm crazy for buying it?"

"No. Fact is, I'm jealous."

Stephen glanced at him, "No sensible surgeon would ride around in a car like this." He shifted down to first and drew up to wait for the streetlight at the intersection of Laurel Canyon and Mulholland Drive.

"I don't know." Alan caught his eye mischievously, "That's only the surface. At heart, I've always been a sucker for speed. I'm an arrested adolescent really." He lay his head back against the headrest and looked at Stephen's hand on the gearshift.

"Last week, after our lunch, I decided to stay in California and not go back to New York. So I bought myself a convertible for a birthday present and became a thirty-six-year-old adolescent."

Alan pulled his tie through his collar and dropped it into the space behind the seats with his suit jacket. He smiled and sat back, enjoying the warmth of the sun, but feeling at the same time the need for something more than a ride in a new sportscar. Last week, after their third lunch, they had separated to go their separate ways for the afternoon. That time, he had been left with a feeling of incompletion. Lunch had not been enough, they had *done* that. Moreover, he had realized that Stephen, out of consideration for his dilemma, would not press him for more than a lunch now and then. Just as with Alexis, he was at an impasse with Stephen.

"You okay?" Stephen jostled his knee affectionately.

"I'm fine. Relaxing. I thought your birthday was next week."

"It is. Are you free that day?"

"For what? Lunch?"

"Dinner's a more serious meal."

"I can't do dinner, you know that." He glanced at Stephen pointedly. "What are we going to do, *eat* our way through this relationship?"

Stephen chuckled, "It's not my fault I'm only your *lunch*."

"Your light's green."

Stephen pulled ahead, swinging left onto Mulholland. The engine released a swift, rising purr as the RPMs climbed. "We'll take Mulholland across the hills to Beverly Glen and then cut back down to Sunset. I'd take Benedict or Coldwater Canyons, but they're off limits."

Take anything, at this point it doesn't matter, he started to say, but looked off instead through a break in the hills towards the San Fernando Valley spread out below them to the north. For one moment, when Stephen had driven up in the car to pick him up in front of his office, he had thought maybe this time Stephen had something better than lunch in mind. A drive together alone through the top of the Santa Monica mountains, this would be their moment. But it wasn't. The drive, like his substitute appetite at their lunches, only left him desolate when the real aching need was to hold and be held by Stephen.

He felt Stephen's hand stroke his arm. "You're not enjoying this at all, are you? Tell me where you'd like to go."

The ache rolled through his whole body. He lifted his head and caught sight of a small dirt road running off at an angle at the far end of the approaching S curve. It was familiar. So was the desire he felt. He had taken the road a couple of times on outings with Alexis and the kids. It ran up the side of the next hill to a flat, empty place on top. "You see that road up there," Alan pointed through the windshield.

"What about it?"

"Slow down and take it."

Stephen braked and looked at him, startled.

"It runs up to the top of that hill. You can see everything from up there, the Valley and the city."

"What is it, someone's driveway?"

"It's just a road. There's nothing up there but a view."

As Stephen eased off the asphalt into the shallow dirt treadmarks, he gave him another look, this time curious and puzzled.

"I'd watch the ruts, this thing has a low center." Alan shifted nervously in his seat. They both went silent as Stephen maneuvered the car along the upper edge of the dirt ruts. Alan stared off towards the snow-capped mountains far off on the north side of the Valley. The tension between them made the drive up the slope interminable. Alan felt the familiar nervous pounding of his heart. A few yards from the crest of the hill, Stephen said in a calm voice, "We'll probably find a lot of teenagers up here smoking dope."

"It's usually empty," Alan said. There was, he realized, an awkward edge of self-consciousness in both their voices. Since that first lunch together until now, they had never been entirely alone together. On the highway a moment ago, he had felt and acted on a very definite impulse; but now, faced with solitude and Stephen, he could only come up with panic. They rounded the crest of the hill. Ten yards ahead, the road ended in a maze of old dune-buggy tracks. Stephen slowed and stopped. "Where do we go from here?"

"Nowhere. This is it." Alan gestured towards the panorama he had promised. A sea of tract houses and snow-capped mountains to the north. The city, Palos Verdes peninsula, and the sea to the south. Stephen turned off the ignition. For a while, they sat in awkward silence, surrounded by four hundred unobstructed square miles of Alan's view.

"It's a clear day," Alan said, "not much pollution."

"No."

"And no people."

"No."

Alan leaned back against the headrest. The ache started in his legs and ran up his body again, painfully. He was paralyzed, though. And he felt childish and foolish. "From up here, the world is very beautiful, I think," he knew his observation sounded idiotic before he even finished it. Without looking, he knew that Stephen had smiled. He kept his gaze directed through the windshield. In front of the car, he watched a ball of dried scrub roll across the ground and hang in the low green brush. The Santa Ana blowing from behind them was coming from the desert. It was warm. He would say something about the wind, he thought.

"Alan," Stephen said before he could speak.

Alan looked at him. He had sat forward in his seat and was staring at him, smiling. "You got me up here, now what?"

"What do you mean?" Alan read the thought twinkling in the pale blue eyes, the same thought he had read that afternoon on the tennis court when Stephen looked up in the sunlight. The look paralyzed him still further.

"You know what I mean. You know what we both mean." Stephen's face came towards him. He fixed his eyes on the curve of his lips. A determined smile played at the edges. He had kissed a man before, this wasn't his first kiss—but then why did it feel as though this was going to be his first? They kept coming towards him, Stephen's lips, and when they were two inches away, Alan realized that his eyes were crossed. He looked up, uncrossed them, and met Stephen's an inch away. As their lips touched, barely grazing, he made a small sound in his throat.

151

Stephen's breath beat against his face. With the edge of his own lips he could feel Stephen's mouth opening. Then it came apart inside him, both the need and the desire, both together, like a dam breaking. Without hesitating now, he encircled Stephen's body with his right arm and drew it to him.

"They're all due today, the tenth." Alexis slid the stack of books across the counter with the bindings facing away from the young girl. She started to turn away.

"Let's see." The desk clerk gestured to her from behind the counter, rotated the books towards her, and began opening the covers. *"Natural Childbirth,* February tenth, *The Lamaze Technique of Natural Childbirth,* February tenth, *The Psychology of Homosexuality, Loving Someone Gay*—" still smiling, she glanced up and, for a split second, rested her gaze on Alexis's stomach, "February tenth, February tenth, February tenth," she went on flipping the covers open, "and February tenth." The detached expression on her young face, Alexis saw, had not altered, "All on time," she confirmed.

"Yes. On time." Alexis started to turn away again. She had put the two books on the Lamaze method on top of the stack to avoid this kind of humiliation.

"When are you due?" the girl asked.

"I'm sorry?" Alexis looked back.

With a cheerful, unassuming expression, the girl pointed to her stomach, "The baby—when is it due?"

"In a month," Alexis smiled, somewhat relieved.

"You're doing it the Lamaze way?"

"Yes," she smiled, then added, "my husband wants to be with me for this one."

"I hear it's wonderful."

Alexis smiled over her shoulder and started away, "I hope so. We'll see."

"Good luck."

"Thanks."

"Alexis!" a muted voice called across the hush of the library foyer. Without turning, Alexis recognized the brittle sweetness at once. In the instant before she turned, her eye caught sight of the book on top of the stack. *Loving Someone Gay.* Its boldly printed title glared back at her. She turned, and felt her insides give way. Before she could take two steps from the counter, Sharon Berrey was already upon her. Behind Sharon, she caught sight of Phoebe coming towards her with an armful of books, all smiles. "Hello, Sharon."

"What a surprise!" Sharon squeezed her shoulders and gave her a quick lip-brush on the cheek, "How *are* you?"

"Fine. And you?" she tried to edge forward, away from the books behind her on the counter.

"Alexis, sweetheart!" Phoebe shifted her books to her left arm and embraced her with her right. Sharon, Alexis saw, had stepped back to tighten the belt around her blue mackintosh. Her gaze rested on the counter. "I called you yesterday," Phoebe was saying, "but you never return my calls anymore!"

"I was out with the builders all day." She tried to move forward.

Phoebe blocked her way, "I've only seen you once since Christmas, darling. What have you been *doing*?"

"Trying to build a house and give birth to a baby."

Phoebe's gaze had wandered to the counter behind her, "It only takes a minute to pick up a phone. You've obviously got time to *read*."

Alexis reached out and took both Phoebe and Sharon by the arm, "I've been studying the Lamaze method. Alan has his heart set on it this time." She began maneuvering them away from the counter towards the front door.

"The *Lamaze* method," Phoebe looked back towards the counter and laughed. "What do you mean, *Alan's* heart?! *You're* the one who's pregnant!"

"We both want it." Alexis colored. They could not have missed the books on homosexuality. She continued on towards the door, followed by Sharon and Phoebe. As they reached the checkout desk, Phoebe shifted the stack of books under her arm. ". . . and Sharon and I got stuck with planning the hospital benefit for Easter. We're doing an outdoor thing in my garden . . ."

Alexis nodded, half listening. She had spent the last few days when she was alone in the afternoon reading the six books on homosexuality in the privacy of her bedroom. She had kept the books concealed behind a stack of old shoe boxes on the top shelf of her closet.

"Alexis, you know, is a genius with gardens," Sharon was saying.

"Yes, dear, but she's one of those women who always tries to hide her light under a bushel," Phoebe nudged her playfully.

As Alexis stepped back to let Phoebe put her books on the checkout counter, she felt a hot flash in her face. Was Phoebe's remark a reference to the books? She had kept them secret, even from Alan.

". . . and I meant to call you and congratulate you and Alan on the gift," Sharon said, talking of the gift Mrs. Beck had made to the hospital in Alan's behalf. Alexis nodded, pretending to listen, but her mind raced off through a catalogue of possible repercussions. Sharon would tell Arnold, Arnold would use it against Alan at the hospital, the gossip would spread to their friends, to Helen and Christopher.

Phoebe gathered her books from the counter. "Now Alexis." She turned towards the turnstile leading to the front door. "You and Alan must come out this Sunday to the house in Malibu. Charles and I are opening it up for the summer, and we're giving a party. Bring the kids, it's an outdoor barbecue."

"I'd love to." Alexis followed her through the turnstile. "I'll ask Alan and let you know in the morning." She moved behind Phoebe towards the library door. Sharon was now behind her.

"And if Alan doesn't want to come, you and the kids come by yourself. I know Alan hates our beach house."

"He doesn't hate beach houses, he hates beaches." She followed Phoebe through the door and stopped to hold it open for Sharon.

"You poor dear." Sharon stepped out under the portico and turned to her. "I hope all this hasn't put you under too much strain."

Alexis let the door swing closed, feeling as though she had been suddenly knocked sideways. "All of this?" She tried to repress the shrillness in her voice.

"The baby and the house, of course." Sharon joined her to follow Phoebe down the front steps. "What did you think I meant?"

"I don't know."

Phoebe reached the sidewalk and turned towards them, beaming. "Now I'm serious! I want you to come out to Malibu on Sunday!"

"We'll try. I'll ask Alan and let you know."

"Fuck Alan. If he doesn't want to come, then let him stay home. Or go play tennis or something with the boys. And if you don't want to drive, you and the kids can get a ride with someone. Angie Fields is driving out in her station wagon with Dr. Milner; you can get a ride with them."

Alexis reached up to shade her eyes from the sun.

"You remember Dr. Milner, don't you?"

"Yes. Of course I remember," she said numbly, recalling that it was Phoebe who had introduced them to begin with.

"I insist you come." Phoebe started towards her white Mercedes, parked illegally at the curb. "You'll have a wonderful time."

"Bye dear," Sharon squeezed her arm and hurried on towards Phoebe's car.

"Good-bye."

As Phoebe turned towards the parking lot at the side of the Beverly Hills Library, she waved. Alexis returned the wave and went on. On her right she passed one by one the jets of water splashing playfully in the reflecting pond. The strain of the last few weeks, her nagging premonition that Alan was seeing someone behind her back, that he would go on seeing the man until it was too late to stop—it was getting to her. She was becoming a chronic paranoid! The clerk at the desk, Phoebe, Sharon—she was reading mockery and laughter into their reactions when there was none! "I must be crazy!" she said aloud and continued across the parking lot. At her car door, she dug into her purse for the keys. But it was true! On the eve of their third child, there was the bitter possibility that, never knowing when or where, afraid now to ask while he was in therapy, always waiting, she would go through the rest of her life sharing Alan with an endless parade of male lovers.

Angrily, she drew out the key ring, rattled through the cluster of house keys, car keys, keys to god knows what, and found the small, rounded door key. Phoebe Amherst, Sharon Berrey, Arnold, Donald, Helen, Christopher, Max—the gossip would spread like fire through dead brushwood. She would live out the rest of her life known by everyone as the loyal, courageous little wife of "that gay doctor." Pitied and laughed at. A zero as a woman.

She inserted the key into the lock and caught sight of her face reflected in the tinted car window. No doubt they had seen it, too—the panic, the anger, the fear.

"So tell me, how'd you get the night off?" At the far end of the living room Stephen squatted before the fireplace, struck the match against the rough stone mantelpiece, and touched the flame to the paper under the kindling.

"You know damn well how I got it off," Alan sat forward on the sofa and smiled wryly. "You were going out to Phoebe's yourself until I called. How'd you get out of it?"

Stephen got to his feet and came towards him on the sofa. "I called Phoebe and told her I'd met someone and wanted to spend the evening with him. She told me to bring him. I told her I couldn't."

"Did you—?" Alan reached for his wine glass on the table.

"No, I didn't. I may be a jealous man, but I'm not destructive." He took the bottle to refill their glasses, "And you?"

"And me—" Alan slid his glass halfway down the glass-topped table. He sighed, thinking of the tightrope he was walking that night. "Alexis said she wanted to go out to Malibu with the kids. She knows I don't like Phoebe's beach-house parties. So she didn't press me. She drove out with the kids alone."

"Relax, Alan. Phoebe and I don't talk about my love life. She doesn't *want* to know." He moved his glass from the far side of the coffee table, where he had been sitting, to the sofa side. "Thanks for coming tonight, it's a real birthday party now."

"It's a day early."

"You mean a *night* early." Stephen sat down on the opposite end of the sofa.

Evening, Alan thought, looking through the sliding glass doors at the twilight settling in the patio. As yet, he had not had the heart or found the appropriate moment to tell Stephen that it would be a short one. Alexis had said she would be home between nine and nine-thirty. In letting him off the party and then telling him the exact hour she would return, she was, he had realized, forcing herself to give him room. Which was more than he dared ask of her, considering the silent pain he had seen in her face these last few weeks. The impasse between them was complete now. The last thing in the world she wanted to hear from him was that a portion of his love belonged to a man and not her; and, rather than ask him herself, she preferred the silent anguish of her suspicion. With luck, perhaps she need never know. But that meant being at home when he said he would be there, at *least* that.

"Alan?" Stephen brought him back.

"Sorry, I was just thinking," he pointed to the long gift-wrapped box propped against the coffee table, "You haven't opened your present."

"I was saving it for the cake."

"You know damn well what it is."

Stephen grinned and reached for the box, "I have pretty good suspicions. You're lousy at disguising things, you know that?" He lay the tissue-wrapped, long, rectangular box on his knees and pulled at the green ribbon.

"What do you mean?"

"It's not the box, it's your innocent, boyish face that gave you away. I knew what it was when you walked in."

Alan watched him tear at the white tissue paper and smiled to himself. "By the looks of it, I'm not the only kid around here."

"I can't help it, I'm a sucker when it comes to presents and gift wraps." He pushed back the paper from around the box. In the candlelight from the table, Alan saw the expression in his profile alter with a faint tremor in the flesh over his cheekbones. He stared at his face, surprised by the small, unconscious eruption of feeling. Stephen said "Guess what? It's the right one." He turned with a childlike look of shock in his eyes. "How did you know?"

"Easy. When we came back that afternoon after the drive, I looked at your racquet in the closet. That one's about had it." Alan suddenly recalled the same look of shock on Karen's face when he had walked in with the bicycle the afternoon of her birthday party.

Stephen propped the box against the sofa cushion and moved down next to him. He reached up and rested his hands on Alan's shoulders. "Thank you. I needed that."

"You're welcome," Alan felt the vibrations of Stephen's pleasure. They poured in, filling him with a sudden sense of joy. He put his hands against Stephen's sides and pulled him forward. The ease and naturalness of his own gesture surprised him. For a while, neither of them feeling the need to speak, they simply held each other with their heads resting comfortably together. The scratch of Stephen's five o'clock shadow was familiar to him now. The male smell of his body somehow no longer frightened him. For the first time, he was aware of its living warmth, separate from his own. He ran his hands over the lean, solid muscles of his back, relishing the warmth through his shirt. Until now, he had never thought of Stephen's body or, for that matter, Brad's or any other man's as anything more than an object of desire and, sometimes, envy. Never as something alive and precious—to be honored for itself. He had only had this awareness once recently, when he had rested his face against Alexis's stomach and heard the fetal heartbeats.

Stephen moved his face into the crook of his neck and kissed him. As his hands opened, moving over his back, the kiss traveled up his cheek to his mouth. Alan felt his mind empty itself of reason and logic. His body spoke with feelings now—wanted the bittersweet taste of saliva and wine, the pressure of rugged flesh against his own. His body answered what doubts were left with a hardening erection.

Saying nothing, doing nothing, they drew apart and looked each other in the eye. Stephen smiled and touched his arm. Together, a little self-consciously (such choices are always delayed with a little inner debate), they stood up. Stephen turned towards the bedroom door. Alan followed, realizing as he jumped the mental hurdles between him and the far side of the room that he was crossing over, knowing without saying it to himself that Alexis now belonged to a wholly separate world inside himself. On the far side of the room, he followed Stephen through the open door into the more softly lit bedroom. A small brass lamp burned on the bedside table next to the big bed with its corduroy spread. The deep brown carpet felt thick and soft under his shoes and muffled the sound of their feet. Alan looked around, nervous, at the chromium-framed lithographs on the brown walls.

Smiling, Stephen reached up and began loosening the tie around Alan's neck. As the tie came up through the knot, Alan took hold of Stephen's tie. It was awkward and strange, standing there together, untying ties. Brad had once tried to take his tie off for him, but he had refused. Stephen worked down the buttons on his white shirt; Alan followed suit. Stephen chuckled at his clumsiness. As the buttons opened before Alan, he caught sight of the hair and skin on Stephen's chest. Their breath was now labored and quite audible in the silence.

With a gentle tug, Stephen brought him down beside him on the bed. Thy rolled together face to face and kissed, this time with their entire bodies. The cool blue sheet warmed with their movements. It was a kiss, Alan realized, unlike any he had enjoyed before with a man, for it locked them together with both need and desire.

He had wanted to hold and be held by this one man for months. It seemed now, with the reality in his arms, that he had wanted it for a lifetime. Beyond the physical pleasure, there was the joy of an emotional rest, the unequivocal realization that he had come home. For a long time, in comfortable silence, he explored Stephen's body with his hands, enjoying the luxury of his freedom.

Stephen rolled onto his back under Alan's weight. His body, Alan realized, knew all the language. There was nothing to say. As he rose up on his knees above Stephen, a thought brushed his mind: Odd. For all the differences, it was the same act that he and Alexis had always taken for granted. He hesitated before he moved again, wondering to himself what pleasure this could be for Stephen. His answer came as a soft sound below him. He began, slowly, a little awkwardly at first. Felt a wave of pleasure roll through his body which, at first, his brain caught and held at bay. Stephen reached up and stroked his face. The touch of his hand freed him again. Again, as before, his mind let go of his body. The censor, he realized, had gone.

I want this man's wanting me, he thought (and the thought came now from his body), want him to pass through and into me, become and belong to me.

He moved his body against and into Stephen's. The sound that came from his mouth was the voice of something breaking apart far down inside him, deeper than the breaking he had felt when Stephen kissed him, a groan of hunger that came up sounding like pain: for with it came also the realization that moments of completeness like this always passed. It was going too fast, and Stephen, he saw, was aware of it. Alan closed his eyes and slowed himself. Stephen's hand circled his neck and drew his face down. They met and kissed. Inside, Alan felt the wave roll through him again; but this time, it did not stop. It passed through his back, into his shoulders and flooded his mind. From the sound and movement under him, he knew he was not alone.

For a long time, with his eyes still closed, he held himself motionless above Stephen. Then he sank down with his face cradled in Stephen's neck. He breathed in deeply, needing air. An inch from his eyes, the sheet became blue again. He listened to their breathing grow slower with the motion of the chests. He found himself counting and comparing their heartbeats. His was faster. But he was also older.

It was there again—he shifted his body—that familiar sense of uneasiness. After a small delay, trying not to communicate his discomfort, he moved from Stephen and lay beside him.

Post coitum omne animal triste est. The words came back to him. The sadness he had feared was with him again. Just a moment ago, and now everything—the world he had dreamed only moments before —had changed. A moment ago, he wanted to hold and be held; now he wanted to retreat.

"Your mind is racing, isn't it?" Stephen said.

"I feel like I'm running in two different directions." He moved again, a little further.

Stephen turned on his side and rested his head against his hand. "You're very hard on yourself. Why?"

"I don't know. Forty years of conditioning, I guess." He glanced at the digital watch on his wrist. Five past eight. Alexis had said she would be home between nine and nine-thirty. He had to be there when she arrived.

"I gather you've got to go now."

"I'm sorry. I told Alexis I'd be there when she returned."

Stephen jostled his arm affectionately. "Okay, don't explain." The hurt in his voice was undisguisable though. "The bathroom's through that door, if you need it. The towels are clean." He got up and crossed to the closet.

Alan swung his legs off the bed. "If you still want to, we can have lunch tomorrow. I'll take you to L'Hermitage for your birthday." He could not recover what was lost, and it sounded like what it was—a door prize.

"Yeah." Stephen started out of the room, tying the sash around his terry-cloth bathrobe. "I'll cut you a piece of birthday cake before you go."

Alan went into the bathroom and closed the door. He stood before the sink, feeling numbed by the thought of Stephen's pain. And guilty. He tried to reason with himself: Alexis had priority . . . Then his mind went blank. Mechanically, he washed and dried himself, refolded the towel as if he had never used it, and padded back into the bedroom.

"Did you find what you needed?" Stephen set two plates of mocha chocolate cake on the dresser.

"Yes, Stephen. Thank you." He tried to catch Stephen's eye but failed. He sat on the bed and began putting his socks on. Brad had accused him of taking what he wanted for himself from both worlds— his and Alexis's, the best of both. Of enjoying both and taking full responsibility for neither. It was happening all over again. But with Brad, he had been clear from the beginning that his "best" would never include love. That belonged entirely to Alexis. For seventeen years. With Stephen, too, he had made it clear that when the crunch came, the biggest portion of his heart belonged to Alexis. It could never be more than lunch. Easy to say. Easy for someone who, until now, had never needed or been needed by *two* people. Bewildered, Alan stood up and put his trousers on. In the mirror over the dresser he watched Stephen replace the spread on the bed. He thought back to those painful departures from Brad's to get back to Alexis on time. Until tonight, he had always assumed that Stephen was stronger, more independent and detached than Brad. He had not counted on coming up against a need as large and as deep as his own. "I meant what I said about lunch tomorrow," he ventured. It still sounded like a consolation door prize.

"Sure," Stephen rose up and looked at him determinedly in the mirror where he was putting on his shirt. "That was our original plan anyway." Their eyes locked in the mirror. In Stephen's face he saw something he had never seen there before, something he had only seen in Alexis's: a resolute determination to win. It took his breath away. "I'm free from one to three. I'll pick you up in front of your office at one-fifteen, as we originally planned." Stephen went back to arranging the spread.

"I'll be there. On time." A pleasurable sensation of relief and absolution flowed down his body and, at the same time, in his mind he saw a fuzzy but ominous picture of possible future disasters. As he fastened his collar button, he realized it was rather pointless to put his tie back on now.

Stephen joined him at the dresser. "It's a beautiful cake, Alan. Thanks."

"You're welcome," he smiled.

"Here." Stephen reached for the two plates on the dresser. One of the slices, Alan noticed, was a thin sliver. Stephen handed him the plate with the sliver. "This one's yours."

Alan took the plate. "Christ, am I *that* fat?"

"You're not fat at all." He sliced his portion with his fork. "You just don't have time for a whole piece. It's eight-thirty. It takes one minute to get to your car and twelve minutes to get to your house. That's a three minute piece of cake," he gave him a broad mischievous grin.

"Jesus."

"Now, you didn't think I was going to let you get away without a piece of your own surprise, did you?"

Alexis looked up from the bedroom floor to the photo on the dresser above her. The Lamaze instructor had said to fix her eyes on some simple, convenient object during the exercises; it would prevent drowsiness and reinforce the reality of the situation, he had said.

The reality of the situation, she thought to herself, took a deep breath, then said silently, "Contraction begins." She began the eight short pants, trying to keep the breath shallow in her throat. The photo was fifteen years old, taken the second year of their marriage, a few months after Karen's birth. She formed her mouth into an O, blew out the air forcefully, then began the pantings again. By the clock on the dresser top, it was now 8:44. Exactly. She had said she would be back from Malibu between nine and nine-thirty. She had returned a little before eight, fed the kids, and put them to bed. On the way out, she had toyed with the idea of returning early. Alan had said he would probably stay home and work around the house; but she had doubted that. *Probably* was one of his guilty compromise words. When she got home, the house, of course, was empty and dark, which meant he had gone out while it was still light.

She blew out the air again and took the third deep breath. Nasty as they were, her motives in returning early had at least been honest. To verify her suspicions. For the last week, like a private detective, she had been clocking him so that when the day of atonement came (and it was coming fast), she would have facts and not suspicions loaded in her gun. Tracking him like this was ugly and small, but as a pregnant woman tied to her house, what ammunition did she have? After all, she was simply applying the golden rule of every practical housewife: necessity is the mother of invention. Of course, her dossier was slim so far. Since she had begun the Lamaze exercises, he had missed the evening sessions three times. Twice for proven emergencies at the hospital, once for what he said was a business meeting. Of course, what he had been doing during lunch hours was a little harder to track down.

For a moment, she lay quietly breathing, staring at the photo, trying to remember how many pantings she had gone through. She had forgotten. Incredible how naive and stupid she looked in the photo, standing there in front of her parents' front door with her arm around Alan, grinning like a schoolgirl. With disgust, she turned away to stare at herself in the mirror on the closet door. She also looked stupid lying on the floor like this with her head, back, and knees propped up on bed pillows. Except for a nightgown and a difference in species, she was going through the same motions as a cow alone out in a field giving natural birth to a calf.

Alexis sat up suddenly, resting her weight on her elbows, and felt the heat of anger explode in her face. Over eleven months had gone by since he had asked her for another child. It seemed like a lifetime ago.

She turned and looked up at the photo again, grimaced, and felt a ripple of nausea run through her stomach. Prim, shoulder-length, little-Mrs.-Goody-Housewife hair. She had worn it that way right through the entire sixties, through three revolutions, women's included, without one single hair out of place. She sat up further, listened to the clock ticking away on the bureau, and gaped at herself in the photo. That silly pose—clinging to him for dear life like English ivy on a stone wall. The beguiled face of a Betty Crocker housewife! After seventeen years, that was the sum total of her talents. She could do laundry, bake pies, do shopping (Oh, yes, she was proud of her little economies!), do the bills, do the house, do *auxiliary* work for a charity now and then to break the monotony and stave off suffocation, she could rise up in the morning to please and fall down at night congratulating herself if she *did*, she could give parties and give birth. She was a *giver*. At thirty-seven, she woke up realizing it was her turn to *take*! But *what*?! Nothing *belonged* to her! And no one *now* was going to take her seriously! Left on her own, she could not earn one dollar in the world! At home, she couldn't even play the piano for *herself* with confidence any more! Like the clock on the dresser, she had simply ticked away.

She looked down at the soft gray carpet under her and watched the liquid drop from her eye—one drop—watched it run down and vanish into the deep, rich wool.

She had not—not in seventeen years, not in almost thirty-eight—done one thing, one solitary fucking creative satisfying thing for herself and for herself alone. The fact was, she was as much a fool now as she had been then, when they married.

She lay back against the pillow and let the tears run freely down her face.

But worse than all the facts of her past was the truth of her future: that she needed and wanted him more than anything else in this world, that she had never in seventeen years thought to separate love from need; that without him she did not exist, never had.

She reached up and wiped her face half dry. Suddenly, from the far end of the house, she heard it—the sound of the back door closing. She turned quickly and froze with her eyes riveted on the bedroom door.

And the wretched truth of their future was, there were no business meetings. She knew it, and she knew he knew she knew it. There were no occasional *men*, either. There was a man. And she would go on blinding herself to it for as long as he cared enough to lie to her.

Beyond the bedroom, the floor creaked under the carpet in the hall. She had heard it often. In a moment, he would come in looking like a guilty child and apologize. Trot out another lie so that he could avoid hurting her with the truth. And she? She would save face by only half accepting it and give him another half-assed warning shot across his bow.

It was 8:45. She had said nine. At least for the moment, he cared enough to honor her feelings by the clock.

The bedroom door opened. He stood with his hand on the knob, startled at the sight of her sprawled on the floor in her nightgown. She gave him a look of resignation.

He said, "You came home early." It was half statement, half question, loaded with guilty surprise.

She waited until he closed the door behind himself to respond. "The kids got tired. We got home at eight."

"I went out at about six." He crossed to the bed and dropped his jacket and tie. "I got bored sitting around the house." The look of exhaustion and strain on his profile was not, obviously, the result of boredom. His hair was a mess, she noticed. The curls on the back of his neck looked damp. Another hurried shower. She said nothing, let the ball lie distressfully in his court. "Have you finished, or do you want me to clock you some?" he looked at her guiltily.

"No, I haven't finished. I've only just begun."

"Which one are you doing?" He came over to where she lay and looked down at her. She saw the flush in his cheeks, the lingering kind of flush he always had when they had made love for a long time.

"One usually begins at the beginning, with number one."

"You know the purpose of the exercise, don't you?" She saw the waver in his eyes, and with it a falling shadow of pain.

"Yes, Alan, I know."

"Your contractions will be far apart at this point. The baby's head is going to be—"

"I know what's going on, Alan, I know what to expect. I've been there before."

His face went pale. "You had slow transitions with Karen. Chris was faster. You'll probably have poorly defined transitions with this one, but it's hard to tell after this many years."

"I have a memory like an elephant." She closed her eyes to cover the tears starting in her eyes.

"Are you ready?"

"Yes." The momentary impulse passed. She opened her eyes again and smiled. "I was just recalling the bloody pain of it those first two times."

"*Pain* is not a word we're going to use this time, remember? *Discomfort* is what they told you to use."

"I know. I forgot." The instructor had told her she could condition herself to think of it as discomfort. Condition herself—like Pavlov's dog, she had thought.

"Contraction begins."

She took the deep breath, the "cleansing breath," as it was called. Instead of staring at the photo, she stared at him, blew out the breath, took another one, and began the pantings.

He glanced away, realizing she was reading his eyes. She blew out, feeling the blood rush to her face.

"Contraction over," he said absently. It was too soon. Above her, in his profile, she saw that he was no longer in the room with her. For the moment, he had withdrawn into his own private world.

On her own, she drew in another deep breath, blew it out, took another, and started the pantings. She had asked him point-blank that night in December if he had loved Brad. He had denied it. The truth was, the only thing that had prevented him from going that far was the accident of death. This time, without blowing, the air merely ran out of her lungs. If he had come that close once, why not again?

"Contraction begins," he said.

She filled her lungs with air. Sex now and then with a passing stranger, she could have borne that as mere *discomfort*. But love—that, even Pavlov's dog could not learn to bear.

"Alexis?"

She let go of the air and looked at him.

"Sweetheart, what's wrong?" He knelt down beside her and took her hand. The expression on his face was that of a frightened child.

The soundless words formed on her lips: "Damn you."

X

"Who moved first, you or George?"

"He did. I finished my residency at Columbia, got the job at Mount Sinai, then moved." Resting next to him on his elbow, Stephen looked down and smiled wryly. Alan settled the back of his head into his hands against the pillow. His right elbow was resting comfortably against Stephen's shoulder. On the wall opposite the foot of the bed he could see only the top of George Demerino's face in the framed photo next to the lithograph. "You mean, you *followed* him out."

Stephen chuckled softly, reached over and rested his hand on his stomach. "I mean, he got his job first and then I got mine."

"But you had a better offer at Columbia."

"I don't believe this. How can you be jealous of George Demerino? That was *five years ago!*"

"I'm not jealous, I'm curious."

"Curious, hell!" There was a victorious pleasure in the laughter now. "You're squirming with jealousy, Alan." He ran his finger down the center of his stomach.

"Lay off, I'm ticklish there." Alan turned onto his right side to cover his embarrassment.

Stephen's laughter subsided. He moved closer, encircled Alan's waist with his arm, and said knowingly, "You're also jealous of a man who's been out of my life for five years."

"Not five. Four. You lived with him for one, remember?"

"Four then." His head appeared over his shoulder. "What is this, anyway? *I'm* supposed to be the jealous side of this relationship."

"If it's been over for four years, what's his picture doing on the wall now? It wasn't there last week."

"I hung it there to remind myself."

Alan glanced back. "Of what?"

"Of past lessons learned." He rested his chin on Alan's shoulder. "It's like a note to myself. It keeps me from falling inordinately in love."

Alan turned onto his back again, looked at Stephen, and lifted an eyebrow. "I thought we weren't going to use that word." He raised his arms and put his head into his hands again.

"I slipped. Sorry." Stephen blew on the hair in his armpit.

Alan winced. "Now don't, I'm ticklish there, too."

"Tell me something. Why is it, every time we're together like this for lunch, I end up feeling and acting like an adolescent?"

"I don't know. You're the psychiatrist."

"It must be the overflow of my frustrated anticipations between Tuesdays and Thursdays."

"Jesus." Alan gave a look of mock despair. Of course, in the last two weeks since that first Sunday evening, he himself counted the days between Tuesday and Thursday and Thursday and Tuesday. There *was* a kind of frustrated anticipation between.

"It's too early, of course, to decide if it's simple infatuation or that other—the forbidden thing."

"It's not the other thing," he smiled, "the other thing takes a long time. Besides, I thought we decided we were going to be sensible, grown-up, professional men and do it like a regular straight businessman's affair. Twice a week in our lunch hours."

"We are. Only I detect a slight change in your agenda."

Alan moved his arm and ruffled Stephen's hair with his fingers, "What change?"

"This is the first time in two weeks you haven't jumped up right afterwards and run into the bathroom."

He let his fingers rest in Stephen's hair and looked at him, surprised. It was true. Until today, he had always made an excuse to get right up and go into the bathroom to be alone for a while.

"I think you should mention this to Schaeffer." Stephen smiled pointedly.

"*Schaeffer*? Whose side are you on?"

"Nature's." He laughed.

"Which reminds me"—Alan sat up on his elbows—"we're supposed to be eating. What time is it?"

"One twenty-eight."

"I'm supposed to be back at the office at *two*! Christ, I've got paperwork to do and an appointment at three-thirty! You're supposed to be *feeding* me now!"

"Me?"

"It's your turn to provide the food."

Stephen sat up, "Measure for measure. God, you're calculating."

"What have you got for us?"

"Sandwiches. Can you eat a sandwich in seven minutes?"

"You get the food, I'll call my office and tell them I'll be ten minutes late."

"What do you think I am, a houseboy?" Stephen got off the bed and shot him a meaningful look as he left the room.

Alan reached for the telephone receiver and dialed his office number. He sat up as Margaret answered, "Doctor's office."

"Hello, Maggy, this is Doctor Stegman. Any calls?"

"Yes, doctor, one. Mr. Rees phoned a few minutes ago and canceled his three-thirty appointment. Said he couldn't get any gas for his car."

"Sounds familiar. Was he sober?"

"*Mellow* would be more like it."

"Well, it's his kidney," he sighed, "if he wants to drown it with bourbon, he has every right. Is that the only appointment I've got for the afternoon?"

"Let's see, I'll check the book." She put the receiver down. Alan looked at Stephen's bedside clock. He had not phoned in since leaving the hospital at 12:15. Alexis had not been home since 9:00 that morning.

"Yes, doctor," Maggy came back on, "that's the only one. You were going to do your paperwork this afternoon."

"Did my wife call in?"

"Not since this morning," she sighed. "Relax, Doctor Stegman. She's got a good ten days to go. God, you expectant fathers are all alike!"

Alan looked down at his naked body. "I wouldn't say that, Maggy."

"Stop worrying and enjoy your lunch. If she phones, and it's important, I'll have you beeped. You've got the beeper, haven't you?"

"Yes, I've got the beeper." He glanced towards his trousers hanging on the door nearby. "I may be a little late getting back to the office, but I *will* be there." Behind him, Stephen came into the room.

"Take your time. I can use the vacation."

"Bless you, Maggy." Alan chuckled and replaced the receiver.

"Did I hear what I thought I heard?" Stephen asked.

Alan turned to see him setting a tray of sandwiches and beer on the bed. "My appointment was canceled."

Stephen got on the bed and pushed the tray forward, "What a coincidence. So was my three o'clock appointment. Help yourself, there's pastrami on rye with lettuce, tomato, mustard, and mayonnaise; dark beer, pickles, and cheesecake. After that, I'll make some fresh coffee."

"And your nap, Mrs. Stegman? When are you going to take *that*?"

"Will you *stop*, Claire?" Alexis laughed. "Between you, mother, and Alan, you'd think I was a pregnant moron!"

"The doctor said you should rest in the afternoons, and you've been running around all morning like a crazy person." She gathered up the pile of dirty clothes from the laundry-room floor.

"The doctor also wants a particular kind of shingle for the roof of his new house, and custom-made toilets." She opened her purse to check for her wallet and keys. "And you don't get those lying in bed all afternoon reading *Cosmopolitan*."

Claire began stuffing the clothes into the washing machine. "It's not my business, but the doctor *could* take charge of a few of those things himself for the next few weeks."

Alexis snapped her purse closed. "Alan's got a hospital full of patients. And besides, between you and me, if I leave the choice of shingles and toilet bowls up to Alan, we'll end up with something like Disneyland."

Claire shook her head and went on stuffing the clothes into the washer.

She turned towards the door leading out into the carport. "Now, I'll pick the kids up at school, drop them back here, and then go on. I have an appointment with Cagle at three o'clock, and that should take about—" She stopped abruptly, feeling something give way far down inside her stomach. For an instant, it registered in her mind only as a pleasant sensation of release, as though her bladder had suddenly and spontaneously begun to empty. But it was not, she realized, her bladder. It was something further down. She stood riveted, staring at the door in front of her, as the warm liquid spilled through her underwear and ran down the insides of her legs. The familiarity of it washed back on her. "Claire," she said softly.

She could feel Claire's eyes on her from behind, startled, alarmed. "Mrs. Stegman—what's wrong?"

"I think—I think my water has just broken."

There was a moment of silence. A few feet away, the washer began to fill with water. "Oh my god," Claire said.

Alexis smiled to herself, feeling the liquid run down her legs. "Thank god I'm not wearing those damn panty hose," she said absently.

"Mrs. Stegman!" Claire grasped her arm.

She turned calmly, "It's all right, Claire."

"Take my arm! I'll help you into the breakfast room!"

"I'm perfectly all right," she said, realizing that Claire had never herself experienced it.

"There's a chair in the breakfast room; you can sit down there!"

"I don't want to sit down in the breakfast room, I had breakfast *hours* ago."

"You come sit down," Claire started into the kitchen, "I'll call the doctor."

Alexis followed her, "*You* sit down. *I'll* call him."

"*Mrs. Stegman!*"

"Better still, get me some towels." She followed Claire across the breakfast area towards the phone in the kitchen. "I just waxed this floor and I'm leaving a mess. *I'll* do all the calling."

"Are there pains yet?" Claire turned with the receiver in her hand.

"Now, Claire!" she took the receiver from her, "Will you please *calm down*? There are no *discomforts* whatsoever yet."

With a look of exasperation, Claire headed back to the laundry room. Calmly, Alexis punched out the number of Alan's office phone. Damn, she thought, I was going to call Cagle on that faggoty-looking stonework he's designed for the terrace!

"Doctor's office," Maggy's voice came on the line.

"Maggy, this is Alexis again."

"Hello, dear. I'm afraid his majesty's out at the moment for lunch."

"Figures," she sighed. "Do you know *where*?"

"Not a clue. He phoned in—oh, about twenty-five minutes ago. Do you want me to beep him for you?"

"This time, I think we'd better."

"Is something wrong?!"

She looked back across the kitchen floor at the trail of liquid she had left, "Nothing you couldn't write off to the human condition. My water broke a few minutes ago."

There was a beat of silence on the other end, "Oh, God. Are you all right?!"

"I'm fine. Actually, it felt rather nice this time."

"Is Claire with you?"

"Yes, Claire's here." She glanced back again to see Claire hurrying in with a stack of bath towels.

"Have your pains started yet?"

"No, Maggy." She detoured around the approaching line of questions. "While you're beeping Alan, I'll call Evans's office and get his wheels in motion. Have Alan call me here, okay?"

"We'll get right back to you." She went off the line.

"Just throw one on the floor here, Claire." She glanced at her list of phone numbers on the wall and dialed.

"I don't know how you can be so calm at a time like this." Claire hurriedly spread a towel on the floor next to her.

"Easy," she said, "I'm a three-time mother."

"Doctors Evans and Ortega," Louise, the receptionist, answered.

"Louise, this is Alexis Stegman," she said, stepping onto the towel.

"Yes, dear."

"I hope the doctor's in, honey. My water just broke."

"Oh, dear. He's out to lunch right now. If you'll hold, I'll beep him."

Alexis felt a flash of panic, "They're *all* out to lunch on the goddamn beeper!"

"Now, calm down, honey. Are you alone?"

"No. My housekeeper's with me."

"Have you started labor?"

"No." She rolled her eyes back, exasperated again by the same line of questions approaching. "I don't feel a thing."

"Hold on, I'll get right back to you."

"No! Don't bother. Just tell the good doctor my water has broken. Ask him to arrange a room for me at the hospital; and if he can, to meet me at the emergency desk. I'll get Claire to drive me down to West Hollywood General."

"I'll do that, Alexis. I'll notify the doctor and the hospital. Now don't worry, everything's going to work out fine."

"Thanks, Louise. Good-bye," she returned the receiver to the hook.

"Now you stay here, Mrs. Stegman," Claire started out of the kitchen. "I'll get your things. I know exactly what you need."

Alexis irritably reached for the receiver again. "A call-back from Alan wouldn't hurt at this point." She punched out the number. Maggy picked up the receiver halfway through the first ring. "Doctor's office." Her voice sounded frantic.

"It's Alexis again, Maggy."

"I've beeped him twice, but he hasn't answered. The only thing I can think of is the battery on his beeper may have died."

Alexis felt a chill run through her body. "That, or he forgot to take it."

"No, he made a point of taking it when he left. He told me to beep him if you called. I know he's *got* it!"

Alexis blinked as her eyes suddenly watered. "Keep trying him, Maggy. And tell him that I'm going to the hospital now. Claire's going to drive me. Evans is making all the arrangements."

"I'll keep after him. You go on now. I'll take care of this end."

Alexis looked up at the cabinet above her. "I want him *there*, Maggy!" she blurted out before she could stop herself.

"I'll do my best, Alexis. Now calm down. You just concentrate on getting to the hospital."

Alexis hung up and looked down at her feet. The last of her water had made a tiny stain on the white towel below her, a yellowish stain the size of a saucer. She reached to her face to suppress the choking sound that came from her mouth. He had promised to be there with her, had told her every night for the last three weeks that he would be with her. The Lamaze idea had been his. She took one of the towels from the counter, bent down, and lifted her skirt. It had not soaked through the skirt. Through her underwear, yes. She would not have to change her skirt. She began drying the insides of her legs. The dream, some months back, where she had sat on the stage at the piano in front of her parents and an auditorium full of strangers, the dream where she had menstruated in public; with a frightening feeling of loneliness and panic, she heard Claire's footsteps running towards her across the dining room, "Mrs. Stegman!"

"I'm in the kitchen, Claire! Now for the last time, will you please—" As she dropped the hem of her skirt and started to rise, she felt a sudden constriction and pain grip her back near the center of her waist.

"What happened?"

"He met someone else."

"Just like that?"

"How else do you meet someone else?" Stephen poured the last of his beer into his glass on the tray between them. "Richard was on the production staff of NBC, where George worked. They met, started seeing each other on the side, and that was the beginning of the end."

"And you found out." Alan settled his head into the pillow.

Stephen glanced at him over his beer. "Unfaithful lovers usually leave clues. It's the last but guilty sign of caring. When I confronted George, he said his feelings for Richard were not the same as his feelings for me, and they didn't get in the way of our relationship. All he wanted was a little time here and there with Richard. For sex, of course."

"You're being ironic with me, aren't you," Alan said.

"The *there* got to be more than the *here*, of course, so I gave him a choice. Stop seeing Richard altogether, or go live with him for good."

"So he pissed off, and you ended up with nothing." He turned away his head on the pillow to avoid Stephen's stare. The clock on the bedside table read 2:25. He should phone his office, he thought, and see if Alexis had called. He should have gone back to his office an hour ago, in fact.

"I ended up with my sanity, Alan."

He turned back and saw that Stephen was looking into his empty glass, pensive now, and a little sad. "You're not the possessive type, are you?" he asked.

"Possessive?" Stephen looked up, "That depends. One man's possessiveness looks like commitment to another."

"You mean, one person can't love two different people in two different ways?"

"As friends, yes. Not as lovers. As far as I'm concerned, the laws of trigonometry apply to human triangles as well. If you change the degree of one angle, you change all three. If you widen one, you narrow the other two. It hurts to have your angle narrowed." He shrugged. "Ask Alexis, she knows."

Alan was silent for a moment. He did not have to ask either Alexis *or* Stephen. He knew. He also wondered if *they* knew that there was no advantage or satisfaction in being the one caught in the middle, in being the source of everyone else's pain. "So what do you suggest we do? Stop seeing each other?"

"If we were sensible, we would."

"If I were sensible, I'd have gotten up an hour ago, gone back to my office, and done my paperwork." Alan sat up on the side of the bed and looked at his trousers hooked on the back of the bathroom door.

"If I were sensible, I'd have gotten up and done my income tax for last year." Stephen moved across the bed and rested his hand on his shoulder.

"You're a psychiatrist, you should know better."

"I'm also a human being."

Alan felt Stephen's head come to rest on his back. "Yeah," he said, "that makes two of us."

"Don't you understand!?" she looked up into the patient face of the nurse behind the reception desk, "His office said he's on the beeper! If he's got it, he can either hear or *feel* it!"

"Mrs. Stegman." The receptionist closed her eyes and gave her one of those smiles of infinite patience. "We have *beeped* your husband, we have *paged* him here at the hospital, there is nothing more we can do at the moment. Now there is plenty of time for your husband to get here. It isn't going to happen in the next ten minutes, and—"

"Don't tell me how long it takes!" she shouted.

The receptionist glanced at the nurse standing next to the wheelchair where they had put her. "The best thing for Mrs. Stegman to do, Alice, is to go up to her room and get comfortable." She smiled again at Alexis, "Dr. Evans has arranged a nice room for you on the fourth floor. Now the nurse will wheel you up, you can get into your bed, and we can start our preparations." She looked down at her as though she was looking at a small, rebellious child.

"And these damn papers?!" Alexis reached for the admission papers in her lap. "Who's going to fill these out?"

"I will, Mrs. Stegman," Claire came around from behind the wheelchair. "I'll take care of everything."

"You've got to go pick up the kids at school. It's almost three." She
stared up into Claire's bewildered face, realizing she was beginning to
sound crazy now. She looked away as the tears broke in her eyes. "He
promised to be here. It was his idea, the whole thing."

"When the time comes, he'll be here, Mrs. Stegman." Claire rested
her hand comfortingly on her arm, "They'll keep beeping him, there's
nothing to worry about."

"Nothing to worry about!" She jerked her arm back savagely. "You
don't know the half of it!" She reached to her face, covered it, and began to cry.

"Alice, take Mrs. Stegman up to her room," the receptionist said,
"and we'll finish up here with the forms."

She felt the wheelchair move, felt the nurse's eyes on her from behind, heard the squeak of her crepe-soled shoes on the terrazzo floor,
heard Claire's and the receptionist's voices fade away down the corridor.
The wheels of her chair made a soft purring sound. The dreaded emptiness she had kept at bay during the drive to the hospital now sank down
on her. He would not come. This birth, this labor would be fast—she
knew it instinctively—and she would go through it alone. Not because
he had willfully and deliberately chosen to stay away—that she could
deal with—but out of witless default, because he happened, at this pre-
mature moment, to be off caring for someone else. She felt the chair
come to a stop, opened her eyes, and saw the elevator doors part before
her. The chair moved forward into the elevator, and the door closed as
the nurse swung her around.

"Here we go," she said, as if talking to the world's biggest fool.

Alexis watched the numbers of the floors pass. And the irony of
ironies is, she thought, I really don't want this child. *He*'s the one who
wants it. *He* should be the one in this wheelchair. The elevator slowed
to a halt, and the doors parted in front of her. "Here we go," the nurse
said like a cheerful recording and pushed her out into the corridor. The
walls were pale blue, a rather sickening maternity blue, she thought. As
they started down the carpeted corridor, she realized she had been here
before; not here exactly, but in some identical corridor with identical
rooms. Those other hospitals. She had ridden down this corridor twice
before. She gripped the arms of the wheelchair, feeling light-headed. It
was all about to happen over again; but this time, instead of exalting
and cleansing, the agony of it would be monstrous and degrading. Room
404, the receptionist had said. They were at 458. Suddenly, she wanted
to go back—far back, years back, to that day in March when Alan had
stood in the garden of her parents' home and asked her—how hesitantly

he had asked—to marry him. Knowing what she now knew, she wanted to go back to that day and choose again, with herself in mind this time. Again, she felt it start in her back; but this time, it shot around her waist and grabbed her high in the stomach. She arched back in the chair and gasped aloud.

"It's all right." The nurse's hand grabbed her shoulder. "Just hold tight, we'll be there in a minute." She wanted to go back, but they were rolling forward, and no power on earth could alter the course of nature. For either her or Alan. Reared back in her chair, she wanted to scream. She stared vacantly down the corridor with her mouth frozen open. It shot through her middle, stabbing her, emptying her mind, leaving only a vivid, unerasable picture: Alan on the driveway of Stephen Milner's apartment building, embracing him.

"Breathe in!" The nurse shook her shoulder and began pushing the chair faster. "Remember your Lamaze exercises, breathe in deeply!"

Without thinking, Alexis forced in a deep breath.

"That's right, keep breathing until the contraction passes."

The chair whizzed forward. It was *that*—to have feelings and needs, and have them so indifferently discarded—which hurt, not his childish deception.

"Breathe, dear! Your breathing will ease everything!"

She tried to recall what the Lamaze instructor had said about first-stage labor, what Alan had repeated a hundred times. *Discomfort* was the word they had seduced her into using.

"Mrs. Stegman, breathe!"

Alexis let the air escape from her lungs, slumped back in her chair, and half-heartedly forced herself to inhale. Pain was pain.

"Alan?"

. . . then he felt it, the thing he had always feared might happen, felt the lower blade of his scissors pass through something soft and spongy beneath the peritoneum sheath he was cutting. The outer edge of the mesentery. He had gone through it. He froze. Above him, the light went suddenly and blindingly white. And then it parted, the entire peritoneum came apart in the explosion of mucous fluid and blood; except it was not the peritoneum he had been cutting, he realized, but the placenta . . .

"Alan!"

He rose up quickly, blinking in the light, "What?!"

"It's okay. Wake up." He saw Stephen sit down next to him on the bed.

"Oh—" He shook his head. "Jesus, I was having a dream."

"I know." Stephen stroked his shoulder. "Here. I brought you a cup of coffee."

"What time is it?"

"Almost five. We both fell asleep about an hour and a half ago."

"*Five.*"

"You needed a nap, so I let you sleep." Alan saw that he was dressed in jeans and a sweater. "You even slept through my typing."

"Thanks." He took the cup of coffee, "I shouldn't have slept that long. My beeper didn't go off, did it?"

"No. Nothing went off." Stephen got up. "Take a warm shower. I'll be out in the living room."

"I'd better call my office." Alan reached for the telephone receiver and dialed his office number. His trousers, he saw, were where he had left them on the hook. Maggy would surely have beeped him by now. Alexis should have phoned.

"Doctor's office," Maggy answered quickly.

"Maggy, this is Doctor Stegman."

"Oh!" There was a gasp of relief. "We've been trying to beep you for the last two and a half hours, doctor! Alexis is at the hospital. Her water broke about two and she's in labor."

Alan sat up, spilling his coffee, frozen to silence.

"Doctor Stegman!"

"What do you mean, she's in labor?"

"Just that! I phoned the hospital a few minutes ago and she's been taken to delivery. Where the hell—" She caught herself. "Where were you?"

"I'm on the beeper, god dammit! Why the hell didn't you beep me?" He stood up.

"We've been beeping you every fifteen minutes for the last two and a half hours," she said as he put his cup down and carried the phone to his trousers on the door.

"Jesus Christ—how is she?"

"She's fine. She's close to delivery, but she's fine."

"Call the hospital, Maggy." He pulled the trousers from the hook and fumbled for the beeper. "Get in touch with Levin in delivery, or whoever's in charge. Tell them I'll be there in fifteen minutes. I'll scrub and go right in. You got that?" he said, pushing the button on his beeper. It vibrated in his hand.

"Yes, doctor."

A leaden weight dropped inside him. "Fifteen minutes, maybe ten. I'm leaving now." He hung up, put the phone down, turned and hurled the beeper against the opposite wall. "Stephen!" The flash of rage passed as quickly as it came. His hands shook as he pulled his trousers on. "*Stephen!*" He looked up to see him standing in the door with a look of shock on his face. "She's in labor. Alexis is in labor. She's at the hospital." His voice shook. His insides were like jelly now. He looked around for his shirt and saw it on the bathroom door handle.

"Oh my god—why didn't they—?"

"They *did*! I had it on the vibrator!" He left his shirt open and stooped to get his socks. "I forgot to change to the tone signal! It was on the vibrator the whole time . . ." His eyes filled and blurred. He had been joking with Stephen when he undressed; his mind had been on sex when he undressed.

"It was an accident, Alan."

"It was stupid and irresponsible." He quickly stepped into his loafers. "There is no excuse." He grabbed his coat and tie, looked around, and started towards the door. "I'm sorry about the wall, I'll—"

"Forget it." Stephen followed him into the living room. "It's a good hospital, Alan, she's in safe hands."

Alan continued towards the front door, wiping his face with his hand. "It was my idea, everything—the baby, this Lamaze delivery—everything. I should have been there." He opened the door into the hallway and hurried towards the staircase leading into the rear of the apartment building. His car, as usual, was parked in Stephen's carport, part of their clever camouflage. Stephen's footsteps were behind him on the staircase. He—no one else—had brought it down on all of them. His selfish, childish "need to look inside now and find myself," as he had announced to Schaeffer that first session.

"How long has she been in labor?"

"Hours!" He pushed through the back door and started across the concrete towards the parking slots under the carport. "There's no point in going through Lamaze alone!" His anger echoed off the wall of the building behind him. "She can't do it without me, she won't! She's no good at physical pain alone, I know her!" As he threw open the car door, the picture of Karen's and then Chris's delivery came to mind; twice, the sight of her drugged, distorted face flashed through his mind. "She's like a little kid with pain!" His voice broke as he tossed his jacket into the passenger seat and started to get in.

"Alan." Stephen grabbed the frame of the door. "She's done it twice before. She's in good hands."

He turned with his hand thrust in his pocket for his keys. "This one isn't like the others!"

"So you fucked up the Lamaze! What's more important now, the baby or the method?!"

"Don't you *understand*?!" he shouted. Even as Stephen stepped back, he realized that the hostility and rage were directed at himself and not Stephen. The pressure of it came apart in his eyes. "It was something we were going to do together. One thing, for once, completely together." He began to cry as he got into the car.

Stephen let go of the door frame. The color went out of his face. "I know," he said.

Alan pushed the key into the ignition lock. "Stephen, I'm sorry."

Stephen nodded and pushed the door closed.

"You're not responsible for this." He turned the key and the motor fired.

"I know that. But I'm involved." Stephen stepped back as he put the car into gear. "You see now what I meant. The angles always add up."

"Now bear down, Alexis! Bear down!" Evans's voice came at her again. As she held her breath, stared up into the white light, and did what she was told, the thought drifted again through her mind: she was a gigantic wooden barrel filled with something, a huge barrel splitting open from the inside. She was splitting open, but it would not come out!

"Come on, bear down!" he commanded.

The light above wavered from side to side. There were iron rings around her middle, she was sure of it; and if they split, her skin would fly apart. There would be blood everywhere, all over the green and silver room. She was going to explode, not from the bottom where it was tearing open between her legs, but from the middle. She rose up towards the light, let the air out with a bellow, then fell back. It was down there now, the pain, between her legs.

"Okay, Alexis, now relax and breathe." His voice was closer now, gentler than before. He was one of the green figures moving around her. She did what he said, she breathed. Above, everything seemed momentarily to clear. It would not stay clear, though. There were eyes above her, men's and women's, staring at her from behind masks.

"Breathe deep and slow," he said from down there where the pain was. He had given her something for the pain, she had begged him for something and he had given it. In her spine. She had waited to ask, she *had* waited, but he didn't come. He had promised to, but he didn't. Why shouldn't she ask for something, if she had to do it alone. It was *her* pain, not his. They were touching her face with something and it felt cool. But it felt like someone else's face, too. The drug did that. You were someone else for a while and that was nice. Alan was a doctor, he would have been in green like the others if he were here. It wasn't his pain, but it was his baby—she shouldn't be using that word, she should say *discomfort*. She would have said *discomfort* if he had come for his baby, but he had left her with only pain.

It was pushing. On a trapdoor down there. The weight of it was on the trapdoor pushing to get out. If she gave a push, one big one, it would go through the door and she would be rid of it. Rid of all the murderous pain once and for all! She drew in air and started to push.

"Hold off, Alexis! Not yet! Hold off pushing till I tell you!"

She stopped pushing. The sound that came from her mouth was smaller than the one she wanted to make, but she choked on it. She was crying now, instead of pushing. It was tearing at her down there, but she was crying for something else, for the emptiness that was bigger than her fullness, for Alan who had given her this but who had not come to help her give it back whole and finished, who had walked off with the reason for her motherhood.

She tensed. It began again. The drug could help that pain, the one down there, but it could not touch the one up here, the emptiness of his absence. She tried to reach up and cover her face, but hands held her arms down. This time the pain whipped around her sides like a twisting razor. It coiled through her stomach and ran down into her belly. She opened her mouth to empty herself with a yell, but heard only a clucking noise in her throat. It was low, pushing against the door like a mountainous movement of her bowels, but it would not leave!

"All right, breathe in and bear down!"

It would go on and on and—"Oh, God!" she shouted—and on and never come out!

"Do what I say! Take a deep breath!"

If she did not do it, she would die. With all the concentrated strength of her will, she broke through the spasm in her chest and drew in air. Above, the lights were turning like a child's kaleidoscope.

"Bear down now! Bear down hard!"

She held her breath and obeyed. She had always obeyed the deep, strong sound of men's voices. Her father's voice. Alan's, too, until these last few months when the scream inside her was louder than his voice.

"Breathe!"

Far down in her belly it moved, something huge and uncaring and separate in its mindless determination to get out. Her body jackknifed on the table, her legs bolted in the stirrups.

"Breathe in! You're getting there!" There was another man's voice and the clatter of metal at the same time.

She breathed in obediently.

"Now bear down, Alexis!" the command sounded monotonous now.

"Bear down, honey!" another voice echoed. She did, and it moved, searing her flesh. She drove down hard this time, willing, demanding that it leave her, for she could not imagine a world now in which she would want it or could bear to live with it.

"Once more, then breathe!"

"Once more, honey!" The second voice, the familiar urgency of it, sent a shock through her body. At his gentle command, she bore down harder than ever before and held her breath.

"Now breathe again!"

"Breathe, Alexis, take a deep breath!" He grasped her hand. She turned her face towards his voice, felt something lift inside her, opened her mouth, and drew in.

"Relax now, and *breathe*," he said from the far end.

"Relax, honey. Breathe easy. Everything is going fine. I'm with you now." His hand squeezed hers. "You're doing great." The hand and the voice, she realized, belonged to the same man and she knew them both, knew what he was saying to her with his hand.

It rose up inside her, lifted her suddenly on its crest before she could either stop it or even name it, the old habit of joy when he was there.

"I'm here, sweetheart." His face behind the mask came towards her. He kissed her forehead. For one brief moment, just as it began again, she could no longer remember why she had felt any pain.

He steadied his arms under the bundle of blankets, veered around a gurney parked in the corridor, and checked the room number he had just passed. She was down at the far end. Evans had arranged for a room at the quieter end of the wing. He started to hurry his pace, then slowed as the red, wrinkled face between the folds of the blankets twisted into an irritable corkscrew. There were whiffs of dark hair on his head; it could go auburn like Alexis's or black like his. The face, more like an irascible prune than a face, could be either his or hers. Or the face of anybody's child. Except that it was unequivocally and beautifully the face of his son.

A young nurse hurrying down the corridor looked at him in his OR greens and mask. A knowing grin broke across her face, she nodded, and continued by. For the second time since he had left the nursery, he felt a surge of pride and, at the same time, the downward pull of guilt. By the time he had scrubbed and gowned and reached the delivery room, she was already in the final moments; the baby's head was visible. She looked up at him in her drugged delirium, clutched his hand, and smiled. In her pale, exhausted face he read the pain she had gone through and the worst of her pains had not been those of labor. For one moment, forgetting she was seeing the world through a cushion of drugs, he had thought there was forgiveness in her eyes. But that would have been absurd to expect, even from a saint. He had come to her not minutes, but hours late; and he knew that she had guessed maybe not the *where* and the *who* of his last four and a half hours, but certainly the *what*. As he gripped her hand in the last moments of the agony, he wondered if *this*

—this small new life, was enough to hold them together now.

Alan glanced again at the room numbers. Another twelve and they would be there. They. He pressed the bundle lightly against him. There was no language for this other feeling. More than pride, more than joy, even more than a sense of human completion. He winced at the word. And though he had felt it twice before, this time it was different; this time, he could see it against the raw backdrop of that other way of life, Stephen's. He knew now what it would feel like never to have it. Between the blanket flaps, the tiny mouth puckered with a bubble of spittle between his lips. And he now also dreaded the possibility that she would take it from him, pushed far enough to conclude that he was now unworthy of it. She had, of course, seen the baby lying on her stomach after the delivery, a little mess of afterbirth and umbilical cord; and he had watched the thrill rise in her face, a thrill disengaged from logic, drugs, and the aftereffects of gas. After a couple of hours of rest, she was going to see him and hold him now for the first time. See *him too* for the first time with a clear head.

Alan took a deep breath, balanced his little burden in one arm, and opened her door. A soft light burned on the table next to her bed. At the sound of the door closing behind him, he saw her eyes open. She looked towards him from the bed. For a moment, neither of them spoke. "I brought you a visitor," he said quietly from behind the mask.

"Let me see," she said. Her voice was faint and tired. She stirred on the bed and drew herself up against the pillows.

"Put this on, first." He handed her a packaged sterile mask with his free right hand, searching her face for a clue to her thoughts as she wrapped the mask around her nose and mouth and tied the strings behind her head.

"How is he?" She raised her eyes, and he read in them, isolated from the rest of her face, the obverse side of his own ambivalent feelings: both fullness and disappointment.

"He's fine. Seven pounds, one ounce. Here." He handed her the bundle. She drew the blanket flaps away from the baby's face.

"He's beautiful." She drew in a breath.

"What did you expect?" He saw her smile to herself behind the mask.

"Funny, they all look alike at this point." She said after a moment, running her index finger over his forehead. "He could be anybody's."

"But he's just not anybody's."

"It seems like yesterday I was holding Chris like this. Do the kids know yet?"

"I phoned about an hour ago. They want me to bring them up to see him."

"Maybe after school tomorrow. Are they behaving with Claire?"

He nodded. "She said they're fine." He saw she was on the verge of saying something.

She hesitated with her brows raised in a question, then said, "And mother and dad?"

"I phoned them, too. They're very proud of your having another boy this time."

"Dad would be. I think mother wanted a girl."

He ventured to sit on the edge of the bed. "Max wants to come to see you tomorrow. Said he had something special for you. He asked me to give both you and him his blessing."

"Him—" She ran her fingers over the soft spot on the baby's head. "We can't keep calling him *him*, you know."

"Did you come up with any more?" He realized they were merely circling each other.

"One."

"What's that?"

"I think you know."

"You mean—?"

She nodded. "Aaron," she said and looked up at him. With her mouth and nose covered by the mask, he could not tell if the look in her eyes was one of forgiveness or merely one of exhausted submission.

He reached over and closed his hand over hers resting on the baby's head. "Alexis."

She glanced down at the baby cradled in her arm. "Don't Alan. Not now."

Under the combined warmth of their two hands, the baby stirred and wriggled his arms. There was, of course, no clear vision in his small blue eyes. He seemed to be looking up at both and yet neither of them.

"We almost named Chris after your uncle, remember?" She looked up at him again. This time, he saw steadfast determination in her eyes. "Aaron Alan Stegman," she said, "that's what his name should be.

XI

"We want it across the front, Jimmy, and down both sides." Alan pointed to the east and west sides of the property. "But not across the back," Alexis added, "we want that left open for the view."

Under his umbrella, Cagle turned and looked back up the muddy slope towards the half-finished structure of the house. "If you had told me you wanted an eight-foot wall around the place at the beginning, I would have designed something different." His chin lifted with indignation. "What you're asking me to do will, in effect, destroy the entire architectural balance of this house." He turned abruptly and started down the slope towards the lower southwest corner of the lot. "If you'll come down here, I will show you what I mean."

Alexis gave Alan an amused look of mock despair and formed the soundless words "What did I tell you?" with her lips.

He reached over and closed her open slicker. "Honey, why don't you go back to the car, you're getting soaked. I'll handle Jimmy."

"Don't be silly, I'm not retreating *now*."

"This clay is like glass when it's wet." He pulled the hood further over her face.

"*Alan.*" She took his hand. "Will you please *relax!* We got him up here in the rain for a showdown about this, and we're going to face him together. Okay?"

"Okay." He smiled and took hold of her shoulder. "But just be careful going down, it's slippery."

"And stop treating me like a pregnant woman." She reached around his waist and squeezed him. "I've *had* the baby. Three weeks ago."

"All right, all right, I'll shut up." He pulled her close to him. Together they started down the rain-rutted slope. She relaxed into him, letting him steer their way down the wet clay. In the last three weeks since Aaron's birth, she had enjoyed his mothering. To some extent, at least.

The ten days of nonstop rain had washed a good inch of topsoil away. The entire backside of the lot was now scarred with deep gashes from the steady flow of rainwater. Gruber, their contractor, had warned that the rains might go on for weeks. "Did Gruber say when they were going to start again?" she asked, searching for a foothold.

"I talked with him again this morning. He said they can't do a thing until the rains are over."

"Never mind, we're doing our best."

"At this rate, we won't be finished until late August." She saw him look off towards the south where the Palos Verdes peninsula was shrouded in a leaden sheath of rain. It was there again, that look of anxious distance in his face. "If we lose another inch of topsoil, we're going to be in *real* trouble," he said, easing her down a sharp drop in the ground.

"If we lose it, we'll replace it when the rain stops, that's all."

"*If* it stops."

"It will, dear. Just *relax*." In the last three weeks since Alan had taken control of Gruber and the builders, he had worked miracles. Alan had forced him to replace the shoddy materials he had used in the east section of the roof. He had coordinated the plumbers, carpenters, and electricians, something neither she nor Gruber had been able to do.

"Fighting Gruber and Cagle is one thing. Fighting *nature* is another," Alan said.

She drew up and let him move ahead, suddenly chilled by the inadvertent reference. A week after Aaron's birth, she had reached the point of asking him where he had been during the hours of her labor, asking whether he was involved with someone or not, but she had been afraid of tipping the delicate balance of their newfound happiness. Alan had kept silent, proving his faithfulness with actions rather than words. Until the rains started, they had divided their attention between Aaron and the house. "Alan?" she asked.

He turned a few feet below her and reached back to offer her a hand. "What?"

"What do you mean, fighting nature?"

Alan looked at her, genuinely surprised. "Just that. We can't do a thing about the weather."

She took his hand and started down, half an eye on the ground, half an eye on his face. He had glanced away, distracted, that look of distance in his face again. Suddenly, she felt the heel of her tennis shoe give way on the slippery clay, lost her balance, and slid forward.

"Watch it!" He jumped forward, grabbed her waist, and pulled her against him. "Jesus!"

"I'm okay." She looked up at his face and saw an expression of panic in his eyes. "I slipped, that's all." She tried to smile.

"It's those damn tennis shoes. Now hold onto me; I told you this wet clay is like ice." This time he encircled her waist and held her firmly, a little too firmly, against him. As they moved down the slope towards Cagle waiting for them at the bottom, she had the curious feeling that *she* was the one supporting *him* at that moment.

"Now from here, you can see what I mean," Cagle said as they came towards him. "Look at the house from this angle," he indicated the house at the top of the slope.

They turned together and looked up towards the one-story rambling maze of wood and half-faced walls. "What about it?" Alan said.

"You wanted something open and sunny that takes advantage of your unobstructed hilltop. You've got seventeen feet from the side of your house to the edge of the lot here. Now what do you think an eight foot wall is going to do to your feeling of *openness?*"

"Protect us from those damn snooping neighbors, Jimmy."

"But your house sits a good nine feet higher than theirs!"

She felt Alan's arm slacken around her waist and turned to look at his face. He looked down, silently battling with his indecision. "We still don't think there's enough privacy," she said to Cagle resolutely.

"*Privacy?*" He lifted his umbrella. "You asked for privacy, and I *gave* you privacy! You don't want privacy, my dear, you want *isolation!*"

"We want to enjoy the house *alone*, Jimmy!" Alan blurted out angrily. "We're not interested in making a Beverly Hills public display!"

Alexis drew herself closer to Alan, feeling the need suddenly to make a final stand for them both. "After all, Jimmy, it *is our home*." She turned her face away from the wind as the sky opened up in a downpour.

"You're both crazy, do you know that?" Cagle started off in the direction of the pool area. "Now come here, I'll show you from the east side what it will look like."

"Honey, I'll go with Jimmy," Alan said as he turned her and drew up her slicker around her neck. "Now you go back to the car, you're soaking wet."

"I don't care," she said, "if he doesn't want to give us what we want, then he can fuck off. It's our house."

"Now relax." He kissed her forehead. "We'll get our wall. Everything is going to be just fine." There was a clap of thunder far down the canyon as the rain began to fall in torrents. "Go back to the car and wait for me. *Please*." Behind his smile she saw both determination and exhaustion.

She nodded, "If he won't agree, then forget it. We'll build it ourselves later. It's just a wall." She left him and started back up the hillside, aware in the back of her mind that ultimately, it really wasn't a lousy brick wall they were fighting for now.

"By the way, Jimmy." Alan came up behind Cagle where he had stopped a few yards from the southwest corner of the pool excavation. "We're giving a party next Sunday to show off the baby. We'd like for you to come."

"Sure, Alan. Thanks, I'd love to."

"Open house from two to five. There'll be food." He noticed Jimmy's gaze fixed on the ground some yards away at the lower end of the property. "Is something wrong?"

"I don't know. Let's have a look." Cagle moved away towards the southern side of the lot. Then Alan saw it, a slight sag in the soil about five yards south of the pool. A thin, almost imperceptible crack in the mud running east and west across the ground. Jolted, he stared at the crack and traced its zigzag path across the lot with his eye, then started quickly after Cagle. "Jimmy!" He came up behind him on the edge of the lot where it dropped off suddenly into the deep ravine behind the house below them.

"Look." Cagle pointed towards a spongy ripple of soil at the very edge of their lot.

"Damn!"

"If it's what I think it is, we're going to have to call in a geologist to look at it right away."

"Jesus Christ!" A few yards down the side of the ravine, a wedge of soil had already given way and collected in a heap against a large sandstone boulder. He had managed to get Jimmy aside to ask his advice about one threatening disaster and had come face to face with another. He looked down into the ravine, speechless.

"It's probably the result of the pool excavation. They may have loosened the whole hillside digging it."

"Which means reinforcing this whole hillside with concrete!"

"We won't know until they look at it. In any case, you'll have to do what's necessary to protect both your land and the house down there. It's your responsibility if there's a slide."

"It'll cost a fortune."

"It could, yes. I'm sorry, Alan. This is a raw break."

"How soon can we get someone to look at it?"

"Tomorrow. I'll have Gruber notify the city and contact a geologist I know. I don't think they can do anything until the rains stop except cover the weak spots with sheets of plastic."

"Right." Alan looked out across the gray shroud covering the city. "We'll do that. We'll cover the weak spots with plastic until the rain stops." It had all been fine until the rains started ten days ago. He had burned off the energy of his free time working with Gruber and his men, had managed not to be alone too much with the fact that it was over now between him and Stephen, that he would not see him again as he had before. As a part-time lover. He had phoned Stephen the day after Aaron's birth, and Stephen had at least pretended to understand why they could not meet for the next couple of weeks. But that was merely postponing the inevitable. The fact was, Aaron had brought him up sharply against the disaster he had been heading towards in these last few months. If he continued to see Stephen, Alexis would find out; and knowing her resolution without asking, he had chosen to throw himself into building something instead of destroying everything. Then the rains had begun, and he had found himself once again idle and alone with his decision.

"Come on, Alan." Cagle tapped the sleeve of his raincoat. "There's nothing we can do here. And it's dangerous." He turned back towards the direction of the house.

Alan followed a few feet behind. The right, the simple and logical thing to do was to tell Stephen and end it once and for all. Tell him that it was a game of Russian roulette that he could not afford to play, not with Alexis. Not with a new child at home. But ending his short affair with Stephen was not going to put an end to the needs that brought him to Stephen in the first place. After ten rainy days of loneliness, he knew that. Even Schaeffer, for all his nodding encouragement and patience, knew that. "Say, Jimmy," he called in a casual voice. Cagle, the only other homosexual he knew well enough to ask advice from, was old enough and experienced enough to know a possible solution.

Jimmy looked back under the shelter of his umbrella, "What?"

"One more thing I want to ask you." He moved towards him where he waited at the base of the slope. In his mind he hurriedly ran through the story he had made up to protect the innocent: He had a friend, a guy he went to med school with, a close friend, a married man with three—no, four kids. The guy has a problem. He asked me if I knew any bisexual or gay men. He loves his wife and kids, but recently he discovered that he's—

"I'd forget about that wall for now," Jimmy said.

"It's not about the wall." Alan closed the few remaining feet between them, racing for a delicate, unincriminating way of putting it: the guy's bisexual. He's fallen in love with a man. He doesn't want to lose his wife, but he . . . The words sounded hopelessly transparent and shallow. As Alan drew up alongside Cagle, he caught sight of Jimmy's thin gold chain nestled in the gray chest hair between the partly open front of his shirt. The Beverly Hills jewelry set, Alexis had called him. "Discreet about it," she had jokingly said later, as though he had thereby merited the world's forgiveness for an incurable social disease.

"It's not about the wall," he repeated, "it's something personal I want to talk to you about, Jimmy. I need your advice."

"Sure." Jimmy's serene face altered with surprise.

"Let's walk. I'll tell you on the way up."

"Alex, honey!" Phoebe's voice rasped over the noise in the room. Alexis looked up from filling Donald's glass and saw her standing across the room beside the piano. Phoebe beckoned her, wiggling her empty champagne glass, and smiled needfully.

Alexis finished topping Donald's glass. "Now enjoy yourselves, there's lots of food over there on the table," she said to Donald and Pat and started through the crowd towards Phoebe.

"We ate, darling! It was delicious!" Pat called after her.

"Where's little Aaron?" Phoebe held out her glass.

"Getting his diapers changed." She began filling the glass and glanced across the piano towards Charles, who was seated at the keyboard, tinkling out a one-note tune.

"Bless his cotton socks. Listen, I brought my Polaroid camera." She leaned against the piano and pointed to the camera. "I want to take a picture for myself of Aaron."

"Not in the mood he's in, you don't. Alan took him back to the bedroom; he's screaming his head off."

Phoebe reached for her camera, "How adorable. An action picture."

Alexis restrained her, laughing. "Not today, Phoebe, he's had enough party."

"Phoebe, dumpling, you're drunk." Charles said from the keyboard, attempting a trill.

"Drunk? Of course, I'm drunk. I always get drunk on sentimental occasions. Baptisms, birthdays, graduations, bar mitzvahs, and weddings. Funerals, too. I'm a sucker for sentiment."

"Here, Charles." Alexis moved his half-empty glass to a napkin on the piano and topped it. "This will loosen your fingers."

"Actually, Alexis, Phoebe is a part-time closet alcoholic. The occasion is only an excuse to demonstrate her capacities in public."

"*Closet alcoholic!?*" Phoebe threw back her head and laughed. "I detest closets! You know what I think about closets?" She leaned towards Alexis, bracing herself against the piano edge. "I think people who live in closets end up hanging themselves instead of their clothes. Don't you think that's true?"

Alexis smiled tightly and stepped back. "I don't know. I suppose."

"Now *there*—!" Phoebe pointed towards Monsignor Driscoll and Helen across the room. She looked back and lowered her voice secretively. "Now *there* is a closet alcoholic."

"Mother?" Alexis laughed.

"The Monsignor, silly."

Monsignor Driscoll was holding a glass of champagne in one hand and gesturing animatedly with the other. Helen caught them staring and gave Alexis a quick look of surprise and disapproval. "Here, Phoebe, have some more." Alexis tipped the bottle to fill her glass again. A month ago, she had a fight with her mother about Aaron's name and the fact that she and Alan had decided against christening Aaron a Catholic. Nor would he be circumcised a Jew. Her mother had obviously brought Monsignor Driscoll along with them to the party to remind her of her little apostacy.

"I really shouldn't," Phoebe said. "One more, and I'll be on all fours."

"Which, of course, is her natural position," Charles said, tinkling at the piano. "Among paleoanthropologists, there is reason to believe that Phoebe is still among the *Dryophitheci* of this earth."

Alexis withdrew the bottle and glanced uncomfortably from Charles to Phoebe. She had heard some weeks ago there was trouble brewing.

Phoebe turned her back to Charles and sipped her champagne, smiling icily. "Charles, on the other hand, has advanced to the stage of *sitting*. Charles, I believe, is what they call a *Ramapithecus*. He can *sit*. He spends most of his waking hours at the office *sitting*. The only reliably *erect* thing about Charles is his—"

At the piano, Charles struck a loud, dissonant chord and momentarily brought the room to silence.

"You missed your calling, Charlie!" Donald said. There was an uneasy ripple of laughter through the room. Helen, Alexis noticed, had turned towards Monsignor Driscoll with a look of alarm.

"Alexis!" Charles stood up at the piano. "You play!"

"Yeah! Come on, Alexis, *you* play!" someone exclaimed across the room.

"Let's hear it for Alexis on the piano!" Phoebe set her glass down and applauded twice.

"I haven't played in years!" Alexis flushed under the smiling stares around the room.

"Nonsense, Mrs. Stegman," Claire said, "you play beautifully."

"She studied with the best teacher in California," her father announced to the room. There was a sudden burst of applause and encouraging shouts. Alexis glanced towards her father, feeling suddenly frightened. "Come on, sweetheart, play something," he smiled reassuringly.

"All right." Alexis handed Claire the champagne bottle and quickly ran through her repertoire in her mind. The Fauré Impromptu. She could get through that decently, at least. "But I really should *warm up!*" she started towards the front of the piano, then realized that Alan was not in the room. She had practiced the Nocturne for *him;* and if she was going to finally play it, she wanted him present. "Claire," she turned to send Claire back to the bedroom for Alan and heard the telephone ring in Alan's study. Max, she thought. He was to have arrived with a friend from the Georgian by two-thirty. It was well after three. The telephone rang again. "I'll get the phone, everybody, and come back!" she started towards the hallway. "I want Alan to hear me, too!"

"Saved by the bell," Phoebe called after her.

She turned down the hall and started towards the open bedroom door as the phone went silent. She could do a decent job on the Impromptu; not concert perfect, but well enough after seventeen years of neglect. Alan would be proud of her for the attempt, at least. She slowed her pace, reached the bedroom door, and started in.

"I know that, Stephen, I understand," she heard Alan say with feeling. She came to a dead halt at the door. Alan was standing with his back to her, bent over the bed with the telephone receiver crooked in his neck. "I know your feelings, and by now you know mine," he said insistently.

An icy chill ran up her back.

"It's not that simple. You're a psychiatrist, you know that!"

She took one step backwards, open-mouthed, and gaped at Alan inserting a pin into Aaron's diaper.

"I know exactly how long it's been since we've seen each other. I remember the day only too well."

The baby lay quietly on the bed, looking up at him. She covered her mouth and stepped back further into the corridor, careful not to make a noise, careful to vanish as she had come. "All right, then, on Tuesday. All I ask is that you don't misread my absence," he said as she kept on moving, sideways now, like a crab.

Alan's voice went on, garbled, unintelligible.

She went into Chris's bedroom which they had turned into a nursery, stepped over toys on the floor, and got inside the bathroom before the champagne came up.

Alan adjusted the telephone receiver against his neck, "I have a new son. What would you have done in my place?"

"The same, I guess." Stephen sighed with resignation. "It must feel wonderful being the father of a month-old son."

Alan straightened the nightgown over Aaron's legs, wondering if there was a touch of sarcasm behind the hurt in Stephen's voice. "Yes, it is," he said.

"I left four messages on your office phone that first week. You could have returned them."

"I debated doing that. I decided not to."

"I wasn't going to ask to see you. I called to congratulate you."

"I didn't phone you because I would have been the one to ask."

Stephen was silent for a moment, "I'm sorry I phoned you at the house. I should have waited and talked with you tomorrow at the hospital."

"It's all right. At least I answered and not Alexis."

"She still knows nothing?"

"No. And there's no point now in telling her."

"I see." There was a moment's silence on the other end. Alan closed his eyes, searching for a gentle way to say what he had only brutally implied. Through the open bedroom door behind him, there was a burst of party laughter from the living room. He had laid out his dilemma to Jimmy Cagle a week ago Saturday in Coldwater Canyon. "You're a fool to get involved with boys," Jimmy had said. "If you need a little something on the side, go to bars or baths; or better still, be discreet and go to another city for a weekend now and then." *Involved with boys* was the expression Jimmy had used, a blanket dismissal of everything beyond sexual desire that Alan had felt for this man over the last two months.

"I love you, Stephen, but we cannot meet anymore. It's finished." Alan opened his eyes and stared at the blank wall behind the bed.

"Is that what you were going to tell me on Tuesday?" Stephen asked after a moment.

"Yes."

"Then there's no need for you to say it twice, is there?"

Below him on the bed, Aaron made a bubble of spittle on his lips. "No," he felt the rope inside him pull apart at the middle. He heard Phoebe's voice calling Alexis from the living room.

"I guess I should have known from the beginning the trigonometry was against me."

"Yeah. Me too."

"If you need me, phone."

"Right. I will."

"Good-bye."

"Good-bye."

He lowered the receiver and began folding the corners of Aaron's blanket around him, then reached up quickly and wiped his eyes, watching the spot he had made dissolve into the flannel.

"You're sure you don't want me to finish up, Mrs. Stegman?"

Claire asked at the door leading into the laundry room.

"I'm positive," Alexis said from the kitchen counter where she was drying silver, "we'll finish the silver and then do the rest in the morning. Good night, Claire."

"Good night. Good night, Dr. Stegman."

"Good night, Claire."

Alexis gave the silver platter another vigorous buff and listened for the sound of the back door closing. It was 9:55.

"What do we do with the ham?" Alan asked.

"What do we usually do with leftover meat?" she retorted. The door leading from the laundry room to the carport snapped closed. She sat the platter on the counter with the other finished pieces. Behind her there was the sound of plastic tearing. They were finally alone. Donald had stayed on after the party to talk business with Alan, leaving her to entertain his boring wife. After eight hours of silent speeches to herself, the time had come, but she could not speak.

"You did a great job with the food. There's not much left," Alan said tentatively.

She reached for the silver sauce dish in the sink. What had maddened her most was the way he came into the living room afterwards carrying Aaron in his arms, looking every bit the loving father and faithful husband. He had made her pose with him for Phoebe's camera with his arm around her shoulder. She had sat down then and played the Fauré badly.

"Max enjoyed himself after he got here. Everyone seemed to, even your mother after she relaxed." She could feel his eyes on her, questioning.

"There's bound to be some joy in two cases of champagne," she said, rolling the sauce dish in the towel. Take him off guard and ask him, that was the way she would do it. Whatever he would come up with on the spur of the moment, his face would not lie. From his silence, she knew he was waiting like a trapped animal for her to make the next move. The refrigerator door behind her opened. "Do you want to save the rest of this mousse?"

"Save the mousse? By all means. If nothing else, we can at least *save the mousse*." She had not intended the bitchiness in that, but the question had just then popped again into her mind: had it been going on since December, since the day she saw them in Milner's driveway? And even before that? She had turned the question in her mind all afternoon, his December lie. But more galling than December was the memory of the months that followed, the Christmas honeymoon, then January and February when he duped her with his little confessions of sexual desire to camouflage an out-and-out love affair. This afternoon she had seen herself for what she was, a naive, gullible, utterly trusting fool, and that burned her gut now more than his infidelity.

"Alexis—" He was on the verge of preempting her.

"Save the mousse, Alan, but throw away the mustard sauce," she hurried on, "and if there's any carrot salad, keep that; but throw away the cucumber salad, it won't keep overnight." In the tense moment of silence that followed, she began arranging the smaller pieces of silver on the tray. She would take them into the dining room now. No, she would ask him now and leave the silver for later. Or was she too damn rattled to do either? Did she, in fact, really *want* to know?

"What's wrong, honey?" he asked.

"Wrong!" She started to lift the tray, then let it drop on the counter with a clatter. "You tell me, Alan, *you tell me!*"

Neither of them moved. Nothing except the second hand on the clock above the sink. The air had gone out of the room. She took a breath. *"You* tell *me* what I think is wrong." He did not answer. A drop of water fell from the faucet into the stainless steel sink and stirred the milky surface of the dishwater. "You're having an affair with Stephen Milner, aren't you?" She looked up to watch the second hand sweep past the six and head for the nine. There was a heavy, defeated sigh behind her. "Answer me, Alan." Still, he said nothing. "Answer me, god dammit!" She spun around to face him, astonished by the sudden exhilaration of it, "You and Milner are having an affair!"

He stood five feet away from her with the box of plastic wrap in his hand, a look of appalled shock on his face. "We were, yes," he said quietly.

The simplicity of his words hit her in the chest like a stone. "It's been going on for a long time, hasn't it?"

"A month."

"Don't lie to me, Alan! This time, I want the truth!"

"I've been seeing him for a little over a month," he repeated.

"I think you've been seeing him for a great deal longer than that!"

"Since the middle of February." The candor in his stare was infuriating.

"You've been lying to me for over a year now, haven't you?" she fired wildly.

"No. I didn't lie. I didn't tell you because you didn't want to know, and you never asked."

"So instead, you did it behind my back and then *pretended* with me!"

"I didn't pretend. I love you."

"You cannot love and deceive a person at the same time, Alan."

"You have always come first, you and the kids."

She stepped away from the counter, feeling the exhilaration of rightness sweep through her. "Did I come first the afternoon Aaron was born?" His face sank, and he looked down at the floor, defeated again. "You were with him while I was in labor, weren't you?"

He nodded and looked back up at her, foundering. "It was an accident. I would have been there. He came early."

At the crippled self-effacement of it, she felt an explosion inside her. As the shrapnel from a year's worth of rage ripped through her gut, she raised her arm and lunged at him. "You bastard!" she shouted, "I went through that hell alone!" But he had caught her arm with one hand and grabbed her shoulder. He held her back from him, stunned. Their eyes locked together. For a moment, nothing in or around them moved. Then his face altered. At the expression that appeared in his eyes, she felt the energy and force of her rage leave her arm and drain back through her body. In his eyes, she saw that she had done what she *had* to do: pushed them both across the invisible line. He released her arm, dropped his hand from her shoulder, and looked at her with grief now. She moved back stiffly until she struck the counter edge, then breathed, trying to control the spasm jerking in her throat. If it was finished, if there was nothing left for her to fight for, she wanted now to hear it, to know. "You're in love with him, aren't you?" she said.

"You come first. I have always loved you first."

"Then you do love him."

"I love him, but I'm not *in* love with him."

She shook her head. "Semantics."

"Not the way you mean."

"You cannot love us both."

"But I do. Only him, I will not—"

"How do you love me? Like a *woman?"* she stepped forward.

"You know what I am, what I've been for the last year and a half."

"Bisexual? I'm not so sure, Alan."

"We have had sex."

"Occasionally."

"Is that the way you measure my love for you?"

"We're married. I will not live with you for the rest of my life like a sister. I will not settle for a sexless marriage. I have a body, too, and I need to be loved as a woman. All of me. Completely. Do you understand me?"

He nodded.

"You decide. You decide which one you want more, me or him, a woman or a man. I'm not a child, love is not a toy, and I will not share it, with a man *or* a woman. I do not want the kind of love that comes without the body, do you understand what I'm saying?"

He nodded again, "I have decided. I decided before you asked."

"I cannot force you to love me in the way I need or in the way I love you. But if you see Stephen Milner again, it's finished." After seventeen years, it was easy to read his face: yearning, resolution, loss, grief, guilt, sadness, and fear. The two traces that ran down his cheeks caught and glinted in the fluorescent light overhead. His eyes, washed clear, were very blue.

He nodded again and made a small, incoherent sound.

She had read what was in his face, but now she also read what was no longer there: the protective power, the fatherly strength, the captivating and seductive command, which until now had sweetened her lifelong helplessness. The things for which, in part, she had married him. The master surgeon, the husband, the father, her tall dark man, she saw, was also a child.

"Mrs. Wilkes was scheduled for a nephronectomy at seven-thirty, Arnie, not at eight-ten." Alan looked down angrily at Arnold Berrey behind his big Danish office desk.

"Calm down, Alan. This is a big hospital. These things happen."

"Twice in one week?!"

"I'll have a word with our OR head."

"Your OR techs came in late this morning and kept me, Dr. Lindquist, and Dr. Hendriks waiting for forty minutes while they set up."

"I said I'll speak to the head of OR, Alan." Berrey's swivel chair squeaked to the rhythm of his rocking.

"Forty minutes represents several hundred dollars of our time."

Berrey gave him a faintly sarcastic smile. "Then add the delay onto her bill. Mrs. Wilkes is on Medicare." Alan felt his face color. "I was only joking." Berrey sat forward and chuckled, "Relax. Sit down and have a cup of coffee."

"I've got things to do, I'm in a hurry." Alan turned quickly towards the door, realizing he was on the verge of an explosion.

"Is that all you wanted to see me about?"

"That's all." He turned with the door half open. "And if it happens again, Donald and I are moving our surgery to another hospital," he said before he had a chance to think.

Berrey's smile dissolved. "I take it that's a threat."

"There are a lot of hospitals in this city that can use the revenue."

"We're still the biggest and the best equipped."

"Ten laproscopes aren't much good if you don't have patients to use them on." He went out, letting the door swing closed behind him. Keeping his eyes on the floor, taking deep breaths as he moved, he started towards the hospital lobby. His outburst with Berrey had been larger than the situation called for, and he now regretted it. He paused at a drinking fountain in the corridor. The cold water felt soothing in his throat. The OR incident that morning had been only the catalyst. The explosion had been building in him for the last seventeen days, since that night in the kitchen with Alexis when she delivered her ultimatum. Alan righted himself from the fountain, wiped his mouth with the back of his hand, and continued towards the lobby at the end of the corridor. In time, if he was patient, everything would come right again. The tension between him and Alexis would pass. In time, this frustrated need for Stephen would pass. In the lobby ahead, he caught sight of the clock: 11:07. He was on time. Alexis would meet him and Fred Cochran at Cagle's office by 11:30. Cochran, their geologist, would give his final report. Cagle had warned him by phone that it wasn't good. The earth under the entire southern end of the lot had come loose and was now threatening to slide. They would have to stop construction on the house for now and concentrate on building a concrete retaining wall across the face of the ravine. What it would cost, God only knew at this point. He slung his jacket over his shoulder and crossed the lobby to the door leading down to the basement parking garage. At the door, he paused to remove his beeper from his belt, check the position of the tone signal, and drop it into his suit coat pocket.

"Alan?" He heard Stephen say behind him as he reached for the door handle. For the last seventeen days, he had known this would happen. He let go of the handle and stood facing the door. His stomach tensed. It was impossible, working in the same hospital, that they should not meet. He turned and saw Stephen coming towards him across the lobby with a faint smile on his face. He looked sober and dignified in his dark brown suit.

"Hello, Stephen."

"How's it going?" Stephen came up with his hand extended; a gesture intended, he realized, to put him at ease.

"Fine. And you? How about you?" He shook his hand and felt the familiar grip. Also felt his face go red.

"I'm okay. Overworked, but okay." He let go of his hand and tried to smile, "How's little Aaron?"

"Great! Gaining weight by the day." He rummaged in his brain quickly for something to add but realized they had both come to the end of pleasantries. "Stephen—"

"I only wanted to say hello, Alan."

"She knows. She overheard me talking that afternoon."

Stephen stared at him, bewildered. "I didn't know. I'm sorry."

"It's just as well. If nothing else, it finally cleared the air."

For a moment, neither of them spoke. Then Stephen said, "Where are you heading?"

"I'm going down to get my car."

"Oh," he hesitated, "do you mind if I walk you down?"

"No. Of course not." He held the door open for Stephen to pass. As he went by, the sunlight falling through the huge front window touched his face, silhouetting a faint tremor in his cheek. Alan recalled the same inadvertent movement in Stephen's profile the night before his birthday when they had sat together on his living-room sofa. The heavy steel fire-door closed behind them in the cement stairwell. Following Stephen down the concrete staircase, Alan let his eyes rest on Stephen's shoulders. Their footsteps echoed up the stairwell, out of rhythm and heavy. As Stephen turned at the first landing, Alan felt a sudden desire to reach out and lay his hand on the shoulders below him. At that moment, rounding the second angle, Stephen looked back up at him, smiled, and started down again. On the second flight, the sound of their footsteps synchronized. The desire carrying him down, Alan realized, was purely sexual, the escape hatch of his bottled emotions. At the next landing, Stephen stopped, hesitated, and then turned around to wait for him. Alan kept walking. He rounded the corner of the steel banister, took three steps across the landing, and knew what he was about to do. He opened his arms and folded them around Stephen. It had happened in seconds, a wordless agreement between both of them. Alan's cheek came to rest against Stephen's. He had not thought they would come this close again. Stephen's hands gripped his back and pressed them together.

"Alan," his name echoed back up the stairwell.

"No, Stephen. It's over," he said. This he knew—he affirmed it again in his mind—this would be the last time. He moved his head back and kissed him—open-mouthed, deeply, lovingly, suppressing the small sounds of momentary joy that came from his throat. Then he drew back and let his arms fall to his sides.

Stephen said nothing. He stepped back and looked at him with astonishment. Two floors above them, a metal door closed. Then came voices, footsteps, and laughter descending.

The footsteps, voices, and laughter came down, moving fast. Stony-faced, Stephen started around him towards the staircase behind. Alan followed him with his eyes, opened his mouth to speak, but realized he had nothing to say. Behind him, Stephen reached out and gripped his shoulder, jostled him encouragingly. The small group of men and women rounded the landing above them. As they started down and saw them, their voices and laughter stopped abruptly. The grip on Alan's shoulder relaxed. And then he was gone.

XII

"**B**y the way." He ran the brush across the side of her head and looked at her in the mirror opposite. "Who was the guy who did it to you?" He smiled knowingly.

"You mean his name?"

"Yeah!" He was playing with her. He knew who had done it.

"Why do you ask?"

"I'd like to beat the shit out of him. It must have been beautiful the way you described it, long like that."

She started to glance away but instead decided to meet the challenge of his provocative gaze. "I did it," she said finally.

He looked down at her head, still smiling, and went on brushing the close-cropped remnants of her hair. To even out the botched job she had done on it with her sewing scissors that morning, he had cut it down to an inch all around. It was now even *shorter* than Alan's. "Why did you try doing it yourself? It would have been a lot easier on you to have phoned *me*."

"I didn't *know* you, Mr. Russo. My usual hairdresser was out of town, and I thought it would be easy to do. I cut my son's hair all the time." She shifted herself in the chair, recalling the scene in the bathroom earlier that morning. "I got your name and number from a friend *after* I made a mess of it."

"Keep it brushed back from your face like this. Later on, when it grows out a little . . ." He went on to reassure her about what he would do to make her "feel more comfortable" with herself in the weeks to come, but she heard nothing of it. That morning, after Alan had gone off to work and the kids to school, she had taken the scissors from her sewing box and locked herself in the bathroom away from Claire. True, in the last two months as she watched her stomach and hips narrow, she had attempted other little changes in her appearance. She had bought French jeans and a pair of boots at the end of April, had hated them, and then compromised with loose-hipped cotton trousers and long-sleeved cotton shirts. Alan's puzzled, indifferent surprise had only made her feel like a worse fool. "Do you use a conditioner?" he asked, looking at her in the mirror.

"Yes. I have a good one at home," she replied and saw the panic in her reflection.

"Don't worry, it will look great in a week or so," he stroked the top of her head. "Now use the conditioner and keep the sides brushed back like a boy's haircut . . ." She glanced down at her hands nervously. The third week of March she had given her ultimatum and he had abided by it for these last weeks; he had not seen Milner, she knew that. He had even gone beyond those negative terms of hers, had almost smothered her and the kids with attention. A weekend in Palm Springs, "to get away from LA" he had said; another weekend in Laguna "before the beaches get crowded." They should have stayed in town, of course, to watch the emergency work Alan had demanded on the concrete reinforcement wall in the ravine. But he had insisted.

"Okay, now what do you think?" The young man stood behind her and rested his hands on her shoulders.

"I don't know. It's a shock. I've never had short hair before." She held her breath and turned her head to the side, more conscious of his hands on her shoulders than her profile in the three-way mirror.

"I think it looks great."

She had told him she could not tolerate a sexless marriage, would not live with him like "a sister." They had had sex in these last weeks, several times. Sometimes even with passion. But she had realized last night for the first time that something was missing. They weren't communicating in it. "I think I look like an aging boy," she blurted out.

"Boyish, *maybe*. Aging, no." He reached up and playfully flipped the hair on the nape of her neck, "It's very youthful on you, Alexis."

He had not used her first name before. She raised her eyebrows. "Oh?" her voice sounded shrill, dubious, and angry at the same time. Last night, she knew Alan's heart hadn't been in it. She had gotten up this morning aroused, utterly unsatiated, and more surprising than that, feeling desperately inadequate and guilty.

"Sexy, too," he chuckled. She felt his fingers run down her neck again, lightly, caressingly. He had done that twice before while he was cutting her hair. She flushed, half with embarrassment, half with anger, and glanced down at the blue smock covering her still distended stomach. After breakfast when Alan had gone, she had returned to bed and lain there like a mad person inventing ways she could attract him again as a woman. She had masturbated, too, thinking of his body against hers as it had once been.

"You don't believe me?" he asked behind her.

"Something tells me you say that to all your customers," she raised her eyes accusingly.

"Not all," he chuckled, "I have both men and women." At his naughty, teasing smile, she averted her face, recalling the vision of herself before the bathroom mirror. In retrospect, she knew that for ten or fifteen minutes she had lost all contact with reality. She had taken her scissors from the sewing box, locked herself in the bathroom, and proceeded to cut her hair. When she finished, she looked like something from a state mental institution. She had awakened at that point as though from a dream, gotten on the phone, and called Phoebe for a hairdresser.

"Something tells me you think all male hairdressers are gay," she heard the hairdresser say. Startled, she glanced at him in the mirror as he stooped down behind her to measure the line of the cut across the neck. "Some are, some aren't," he said and smiled. His head was level with hers. She could feel his warm breath on her neck. "Me, I'm into women."

"Really?" she felt her throat tighten, "And what kind of women are you into?" she asked as he turned her head from side to side, judging the line. She caught sight of the naked fourth finger of his left hand. Until now, she had ignored the flirtation, telling herself it was merely the usual hairdresser's flatteries.

"Good. The back and sides are straight." He ignored her question, stood up, and crossed to the long counter in front of her. She stared at his back. Over six feet, broad-shouldered, and uncharacteristically masculine, his muscular good looks had in fact raised the question earlier in her mind. As with Alan, there was no way to tell from appearance alone whether he was gay or straight. Or both. Russo looked Italian. "What kind of woman?" he said finally, tearing the bill he had been writing from the pad and turning towards her. "A mature woman with natural, unaffected good looks. A little shy, maybe, soft-spoken and refined. I like women who keep their sex guarded." He grinned and handed her the bill, "It's my nature, I'm Italian."

"Really?" she reached up to remove the smock from her neck, "I would have sworn you were Swedish."

"Here." He laughed and moved behind her. "I'll take that." He drew the smock away from the front. "Be patient with your hair. After a few days it'll begin to take shape. If you want to come back at the end of the week, I'll even it up for you."

"Thanks. I'm sure it's going to look fine." She stood up quickly and adjusted her blouse over her slacks. Next to her, he looked massive, a good foot and a half higher.

"Sexy," he said softly.

Alexis glanced at the customer seated in the next chair and reached for her purse on the counter. "Don't you mean *foxy*, Mr. Russo?" she asked, then immediately regretted her sarcastic hostility, realizing that it came from elsewhere. From her frustrations at home, from her habit of mental monogamy. "I'm sorry." She turned to him. "I didn't mean that."

"I don't like being stereotyped any more than you do, Alexis. I meant sexy." He shook the hair from the smock.

"Thank you, Mr. Russo. I feel flattered." She opened her purse and dug for her change purse.

"The name is Giovanni. G-i-o for short, but it's pronounced Joe." He looked at her as she opened her purse and drew out a five. Alan had looked at her that way, even less than a year ago, but not since. She felt an uncontrollable flush spill into her face. "Thank you, Gio." She handed him the five-dollar tip and smiled forthrightly. His eyes were brown, the color of chestnuts.

"Thank *you*, Alexis." He seemed not to notice the tip. He caught her hand before she could draw it back, turned it over, and placed a small card in her palm. "Here's my number. Call me. Anytime." His mouth was playful.

"Anytime?" she asked on an impulse.

"I put my home number on the card." Under the black mustache, his lips moved as he swallowed.

"It may need trimming. I'll call." She turned towards the front desk at the far end of the room, "Good-bye. And thanks," she called.

Moments later, she pushed through the front door and stepped out onto the sunlit sidewalk along Robertson Boulevard. She opened her purse and slipped Giovanni's card into an empty slot. Halfway down the sidewalk, heading towards her car, she paused to look at herself in the glass of a store window. The haircut, of course, looked ridiculous. But it, unlike some other things, would grow back by the end of summer. She touched the belt around her waist. She had lost a good inch since she last checked. Alan had scarcely noticed. Giovanni had said be patient. She started towards her car, feeling suddenly and curiously buoyant. She had an hour and a half to kill before the kids got out of school. Saks's sale of winter dresses was still on. Some of them were designer clothes, like the silk crepe she had seen with Phoebe. Alan had said to go back and buy it, if she wanted it. She inserted her key, opened her car door, and got in.

Call me. Anytime. It was silly of him, but he meant it. She turned on the motor, put the car in reverse and eased against the bumper of the car behind. She hadn't bought a dress like that in a year! It was too small now; but if she dieted, by next winter it would fit.

I put my number on the card. He had said it quite flagrantly and he meant it, too.

She put the car into "drive" and moved forward. I look like shit now, she said silently but determinedly to herself; but next winter, in that dress, these ashes will *glow*.

The young man behind the check-in window glanced dubiously at Alan's suit and tie. "Are you a member, sir?"

"No, I'm not." Alan smiled at him uncomfortably through the glass.

"This is a private club, sir, and you need a valid membership card or three pieces of identification with a picture." He looked down, busying himself with his paperwork.

"Three?"

"That's right, sir."

Alan took out his wallet. He recognized the tone and attitude from some of the hospital receptionists, but it still succeeded in intimidating him further. He removed a handful of credit cards and his driver's license. "These okay?" He dropped the cards into the slot under the window. The young man began filling out forms.

"That'll be six dollars for your membership and six for the room, sir." Alan returned the forms with a twenty-dollar bill. "This is your membership card." The young man pushed a small card towards him with his change. "Please sign it." He took the card. On it, printed in black letters, were the numbers 8709. No name, only the street address. Anonymous, as he had hoped it would be. Stamped in the lower left-hand corner was the expiration date, six months from today, May 16. He signed it. "You keep the card." The young man pushed a towel under the slot. "Check your valuables and pick up your room key at the window inside." He pressed a button that sounded a buzzer at the metal-faced door on Alan's right. Alan took the towel, opened the door, and stepped into a carpeted, softly lit hallway. Ahead of him, in what looked like a lounge area, several young men stood talking near a row of vending machines. Except for the white towels around their hips, they were naked.

"Can I help you?" another young man behind a long window on his left asked. The window had verticle wooden bars. Alan turned towards the window, noticing on his right another room divided by lines of gray metal lockers. Disco music blared from a speaker somewhere at the end of the hallway.

"Is this where I pick up my room key?" he asked nervously, feeling out of place in his dark gray suit.

"You got it." The attendant smiled agreeably. From the opposite wall, he removed one of the long, narrow metal lock boxes, opened it, and laid it on the counter. "Do you want to check valuables?"

"Yes. Please." Hurriedly, awkwardly, Alan removed his watch, took his wallet, and placed them in the box. The young man returned the box to the wall, locked it, and came back with two keys attached to an elastic band. "Here's your key. You're in room 39. Do you know where it is?"

"No, I don't." The nervous cramp in his stomach tightened.

"Through the lounge there." He pointed off to Alan's right. "Turn right, follow the corridor around. You can't miss it. The rooms are numbered on the doors. Have a good time."

"Thanks." He took the keys and started through the lounge area towards a door opening into a corridor dimly lit with pink and amber. The four young men in towels near the vending machines glanced at him assessingly as he passed, then went back to talking. Alan turned into the corridor, aware that he had just been evaluated and rejected. On his left was a line of dark-painted doors with white numbers stenciled on the front: 31, 32, 33 . . . He made a left turn and continued down, wondering if the sex he had so powerfully needed an hour ago was worth this much anxiety. Another left turn. He wondered if he should turn back, hand in his key and leave. Yesterday. That's when it had begun. When he'd seen Stephen leave the hospital and get into someone else's car. He had not seen the driver, but he imagined the man it *might* be. A right turn now—34, 35, 36 . . . He had carried his jealousy home in the form of moody irritability, and Alexis had been its victim. By this afternoon the jealousy had gone from irritability to anger to a burning need for sex with almost any man. Another left turn. Alan stopped. The doors and corridors now went off in every direction. He had wandered into a labyrinth! The numbers now ran backwards. 28, 27, 26 . . . Everything looked the same. The doors—all painted black; the walls—all the same brownish-looking red under the overhead pink and amber lights. The color of a fresh bruise. Except . . . He moved on down the corridor ahead. Except the wall on his right which was gray and decorated with a painted mural of naked males. Alan moved on and turned right into what seemed like another wing of the building. 37, 38. At 38 the door was open. Inside, he saw a young man lying on a double bed alongside a plate-glass mirror. In the soft spill of light from an amber spot over the bed, the young man looked up at him, scrutinized him, then turned his face away. He was naked, Alan saw, with his towel draped over his slender hips. Dark-haired, dark-mustached, his handsome face had a serene expression of experienced disinterest. Alan moved away quickly, embarrassed and a little hurt by the young man's interpretation of his intrusion. 39. In the dim light, he fumbled at the lock on the door with first one then the other key. The door opened into a room like all the others. An amber-pink spot burned over a double bed extending along the plate-glass mirror. He closed the door, stood for a moment in the narrow space between the bed and the adjacent wall, then sat down on the edge of the bed. He looked up towards the speaker overhead blaring disco music and saw there was no ceiling to the room. It was a cubicle. He looked down, took a deep breath, and realized his pulse was racing. He was frightened. He had come here riding on the crest of a desire he knew was as much emotional as sexual; now there was panic instead of desire.

Alan looked at his wrist for his watch and remembered he had left it behind in the lock-box. Alexis would be home by now. In another forty-five minutes, she would begin to wait for him, begin to wonder. Thirty minutes was really all he needed, he was sure. He stood up and began to undress, hanging his clothes on a hook screwed to the wall. From the next room, over the open ceiling, there suddenly came the punctuated groans of someone's orgasm.

Naked, Alan turned towards the bed for his towel and saw a thin roll of fat around his lower abdomen, the middle-aged price men paid for the good life. He took a deep breath, tightened his stomach muscles against the threat of still more discriminating glances, and wrapped the towel around his hips. There was only one inch at the end to tuck it in with. It would come off before he got half way down the hallway. He fussed with the towel for a moment, realized he was only stalling for time he did not have, reached for his room key and went out.

A bar would have been easier, he thought, standing outside his door at the junction of two corridors. Except, the bars were *too* public. West Hollywood General was a big hospital, there were gays who worked there and they went to bars. Sooner or later he would have been seen. OR techs talk, the gossip would have gone around and eventually he would be publicly classed as a "closet queen." Until now, he had thought the baths were the safer of the two choices.

The figure coming towards him could be from anywhere. An average-looking blond in his mid-thirties with wire-framed glasses, which seemed out of place on a man wearing nothing more than a small white towel. As Alan stepped back for him to pass, the young man paused, glanced over his body and smiled. Flustered, Alan nodded and returned the smile politely. The blond observed the confusion in his face, shrugged and moved on. The thought came back again: I'm out of place here, I don't belong. Hurriedly, he started off in the direction from which the blond had come. I don't belong either here or in Stephen's more comfortable world. He paused at an open door and saw the vague outline of a balding fat man lying on his bed in near darkness. He must have turned out his light to disguise what everyone could plainly see. Why would a man like that come to a place like this? he wondered, moving on. But then why would he? Two months ago, Cagle's warnings about the dangers, personal and professional, with any one man had shaken him profoundly. And Alexis. Her terms had named only Stephen, but she had meant *any one man*. Alan made a left turn at the end of the corridor, and found himself in a longer corridor decorated with exaggerated murals. He realized that he was lost now. More rooms, more open and closed doors, more industrial carpeted corridors. He leaned against one wall and stared at the mural on the opposite, trying to revive his desire. Two young men passed him, talking in hospital-low voices. They were both dark-haired, the same height, with slim-waisted, muscular bodies. They appeared to be friends. He thought of Stephen again. And then Alexis. Himself between the two. Tacitly, Alexis had understood since January that there might be an occasional stranger, but she did not want to know about it, and it must not come between him and home. Must be something he did in dangerous secrecy, alone. Without even the self-imposed limitations of a Cagle. Nothing remotely resembling his sex with Stephen. A way of life he had yet to learn.

Two doors down on the opposite side of the corridor, he watched a man in his late twenties, an average-looking curly-haired man, pause before the open door of a room. Reflected in the mirror along the bed lay a dark-haired man in his mid-thirties. Cautiously, hesitating as he went, the curly-haired man moved towards the open door and went in. In the mirror, Alan could see him beside the bed. He reached down and ran his hand along the other man's leg slowly, cautiously, almost politely. So there's a technique, Alan thought. He had wondered how it was done. Alan felt his own body warm. He moved slowly in the direction of the room and reached the door as it closed with a soft thump. The clock at the far end of the corridor read 5:12. If he was to do it, it had to be done now, in the next seventeen minutes.

A moment later he reached an open door and paused, just as the curly-haired man had done. Inside on the bed lay a dark Chicano-looking youth. He was short but had a handsome face and solid, lean body. Alan stared in, waiting, feeling his heartbeat quicken with nervousness. He waited for the young Chicano to make the first move as the etiquette required. The guy did nothing, merely stared at him with indifference, his arms resting idly on the bed. If anything was going to happen, *he* would have to be the one to make the first move. He reached under his towel, feeling aroused but foolish, and began fondling himself. At that, the young man turned on his bed, reached for a cigarette and lit it, keeping his face averted. Alan let go of himself and moved away, feeling trapped between desire and frustration. He had assumed it would be quick and relatively easy, more of a free-for-all than this ego-shattering game of physical roulette. Maybe he wasn't the most gorgeous man that ever crossed Sepulveda Boulevard, but he wasn't all that much of a turkey, either!

He turned into still another corridor, where the lights were dimmed to a more encouraging level of darkness. Ahead, he saw himself reflected dimly in a mirror. Then another. He stopped dead in his tracks, realizing he had wandered into a maze. The narrow passageway zigzagged crazily through a hall of mirrors, like a fun house. Overhead, disco music with zigzag sounds of electronic percussions ran off into space. Someone came towards him in the pale blue light, a body reflected twenty times in the mirrors; a short, thin body with black curly hair. A hand reached out and stroked his chest, gently. Alan looked down at the small, homely, almost ugly young face turned up towards him. "Sorry, I can't," he stammered and moved away, feeling his way along the mirrors. It works both ways, he thought with unalterable regret.

He was in a big room. A faint reddish light spilled down from high above. Slowly his eyes adjusted. In the center of the room, two feet off the floor, was a huge bed. In the dim light, he could see bodies around the bed, moving—standing, kneeling, embracing, and kissing. Two guys were on the bed; they appeared, at first, to be only one. Alan took four steps, drawn forward by what he saw, tense but aroused. A hand reached out and stroked his shoulder, moved around to his chest, then went away. He felt a leg pass by, grazing his own. He moved closer, came face to face with a guy, felt his eyes move down and then up his body, saw him pass on into the darkness. Even here it was all cautious, slow, reticent. Almost polite. He was now in the middle of some fifteen or twenty guys. Surrounded. His fingers touched an arm, ran slowly up to the shoulder, across the guy's back. A clean-shaven face turned towards him and came forward. Alan felt a hand under his towel. He gave in almost at once to the caress and reached out to put his arms around the guy's waist. The man folded against him easily. Alan could feel the beat of his own heart against the other man's firm, hairless chest. He closed his eyes. Anonymous and silent as it was, right or wrong, crazy or sane, it felt good, holding another male body. A warm, elementary kind of goodness. Not, maybe, the substitute for Stephen he had been looking for; a passing thing, surely, but also a momentary, much-needed relief.

He opened his eyes, turned to kiss the guy, and caught sight of the back of a head a few feet away. A familiar head. The gray, neatly trimmed hair, the tanned neck, a thin gold chain. Startled, he stepped back. The light was too dim to be sure. But it *could* be. Cagle had suggested the baths to him "as an outlet." The man in front of Alan stood staring at him, puzzled. If the gray head turned, if it *was* Cagle, even if he already knew about him—in the next instant, Alan was pushing his way between the clutch of bodies towards the door at the far side of the room. He guided himself in the mirrored maze with an outstretched hand, found his way and hurried along the corridor, trying to remember the direction to his room.

Even the mere *chance* of seeing Cagle! It had felt at that moment like a humiliating defeat, a concession to Cagle's sixty years of empty lovelessness.

In his room, Alan sat down on the edge of the bed and looked at himself in the mirror, ashamed and frightened. He looked like a kid, holding his sock out like that with both hands, a juvenile delinquent in the body of a forty-year-old, married, successful surgeon. In the future, when the need arose . . .

"I know a guy who looks like you, he's from Long Beach." From the next room came the sounds of voices and low, playful laughter.

Some were luckier. He pulled on his socks, stood up, and reached for his shirt and trousers. Others, trying to hold two worlds together and running from both, had no choice but to live half their lives in darker, more secret places.

Four minutes later, Alan stepped out of the baths and let the plain metal-faced door slam closed behind him. Fifty feet away, on the way to his car parked at the end of the block, he took a deep breath, for the moment relieved.

It was only 5:44.

"Daddy! Look at mom!" Karen shouted gleefully from the table.

Alexis turned from the cabinet with the stack of dinner plates in her hands as Alan came through the door from the laundry area. "Oh, Karen be quiet," she said as she lay the plates on the counter and glanced at Alan. "If you say one word about it, I'll kill you." She gave him a warning smile. Alan stood in the doorway with his briefcase in one hand and his suit coat draped over the other arm, staring at her dumbfounded.

"Mom cut all her hair off." Chris giggled at the table where he was shaping a piece of green construction paper.

"I told you what he'd do," Claire said, busying herself with the salad greens at the sink.

"Mom did not cut all her hair off. A rather large Italian hairdresser by the name of Russo cut off all of mom's hair." She turned towards Alan for his reaction.

"What did you do *that* for?" he asked.

"I don't know. Impulse. It looks ghastly, doesn't it?"

"I don't know. I'm still in shock."

She noticed his own hair, which stood up on the top of his head in a crazy twist of black curls. "Well, yours doesn't look much better, you know." She smiled and turned on the broiler.

"Look daddy!" Karen held up a piece of half-cut red construction paper.

"Hey! What is it?" He caught her up in one arm and set his briefcase on the breakfast room table. His gaze was still on Alexis's new hair-cut.

"It's a present for my teacher. It's going to be the roof on the schoolhouse I'm building."

"Wow!" Alan laughed and hugged Karen. "Why don't you make me something?"

"Okay." Karen squeezed his neck.

"I'm making a valentine!" Chris held up the paper he was cutting.

"Valentine's Day is already over," Karen sighed. "You're too late."

"I don't care, I'll keep it for next year."

"Now, kids," Alexis said from the kitchen area, "let your dad rest for a minute." She started towards him in the breakfast room mildly surprised by his attention to the kids. It was unlike him when he first got home from work.

"I talked to the reinforcement people," Alan said, studying her head, "there's been a minor slide in the ravine. We ought to go up and look at it after dinner."

"Jesus." Alexis reached for the jacket on his arm, "Is it serious?"

"They say not. It's just begun, though."

She kissed him on the cheek. He looked tired and worried. "Are you all right?"

"I'm fine. Tired, but okay."

"Gruber phoned and said they can start construction again next week. That is, if the concrete has dried on the wall." She opened the jacket and began emptying the pockets on the table. "For crying out loud, Alan, what did you do to this jacket?" Besides being wrinkled, the jacket had a large stain on the sleeve that looked like grease.

"I dropped it on the ground," he said and turned to look at Chris's valentine.

"Alan," she held up the jacket, "it's your best suit!" She drew out a handful of keys and change. With the keys came a small green card. It dropped on the table. She glanced at it. "8709, what's this?"

Alan looked up from Chris's valentine, startled. "Oh—that. It's nothing. Just a joke someone played on me." He turned away, visibly uneasy. "Now why did you decide to cut your hair off? It looked great the way it was."

"I just wanted to." Alexis glanced back at the card next to the keys and change, puzzled. Below Alan's signature, next to the printed word "countersigned," was a second signature: Walter F. Harding. And below that, "Expiration Date, Nov 16."

"You look like a *boy*," Alan laughed somewhat ironically.

Alexis glanced a second time at the card. Odd, she thought.

XIII

Gradually, his eyes adjusted to the darkness in the theater. He could make out some ten or fifteen heads silhouetted against the cheap technicolor light from the screen. "I'm here to repair your electrical wiring," the dark-haired guy in overalls on the screen was saying to a curly-haired blond standing on a ladder. The blond was dressed like a garage mechanic. Alan removed his damp raincoat. Most of the men in the theater, Alan saw, sat alone; but in the deeper darkness along the walls, there were a few pairs. Nervously, Alan sat down in the fifth seat on the fourth row from the back, took a quick breath, and folded his damp raincoat over his lap. The blond on the screen started down from his ladder. The electrician reached up to feel his crotch on the way down. Alan glanced at the illuminated digital numbers on his watch. It was 12:26. He wondered how long the dramatic preliminaries would take. He had promised to meet Gruber, their contractor, in Cold-water Canyon at 1:30. It was a good thirty-minute drive from here. His hands were shaking. He gripped the armrests and looked again at the screen. The mechanic and electrician stood face to face, undressing each other now. Their faces and arms were colorless in the overbright artificial light, the sound of their movements muffled and dead, like the sound-track of a home movie. From the aisle behind him on his left, Alan heard the soft squeak of a theater seat. Startled, he glanced to the side and caught sight of a figure in the row behind him. He had meant to sit alone, rows apart from anyone. He looked back towards the screen and wondered if he could change seats now without calling attention to himself.

On the screen, the two men were naked. They came together and kissed.

If he was going to do it, it had to be quick and secret. Like the first time. In that West Hollywod gay porn theater two weeks ago, there had been only two or three men. He had come in, done it, and left. But he couldn't go back there. Afterwards, on the street in front of the theater, he had seen Dr. Kreutz's black Cadillac pass just as he came out. It was a coincidence, but professionally he couldn't afford another coincidence like that. Nor could he afford to be seen in the bars or baths.

They were lying down now, still kissing. A kiss wasn't what he had come to see. Alan turned his face up towards the dark ceiling and blinked away the sudden sting in his eyes. He had come to look at the sex, the rest was pointless. A quick look, a furtive ejaculation, and then back into the street, into the light, into his other world where everything was peaceful and secure. He had done this once before, when the pressure inside him had reached the breaking point. It was wrong and stupid and even childish, but it put out the fire and harmed nobody. It left him free for a while.

The blond turned around to take the dark one's cock in his mouth. He recalled the first time he and Stephen had done that, in mid-February, their second time together. In the last three months, he had passed through light-years, it seemed. He had reached a kind of plateau now. For a couple of weeks after their last meeting in the hospital stairwell, he had nursed his jealousy of Stephen and his anger at Alexis and himself in silence.

The sounds they were making on the screen sounded empty and forced, exaggerated for the pleasure of the audience. In time, Stephen would become only a memory. He was already getting better at preventing himself from daydreaming about Stephen when he was alone. This foolish nostalgia was beginning to embarrass him. In time, the need to be loved and to love in that way would go. In time, he would only have to deal with these periodic flashes of desire. They would always be there.

The camera moved along their bodies now, resting on the dark one's face for a moment. The effort was almost convincing. Alan's desire came and went, and in between there was a kind of peace. It was now a matter of putting out the fire and moving on. Alan glanced around nervously. If he was careful, the figure behind him would notice nothing. As he moved his fingers to his zipper, he pretended to be adjusting the raincoat over his lap. He could be done with it in a moment and gone. Even if the guy behind him *saw*, what did it matter? He was a total stranger. It wasn't like doing it in front of Alexis or Stephen or anyone else he knew. It was still a secret. He was in a cheap East Los Angeles porno house, miles from anyone who would know or care about who he was or where he came from or *why* he had come there. They were all total strangers here, all doing what they *had* to do for their own reasons, whatever they were.

His damn zipper was stuck. He pulled at it, but it would not come down. He shifted his body forward in the seat to free it. He pulled at the tiny clasp again, and it made a soft purring noise as it went down. He hesitated, wondering if the noise was audible over the groans from the screen. He waited. His hand under the raincoat was shaking now. He took a deep breath, then heard a movement behind him. His heart leapt in his chest. He glanced to his right and saw in the corner of his eye that the man behind him had gotten up and was moving off towards the aisle. Under his raincoat, Alan moved his hand away from his open fly and rested it on top of the coat. Kept his eyes dead ahead on the screen, where the dark-haired one was kneeling face forward now, on his haunches, doggy-style, as they called it. A shadow moved towards him in his own row. Before he could stop himself, he glanced sideways and caught a glimmer of light reflected off a pair of glasses. A man, young, in his mid-twenties, wearing a dark T-shirt and jeans, came towards him and, without hesitating, sat in the next seat. Alan turned back towards the screen and kept his eyes dead ahead. Carefully, he moved his hand from under his raincoat and rested it innocently on his leg.

The blond on the screen was ejaculating into the camera, helping his audience with low, off-camera groans. Beside him, Alan could see the young man's eyes on him, could feel the presence of his body all the way down the right side of his own. The closeness both terrified and aroused him.

Schaeffer, when he had told him last week about the porno theater, had asked him if he had done it, in part, out of a taste for danger. "No," he had replied, "it was an escape hatch for me at the time." He wasn't sure now.

He felt his erection harden under his shorts and realized that if they were to do anything, he could not be the one to initiate it. He was too scared to make the first move. Then it happened. On his right leg he felt a slight pressure from the young man's left leg. He hesitated, pushed back the sudden rush of awful possibilities that crowded into his mind, and then moved his leg slightly. The young man responded, reached towards his left leg and stroked his thigh with the back of his fingers.

On the screen, it was the dark one's turn.

Alan held his breath, moved his right hand along his leg, and touched the young man's fingers. A picture of his fingers touching Stephen's that afternoon at lunch came to his mind. It was not the same kind of touch. The young man's fingers left his and moved across his leg towards his fly under the raincoat. With a last, quick glance over his shoulder, Alan drew the hand under his raincoat and guided the fingers to his open fly and felt them slide through the flaps of his boxer shorts. It would be awkward, but it could be done. He stirred in his seat, moved his hips forward, and let the young man pull his erection forcefully through his undershorts and fly. For an instant, he felt exposed and threatened under his raincoat; then closed his eyes and yielded to the gentle, experienced movement of the hand.

At first, he was not even aware that something behind them had moved. When he opened his eyes, it was only a vague, distant shadow. Then it was behind them, directly behind and over them. From the corner of his eye he saw the head bent forward between them, felt it come close to his neck, heard the breath, felt a cold chill ripple through his entire body.

"I'm a police officer." The voice was soft, almost intimate. "I want you to get up and walk quietly with your hands to your sides to the lobby of the theater. I won't cause you any embarrassment if you co-operate. Don't try to make a break for it or you'll get hurt. I have a fellow police officer with me." The head lifted and went away.

For a moment, in the vacuum of silence, neither he nor his partner moved. Nothing moved. From the screen, there was the sound of an orgasm, but it seemed to come from another world. Alan realized he was paralyzed.

"Shit." Next to him he heard the young man get to his feet and start angrily down the aisle.

In his mind, he thrust out for some alternative, tried to form a clear, rational thought. One word came to him. *Finished.* It dropped into his mind like a pebble into a pool. He saw it ripple out like a wave through the surface of a stagnant pool, saw it spread through his entire life. He tried to stop it, anchor it, but it went on. Like the falling pebble, he saw himself founder and sink to the bottom. *Finished.* For one foolish moment of sexual relief, he had sunk his entire ship.

With both hands, he reached under his raincoat and fumbled to stuff the limp evidence through the flaps of his shorts, then pulled at his zipper. It stuck halfway up, wrenching a tuft of pubic hair. Even now, he was absurd. They were waiting. He would never get up now. He moved his hips forward in the seat, eased the zipper up. His hand now shook uncontrollably. If he did not get up soon, they would come back. He grasped the back of the seat in front of him and pulled himself to his feet.

"What about a lighter? Does he smoke?" the saleswoman reached under the counter for a small gold cigarette lighter.

"No, he doesn't smoke. Could I see the wallet again?"

"Certainly." Instead of the lighter, she brought out the brown morocco wallet. "A wallet's always a nice gift."

"Except he has a perfectly good one already."

The saleswoman forced a patient smile. "Is it for a particular occasion, a birthday or something?"

"Our wedding anniversary. Seventeen years."

"I see. Well, that shouldn't be too hard." She scanned the array of expensive little gifts arranged under the illuminated glass. "What about something for his office? What kind of work does he do?"

"He's a surgeon," she said irritably and replaced the wallet on the counter.

"Then what about a lovely leather box for his desk?"

"No, I think not."

"A key chain?" She pointed to a 14-carat gold chain.

"He uses a sixty-five-cent steel ring for his keys," she said hopelessly. None of it—boxes, wallets, key rings—was going to bridge the space that had widened between them in the last six weeks. In former years, her joy had always been in the thought behind the gift.

"Perhaps if you gave me an idea of what you'd like to spend."

"It's not a question of cost, it's a question of value." She averted her gaze from the puzzled stare of the saleswoman. She could buy the entire case and none of it would replace the value of what she was afraid had been lost in these last weeks since her ultimatum. She had solved one problem and created another.

"Have you tried in the men's department?"

Alexis smiled bitterly and thought *Oh, yes. In* one *man's department, I have tried for seventeen years.* "He doesn't need any clothes," she said.

"I gather, then, he's one of those men who has everything."

"Yes, that's it. He has everything." Everything but the wife he so abundantly provides for and the lover he wants and needs.

"In that case, why don't you—"

"I'll just take the wallet," she blurted out.

"Certainly." The saleswoman looked up surprised and relieved. "I'm sure he'll adore it."

"Yes. It's very nice." Anything to finish and get out. She glanced toward the storefront window. The rain had started down again. She had spent an hour running up and down Rodeo Drive looking for a meaningful gift. Enough was enough.

"Will this be cash or charge?"

"Charge." She opened her purse and took out her billfold. In the small slot in the black silk interior of the purse her eye rested on the protruding edge of the card Giovanni Russo had given her. She pushed the card down and removed her MasterCard. "Do you take Master-Card?"

"Certainly." The saleswoman took the card and reached for charge slips.

A wallet. She was a fool. She had hit every store from Hermès to Gucci looking for something unique that would tell him a week and a half from now what she herself could not put into words. That she needed and loved him more than anything else in this world; that without *all* of him, she did not exist. She was bribing him with a wallet.

"Mrs. Alan A. Stegman?" the saleswoman looked at the card and asked.

"That's right."

"Is this his correct address?"

"His?" Alexis smiled at her thinly.

"Yours."

"Yes. That's our correct address." She had been asked that before by other salespeople; but now it struck her as condescending. Her charge cards had been in his name for years. The saleswoman began writing up the slip. She had never questioned her identity as Mrs. Alan A. Stegman.

"Some women use their maiden names, others use their husband's," the saleswoman said to reassure her. Alexis watched her writing out the figures. The mocking irony was, of course, that she was buying Alan a gift with his own money! Bribing him with his *own* credit. She stepped back, appalled. The truth was, she herself owned *nothing*! Other than the savings she had accumulated from stocks her father had given her, stocks put aside for the children, she *had* no money. She could pay for nothing with money of her own. As a person in her own right, she did not exist as far as the world was concerned. She stepped forward, more pained than angry, "Forget it," she said and reached for the MasterCard.

"I'm sorry?" The saleswoman looked up, surprised.

"Forget it." She dropped the card into her purse. "I don't think I want anything after all." She snapped the purse closed.

"But—"

"Thank you, but I've changed my mind." She started off towards the front door. The sum total of her potential in the real world was zero. After seventeen years of marriage and almost thirty-eight of life, she was, at best, equipped to be someone's nanny or someone's maid. There are no openings in this world for housewives and mothers. She paused with her hand on the glass door. Outside Rodeo Drive and its glamorous sidewalks had come to an expensive standstill in the rain. She had twenty-five minutes to meet Alan and the contractors at the house in Coldwater Canyon to view the rain damage to their uncompleted retainer wall. Work on the house was again at a standstill. As Alan had said, it was not contractors but nature that was against them.

As she pushed her way through the door into the street, she caught sight of her reflection in the glass. Her hair was growing out now but the ends were ragged. Perhaps it was time to call Mr. Russo and have him even things out.

"Your home address?" The officer typing the booking form looked up at him through the glass partition.

Alan gave it.

"Is that your wife's address?"

"Yes." Alan turned towards the officer on his right leaning against the partition separating the prisoners from the booking officers. "Is this necessary?" He indicated the handcuffs behind his back.

"Business address?" said the voice behind the window.

"Answer the question." The arresting officer pointed to the window impatiently.

"You don't have to keep us handcuffed now," Alan said angrily, "none of the others have them on." He looked back at four men seated on a bench across the room, waiting their turn to be booked.

"Business address?" the voice repeated.

"You handcuffed me around the metacarpal bones! My damn wrists are swelling; you know that, don't you!" Alan glared at the arresting officer.

"You answer the questions, buddy! I'll decide when the cuffs come off!"

Alan gritted his teeth and turned towards the circular hole in front of him. He gave his Wilshire Boulevard business address and then took a deep breath, trying to clear his head. There was a biting pain in his wrists behind his back. Mechanically, one after the other, the questions came at him through the circular hole. Between questions and answers, Alan turned to look around the room at the thick mesh over the windows, at the drunks huddled on the benches, at the acrid-smelling pool of urine on the gray vinyl floor.

"Bullock's. I work at Bullock's," the young man he had been arrested with said into the adjacent window. His voice was pitched high now, shaking with terror. He had said he was twenty-two years old. He looked nineteen.

"Look, man, you're wasting my time!" the officer on his right said, "answer the fucking questions!"

"Wife's name?"

"Alexis Stegman." This is not real. I am not here, and this place is not real. She would not believe him when he phoned. A porno movie theater. She would neither understand nor believe him. He went on answering the questions, but his thoughts ran off at crazy tangents. She would be waiting for him at the house in Coldwater Canyon. Knowing her, she would have waited for an hour and a half. But he was dead. Somewhere between the hospital this morning and now, he had come to an end, had died, did not now belong to Alexis or her world.

"All right, let's move." The voice on his right was exasperated. He felt a hand on his arm, pulling. Then a heavy steel door across the room opened and he was led into still another room.

"Where are we going?" he heard Robbins, the young man, say behind him frantically.

"Fingerprints," his arresting officer said.

Seated on benches in the middle of the room were some eight or nine prisoners, waiting to be fingerprinted. They did not wear handcuffs, Alan noticed. A glass window ran down the left wall, separating this room from another room painted yellow. "I'll take this one in first." His arresting officer steered him to a door. "You keep the kid out here." He gestured to an officer behind the glass to open the door. The pain ran up both arms into his shoulders. A middle-aged, plain-faced officer in uniform stood in the open door, looking at him with indifference. "Norton was down here looking for you a little while ago, Chuck," he said to the arresting officer guiding him into the room.

"Did he say what for?"

"Wants you to sub for Jennings tonight."

"Christ! I subbed for Jennings *last* night! It's McCarthy's turn! I've had it with these fags!"

"Talk to the Sarge, I only take prints." The door closed with a solid metal thud.

"This one's a doctor, Jimmy, so treat him with respect." The voice was mockingly patronizing. Alan felt the right cuff slip from his wrist.

"Takes all kinds." The fingerprint officer crossed to an old-fashioned desk in the center of the room.

"When you've finished with this one, Tom has the other one." The cuff came off his left wrist. Behind him, Alan heard the door open and close with a dull thud.

"Okay, over here," the officer motioned him towards the desk. Mechanically, Alan moved forward, rubbing his wrists. "Give me your right hand." Alan held out his hand and looked at the clean-shaven, ordinary face intent on pressing his fingers into the ink pad on the desk. "Index finger," he said and pressed Alan's finger against the card. Running from himself, Alan thought, hiding, apologizing time and again to Alexis when he gave in to his feelings, telling himself for months that it would pass—"Relax it." the officer jiggled his fourth finger—hating himself when it did not pass and he stole off to put out the fire secretly—

"Come on, mac, relax your hand." The officer shook his left hand. "Let it go limp. Gimme a limp wrist." Stealing a moment here and there to be with Stephen, loving him and hating himself for loving him. "That's right, limp. Nice and limp." The officer smiled to himself. Alan looked at his face, astonished, realizing he had never been spoken to in that way. He was being addressed like a delinquent child. Worse. Like an object. "Now your third." *I've had it with these fags!* The impersonal contempt of the word had fallen on his head like a stone. A judgment that left him defenseless and silent. For it was, whether he admitted it to himself or not, his own judgment of himself. "Now your pinkie." His fifth finger rolled over the card. *Raus mit den Juden. Kill faggots*. The graffiti on the Berlin wall in his dad's picture book of the war. The graffiti near the Santa Monica pier. He looked down at his black prints on the card and suddenly wondered if his Uncle Aaron had been printed before they loaded him into the train for Auschwitz.

"All right, go to the sink over there and wash your hands." The officer pointed to a wash basin on the far side of the room.

"So be it," Alan said to himself, turned, and crossed obediently to the sink. He turned on the tap, wet his hands, and reached for the bar of soap.

"Make it fast," the officer said across the room, "we've got others waiting."

"I take it that by law we're allowed to make a phone call," Alan said, lathering his hands.

"You can call your lawyer from the cell upstairs."

"Whom I choose to call is my business," Alan said, curiously restored in his confidence. "I may call my lawyer. Then again, I may call my wife or I may call my lover." Behind him, the silence was heavy and uncertain. He put his hands under the water and watched the inky lather run from his hands, feeling relieved by what he had just said. Further down the wall on his left, a door opened and from the corner of his eye he saw the blue-clad figure of another officer step into the room.

"You guys got anyone for me to take up to the tank?"

Alan stared at his hands under the water, startled by the familiarity of the voice.

"That one," the other officer replied.

"What's he in for?"

"Lewd conduct in a porno house."

"Jesus, that makes eight already today! Palmer and Henderson must be working overtime." He recognized the Chicago accent. "Say! You at the sink." Alan did not respond. He watched the lather slowly drain down the hole in the sink. For an instant, the feeling of humiliation and shame flooded over him again. In a moment, he would have to turn and face the young officer. Martell. He remembered his name now. Martell would know him at once. For the moment, he could not bring himself to turn around. "Dry your hands and get moving," Martell ordered. A year ago, December. He recalled the afternoon. The look of fear and despair on the young man's face. "Did you hear me, buddy?!" the voice rose angrily. Keeping his back to both officers, Alan pulled a paper towel from the dispenser overhead. "I'll take this joker upstairs and come back for the next one later," Officer Martell said. Ten days before Christmas. Martell had come to him at his office, told him he could not afford to pay for the cervical procedure his wife needed. He was unemployed at the time and had no insurance. He pleaded with Alan to give him a break. He had applied for police school, would pay him back later in installments. His wife wanted *him*, he had said, to perform the operation. She was terrified of surgery, but she trusted him. "All right, let's go." He had performed the surgery but had never received the promised installments. Alan wadded the paper towel into a small ball, dropped it into the trash can, and turned with a feeling of sadness and embarrassment. Not, curiously, for himself but for the young officer.

Standing five feet away, Martell opened his mouth to speak, then stood riveted with a look of bewilderment on his face.

"All right, officer, I'm ready," Alan said calmly.

She leaned back in the rocking chair, adjusted Aaron in the crook of her arm and began rocking again. She could hear the children playing on the swings outside. It was 7:20 by the clock on Aaron's bureau. Her mistake—she rested her head against the rocker—her mistake had been in trying to win him back by pleasing. As though by asking herself in advance what he might want of her, by keeping one step ahead of his needs, she might by some magic combination of little surface pleasures bring him back to her. A haircut, a wallet, her obsessive punctualities. She had met the contractors at 1:30, had forced them to wait with her in the rain until 2:15. They had gone down to see the damage from yesterday's slide. In Alan's place, she had agreed on the additional money needed to repair the problem. She had waited for Alan until almost 3:00, when she had had to collect the kids. She had left the house wishing that the whole damn thing would slide down the hill, that they had never started it to begin with.

She lifted her head and opened her eyes, suddenly aware that the telephone was ringing. She sat forward, listening to the second ring through the closed nursery door. Outside, the children's voices were moving towards the house. Karen or Chris would answer it. Claire had gone off to a movie in Westwood at six. To hell with him, she thought, and sat back again. Three times that afternoon she had phoned his office, then the hospital to have him beeped. The old story again after six weeks. Only this time, she had drawn the only logical conclusion left: he had spent the afternoon with Milner and, in doing so, was telling her that he made his choice.

"Mom!" Karen called from the far end of the hallway.

Wearily she got up and crossed to the crib with Aaron. She laid him down in his blanket and turned towards the door.

"Mom!" Karen called just outside the door.

"Don't shout." She stepped into the hall, closing the door behind her. "The baby's asleep. Who is it?"

"I dunno. Some man."

"Didn't he say who?" She turned down the hall towards their bedroom.

"No. He wants to speak with you."

"All right. I'll take it in here. You go back to the front and hang up that phone." She entered the bedroom and hurried to the phone by the bed. For some reason, she felt suddenly frightened. "Hello?" she blurted loudly into the phone.

"This is Sergeant Fowler of the Los Angeles Police Department. May I ask who's speaking, please?"

"This is—I'm Mrs. Stegman," she caught her breath.

"Mrs. Stegman, I'm calling to verify an address. Is your husband Dr. Alan A. Stegman?"

"Yes." Her heart leapt.

"And you both reside at . . ." she listened to him give their address, feeling the blood drain down her body.

"Yes. Why? Is something wrong?"

"We're holding Dr. Stegman in custody here at the Parker Center and we need to get verification of his home address before we can release him on his own recognizance."

"In custody! What do you mean?" She glanced over her shoulder and saw Karen standing in the bedroom door. "What's happened?!" she motioned her to leave.

"Your husband's been arrested, ma'am."

Gesturing angrily, Alexis grabbed the phone, crossed to Karen and pushed her back into the hall. She closed the door quickly. "Arrested for what?" She tried to lower her voice.

"He's been charged with lewd conduct in a public place."

"If this is your idea of a joke, it's not funny! *Who is this?!*"

"Sergeant Fowler, LAPD. I'm afraid it's not a joke, ma'am."

"Where is he?" she broke in, "I want to talk to him! Put him on the telephone!"

"I'm sorry, we can't do that."

"What do you mean you can't do that?" she shouted, "What is your name?!"

"Fowler." There was an impatient sigh on the other end. "If you have any questions, you can phone the information desk; they'll tell you what they can. I'm afraid that's all I can say now."

"You listen to me! Don't you dare hang up! I want to talk to—!" There was a click at the other end and the line disconnected.

She stood motionless, holding the phone, listening to the dial tone, staring through the bedroom window at the summer sunset reflected off a distant neighbor's window.

Lewd conduct in a public place.

A thought went through her mind, brushed across her awareness like the chilling brush of a spider's web across the face: she had spun out a web of her own needs and now she had finally trapped him.

"Calm down, Alan, it can't be helped." Stephen's voice was composed, firm.

"The only reason they were going to let me out on my own recognizance was because I'm a surgeon and I live in Beverly Hills." With the receiver to his ear, Alan reached through the bars of the cell and pulled the portable telephone box towards him. "When they took me down to arrange the release, a couple of those underlings behind the desk made jokes about the faggot doctor. I lost my temper and told them off."

"Forget it, Alan. I'll contact a bail bondsman and have him meet me down there within the hour with the five hundred dollars. In the meantime, calm down."

"I don't have to take that shit, Stephen!" he looked through the bars at the young officer who had wheeled the telephone into the cell block. He stood at the end of the passageway between the two lines of cells.

"*Alan*," Stephen said sharply, "keep your mouth shut until I get there. I've been through this before with other friends. You're only making things worse."

"Okay, okay." Alan let his eyes run along the three cells opposite where six or seven prisoners were watching him, waiting their turn for the phone. He had been the first to use it.

"Does Alexis know yet?"

"No." He leaned against the bars, resting his forehead against the rung. "Unless she thought to phone the police. She may have; I've been here now for close to seven hours."

"Do you want me to call her?"

222

"No!" he caught himself. "Please don't. I want to tell her myself. I have a lot to tell her."

"Hey, doc! Get the fuck off that phone! You can talk to your fuckin' boyfriend when you get out on bail!" a prisoner two cells down called. The young man was stretched out on his bunk, shirtless, dressed in a baggy pair of white dungarees.

"Do you want me to call your lawyer?"

"No. Walker's wife is a friend of Sharon Berrey's. It would be all over the hospital by morning." He knew it would come, the public exposure, the scandal. But he needed time to prepare himself and Alexis. "I'll find a lawyer tomorrow. I'm going to need," his voice wavered, "I'm going to need all the legal help I can get." He thought of his work and the mountainous cost of the house in the same instant.

"More than that, you may be needing a friend."

"Yes," he closed his eyes, "I do." He had called Stephen rather than Alexis because Stephen was the one person in the world who would not meet him at the jailhouse door with a silent judgment. Stephen would not ask him for an explanation.

"Look, you rich honky queen, get off that motherfucking phone!" a tough, husky voice shouted. Alan looked up at the black face staring at him from the opposite cell. The man's eyes fixed him with savage desperation. The officer at the end of the passageway started towards the black man's cell.

"I'll be down within the hour," Stephen was saying, "but in the meantime, try not to antagonize the police."

"Will you get that faggot off the phone, officer," one of the young drag queens housed two cells down drawled, "I've got to call Denny's and have them send in some *food*. That meat loaf you girls made for us was *shit*."

There was a burst of laughter, catcalls, and applause down the length of the cell block. Another voice broke in over the laughter, "Listen, officer, that girl over *there* is doin' nothin' but making a date to fuck her boyfriend when she gets out! I'd book her on attempted sodomy if I were you and save yourself the trouble later!" The laughter rose again, echoing off the bare plaster walls.

". . . and they'll interpret any complaint you make as a refusal to cooperate, Alan." Stephen's voice seemed to belong to another world.

"Listen, ladies." The officer stood before the cell holding the two drag queens. "Keep it up and we'll cancel your phone privileges till morning."

The laughter in the cell block died away.

"They're not afraid of you, Alan; if anything, they're afraid of themselves. But now they've got the power."

"Okay, sweetheart, time's up." The young officer rested his hands on his hips, "Let your buddy there have a crack at it."

There was a loud round of applause and jeers from the others.

"The fact is, Alan, you're a homosexual," Stephen said, "and what you're asking for now is permission and justification. But the police can't give you that. Only you can give yourself that."

"The others are waiting," Alan murmured into the phone.

"What you must look for now is justice, and you'll find that in a court of law, Alan."

"I understand." He looked down at the dark cement, "Please come now."

"I am, Alan. Be calm."

Alan reached through the bars with the receiver and settled it back on the hook.

"About fuckin' time." His cellmate, Vernon, pushed by him to the phone.

The diced chicken had curled and its sauce had evaporated; the snow peas were limp and the steamed rice had dried solid. Alexis replaced the tops on the three Pyrex dishes and stood listening to the silence. At 7:20 she had phoned the police station desk to learn that he would be released on his own recognizance. Then at 9:15 she had phoned again, only to learn that he was now forced to post a bail bond of five hundred dollars. When she insisted she would come down with the money, they told her someone else had come in with the bail. Absently, she looked down at the line of tiny black ants threading its way between a pea-sized morsel of Chinese chicken and the edge of the butcher-block table. She picked up the morsel and tossed it into the sink a few feet away. For a moment, she continued to watch the little army moving back and forth between the spot where the chicken had been and the edge of the block. It was useless; the object of their hunger was gone now, but they went on anyway. With a rush of anger, she crossed to the sink, grabbed the sponge and turned on the faucet. She was going mad, she thought. She held the sponge under the faucet, filled it with scalding water and crossed to the table. With a swift stroke, she swept up the trail of ants, turned the sponge over, and watched them curl up and die. She had won all her little battles, but she had lost the war. At the sink again, she held the sponge under the water and watched the tiny corpses swirl down the drain. Lewd conduct in a public place. She tried again to picture what he had done: homosexuals did things in public toilets, she knew that. He had told her what they did under the Santa Monica pier. But *Alan*—she turned off the faucet—he was not that kind of man! The dribble from the faucet made a rat-tat-tat on the stainless steel bottom of the sink. The dribble slowed to a single drop that clung to the faucet mouth, then fell.

There was a dead silence in the room.

Between now and his arrival, if she did not find something useful to do, she would go mad. Turning from the sink, Alexis looked around the kitchen. Everything—pots and pans, the counters, cookbooks, utensils—everything was perfectly arranged, as always. There was nothing for her to *do!* Except the silver. On an impulse, she started towards the dining room, then stopped and looked at the top drawer of the counter under the telephone. The drawer where she kept all the odds and ends she had no other place for. Countless times, she had told herself she would have to do something about the mess inside. She opened the drawer, stared down at the cherished little collection of her venal economy, and realized that none of it had been or ever would be of the slightest use. Mad as it was, she could at least *clean out a drawer!*

She moved quickly, feeling an odd sense of exhilaration, drew up the plastic garbage bin, and began emptying the drawer. The preserving jar tops, the potholder, the fuse. He had called Milner, not her, to come down with the money, she was sure of it. After her little scene in the kitchen six weeks ago, *Milner* was the one he trusted. In a crisis, she was useless! In her battle to hold onto him, she had made herself useless in a crisis! A broken can opener, a large nail, a flattened roll of electrical tape, one half-melted votive candle against the night when the lights would go out—

His car door closed outside under the carport.

Startled, she hesitated, caught her breath, then scooped up the remaining contents and dumped them into the trash. She left the drawer open, hurried to the sink, and began going through the motions of washing the counter with the sponge. She would be busy when he came in.

His key rattled the lock in the back door.

With the soapless sponge, she began scouring the bottom of the sink, feeling in her stomach the nauseating coil of panic, dread, and fear.

"Alexis," he said quietly from the breakfast area. She turned the faucet off and faced him. He was just inside the door, holding his raincoat in one hand and his briefcase in the other. His wrinkled white shirt was open at the collar. "I've—" He went silent, looked at her for a while, and read what was in her face. "You know already," he said.

"Yes." For a moment, they did not move. "They telephoned me to verify your home address."

He nodded absently, laid his raincoat over the back of a chair, and set his briefcase on the floor.

"Are you all right?" she asked.

He nodded again.

"It's late, you must be hungry. Did they feed you?"

"I'm not hungry." He came towards her around the stove partition.

"There's Chinese food. I kept it hot, but it dried out in the oven. I could fix you a sandwich." Her voice sounded strident.

"No. Nothing," he stopped by the stove. "Did they tell you why I was arrested?"

"They told me the charges. Nothing more."

His face clouded with pain and exhaustion. "I wanted to be the one to tell you."

"Alan—" She stepped forward to stop him.

"I was arrested in a porno movie theater."

"Alan, *please*—"

"I was charged with lewd conduct in a public place."

"Tell me later, not *now!*"

"No. I want you to know *now*. Not later. We've had too many laters."

"There are things in the refrigerator, I'll fix you something." She started by him towards the refrigerator.

"Alexis." He took hold of her arm. "I was in a porno movie theater! I was arrested!"

"I *know* you were arrested! But it's done, it's over!" She tried to pull free.

"No!" He held her firmly. "It's not over! I was charged with a felony! There will be a trial!" His eyes were startlingly blue in the muted fluorescent light. She raised her hand to stop him. "It will be public knowledge, Alexis!"

"I don't care, it doesn't matter!" She pulled free and bolted towards the refrigerator. "People are arrested all the time, it does not matter! Charles Amherst was arrested last week for drunken driving." She threw open the door and looked at the food on the shelves.

"I was arrested for a sex offense, not drunken driving."

"There's ham from last night and some of the children's sandwich meat," she said, rummaging on the top shelf.

"I went into a porno house." He went on, determined now. "A man sat down next to me—"

"And there's cheese!"

"A man sat down next to me and I let him—"

"I'll make you a cheese sandwich!"

"—I exposed myself. The vice squad was there. They arrested us both." It was coming too fast, they were only words.

She reached for the package of American cheese, "Here! I'll use *this*."

"It was a gay porno house. I was arrested for a public homosexual act, Alexis."

She reached to her face with one hand and held onto the door with the other. "Please don't do this to me, Alan."

"I want you to know everything! From the beginning! Do you understand me?! No more illusions, Alexis!"

"Just tell me what you want and I'll make it!"

After a moment, he said, "A drink. I'd like a drink."

"Yes." She swung the refrigerator door closed. "I'll make you a drink." Without looking back, she headed towards the dining room. Distance. For the moment she needed distance. From the kitchen to the liquor cabinet in the living room, she would have time and space to collect her thoughts, get hold of herself. It was falling too fast, too much too fast. Everything running out like water down a drain. And she was not prepared, not yet.

"There's no ice," she said shrilly, opening the lid to the ice bucket as he came into the living room behind her. "I'll get some." The top slipped from her fingers and clattered against the cabinet top.

"No. It isn't necessary. Just plain scotch." He watched her pour out a full glass of Johnny Walker. Her hands shook. "Do the children know?" he asked.

"No." She poured another glass, then turned to him stiffly. "Not yet."

He took the glass. "Are you all right?"

"Yes." He could see, though, that she was not all right. She was merely numb. She went to the far end of the sofa and sat down.

"Do you want to talk now?" Staring at something on the coffee table, she nodded vacantly and sipped her drink. He sat down at the opposite end of the sofa, careful to give her room. "Alexis." He looked at her, appealing for her attention. Her face colored with pain.

"Why didn't you call me to come down and post the bail?" she asked.

"I couldn't."

"Why?"

"You know why."

She sipped her drink and winced; she hated scotch. "You called Stephen Milner, didn't you?"

"Yes." She stared at the box of cigarettes on the coffee table, obviously wanting one but unable to reach out. He looked at her, unable to speak. "Alexis." He sat forward after a long while and forced out the words. "I want you to look at this clearly and coldly because," he cleared his throat, then went on, "because in a matter of days what happened this afternoon will be public knowledge." She shook her head and sat up rigidly. "I want you to think—think *hard* now about yourself, what you're facing." He had worked it out in his mind on the way home in the car after Stephen left him.

"You were arrested in a porno house. It's not the end of the world."

"There will be a public trial in a criminal court. Everyone will know—your family, our friends, my business associates. There will also be a public hearing before the medical board on charges of moral turpitude."

"So what?"

"It will happen. If the medical board rules against me, I will lose my license to practice medicine. If I do, we'll lose everything. We're in debt, Alexis. Do you understand me?" She raised her glass and drank a full half of the liquor. "Knowing that, I want you to think about yourself now. Yourself and the children. I want you to do what is right for yourself and them."

"It doesn't matter. I don't care what other people say or do."

"Alexis, look at me."

"I don't care." She turned to him but her eyes, he saw, were blurred with tears. "I love you."

"You—" His face went cold. "You love me as I was, not as I am."

"You're my husband, the father of my children."

"See me as I *am,* Alexis, not as you *want* me to be!"

"I know what you are. It doesn't matter, we'll work it out."

"How? I am not the man you married, not any more. The life we've had up to now is finished."

"You were arrested for a little sex thing in a porno house. I—I forced you into that kind of place."

"It goes beyond what happened today."

"You're saying you want to be free to lead a bisexual life, aren't you?"

"I'm saying that the marriage we once had is over. If you stay with me, it will be different."

"Stay with you?" she turned to him, astonished.

"After this, our life is going to be different. I can't promise to love you as you need to be loved." He looked down at his hands. "Sexually, I mean. It may happen—from time to time. It may happen, but you can't depend on it. If you stay with me, I will care for you," he hesitated, searching for words, "I'll love you better than a friend. I'll provide for you and the kids." He cleared his throat, then said, "But you must do it knowing that I'm a homosexual." Neither of them moved. For a moment everything was still. There was only the distant, familiar sound of the grandfather clock in the foyer. Then his eyes filled. The tears clung to his lashes, dropped and ran down his cheeks. He watched her face, knowing its movements by heart.

"Alan." She made a small, open gesture with her hand.

He lowered his drink to the table, closed the space between them, and held her.

XIV

"**Y**ou're being destructive. It was bound to come out sooner or later," Phoebe caught up with her again, breathing harder this time.

"Four days after the arraignment? If Burt and Sally McGregor know, then"—she took a deep breath—"everybody knows!" They rounded the neck of sand. Thirty yards ahead, the long stone jetty separating Phoebe's section of the beach came into view.

"*So what?!*"

Alexis fixed her eyes on the jetty, determined to keep her jogging pace to the end of the stretch. She thought back to the humiliating moment an hour ago when she had arrived at Phoebe's Malibu beach house with the children and overheard the McGregors discussing Alan's arrest with another couple. She had taken the kids down to the beach at once and sat with them while they built a sand castle, too embarrassed and humiliated to join the others on the patio. She had known it would come, but not so soon or so suddenly.

"McGregor's a criminal lawyer. He was in court last Thursday," Phoebe said.

"And, of course, he told Sally."

"Oh, for God's sake."

"Who took herself right to the telephone." Alexis slowed as they approached the line of massive stones running across the beach into the sea. She drew up, felt her heart pound in her chest, and bent over to rest her hands on her knees.

"I'm sorry you were embarrassed," Phoebe said, panting.

"You said to bring the kids out to the beach for a quiet Sunday afternoon." She looked out angrily at the huge waves rolling over the jetty rocks. "You did *not* tell me everybody I knew in town would be here. Thank God Alan didn't come."

"He should have. It would do you both good to face this squarely." For a moment, they both looked out in silence at a sailboat offshore, straining its white sails in the wind. "What are you going to do?" Phoebe asked.

"What do you mean, what am I going to do?"

"You know very well what I mean." Phoebe adjusted the magenta silk scarf around her hair.

"I'm going on a diet and I'm going to lose every last inch of this bulge." Before Phoebe could say anything, she began walking back down the beach.

"Alexis."

"I don't want to talk about it."

Phoebe came up beside her. "For the last ten days, you've been acting like a goddamn martyr. What are you going to do, close yourself up with Alan in that new house and torture each other for the rest of your lives?"

"We'll manage."

"How? He's told you he wants to live as a homosexual, so where does that leave you?"

"Sex isn't everything." She looked away towards the line of expensive beach houses crowded one against the other. A hundred yards down the beach, Karen and Chris were playing with the other children on the edge of the surf.

"I only know one marriage that works without it; and that's because neither one wants it."

"We had sex eight days ago, and it was just fine," she started off at a slow, even trot.

"You're a fool, my dear." Phoebe caught up with her, "It's not going to work; you're deceiving yourself."

"Oh?" She increased her speed.

"You've had ten days." Phoebe moved up beside her. "Have you thought about twenty-five years?"

"I've known for six months. It's been going on for over a year now."

"What do you mean?"

"His first boyfriend died. Then, thanks to you, he found another one."

"What do you mean?"

"Stephen Milner."

Phoebe caught hold of her arm and pulled her to a halt. "I don't believe you."

"No?" Her anger now felt like triumph. "Then ask your friend Stephen. They met at Karen's birthday party last year." She turned and started off again. The surf rolled up and broke around her legs.

After a moment, Phoebe called after her, "You blame *me!* Is that what you're saying?!" The water splashing against her thighs was cold. She edged up the slope of the beach. She heard Phoebe's feet coming up behind her on the sand. "With or without Stephen," Phoebe's breath punctuated the air, "Alan is gay. It's not going to change. And you— if you try to hold onto him—you're going to destroy both yourself and him." Alexis kept her eyes on the kids ahead. She would collect them, get dressed, and leave. "Sooner or later, you're going to divorce him," Phoebe gained on her. Her hair had fallen loose from the scarf and was blowing over her face in the wind off the sea.

"Divorce is your answer to everything, isn't it?"

"Do it now. Divorce him, get what you can out of him, take the children, and make a life for yourself."

"I could get the new house, don't you think?" She looked down the beach towards Phoebe's quarter-of-a-million-dollar, two-story, raw-wood beach house, part of her settlement from Alistair, her second husband. "And a hefty allowance for the children. Alan is very generous."

"Listen to me!" Phoebe took her arm, pulled her back and faced her. "You're afraid to face the world on your own and you're using the children as an excuse!"

"Let me go!" She pulled free and stumbled backwards in the sand. Twenty yards down the beach, the adults watching the children turned to look in their direction.

"You're a child yourself! You've always been a child! You were a child ten years ago and you're *still* one! You don't need a husband, you need a *father!*"

"Damn you." She covered her face.

"You don't love Alan! You merely *need* him!"

"Shove it, Phoebe!" she shouted over the wind. Fifteen yards away, Karen, Chris, and four other children turned to look at them in amazement.

"Let go of him! Let go before it's too late!" Phoebe called after Alexis as she headed up the slope towards the children.

"Get your things," she said to Karen and Chris, reaching her towel and beach bag. They stood four yards away, staring at her. "Don't just stand there, do what I say!" she shouted, ignoring the nearby group of silent adults. With her towel and bag, she started towards the patio overlooking the beach. Behind her, the children hurried towards their things. She would have to pass through some thirty people in the patio and then through others in the living room. But it did not matter now. There was nothing more they could say about her or Alan. Now all she wanted was to be free of them all. Alan would be home with Aaron. She would make dinner, feed the baby, read for an hour and then sleep. She pushed open the low wooden gate and crossed the patio to the steps leading up to the living room. Several people turned to watch her pass.

"Hello there!" a familiar voice called. With her foot on the first step, she turned to see Giovanni Russo heading towards her across the patio. He looked even taller in a bathing suit than he had in clothes. A broad smile broke across his tanned Italian face. "You're not leaving, are you?" He came up, holding a drink in a plastic glass.

"As a matter of fact, I am." She looked towards the children making their way through the crowd.

"It looks great." He indicated her hair.

"Really? Do you think so?"

"Yes, I do." He started to lean on the banister next to her. "I think you look sexy with short hair."

"Frankly, at my age, Mr. Russo, I think I look rather infantile." She turned and started up the stairs.

"Tell me." He looked up at her directly in the eye. "Do you have something against me in particular or just men in general?" Karen, followed by Chris, reached the staircase, stopped, and looked up, puzzled.

"At the moment, let's just say people in general." She swung around and opened the door into Phoebe's living room. Inside, she paused long enough to scan the people grouped on the overstuffed chairs and then continued towards the hallway leading to the front door. Yes, that was it. Against people in general. Against people like the McGregors in the corner by the fireplace who had the complacent habit of dining off other people's misfortunes. Like the Malibu Meads and the Frasers and the Bonnets, smiling as they watched her retreat. She left the front door open for the kids and hurried down the walk towards the gate into the street. Yes, and against Alan, too, for having walled her off in a marriage without hope of physical warmth or any human gratification beyond what she could merit as a housewife and mother. She pushed the gate open and crossed the asphalt drive to her housewife's station wagon, opened the driver's door, threw her beach bag into the seat, got in, and slammed the door.

And more than all the rest, against herself for her blind, passive acceptance of her fate and her rejection of life. She was thirty-eight, ill-equipped to survive in the world on her own; and now, at this late date in life, too frightened to try. She had abnegated to Alan the power to choose for herself. Yes, Phoebe was right, she was afraid. Without Alan, she was nothing. All along, without knowing it, she had been weighing her worth on the scale of his good favor under the illusion that love was something merited by conscientious efforts to please. Like the gold, silver, and green stars on the children's report cards. Like the gold ones her mother had given her as a child for being a good little girl.

The children came through the gate. She saw in their small faces a look of wonder and confusion. She turned away, wondering how she could explain what they already knew but did not comprehend: that their mother, at heart, was a coward. Worse. She had reached that point where she needed to believe even her hairdresser's lies.

"I left the message on your service just before I scrubbed," Alan said, pulling up the knot of his tie in the locker room mirror. "I said I'd phone back. They shouldn't have sent you up here to surgery like that."

"They didn't." Stephen stepped into view behind him in the mirror. "I came on my own steam. I haven't seen you since the night of your arrest, and I haven't talked to you since the arraignment."

"It's easier this way. On both of us. Every time we see each other, it—" For the second time, from the far end of the corridor outside the doctors' locker room, there was the muffled sound of nurses' voices. Alan reached for his jacket in the locker and started towards Stephen leaning against the door. "Let's get out of here." This time, his embarrassment was outdistanced by anger.

Stephen stepped aside and held the door open for him to pass. "What's wrong, Alan? You look like you're going to explode."

He ignored the question, stepped into the corridor outside the operating rooms, and started towards the door leading out of surgery. Behind him, at the opposite end of the corridor, the two nurses arranging surgical instruments went silent. He knew, without looking, that they had turned to stare at Stephen and him.

"Christ, man, hold on. What's the hurry?" Stephen caught up with him as he started down the long hospital corridor towards the elevators.

Alan detoured around the question to the reason he had phoned in the first place. "The trial date's been set for July twentieth." He took a deep breath and kept his eyes dead ahead.

"That's a month away. Slow down."

"My lawyer will try to get the charge reduced to trespass or battery." He kept his pace, measuring the hundred-foot distance to the exit. It had happened twice before, two days ago in the elevator with two orderlies and then yesterday in the cafeteria with three nurses. The looks, the whispers.

"It's your first offense. He'll do it."

"Whether or not he does, there will be a hearing before the medical board of quality assurances on charges of moral turpitude."

"That's automatic. You have a good record as a surgeon. They'll put you on probation, if anything."

"And after that, a hospital hearing." Half an hour ago when he came out of the operating room, Alan had heard a joke running between the nurses around the bend in the corridor.

"Alan." Stephen took his arm and pulled him back. "You've known about this from the start. What's happened?"

He slowed down, but kept moving. "I phoned you before I went into surgery to ask a favor. I'm going to need witnesses for the defense at the trial. People from the hospital staff." The flush in his face, he realized, betrayed his anger.

"That goes without saying. You know I will."

"Think before you decide. People are going to talk."

"People already have. They've been talking about me for the last four years. Only they know it doesn't matter to me."

"You're real tough, Stephen. You always have been."

Stephen took his arm again and pulled him to a halt. "I know what's happened. Those nurses back in surgery." He swung him around to face him. "I saw the way they looked at us when we left."

Alan looked down vacantly at the carpet. "When I came out of surgery a while ago, they were talking about working with a closet queen on a vasectomy." He tried to look at Stephen but couldn't, feeling ashamed of his helpless retreat.

"Closet queen. Is that what they said?"

Alan nodded. His shame flowed back over his anger.

"You knew this was going to happen, didn't you?"

"Yes, I knew. But I told myself I was tough enough to handle it. I'm not. It would have been easier if I'd been charged with murder."

Stephen glanced towards the open door of an empty hospital room. "Alan," he reached up and touched his shoulder. "There's something I want to tell you. Alone." He motioned him into the room.

A moment later, facing the window of the room, Alan heard the door close behind Stephen. They had not been alone together, he realized, since the night of his arrest. The silence in the room made him feel curiously exposed. He stared down through the window at a group of nurses hurrying across the street on their lunch break.

"Alan," Stephen said from the far end of the room.

"I'm listening."

"Back in November when we met, I knew you were attracted to me. I knew why, too. Because, unlike you, I seemed to have it all pulled together. You thought it was tough of me to walk out on the jokes that afternoon at Karen's birthday party."

Alan looked up, surprised.

"I wouldn't have done that three years before. When I moved out here, I was in the closet. In my residency at Columbia, I was in the closet. Word got around, though. People found out that I was a homosexual and had a lover. When it got out, I panicked. I moved out here with George, in part to escape."

Alan turned to face him. "Why are you telling me this now?"

"Because you're making the same mistake I made. That first year with George, nobody here at the hospital knew about him. I made sure of that. I wanted my job and I was prepared to please. I kept George a secret for a year. I made him feel ashamed. Who wants to be called a lover at home and a buddy in public? He left me for Richard." Stephen came forward and stopped at the foot of the bed. He stared at him with a look of pain and loss. "Private self-contempt and loneliness are high prices to pay for the luxury of good public opinion."

"The problem is different for me." He looked away. "I have a wife and three children to live with."

"Is it Alexis or you who's decided you're a pathetic little fairy?"

He stared at the wall, silenced.

"Has she ever used it against you? As either a human being or a man?"

"No." He turned and locked eyes with Stephen. "She's trying to accept me as I am, but it's hard. I pulled the rug out from under everything for her."

"Maybe for a while. She's stronger than you think, Alan."

"She's stronger than she thinks, too," he said, thinking back to Sunday afternoon when she returned from Malibu with the kids and talked about facing their friends squarely with the truth. Behind her words, he had seen anger, not towards him but towards herself: "I've been living in the climate of other people's good opinion for thirty-eight years, Alan!" He moved a step towards Stephen and added, "On top of everything, she's beginning to put distance between us." His voice was faint and hoarse.

"Has she said something?"

"No. I don't think she looks at it as distance."

"And you're scared now, aren't you?"

He nodded. "I'm almost forty-one. I'm new to all this. I'm supposed to be married, and yet I'm supposed to be gay, too. Now, even publicly gay. Even single, I wouldn't know how to be gay."

"It's not a role. You don't have to *do* anything."

"That's not true. When I'm being my gay self, everything I do seems different."

"Maybe feels different."

"*Is* different. You know it is."

"The trigonometry is the same." Stephen smiled.

"Then what about you and your lover George? Like you, I can't picture myself showing up at a straight medical cocktail party with a male lover."

"Maybe what you need to begin with is a friend. A gay friend."

"Come to think of it, you were pretty good at that."

"I tried." Stephen's smile widened.

"You're right," he said, "the ends *are* ragged." He let the back of his fingers graze the nape of her neck. "I'll even it up and then shape it, how's that?"

"Fine." Alexis took a quick drag on her cigarette and stubbed it out in the ashtray on the counter in front of her. From where she sat on the kitchen stool, she could see him behind her, reflected in the plate-glass mirror on the opposite wall.

"Do you want it as short as before?" He was looking down at her head, smiling to himself. The bottom of his T-shirt had lifted, showing a dark ribbon of hair down the center of his stomach.

"No, just the ends, I think." She reached for her wine glass on the counter and swallowed what was left. She felt suddenly ridiculous. He had seen through her pretext from the beginning. He was playing with her.

"What's the big event?" he reached around and refilled her glass from the bottle in front of her.

"A party. My husband and I are going to a party." He had filled her glass twice before. She was getting drunk, her speech was slurred now. He knew it, she knew he knew it, and she didn't care. She would have to be drunk to go through with it.

"That's right. You've got a husband." He ran his comb along her part. "A surgeon, isn't he?"

"How did you know?"

"Phoebe told me."

"Of course. You were around that Sunday for the dissection." She reached for her wine glass again. As she sipped, he ran the comb across her head, slowly and gently. The touch of the comb's teeth against her scalp made her skin prickle.

"If you're referring to your husband's run-in with the law, yes, I know about that."

"Then you must know the McGregors."

"A lot of people were there talking, so what? Beverly Hills is a small town." He began combing her hair from the front backwards. In the mirror she could see the expression of playfulness in his face. "There are two topics people talk about in a small town, the price of property and each other. To tell you the truth, we weren't that interested in your husband. Now if he was a movie star and married, and then got himself arrested in a gay porno house, that's different."

"Are you going to cut it or comb it?"

"I'll comb for a while, then cut. You've got nice hair to comb, I can feel the electricity in it." He ran his palm across the top of her head. "Some women have voltage in their hair, some don't. I think yours is a little cross-circuited at the moment." He rested his left hand on her shoulder. She felt the flush start up her neck. "I can see where your anger is coming from. You woke up one day and discovered you were married to a gay." She sipped her wine, held the bitterness of it in her mouth for a moment, then swallowed. "So what do you do? Take out the whip and beat yourself; and when you've done that for a while, turn around and beat him." He moved his hand and squeezed the base of her neck gently. "Why don't you give it a rest?" His stomach pressed against her back. "By the way, what's your—?" He stopped but kept moving his fingers on her neck. For one instant, she thought he was going to ask her sign.

"My what?"

"Your deadline for getting out of here."

"I don't exactly have one," she heard herself say.

"Good. Then drink your drink while I tend to your hair." He went back to combing. It was a pointless activity, and they both knew it. His stomach against her back was warm.

"Stop pretending you're combing," she said.

He stopped combing and rested his right hand on her right shoulder. "Okay," he said.

"It was a pretext and you know it." She leaned back against him, letting her head fall against his chest, and felt suddenly light-headed.

"Did you think you needed a pretext?" He leaned over to kiss the top of her head.

"Yes. I've never done this before. And I'm frightened."

"Of *it* or yourself?"

"I don't know. Of both, I guess." Reflected in the mirror, his dark head came down again towards hers. This time, he kissed the side of her head over her ear. The arms encircling her from behind were gentle but powerful, dark-haired and tanned. A thought came to her as she watched him. "Tell me something," she said. A thrilling nervousness ran through her body as his arms closed around her.

"What?"

"Do you think you're as convincing in the flesh as Warren Beatty was in the film?" She recalled the night Alan took her to see *Shampoo*.

Above her, Giovanni chuckled, "I think I'm a little taller in the flesh." He drew the towel from her shoulders and dropped it on the floor, then moved around in front of her. Her eyes were level with his chest. She felt her heartbeat racing out of control. His hand lifted her chin. Tall as he was, he bent down and kissed her once on the edge of her lips, then opened his mouth and kissed her again, this time fully. She wanted the enveloping warmth of his body around her. Without separating her mouth, she edged off the stool and let him surround her body with his, vaguely astonished by the ease of this, her first encounter with adultery. In the first rush of excitement, she was unaware of how long they kissed before he drew back and said, "Let's go and get comfortable." She nodded and smiled and let him lead her by the hand into his bedroom. Silently, she let him unbutton her blouse and free her from it, let him take off her clothes, piece by piece, until she was entirely naked. His own clothes, jeans and a T-shirt, came off easily. As he moved towards her, erect, intent on her body, she wondered if he saw the little marks of age on her breasts and thighs. His arms closed around her and she felt contained and deliciously powerless against the warmth of his naked body. He lowered her to the bed and came down slowly over her. For a moment, again, she doubted the truth of his desire for her. He kissed her open-mouthed and with his tongue. She returned the kiss, still not sure of herself. He moved his body over and around hers, made small, feverish sounds as he kissed her mouth, her shoulders, her breasts. She felt the rigid pressure of his erection against her thighs and stomach, knew but could not fully yield to the fact that his pleasure was not faked. She began to explore the solid beauty of his muscular body with her hands, took his erection to feel its shape and reassuring hardness. Then he did something that startled and, at first, dismayed her: he turned face downward and entered her with his mouth and tongue. Alan had done it now and then, but this was different. This man, Giovanni, had lost himself in the pleasure of her body, the taste and odors of her flesh. She was aware suddenly of a strange feeling of freedom, and with it came a sense of joy and affirmation. He raised himself and looked at her. "You don't like oral stuff?" he asked and reached over to tickle the skin around her navel. The faint light through the blinds caught the moisture on his face around his smile.

"Yes." She turned to roll against him. "I do." She ran her fingers through the dark pubic hair and closed her hand around him. Somewhere far back in her mind something old and forgotten but familiar—a weight—seemed to lift. This time, she did not close her eyes or hesitate or feel ashamed as she so often had with Alan. She opened her mouth and yielded to her impulse to reciprocate.

An hour later, the full force of what she had done hit her as she stood naked before Giovanni's bathroom mirror, retouching her face with the makeup she had brought in her purse: in seventeen years of marriage, she had never had sex like that with Alan. Their sex had been good, god knows, but not like what she had just experienced. She stared at her own face for a moment as though seeing herself as a woman for the first time. Then she smiled and carefully evened out the line of her lipstick.

"Tomorrow? I'll phone you about that." Giovanni looked up and grinned at her as she came into the living room, digging in her purse for her checkbook. "Look, I've got to get off. I'll call you back later." He motioned for her to sit down. At the oak table by the door, she opened her checkbook and scribbled the word "cash" across the line, smiling to herself.

"Did you find everything you needed?" he asked.

"Oh, yes. Everything." She finished the check, tore it out, and placed it on the table.

"I put some cheese and stuff out in the kitchen in case—"

"I'm sorry." She turned to face him. "It's already after dinner time. I must go."

He started to draw her towards him. "But I thought you said—"

"Giovanni." She pressed her hand against his chest. "I *must* go. I'm sorry."

"Why don't you give yourself a break?" He concealed his surprise and deflated masculine pride behind a clumsy shrug.

"I did." She kissed him lightly on the chin. "And it was lovely, believe me."

"Is that *all?*"

"I have a husband and three children at home."

"So?"

"So Alan will be worried, the kids have to be fed, and the baby put to bed." She turned towards the door. "Everything will go on as before, you know that."

"What's *that?*" he pointed to the check.

"A check for the haircut," she smiled teasingly.

"Please."

She opened the door. "I insist." She looked back and smiled playfully at him. "It's part of the fantasy I had when I saw the film."

"The *what?*" he called after her as she walked down the apartment corridor.

It was 7:05 when she pulled into the carport. When she opened the back door and stepped into the laundry room, she paused to listen for voices. She had expected to hear Alan and the kids eating in the breakfast area. To her surprise, the house was silent. She ran her fingers through her hair, tried to assume a relaxed expression, and entered the kitchen. The breakfast table was littered with the chaotic remains of cheeseburgers, french fries, and soft drinks. Then from the direction of the backyard came the high-pitched squeals of the kids. She started towards the living room.

"Mom!" Chris shouted as she pushed open the glass door and stepped onto the patio. He was holding a glittering sparkler in his outstretched hand. A few feet away, Alan was lighting a sparkler for Karen. Nearby, Claire turned with a look of surprise. Alan glanced back at her and stood upright as Karen's sparkler ignited.

"What happened?" His face was a map of bewildered concern.

"I had errands to do." She moved calmly towards them. "By the time I finished, it was rush hour." She recalled the occasions Alan had returned with his rush-hour alibis.

"Look, mom!" Chris held his sparkler up. Karen merely stared at her, baffled by the reversed order of late returns.

"You had me worried," Alan said.

"I got caught in traffic." She touched Chris's head, "I see daddy got you hamburgers and sparklers."

"We got firecrackers, too," he said.

"I hope you got mommy a hamburger. I'm starved," she said for Alan's benefit but kept her gaze on Chris's sparkler.

"There's a cheeseburger and a chiliburger left, Mrs. Stegman," Claire said with a little uncertainty, "and a bag of french fries."

She had turned her story over in her mind on the way home and had settled on the simplest and most credible lie possible for a housewife: shopping and traffic. "A cheeseburger sounds divine."

"You should have called home," Alan said.

"How? I was in the middle of traffic." She smiled to herself, remembering the same words coming from his mouth, and turned towards the door into the living room.

"I'll go help mom," Alan said, "Now remember, two sparklers apiece. Otherwise you won't have any left for the fourth. Claire, you stay and watch them."

In the kitchen, she crossed to the sink on the pretext of washing her hands. The fourth. In two days it would be the Fourth of July. Sixteen days until the trial. This afternoon she had all but forgotten the trial.

"I waited till six-thirty." Alan came into the kitchen. "Then I went out and got hamburgers."

"I'm sorry, but there were things I had to do."

"Where did you shop?" he asked. She heard the testing note of doubt in his voice.

"Bullock's Wilshire, Robinson's," she said, then added for the sake of plausibility, "and Zody's over in Hollywood." She turned the water on full to forestall another question, aware that, like her, he needed only the sound of the voice to detect a lie.

"I'd say you got off pretty well, Alan. I gather they don't always reduce the charges to simple battery." Berrey put the match to his pipe and sucked in.

Jeff Marks, seated on Berrey's left, sat forward. "In fact, with judicial elections coming up in November, you were quite lucky. In an election year, judges tend to be a little harder on homosexuals than they are when—"

"Jeff," Berrey interrupted and chuckled. Marks glanced at him and went silent.

For a moment, Alan continued with the doodle he was making on his prescription pad of Marks's angular, ascetic-looking face. He drew in the wire-framed spectacles while he weighed his response. Berrey had said nothing about bringing Marks along to the meeting when he phoned that morning. So far, there had been no explanation; Berrey had done the talking. He looked up at Marks's keen gray eyes behind the thick spectacles. "I wasn't tried for being a homosexual, Jeff, I was tried for lewd conduct in a public place." He lowered the point of his pen to the pad to stop the nervous trembling in his hand.

"Let me come right to the point, Alan." Berrey shifted uncomfortably in his chair. "The criminal proceedings are over. You came off well there. On the other hand, the medical problems are just beginning." Alan began coloring in the dark, intensely alert pupils of Marks's eyes. "As you know, in a month or so, you face a hearing before the state board of medical quality assurances. Probably the first week of September." He paused for a reaction. Alan gave him none. "*Now,* depending on the outcome of that, you may also face a hearing before our hospital board on the question of your hospital privileges."

"There won't be a hospital hearing if they revoke my license," Alan said without looking up.

"I doubt they will do that. You have a very good medical record, Alan, you'll come off with a period of probation."

"On the other hand," Marks jumped in, "in the case of the hospital board, we think you might lose your privileges at West Hollywood General."

"*We?*" Alan fixed the oncologist with a puzzled stare.

"Dr. Marks here will be one of the physicians on the board that reviews your privileges, Alan," Berrey said tightly.

"I see," Alan scribbled in the tufts of gray hair over Marks's ears.

When the flash of ominous heat in his face had passed, he asked, "Lose my privileges? Why?"

"Jeff here was the oncologist for the follow-up therapy on a surgical case you assisted on last year, Alan. A young man by the name of Bradford Hollis."

"In the two months he was in therapy, and particularly in the last two weeks when he was hospitalized, you used to visit him pretty regularly," Marks said.

"He was a friend of mine." Alan wanted to look Marks in the eye but couldn't.

"Jeff believes that your relationship with Mr. Hollis went considerably further than friendship, Alan."

"On occasion, when I visited him in those last two weeks, Mr. Hollis used to confuse me with you," Marks cleared his throat, "On several occasions, he said rather embarrassing things. Homosexual talk, that kind of thing."

Alan felt the veins in his neck pulse against his shirt collar. Flushed, he looked up, caught hold of his anger before it exploded, and said, "People in the last stages of cancer have periods of delirium." He riveted Marks dead in the eye for a moment. "He was in delirium, deep delirium, and you know that, Dr. Marks. And if you intend to use the fact that Mr. Hollis confused you with me in a hospital hearing, you'd better have evidence for the conclusions you draw from that. Otherwise, I'll sue you for slander."

Marks glanced again at Berrey. His face was ashen now.

"Get to the point, Jeff," Berrey said impatiently, "we're not concerned with Mr. Hollis's delirium."

Marks picked at the twill on the arm of his chair for a moment, then said, "During July and August of last year, Mr. Hollis was an outpatient receiving regular chemotherapy and radiation treatments. At the beginning of September, he was admitted as an inpatient. During those two and a half months, you often visited Mr. Hollis in the radiation and oncology departments." Marks paused. Behind the glasses, his gray eyes jerked back and forth, nervously. He seemed aware that his little speech sounded stilted and prepared. "Especially during his last two weeks as an inpatient."

Berrey glanced at Marks and cleared his throat again, annoyed. "Dr. Marks complained to me at the time that you were exerting influence over his patient. The oncology and therapy departments are not in your sphere of activity."

"Towards the end, there was considerable talk among the staff about your relationship with Mr. Hollis." Marks got his second wind and went on. "Two of the nurses on my staff complained to me that the homosexual nature of your relationship was causing embarrassment to both patients and staff." He broke off abruptly.

The pen fell from Alan's fingers and struck the desk top.

"The point is," Berrey interjected, "West Hollywood General has very strict codes concerning the behavior of physicians and patients. Some of them fall under the heading of moral turpitude." Alan was only half listening to the deluge of words. He stared at the bookcase, counting off the battles he had waged in the last few years of Berrey's administration: nursing staff cutbacks, operating rooms closed down, the disastrous pharmaceutical contract.

". . . and the reason we're telling you this now, Alan," Berrey was saying, "in advance of the medical hearing, is to give you time to consider taking action yourself before the hospital is forced to act." His words sounded like pebbles bouncing across a stone floor. "A number of us at the hospital feel you could avoid a considerable amount of professional and personal embarrassment if you simply resigned."

Alan sat back in his chair in the silence that followed and waited. The warm summer sun slanting through his window made the brass letter opener look like hot gold on his desk. "This has nothing to do with moral turpitude or hospital policies, does it, Arnie?" he said finally, cutting through the silence.

Berrey's face colored. "We serve a normal, middle-class American community. There are other hospitals in the city where your problem won't be quite so visible."

"Or anything whatever to do with the fact that I'm a homosexual. It comes down to my view of patient health care versus your view of hospital profits, doesn't it?"

"Of course, no *reputable* hospital would grant privileges to a surgeon whose privileges had been revoked by another."

"For instance, to name but *one* of the cobs in your professional craw—the fact that I'm going to chair the committee that's going to force you to continue accepting nonpaying Medicare patients into the hospital."

Marks leaned forward to appeal. "Your chances of winning in a hearing are slim. You'd be a fool to fight it."

In the look of pathetic guilt in his face, Alan knew that the promotion Marks had always wanted to head of the oncology department was now assured. He kept silent, feeling his mouth go sour.

"Think it over, Alan." Berrey started to rise. "We're in no hurry. I know you've got other worries, the new house and all. There's plenty of time," he started towards the door as Marks rose to follow. Of course. The house. Alan thought of the hundreds of thousands that would have to be paid off. As usual, Berrey had worked out his plan in every detail. He watched the door to his office close behind them. His gaze came to rest on the brass letter opener. Berrey had once jokingly confided in him that his ultimate ambition was to return to Boston, his hometown, and take over the administration of the bigger, more prestigious Massachusetts General. For the first time in his life, Alan felt the raw, unrestrained desire to kill. Slowly, he stood up, turned his back to the door, and crossed to the window. He looked down at the single eucalyptus tree struggling up out of the small garden between the two buildings. Beyond the tree, suspended on a platform connected to the roof by ropes, two men stood listlessly washing the fifth-floor windows of the opposite building. Twenty years ago, in med school, he had dreamed of being a great surgeon by the time he was forty. He was a good, not a great surgeon, and the respect he had wanted as a young man really went no further than the day-to-day gratitude of his patients. All that was left of the dream was the day-to-day pleasure of success. He was tired now. It was enough.

There was the sound of his office door closing behind him. Donald came up beside him at the window. After a moment, he said, "I gather it was bad."

Alan nodded, watching a blue jay that was flying west into the sun turn into a tiny dark speck and vanish.

"I have a suggestion." He felt Donald's arm encircle his shoulder, felt his hand pull at him affectionately. "Let's close shop for the day, take my car, drive out to the coast, and have dinner. The two of us."

"Shhh." Alexis motioned to the kids standing behind her against the living room wall. Karen covered her mouth to suppress a giggle. Claire smiled and nudged her. Alan and Donald were in the kitchen now, talking. So far, he suspected nothing. Donald had phoned her twenty minutes ago from his office to say they were leaving. The plan was for them to stop by the house on the pretext of dropping off Alan's car before going on to Malibu.

"Where is everybody?" Alan said, moving through the dining room.

"Beats me," Donald replied. Alexis smiled to herself. Beside her, Chris wiggled excitedly. She glanced at the balloons and crepe-paper streamers the kids and Claire had hung around the room.

"Alexis?" Alan called. She recalled how she had insisted last year that they decorate the den; but this year, with the house sold, a little mess in the living room would not matter much.

"Alexis!" Alan called, approaching the foyer.

The first thing he would see would be Karen's fastidiously cut paper sign saying "Happy Birthday Daddy." Last year, it had been a crooked crayon drawing.

"*Alexis!*" Alan called again, worried now, and turned from the foyer into the living room.

On cue, she, Karen, Chris, and Claire stepped from behind the wall as Alan and Donald came through the archway and halted. "Surprise!" they shouted in unison. Alan stared at the decorations and presents, speechless. "Happy"—Alexis began the song, and the kids, Claire, and Donald joined in—"birthday to you! Happy birthday to you! Happy birthday dear daddy!" ("Alan!" Donald sang, and Claire trailed behind with "Doctor Stegman!") "Happy birthday to you!" There was a burst of applause, laughter, and shouts from the kids. Alan stood paralyzed, his face blank with shock.

"It worked!" Donald exclaimed.

"He didn't suspect a thing!" Claire cried.

"Alan," Alexis moved towards him laughing, as the kids pulled at his arms screaming, "We did it! Mom, we did it! He didn't know *anything!*" In his crib across the room, Aaron began to cry. Alexis kissed Alan. "Didn't you even *suspect?*"

"Nothing!"

"He didn't even know it was his birthday!" Donald laughed.

"I forgot." He shook his head and hugged her, "I completely forgot."

"This morning at breakfast I almost let it slip!" Claire said.

"Daddy! Come on! Come look at your presents! We've got a cake, too!" Karen and Chris tugged at his arms and led him to the table where the cake and presents were laid out.

Under the pleasure in his face, Alexis saw a look of intense strain and exhaustion. She caught Donald's eye and crossed to him. "He looks worried. What happened?" she said softly under the noise.

"He'll tell you later." Donald put his arm around her shoulder as they started towards Alan.

"This one's mine to you!" Karen held up the box she had wrapped.

"And this one's mine!" Chris handed Alan his present.

"And who made this chocolate cake?" Alan grinned.

"Claire did the cake," Alexis said, "And it's solid homemade chocolate."

Alan read the sign taped to the wall over the table. "I know who did this." He ruffled Karen's hair.

"She cut it out herself!" Chris exclaimed.

"Look at him," Alexis laughed, "he's like a five-year-old!"

"I can't believe it!" Alan shook his head, still recovering from the surprise. "I completely forgot!"

Small wonder, Alexis thought to herself and exchanged a knowing glance with Donald. "What do you want to do first, eat dinner or open presents?"

"The presents! Do the presents first!" the kids shouted.

"Presents first." He winked at her, "I can't sit through dinner in suspense. "Okay." He picked up both boxes. "Which one is first?"

Chris caught Alexis's eye and grinned. "Mom's. Mom's present first."

"Mom's going to do hers first," Karen said.

"Okay." Alan looked at the table with only the cake on it. "Mom's is first."

"I'm afraid it's not gift-wrapped," Alexis smiled.

"It's not something you can see, taste, touch, or smell, either, Doctor Stegman," Claire announced proudly.

"You have to sit down for it, daddy." Karen took his hand. "Over here." She pulled him towards the sofa. Chris, Claire, and Donald followed. Alan glanced at her, puzzled and amused. Alexis turned to the piano and quickly took out the sheet music from the bench. Out of the corner of her eye she saw Alan's expression of surprise as he sat down. She had hoped to do it from memory, but time had not allowed that. She opened the pages on the stand and sat down. Her fingers felt stiff. It would be good but not great. There hadn't been enough time to practice thoroughly in the last week. On the sofa, Alan took Aaron from Claire and began rocking him. Alexis waited for the crying to subside as it always did when Alan rocked him. She thought back to Alan's last birthday, when she had announced her pregnancy to him at Ma Maison. That was the day he had operated on his friend, Bradford. Alexis glanced towards Alan and smiled again. Only recently, he had accidentally found a photo of Bradford taken a few months before he died and had showed it to her. Bradford had been a handsome man, she thought, and virile-looking. Strange, she thought to herself, in the last year so much had happened to them both, so much had changed. Across the room, Aaron gave two feeble cries of complaint, then chortled and was silent. She looked at Alan. In his smile, she saw a glow of pride. With her hands over the keys, she read the first few bars of music to remind herself. It was a small gift, almost foolish, and even a little corny as the world might see it. But it was something entirely her own, and Alan would understand that. She struck the opening chords of Copland's Piano Fantasy.

There was a shudder, and with it a deep groan from far down in the earth under the hill. He watched it, the long zigzag crack opening in the concrete above him. The earth moved again, pushing against the retaining wall. The crack widened further. Dirt and small stones spilled out and rattled down the concrete face.

"Alan—!" She was far away, somewhere out in the darkness, beyond reach.

Then another shudder. It was coming down, the wall, all of it. Coming down on him. His feet went up and down, making a sucking noise in the muck. They would not come out.

"Alan!" *She sounded closer.*

The crack widened, and the rumbling ground poured through it. He raised his hands and opened his mouth to scream. Nothing came out.

"Alan!" *There was a hand on his shoulder, shaking him.*

Alan sat up, opened his eyes, and blinked. He was not sure where he was. Then he saw the bedroom in the darkness. She was beside him on the bed, her hand on his shoulder, stroking him. He breathed in, relieved.

"Honey, you were dreaming."

"Yes."

"Are you okay now?"

"I'm okay. Thanks." He lay back down and breathed in again, deeply. "I'm sorry I woke you up."

"You were having a nightmare." She stretched out beside him.

"About the wall. I was dreaming about the retaining wall. It broke and the hill came down."

"Alan." She rested her hand on his chest. "The retaining wall is up. It's dry. It's not going to come down."

"I know."

She ran her hand across his chest, ruffling the hair, "It's the hearing the day after tomorrow. That's what you were dreaming about."

"A lot depends on it."

"You're still worried they're going to question you about your private life, aren't you?"

"There's a lot they can ask."

"The hearing concerns your professional life. Your private life is something else. It doesn't concern them." She kissed his shoulder and moved closer, putting her arms around him.

"I know. I wish I believed it."

"You're a good surgeon. You're so good, you're almost stuffy. They'll like that." She rested her chin on his shoulder in the crook of his neck.

"I wish you could be there. In the front row. I could use your testimony."

"It's better this way. It's time you fought for yourself."

In the last few weeks, her encouragements sometimes made him feel close to her, sometimes made him feel distant and apart. He could never quite decide which. He turned onto his side and pulled her into him under his arm. "I need you, you know that."

"I know." She ran the tips of her fingers down his back. "I only wish we needed each other in the same way."

"Alexis, will you please stop for a moment!" Her mother followed her around the northwest corner of the house.

"Look." She turned a few yards from where two workmen were recalking the panes in the kitchen windows. "I will not argue with you about this. We've got twenty workmen up here this afternoon, and I've got things to do! The answer is *no!* Okay?" She turned towards the workmen. "Now that's much better. I noticed a few places in the bedroom windows where the rain did the same thing. I think they need recalking as well."

"Yes, ma'am," the older, craggy-faced workman said.

"Honey, I think we ought to let Alexis get on with her work," her father said, following them around the side of the house.

"We'll go in a minute, Christopher." Helen continued behind her towards the back door leading into the kitchen. Exasperated, Alexis scraped the mud from her tennis shoe and stepped into the newly painted kitchen. The warm yellow paint on the walls glistened here and there where it was still damp. She passed the area where the built-in stove, oven, dishwasher, and refrigerator would soon be installed and went into the breakfast area, overlooking the terraced back end of the lot through broad, sliding glass doors. The yellow Alan had chosen gave the room a soft, rich glow, perhaps a little too warm for such a hot late-September afternoon, but with plants, maybe—

"Your father and I finished lunch early, and we merely drove up to—"

"I know exactly why you came up; you found out this morning the results of Alan's medical board hearing."

"We had hoped after the trial that that would be the end of it."

"Six months' probation? I think he came off rather well."

"It's turning into a public scandal, Alexis."

The workmen laying the bricks in the terrace around the pool were leaving splotches of wet cement on the bricks. She would have to speak to Gruber about that. "As a matter of fact," she turned and headed towards the dining room. "You can prepare yourself now. There will be a second hearing. Before the hospital board."

Helen's audible sigh followed her. "Then you must listen to your father and me."

"I haven't the slightest intention of leaving Alan alone at *this* point."

"We were merely suggesting that you take the children and Claire and go away for a while. Until after this mess is cleared up. You really owe it to the children."

The raw plaster on the dining-room walls would have to wait for paint until Gruber replaced the four hardwood boards in the floor discolored by the roof leak in July. "Owe it to the children or to you, mother?"

"For once, Alexis, be sensible." Helen's voice ricocheted off the bare walls. "Take the children up to the house in Tahoe until Alan has finished with these hearings. You cannot allow three small children to get mixed up in this."

"I detest the Tahoe house, I always have. Besides, we have this one to finish."

"For heaven's sake, the man is *sick*. You can't subject the children to that kind of influence."

"Now Helen," her father cautioned from the far side of the room.

"Actually in my opinion, mother, Alan is healthier now than he's been for the entire last year." She crossed to the window and ran her finger through the plaster dust on the sill.

"I assume you know what people are saying about you both," Helen said in a measured voice.

"Yes." She turned to face her mother, who stood in the center of the large, empty room. "They're saying 'poor Alexis Stegman, she finally woke up after seventeen years of marriage to the fact that her husband is a homosexual. And now, poor thing, she's stuck with the bastard for life.' "

"That's enough, young lady." Her mother stepped forward.

"At the hospital, Alan is treated like a social leper." She contained a rush of anger. "Not by everyone, thank God, but by some. I know very well what's going on around us, mother, and I will not be brought down by"—her anger broke free as she started towards the living room—"by *squalid little people!*"

Halfway across the living room, her mother caught up with her. "Have you lost your mind?!"

"Now Helen, let's not lose our heads," her father cautioned, following.

"Aside from the public disgrace and the fact that he's facing professional ruin, you have two small sons and a daughter to consider! Do you want them to grow up under the influence of that kind of man for a father?"

Alexis spun around, "What do you mean, *that* kind of man?"

"You know what I mean."

"You mean he's one of *those* people, as you call them!" Helen's face hardened with indignation. "The word is 'homosexual,' mother! And the person you're referring to happens to be the man I've lived with for seventeen years! He happens to be a loving, generous, and responsible father! I don't *enjoy* his being a homosexual, but that's what he is, and I have to live with it! And as far as the children are concerned, they will just have to come up with a little more understanding and loyalty than most!" Again, she started off, this time towards the corridor leading into the bedrooms and nursery. As she passed her father, he looked down at the floor, red-faced and ashamed.

"Now, Helen," he said, "let's discuss this when—"

"I want to talk to her *now!* Before the damage is done, Christopher! Before it's *too late!*" Her mother's voice echoed through the empty house. Alexis moved quickly down the long white corridor, leaving behind the muddled echo of her mother's strident and her father's cajoling voices. As a child, it had confused and saddened her to watch her father succumb time and again to Helen's crushing emasculation. Now, after forty years, even though the battles were already lost before they were fought, they still went through them. The war was as old as their marriage, and they waged it comfortably now, without even knowing they were fighting, merely out of habit.

The master bedroom. She stood just inside the door and scanned the rich terra-cotta-colored walls.

". . . have them brought up under the influence of *that man!*" Helen's voice rose over Christopher's. The determined sound of her heels approached down the hardwood corridor floor.

Alexis crossed the bedroom, surveying the terra-cotta walls and the freshly painted, white-enameled woodwork. This room, more than the others, they had planned down to the smallest detail: down to the huge Bokhara rug they had bought back in April. The room was their space, entirely separate from the children. She stopped where the bed would go and looked down at the floor. Whatever she had forced her mind to accept, the painful truth was that the body and heart would not let go. Not that easily. The memory of what was and the thought of what could have been still held her back, pulled her down; and the aching loss of his body and heart together, the whole of Alan, filled her with panic, fear, and emptiness. In time, she would force herself to let go of him; in time, she would learn to be alone.

"I beg you, Alexis. Please listen to me." Her mother's earnest plea filled the bare room.

"We're only trying to help you," her father added.

"You have your children and yourself to think of first," Helen continued towards her across the room.

"Exactly. That's what I'm doing."

"If you choose to throw away the best part of your life on a man who can provide you with little more than a roof over your head—and that's doubtful—it's your business. But the kind of home you provide for your children is another matter."

"I think the Bokhara we bought will look lovely with the terra cotta."

"Listen to me, young woman." Helen came around to face her.

"I have done that, mother, for the better part of thirty-eight years! I am not a young woman any more!"

"You two lower your voices," Christopher said.

"For God's sake, daddy, say something of your own for once or shut up!" She turned to Helen, "What do you suggest I do, divorce him?!"

"I did not say that."

"Then what? Go off to Tahoe on a permanent vacation?"

"Do one thing at a time. Take the children away until the hearing is over."

"*Then* what?! We're still married, he's still my husband and their father!"

"Separate. Make a life for yourself and your children." She hesitated. "Eventually, there's every chance you could get an annulment."

"An *annulment?!*"

"Divorce is out of the question. You're a Catholic. Your father and I talked the matter over with Monsignor Driscoll."

"You did *what?!*"

"Monsignor Driscoll says an annulment is quite possible."

"You mean, you and daddy will pull strings in Rome, on the basis of the fact that Alan is a Jew!"

"Based on the fact that you were not married in the Church to begin with."

"You were against my marriage to Alan in *or* out of the Church!"

Helen lifted her chin indignantly. "That you've thrown away your religion as well as your life is not really at issue here."

"We came here, honey, to offer our help," Christopher ventured from across the room.

"Offer it or impose it on me? Mother is still under the impression that I'm sixteen years old!"

"I think you're naive and childish, yes. I do."

"If I'm naive and childish at thirty-eight, it's because you've been sitting on my face for thirty-eight years!"

"I think your language is uncalled for."

"Then leave! In the first place, nobody invited you here this afternoon! You came to meddle under your own steam, and I will not have it!"

"In that case, we're wasting our time." Helen started towards Christopher. "We might as well go, dear."

"The truth is, mother, you've hated Alan from the beginning! You hated him the first time I brought him to the house! You burned the roast out of spite that night he came to dinner."

"Now, Alexis." Her father, caught between them, made a lame gesture of appeal.

"Forget it, daddy! It's too late. You've let her do your thinking for you too long." She walked slowly towards the two of them, unable now to hold down what came rushing up inside her, what she had harbored in silence for years. "Eighteen years ago I fell in love with Alan, and I married him. You have never forgiven me for that disappointment, have you? When I had his children, you managed to swallow your disgust; oh yes, you even managed to love the children in your way, but you hated their father. In the end, you were forced to tolerate what you could not change or control. Why don't you admit it—you've been waiting for this marriage to fail all along, haven't you?" She caught her mother's stricken gaze, held it for a moment, then averted her face towards the window. "In your heart, you despised Alan as a Jew to begin with, and now it must be doubly satisfying to despise him as a queer as well." Her tongue felt thick in her throat. "You must feel terrific now, telling yourself you were right all along." The sunlight through the window doubled the sting in her eyes.

"Alexis," her father's voice sank.

"In the future, if Alan and I decide to separate or divorce, it will not be because he is a homosexual or because of the children. It will not be for any of the reasons you might think."

"Christopher," her mother said, "let's go. I have nothing more to say to her."

"You go to the car," he said quietly, "I'll be along in a minute." Her mother's footsteps sounded small on the corridor floor.

"I'm sorry, daddy, but it had to be said. It's been a long time coming."

"I just want you to be happy." He came up beside her.

"I will be. But it has to be on my own terms. Not yours or mother's or even Alan's. It will take a long time to heal this wound."

He turned her towards him and embraced her. The warm, supportive, caring kind of embrace she had known as a child. "I understand. You go ahead and do what you have to do."

"Yes." She drew back, "I will, daddy. Slowly, a little at a time."

She watched him go, listening to the squeak of his crepe soles. There was a curious feeling of hurt and sorrow now, as though something she had missed in childhood long ago was now lost for good, beyond recovery. She turned to the window and looked out towards the front drive. Her mother sat waiting in the passenger seat of the car. She looked surprisingly small in the huge black Cadillac. Her father came out the front door, walked slump-shouldered around the back of the car, and got in. His hair was white in the afternoon sunlight. Seated together, they looked for all the world like what she knew they were not: two happy, comfortably rich old people whiling away their autumn years with an afternoon drive.

At least, if nothing else, she and Alan would not be living out their lives maintaining the fallacy of appearances.

XV

"Where to?"

"Anywhere."

He veered to the left lane and prepared to turn from Benedict Canyon Drive into Sunset Boulevard. "They finished the electrical work yesterday. Want to drive up and see it?"

"I'd rather not go to the house. Let's just drive for a while."

"Okay." He maneuvered back into the right lane. "Whatever you say." As he swung right onto Sunset, he glanced at her profile. The tension was still there. A half hour before, while he was reading in his study, she had come in to ask if they could take a drive together, alone. By the look in her face, he knew she had something important to tell him. She was tense. As usual, the Sunday afternoon Beverly Hills traffic was slow, mostly families and couples taking drives. He kept to the far right-hand lane and edged up behind a blue Pontiac carrying a young couple with two children. The children, kneeling backwards on the passenger seat, stared at them through the rearview window. "They put the white fixture in Karen's room and the blue one in Chris's," he said to make conversation, "but I don't know which ones to use in the nursery or the study." In the last few weeks, she had given over the last decorating decisions to him: the choice of ceiling fixtures, the choice of colors for the children's bedrooms and the nursery.

"You like the brass lamp in your study now," she said, looking out towards the stately line of mansions along Sunset. "Why not brass in the study? It would look fine with the walnut paneling."

"You hate brass."

"Some brass, not all."

"You don't like the lamp in my study now," he said testily.

"It's your study, Alan. I think you should have what you want."

He swung into the left lane to pass the blue Pontiac. She was avoiding the issue again. In the last few weeks, he had felt threatened by her newfound independence. Far back in his mind, an alert had been sounded, but he had chosen to keep silent. "The children's rooms are not mine, Alexis. The living room and kitchen are not mine. Why are you leaving all this up to me now?" He pressed on the accelerator and started up the slope of the first hill leading into Bel Air. She opened her purse and took out a cigarette, but did not reply. "The escrow on the old house is going to close on the first of October. The Altounians want to move in on the second. That gives us a little over two weeks to finish. You know I've got lousy taste; so why, for the last three weeks, have I been the one to pick out fixtures and paint colors?" He had the sudden and unnerving premonition that they were not going to argue about paint and fixtures at all.

"Because"—she lit the cigarette and blew out a jet of smoke— "it's time you made choices for yourself."

"What do you mean—choices?" He edged to the right, looking for an opening in the two-lane traffic, but both lanes were congested. Choices—he knew she did not mean paint and fixtures, or even the house itself.

"Alan," she gripped the support handle to brace herself as they started around the first slope of an S-curve, "there's something I have to tell you. Now."

"What?"

On the left swing of the S-curve she said, "I think you know." The alarm that went off in his brain sounded through his entire body.

"Know what?" he asked, stalling for time he knew had already run out.

"I think we should separate, Alan." She sat back against the seat rigidly. The bright afternoon sunlight was lost momentarily behind the dense eucalyptus and fir trees on their left. He let go of the accelerator. The car slowed on the steep grading of the slope. He repeated her words silently, staring at the faces of the children in the blue Pontiac as they passed, waving and laughing.

"Alan." She took hold of his arm. He realized the car was coming to a dead halt with traffic behind them, but he could not move his foot to accelerate. "Alan!" She shook his arm. He turned the wheel and rolled to a stop against the street curb. Out of habit, he pressed down on the clutch and braked. For a long while, they sat on their separate sides of the car, silent. He had known she was debating with herself, had felt her restless detachment when they were together, had told himself time and again that the debate would end sometime in the far-off future, long after they had moved into the new house, long after the hearings. One, two, or three years from now, when they had grown comfortable with the idea.

"Why?" he heard himself ask hoarsely.

"It's finished, Alan. We're just pretending."

"Why now? *Why now?!*" he broke in, but his voice died away. "Why so soon?"

"Because I am in love with you in a way you are not and never will be with me. And living with you like this is a torture. I will not move into the new house with you. I can't. If I move into that house, I will never leave it. It will begin all over again, and I will never leave."

"We don't have to move."

"Alan—I've been a wife and a mother for you and the kids for seventeen years! I cannot go on living with you as a *sister* for the rest of my life!"

"We'll postpone the move. I'll rent a place," he said numbly.

"It's already happened, Alan! We can't postpone what's already happened!"

Separate. He took the thought to its logical conclusion, but pushed the result away and said, "You could have waited until after the hearing."

"No." She covered her face with her hand. "You've got to do it on your own. I can't defend you anymore, not against yourself. You've got to fight for yourself now. No one will know, only you and I."

Despite the noise of the cars passing there was dead stillness in the car. "Know what?" he asked shakily. She began to cry softly. "In other words, you want a divorce, too," he said. She put both hands on her face and bent forward. He released the brake and accelerated slowly, squeezing left into the traffic moving up the hill. He thought back helplessly through the past few weeks. She had left clues. He had blocked them out of his mind. She had been quietly planning her moves all along—withdraw, separate, and then divorce. Her encouragement before the last hearing had the bitter taste of betrayal in it now. He glanced at her. She was sitting upright, staring vacantly through the windshield.

"For the time being, no one will know. Until the hearing is over, I will be on a holiday with the children. I will arrange to move you into the new house. When I come back, I will stay in Malibu at Phoebe's house. No one need know we've separated except you and I. In time, people will accept the fact."

Alan kept his eyes on the car waiting beside them at the light on the corner of Sunset and Beverly Glen Boulevard. In the station wagon was a young woman with four small children, two boys and two girls. The little girl in the front passenger seat, barely tall enough to see through the window, was looking at him impassively. Karen, Chris, Aaron—he had imagined what it would be like to live without them but had never thought it would happen so soon, while they were so small. Aaron hardly knew him. Alan could tell, without seeing her mouth, that the little girl in the car next to him was smiling. He turned away, felt his eyes fill, and gunned the accelerator as the light turned green. After a moment, he said, "The children. What about them?" She had all the artillery on her side, he realized, but he had to fight for something.

"They're yours as much as mine."

"They can't live with both of us." He swallowed thickly.

"I know that, Alan. We can come to an agreement. We can consider what's best for them and come to an agreement."

"What's best for them is having two parents."

"We can't give them what we haven't got. What's left of our marriage isn't enough to raise children on. They would hate us for it."

"Then it's a foregone conclusion." His voice sounded small now. "No court is going to give a homosexual custody of his children."

"*Please*, Alan!" she began to cry again, "I won't fight you for them! They're yours as much as mine!"

He had known all along what would be best for them. He could give them love and support and protection, surround them with the security of a seven-hundred-thousand-dollar Beverly Hills house, educate them, feed and clothe them, be with them in the evenings and through the nights. He could give them everything they needed except his own belief in himself as a man. That kind of stability. In time maybe, but not now. He accelerated, passing the intersection at Hilgard, and started down the hill bordering the UCLA campus, coasting at fifty.

"*Please*, Alan," she put her hand against the dashboard as they rounded the curve at the bottom.

They would grow up remembering him as the man who *had been* their father. They would never really know or believe that he had loved them more than himself or the entire world put together. They would know him only as the man who provided things from a distance. They started up the long slope leading to the western gates of Bel Air. She had fired off her guns and blown away their marriage and their children. He was now left with only hurt, anger, and a feeling of rejection as sharp as a scalpel's passage through an unanesthetized nerve. "Have you met someone else?" The wound of her rejection bled through as jealousy now. "Is that what's behind this?"

"Oh, Alan," her voice sank, "I wish it were as simple as that."

"If what's missing between us is sex, you can find that easy enough on the side."

"It isn't just sex that's missing."

He thought of the long period between Stephen's departure and his arrest, the emptiness of sex in those long weeks. He pushed that thought away and flailed out wildly, "How do you *know?!* You could give it a try!"

"I did that, Alan. I tried back in July with my hairdresser. It wasn't enough. I don't want sex without love."

The shock left him open-mouthed and speechless for a moment. They passed the ornate white stone western gates of Bel Air. "I don't . . . I don't believe you."

"Ten months ago, I didn't believe you, either. For months, I didn't believe what was right in front of my nose." She lowered her face and touched her forehead with her fingers. "I know what you're feeling now. Rejection hurts. But just remember, you're not the first." Next to him, he heard a faint repressed sound come from her mouth. Her pain went through him and left him with a feeling of nakedness and shame. Silent. He let the car coast down the curving slope between the rows of neat, middle-class, family-style houses and tidy lawns. Ahead, beyond the San Diego Freeway running north and south through the Santa Monica mountains, the afternoon sun was just dipping behind the crest of a jagged, treeless hill.

They had preeempted each other, they were at a standstill. He veered right off Sunset down the exit ramp. Her hairdresser. He could not believe it. But then had she not found it hard to believe he was sleeping with men? Her *hairdresser.*

He turned up the entrance ramp into the northbound traffic, tried to summon up a feeling of jealousy, but came up only with shame. She had spent almost two years with his rejection. Maybe—maybe if they tried one more time, if he made changes; if he always, whenever the other need arose, kept his need and love of her in mind—maybe he could make it work again. "Stay. I'll do anything you want," he said, knowing it wouldn't work.

"I've spent the last year and a half trying to force you to *do* what I want. It isn't a question of *doing* anything."

"I love you. Maybe it's not the kind of love you married me for, but it's—" He wanted to say it was more love than most people could hope for in a lifetime of marriage, but could not—"but it's everything I've got!" he said.

"I know that!" Her voice was shaking. "I wish to God it was enough! Every night I lie in bed with you, I lie there wishing it was enough! I cannot force you to be what you are not, Alan!" She started weeping, openly now.

Her voice had carried over the noise of the freeway through the open windows. In an old Chevrolet Impala riding alongside them, three teenagers, two boys and a girl jammed into the front seat, looked through the driver's window at Alexis and laughed. Alan sped up and swerved into the lane in front of them. They were on the downward slope of the hill now, heading into the San Fernando Valley below. With the added acceleration, he was now doing seventy-five. The Impala was directly behind him, keeping pace. The three kids were laughing. He looked away from the rearview mirror. A hundred times he had told himself: *this time things will change.* They had not. He had begun with sex and emotional infatuation and had ended with sex and love. Had it been with a woman, Alexis might have held on and fought back.

In the rearview mirror, he caught sight of the Impala pulling up alongside them in the right lane. The three young faces were grinning. He looked ahead, held his speed at seventy-five, and thought how simple life is for the young.

"Sometimes, when you fall asleep, I lie there hating you for not being what I want you to be!" Alexis went on, oblivious of the car alongside them.

"Give him hell, lady!" the driver of the Impala called out and laughed. With his black hair combed back in a punk fifties imitation, his tough, crude face looked complacently stupid. Startled, Alexis glanced at the three laughing teenagers, then averted her head towards Alan.

"Come on, man! Have a heart!" the driver shouted.

Alan reached up, shoved the air with his middle finger, floored the accelerator, and left the Impala lumbering behind. He took hold of Alexis's hand.

"It doesn't matter."

Again they did not speak for a long while. He took the Ventura cutoff from the San Diego Freeway and turned east.

"It's getting late. Let's go home," she said.

"I am."

He drove in silence, holding her hand when the road permitted. From the Valley to the Los Angeles side of the hills, the road climbed through a deep ravine towards Mulholland Drive at the summit. On the last hairpin curve, the entire San Fernando Valley came into view behind them, a flat checkerboard of shopping centers and tract houses stretching northwards towards the Santa Susana and San Gabriel mountains. He had last seen the Valley from this height the afternoon he and Stephen took a drive in Stephen's new sportscar. The afternoon he first kissed him. Now, through the noxious, ochre-colored layer of pollution, the landscape looked desolate and overcrowded. At the top of the hill he slowed for the intersection. "Please wait. If for no other reason—because I need you now." With a feeling of panic, he mentally calculated the distance between here and Benedict Canyon. They would be home in five minutes. He felt like a man counting out the last seconds of his life before a firing squad.

Alexis looked down silently and crumpled the empty cigarette pack in her hand. The light went green.

Alan turned left onto Mulholland and started east across the summit of the hills. "If for no other reason—because I depend on you. I always have. It's my nature." A quarter of a mile down the road, he saw the turnoff into Benedict Canyon. She took a Kleenex from her purse and wiped her eyes, still said nothing. "And because I'm scared shitless of what's ahead for me." He eased up on the accelerator. If he did not turn off into Benedict Canyon, they could drive on to Coldwater Canyon ahead. They could drive by and look at the house: she would see it and realize all the good things they had planned.

"I was with you for the first hearing; but you won that one because of what and who you are, not because you fought for the right to be a physician who happens to be a homosexual. I'll be with you in spirit for the second one; but this time, you'll have to believe in and fight for *yourself*."

He let the car roll to a stop at the junction of Mulholland and Benedict Canyon. "We could take a few minutes and go on to Coldwater if you want," he said quietly.

"No, Alan. I don't need to see the house now."

"I'm not scared of Arnold Berrey's hearing, I'm scared of what comes afterwards." He held onto the steering wheel, hating but yielding to his admission, for it was the only appeal left for him to make, "I'm scared of the world. I'm forty-one years old. I've lived in a straight world for forty of those years. And now I'm supposed to live in the gay one. I don't know that world. I'm afraid to learn it. I'm too old and too conservative to be comfortable in it. I don't belong in either world. And if you leave me, I'll—I'll be alone."

It was quite still in the car. She looked up. "With or without me, you would be alone. You'll be alone until you find a way to love yourself again. Not for what you think the world might like you to be. I don't mean that. I mean, love yourself for the gifts you have and the man you *are*."

"They finished bricking the drive yesterday." He tried to sound hopeful. "You haven't seen how beautiful it looks."

"I love you. I will always love you, but it's finished. Let's go home now." She reached over and gently covered his hand on the steering wheel.

"Daddy says there are lots and lots of seals in the ocean, and they come out and sit on the beach with the people," Karen said.

Alan chuckled, "Well not exactly with the people. The coast of northern California isn't like ours. It's mostly cliffs and rocks. During the day, the seals come out and sit on the rocks to sun themselves."

"Can we play with them?" Chris asked.

Alexis touched the Pyrex coffee pot to see if it was still warm enough, glanced at Alan and smiled.

"No, they're wild. But you can walk down close and look at them. Mom's promised to take lots of pictures of you for me. You and the seals." He looked at her.

"Will you, mom?" Karen asked.

"Of course." She held his eye encouragingly for a moment. "I'm going to put the whole trip on film for dad." By this time tomorrow, she, the children, and Claire would be having dinner at the inn in Mendocino. It would be strange, that first dinner without him.

"Are there shells on the beach?" Chris asked.

"Whoever heard of a beach without shells?" Alan said.

"I'm going to collect a lot of shells for my new room. I'm going to bring some for you, too, daddy," Karen announced.

"I'd like some shells for my room too." He glanced again across the table.

"Coffee?" Alexis reached for the pot.

"A little." He held up his cup. On the delicate matter of when and where to tell the kids, they had both agreed that it should be later and a little at a time. She would take them on a week's holiday while the movers were working. In the excitement of travel and new surroundings, she would find a way to tell them they were not going to return to the new house. They would go on having their holiday in Phoebe's house in Malibu. "Thanks," Alan said. She returned the pot to the table. In the weeks since she had asked for the separation, they had masterminded a plan that would keep their decision to separate and eventually divorce a secret from everyone, except Claire. Claire they could trust. Max, Alan had insisted, should know nothing, not even the facts about his arrest, trial, and hearings, until later. Perhaps never.

"I'm full, mom," Chris said. "Can I go play with my new Frisbee now?"

"It's my Frisbee, too," Karen corrected.

"Now listen, you two ragamuffins." Alan reached out and grasped one hand of each. "I got that Frisbee for both of you. I want you to share it. Besides, you can't play Frisbee by yourself, anyway. Is that clear?"

There were groans and sighs from both sides of the table.

"Say 'Yes, dad,'" Alexis scolded, "And 'Thank you.'"

"Yes, dad," they both sighed, "Thank you." Karen looked at her, "Can I go now, mom?"

"Ask your dad," she replied, coolly.

"Okay." Alan released their hands, "You can play with it in the backyard, but stay away from the pool." Karen and Chris bolted from the table and headed through the kitchen towards the dining room, chattering loudly.

"If they wake Aaron up, I'll kill them." Alexis spooned sugar into her coffee.

After a lull, Alan said, "You cooked a good dinner."

"Thanks. Considering the entire kitchen is packed away, it wasn't bad." She thought ahead to the quick junk food Alan would cook for himself in the new house. She would worry about his meals for a long time, always the solicitous housewife.

"I picked up the airplane tickets and arranged a car for you at the airport in San Francisco. A station wagon. It'll take you about three or four hours to make the drive, I figure. If you arrive in San Francisco at one, you ought to be in Mendocino before six, at the latest."

"I must be crazy, traveling with two noisy brats, a seven-month-old baby, and a crotchety old nanny."

"You'd better get used to it." He lifted his coffee cup. They had postponed the decision about the custody of the children until everything else was settled. Besides, there was no hurry. In the last few days, though, he had dropped hints about his own decision.

"By the way, if you haven't finished packing all the stuff here, just leave it. I'll do it."

"I've almost finished. Except for the kids' clothes." All the boxes would go to the new house. Alan would store their things in one of the empty bedrooms; later, when the separation was a fact and she had found a place of her own, the boxes could be moved.

"I think Karen suspects," Alan said.

"How? All I've said is that we're going on a holiday while the movers are working."

"She asked me why you were putting your things in separate boxes from mine."

"That's funny, she got quite indignant when I packed her toys in the same box with Chris's."

Alan sipped his coffee again and then looked down thoughtfully for a moment. "I'm going to miss them."

"Alan—" She reached across the table and took his hand. "How many times do I have to tell you? You are their father. You will always be their father. They'll always need you as a father. I cannot and will not take that from them." She squeezed his fingers, "I know what you've decided. You're going to give me custody, aren't you?"

He nodded. "Yeah. That's best for them."

"If that's what you want, then so be it. I'm not asking you for it, just remember that. And whenever you want, whenever they want, you'll be together. I promise you."

There were loud, angry shouts from the backyard.

"Damn them." Alexis glanced in that direction as Aaron's crying started from the nursery. "And there goes the baby."

"With those three, you've got a rough job ahead. I'll always be around when you need help, though."

"Good." She let go of his hand and smiled. "In that case, you can start right now. What they need is a good whipping."

Alan laughed, pushed his chair back, and got up. "You mean, I do a better job of that than you?"

"You use a belt, I only use a switch," she smiled.

"Then I guess it's time you tried using both."

She watched him cross the kitchen into the dining room. He moved calmly, without her kind of angry rush. In the children's adolescent years to come, she would need his firm but gentle way of leading them. When he had gone, she got up and began clearing the table. Instead of the sound of a whipping from the backyard, she heard a sudden burst of laughter. She set the dessert dishes down and started towards the back of the house. At the sliding glass door in the living room, she saw Alan on the lawn with the kids. He was beside Chris, demonstrating how to throw a Frisbee. She pushed the door open and stepped out onto the patio.

"Curve your arm around it this way," Alan tucked Chris's arm around the Frisbee. "That's right."

"Oh, daddy," Karen said from across the lawn, tugging dramatically at her T-shirt, "what do you expect from a midget?"

"Cool it, Karen," Alan said, "he'll get it right."

"Shut up, Karen," Chris said in deep concentration.

Alexis closed the door quietly behind herself and stood watching. Strange, their last night together was to be like any other: a noisy meal, a game with the kids, nothing out of the ordinary. And as usual with Alan, not even the necessity of a spanking. Seventeen years, the better part of their lives, should have been ushered out with more flourish.

"Now use your whole arm and let your wrist curve out with it. Let it go nice and easy." Alan stepped back. With concentrated effort, Chris sent the plastic saucer sailing off towards Karen.

"I did it!" Chris shouted.

"You see!" Alan laughed. The Frisbee dropped to the ground a few feet from Karen's feet. "All it takes is a little technique and a little confidence." He glanced back, caught sight of her near the door and smiled. She returned the smile.

"I'll do it now!" Karen retrieved the Frisbee from the grass. Alexis leaned back against the door. In time the wound will heal, she thought. It will close and heal like any other wound; but now, losing him had all the pain and grief of a death. Karen sent the Frisbee gliding low over the ground towards Chris.

"Is that right, daddy?" she called.

"Perfect! You've got it!"

"It's my turn!" Chris darted for the Frisbee. Honest, diligent, brilliant at his work, a little stodgy, sometimes peevish, always sensitive to small things—she watched him against the dark foliage of the garden shrubbery, hands on his hips, smiling—a protective, loving father, a loving husband for as long as the love had lasted, faithful until his nature had pulled him in his own direction.

She looked up towards the tops of the cypress trees at the far end of the pool. They had grown four feet since they had moved in. And cypresses grow slowly. A good man, she thought and smiled to herself. And, God knows, a good man is hard to find.

Alan coasted down the drive, came to a stop under the carport, and turned off the ignition. Alexis's station wagon was parked on the left. He sat for a moment listening through the open window to the chirp of a bird in the trees. He had always welcomed the quiet when he pulled into the carport after work and turned off the ignition. They had chosen this house for that very reason, its quiet isolation from the street. For the first time, though, it had the feeling of stillness about it. Alan reached for his briefcase, then remembered he had left it at the office on purpose. He would not tackle any paperwork this evening, his first evening alone. He got out and crossed to the back door. Banjo appeared around the corner and came towards him, wagging his tail. He looked relieved to see someone. Alan bent down and scratched his head. "What's wrong, fella, have they gone?" Banjo looked up at him and whimpered. Alan turned the key in the lock and held open the door. "It's okay, come on in." Alexis had forbidden the kids to let the dog into the house at dinner time. It was one of her rules they never broke. Banjo hesitated doubtfully, then scampered by into the utility room. In the breakfast area, Alan looked around at the empty kitchen. On the counter, he noticed a dinner plate with silverware wrapped in a paper napkin in the center. He crossed to the plate and saw the note under the silverware. *Dearest, your dinner is in the fridge. Please heat it in the oven before eating, it will be terrible cold. I left Banjo's food in the sack in the utility room. Also, Mr. Hendricks phoned to say the movers will be here at eight tomorrow morning. Count on ten. There are clean towels for the night in the bathroom, and clean sheets on the bed. Don't forget to pack them tomorrow. And please, please get a good night's rest. Don't stay up all night worrying about us or yourself or the bloody fu-*

ture. It will work out for ALL of us. Do I still sound like a nagging housewife? We'll phone from the inn tomorrow. Rest well. We love you more than you will ever know, X, Alexis. Below that, the children had each written a line. *I will take a pik*—Karen had inked out the rest of the word, then continued in her neatly measured longhand—*a picture of the seals and bring you some shells. Love, Karen.* Chris, obviously with Alexis's help, had written in his huge, crooked newly learned longhand: *I took my Frisbee. Love, Chris.* The S's were backwards. Alan folded the note, put it in his pocket, and opened the refrigerator door with a feeling of sudden helplessness. There were foil plates of fried chicken, green beans, corn, and muffins on the otherwise empty shelves. He stared at the food under its plastic-wrap covers. At that moment the last thing he wanted was food, even though it was his favorite meal. On his way through the dining room he paused to look at the boxes stacked against the wall. He continued on, listening to the sounds of Banjo's unclipped nails on the bare floor. It was 5:05. He stood just inside the archway and surveyed the living room. The larger pieces of furniture were still in place, but the small things were gone. He sat down at the far end of the sofa. Banjo came towards him, wagging his tail, looking puzzled. "Kind of quiet around here, isn't it?" He scratched the dog's head. He kept on scratching, realizing he had come to rest here on the sofa with nothing better to do. He could read a book or his medical journals if he knew what box they were in. He could listen to the stereo if the equipment hadn't been packed away. He could sleep, except for the fact that he wasn't sleepy.

The only sounds in the house were Banjo's rapid breathing and the ticktock of Alexis's grandfather clock in the foyer. He remembered a similar silence: the quiet he had felt in his parents' bedroom that afternoon ten years before, the day after his mother had died, when he sat alone in their room and saw all her familiar things still about. A feeling of absence after a final departure; the eerie lifelessness of a place when the human beings who have dwelt there finally depart. He felt edgy. What was he to do? He could sit here scratching the dog's head for the next five hours. He might go to a movie.

Abruptly, he stood up. What he could not do was stay here alone in this house. He would drive up to the new house and plan for tomorrow's move. "Say, how would you like to take a drive up to your new house?" he asked Banjo. Banjo wagged his tail. On the back porch, Alan poured out a heap of dry dogfood into Banjo's bowl, waited for him to eat, then called him hurriedly to the open driver's door of his car. "Come on, boy, this time you can ride up front."

Ten minutes later, Alan swung into the newly bricked circular drive and came to a stop before the plain but massive oak door. Except for the small spaces of unlandscaped ground on either side of the drive, the facade of the house looked finished. Alexis had hunted down the big antique oak door over a period of months. It looked solid and elegant. Alan got out with Banjo at his side and walked into the marble-floored foyer. In the living room, the afternoon sun slanting through the sliding glass doors at the far end warmed the wood floor and the white plaster walls with a deep rich yellow. It was 5:40. They would be arriving at the inn about now. He stood at the glass doors overlooking the patio and let his eye sweep across the stone-walled terrace to the pool area at the lower end of the lot. Alexis had wanted to plant the terraces so as to have something blooming at all times of the year. She had talked endlessly of the garden, the first one she would be able to plant from scratch. But it was huge, bare, and lifeless. Later, maybe, when there was time, he could hire a landscape artist to fill the spaces.

Maybe Stephen would know what to plant. It wouldn't hurt to phone him. The lowering sun was hot on his face. He drew in a deep breath and felt a curious numbness come over him. Except for Banjo, the house was entirely empty, silent. It would never—except on the children's occasional visits to that virtual stranger they obligingly called "daddy"—it would never be really noisy again. Slowly Alan walked towards the corridor leading to the bedrooms. He tried to turn his attention to planning where he would place the furniture tomorrow but realized he didn't much care. All he had brought up this evening from the old house was the silence and the children's dog. He turned his back on the small, pale blue room that was to have been Karen's. He rested his forehead against the opposite wall of the corridor, closed his eyes, and tried to frame the word *alone* with a single meaning. He could not. It spread out boundlessly and embraced his entire life. He was now a husband without a wife, a father without children, a homosexual without a lover. He was one of those successful Beverly Hills bachelors with a big house and a little dog, like Jimmy Cagle. He stepped back from the wall and looked down at Banjo whimpering expectantly at his feet. The whole wonderful circus had packed up and gone, leaving the freak show behind.

He smiled at Banjo. The whole wonderful circus but one: an old man whiling away the last crotchety years of his life in a rest home by the sea. Funny, Alan thought, at least we have something in common now. We're both alone. "How about another ride?" he asked Banjo.

Again, the ragged little mongrel whimpered and squirmed.

Alan turned back down the corridor, heading for the front door. Max would be finished with dinner when he got there. They could sit on the verandah, have coffee, talk about the old man's arthritis, maybe take a stroll along the palisade. He had not visited Max in several weeks, had not really wanted to since the hearings began. He dreaded the old man's intuitive questions.

Forty-five minutes later, Max turned onto the sidewalk running through the park along the palisade and looked back in the direction of the Georgian behind them. "What time do you have?"

"Five after seven." Alan glanced out towards the horizon where the huge autumn sun hung over the rim of the Pacific Ocean.

"Let's go back now, son. I have a game of backgammon with Sylvia Baehr at seven-thirty." For the second time, the old man's eyes scrutinized his face, puzzled.

"Sure. Whatever you say." Alan turned. Together they began retracing their steps. For the last fifteen minutes, they had talked of Max's arthritis; then, as usual, silence had fallen. In another five minutes, they would be back at the Georgian and it would be too late. Alan kept his eyes on the big yellow disk behind the haze over the sea.

"Where's Alexis? I thought she always has dinner for you at seven."

"Not tonight."

Max glanced at him, "Why? Where is she?"

"In Mendocino. She took the kids up to Mendocino."

"For what? I thought you were moving tomorrow."

"Dad." He took Max's arm and stopped him. "I have something to tell you."

The old man turned to him with a look of alarm. "Tell me what?"

"Alexis and I are getting a divorce."

There was a long silence as Max stared at him, expressionless. The fronds of the palms overhead moved in the breeze off the ocean. "A divorce?" The word sounded enormous on the old man's lips.

"We're only going to separate, at first. The divorce will come later."

Stunned, Max turned and started off down the sidewalk.

"Dad," Alan called to him.

The old man muttered something to himself in Yiddish.

A moment later, Alan caught up with him. "It's the best thing for both of us. We both agreed on it."

"I knew something was wrong. Back in December, I knew. I thought you had fixed everything."

"I tried. We both tried. It's not something we can fix."

Max turned away towards a park bench, dragging his cane behind him on the walk. "I want to sit down," he said. He lowered himself to the bench and looked out towards the sea.

The bottom edge of the sun touched the rim of the ocean. Alan followed him to the bench and sat down, three feet away at the end. The worst, Alan realized, was still to come. For the moment, the two of them watched the fiery yellow ball soften to pink. Then Max gave a heavy sigh.

"Do you want to know why?" Alan's voice quavered. He felt suddenly like a small delinquent boy.

"I thought you had fixed everything."

The bottom of the sun dipped into the ocean. "I'm a homosexual," he said. He sat forward and rested his hands on the edge of the bench. Three feet away, Max sat motionless and silent. "I'm gay, dad."

"I heard you, son," Max said softly, "I'm not deaf."

Alan realized he did not know where to go next. After a while, he said, "I found out a little over a year and a half ago. It happend slowly, over a period of time. I don't know why it happened. It just did." He heard the apology in his voice. He had sworn on the drive out that he would not apologize.

Max muttered something to himself in Yiddish again.

Alan sat up. "I don't speak Yiddish, dad, you know that," he blurted out, unable to hide the anger in his voice.

Absently, the old man leaned forward with his hands gripping his cane. "I thought of everything," he said heavily, "everything but this."

"Well, now you know."

"You're a grown man, Alan. You have a wife and three children."

Alan averted his face. It was pointless trying to explain. They were worlds apart.

"Do you *want* to be that?"

"I have no choice. I am."

"You and Alexis were happy together, I thought."

"We were. But not now."

"She doesn't want to live with you like that."

"She's a human being. She's a woman. What's in it for her?"

"It's a terrible thing—" Max looked away and caught his breath, "It's a terrible thing to come to at your age. Your mother would never have understood."

He sat back, feeling the rigid wall between them. "She doesn't have to."

"No. I'm glad of that." Max lowered his head against his hands on the cane for a moment, then sat up. "I'm sorry for you, I'm sorry for Alexis, and I'm sorry for the children." With his gaze still on the lowering sun, he slowly rose to his feet. "I want to go back now. I'm tired." His voice was heavy and defeated.

Alan watched him shuffle across the narrow strip of grass towards the street. He had expected a paternal Jewish complaint, but not this. Not silence and retreat. He had not asked for approval or acceptance, only a fair hearing. With all the facts out in front. The old man could condemn but not dismiss him. With a rush of anger, he got to his feet and started after Max, who was just reaching the pedestrian crosswalk. "You might as well know all of it, dad." He drew up alongside as the old man stepped from the curb, balancing himself with his cane.

Max started slowly across the wide avenue fronting the Georgian.

"You can make your own judgment! But at least make it with all the facts!" He fixed his gaze determinedly on the green pedestrian light thirty feet away. "A year and a half ago, I met a young man . . ."

Restrained by Max's slow, halting pace across the avenue, he began the story from the beginning. He talked quickly, giving only the facts, trying not to confuse the issue with feelings. His meeting with Brad, his own double life, his refusal to confront himself until it was too late.

The pedestrian light had turned red and then green again when they reached the opposite sidewalk. With his head lowered, Max turned right towards the Georgian, a half block away.

"That afternoon, I went to the intensive care unit where they had him . . ." Alan told him of Brad's request and his failure to comply.

Max paused, looked up at him for a moment, perplexed, then continued walking. His breathing was rapid and heavy now.

But even then, Alan went on, he had not accepted his homosexuality as a fact; not until Stephen and he had fallen in love, not till months later when love had taught him what sex had only threatened him with.

When they reached the Georgian, Max took hold of the brass banister and started up the front steps, making soft inarticulate sounds as he went, keeping his face averted. Alan followed, telling him everything now, realizing that it felt cleansing to tell it. ". . . and then after Aaron was born, and I knew I could not see Stephen again, there was a period —I can't describe it—of despair."

Instead of continuing to the front door, Max turned down the verandah towards the table and chairs at the far end.

"I compromised with Alexis by having sex with men, with strangers, in out-of-the-way places," he hurried on, editing out the question of his feelings. "One afternoon, I went to a gay porno house. A movie theater." He waited for Max to lower himself into one of the wicker armchairs.

"Yes, I'm listening," the old man said after a moment. His voice was distant and faint, weighted with dread.

Alan lowered himself into the armchair next to Max. Beyond the palisade, the color had drained from the sky over the sea. "The police were there," he said, "I was arrested."

"I see." His father's voice was now almost inaudible. He leaned forward and rested his head in his hand.

"A month later, I was tried and put on probation," he went on, glossing over the medical assurances hearing, "and now, there's one

270

more hearing. Before my own hospital board. They'll review my hospital privileges. Arnold Berrey wants me off the staff. I guess this will be the hardest one. This time, I'm going to be tried by people whom I know, by my own colleagues. Berrey will force me to defend myself as a homosexual. I'm not sure I can do that." He glanced at Max, then went on, aware now that the old man was weeping. "The fact is, I'm ashamed of what I am. I've tried, but so far I can't defend it, even to myself."

Slowly, Max lifted his head from his hand. His eyes, Alan saw, were fixed vacantly on the wrought-iron railing in front of them. In the glare of passing headlights on the street, he saw the tears wash down the old man's face. "Like being a Jew?" Max asked softly.

Alan stared at him, surprised. "What do you mean?"

"Forgive me. I'm an old man now. Sometimes I don't see things clearly at first. Some things in life are merely given, I guess. Like being born Jewish."

He looked away, stung. "I'm not ashamed of being a Jew."

"You were as a boy. You were deeply ashamed. As a man, you have found ways to appear gentile."

"If I were ashamed, I would have changed my name."

Max nodded and turned to him. "Your Uncle Aaron did just that."

"He what?"

"Changed his name. In Austria, before the war, your Uncle Aaron was a respectable Jewish lawyer. When the Germans took Poland, he saw the handwriting on the wall. He came to me and said he was going to change his name and leave Vienna. I told him he could change many things, but he could not change some things. He was a man, he was my brother, and he was a Jew. That would always be." Absently the old man turned to look towards the sea. "He would not listen. He changed his name to Franz Heydrich. He falsified his papers and moved to Salzburg. He did not look Jewish." Max lowered his eyes, then shook his head sadly. "Heydrich. Of all names to please them with. He was arrested in forty-three. He denied before the Gestapo that he was a Jew. He played the cello, said he was a cellist from Innsbruck, and a Catholic. They did not believe him. They sent him to Auschwitz with his cello." Max lifted his hand and covered his face for a moment. "Years later, I met a man who survived. He was with Aaron on the train to Auschwitz. He told me Aaron arrived insisting to Mengele that he was a gentile."

"Dad—" Alan reached out towards Max's arm.

"Let me finish. You must know this now. That winter, he played in the death camp orchestra, trying to gain time, When the time came, though, he still denied what he was. By then, only he believed his lie. He went to the gas chamber denying even to the Jews with him that he was one of them." Max's face went suddenly ashen. He stared out towards the street, reliving an old pain. "He was the only one I know of who died saying that," he said after a moment.

Alan took a deep breath. "You never told me."

"I was ashamed to tell. Your mother was ashamed to tell."

"I always thought you both honored him so."

"He was a man, my brother, and a Jew. But out of so many millions, I think he was the only one who really died in vain." Max turned, caught his eye and held it for a moment with a frightened expression. "You also have his blue eyes." He reached towards Alan's hand lying on the arm of his chair.

Alan looked down at the soft, pale hand resting on his. "I was angry when you left me in the park," he said. "I followed you back here to have a fight. I wanted you to read the Law to me, the way you used to."

"Back in the park, I forgot the Law. The Law says you must not yoke a small animal to a large one. There are many kinds of life. The Law was given to protect it, not destroy it."

He let his hand lie under Max's hand. He could not remember when his father had last touched him, or when he had touched his father. Maybe Max had touched him as a child; he could not remember. "I understand, dad." He freed his hand, reached around the old man's shoulder, drew him close, and held him.

"Be yourself, son, be at peace," Max murmured, patting him on the back, "some things are merely given." Alan took a deep, freeing breath of cool ocean air. For a moment, without effort, they held. Then Max moved back and touched his wrist. "Is that watch right, son?"

"I set it this morning." He looked at it. "It's seven thirty-five."

"Then Mrs. Baehr is waiting. She cheats when I come late." He reached for his cane and started up. Alan took his arm and helped him to his feet. "What are you doing on Sunday?" Max asked.

"Nothing." Alan shrugged and smiled. "I'm free."

"Good. So am I." He began moving towards the front door, "I've never been to the Getty Museum up the road. Have you been to the Getty Museum?"

"No. Never."

"I'll take you to lunch first. You'll probably need a good meal to get you through the museum." He switched his cane to his left hand and reached for the heavy brass door handle.

Alan took the handle and opened the door. "You used to like seafood. There's a good place up towards Malibu."

"The red snapper out here isn't as good as the kind we used to get even in Detroit, but it's passable. I like snapper."

Alan took hold of Max's arm and led him into the lobby. "I'll phone the museum tomorrow. We need reservations for the Getty. Say eleven-thirty?"

"Eleven." Max grinned. "Old folks need to eat by noon."

Alan pressed his arm and smiled again. "Eleven sharp." He let go. Max turned and started towards an elderly woman seated at a table across the lobby.

On the steps outside, Alan stopped to watch another elderly couple strolling under one of the old-fashioned lamps in the park across the street. He recalled the winter night when he walked the length of the park to the Santa Monica pier. It seemed a lifetime ago.

He went down the steps and saw his car by the curb. Banjo stood in the passenger seat waiting, alert and excited.

When they returned, even Banjo would have to go. He belonged to the kids.

Alan turned back in the opposite direction towards the crosswalk to the park on the palisade. By now, Alexis, the kids, and Claire would have finished dinner, Alexis would be having trouble stopping the kids from running wild through the lobby, and Claire would be with Aaron in the room. He knew the scene by heart.

He started down the curving sidewalk between the tall palms. A few strollers came towards him out of the darkness. In the excitement of their adventure, Karen and Chris would run wild for a while. Eventually, Alexis would have to spank them. She would use her hand rather than a belt. Then put them to bed. When she got the kids to sleep, she would go down to the bar in the inn, sit at a table by the window overlooking the sea, and have a drink. Alone. She would think of him, wonder where he was, whether he had heated his food before eating it.

He looked up through the fronds of the palm trees. In the cloudless, moonless September sky he saw the shallow end of the Milky Way. She would walk on the big terrace over the sea and see the same sky.

At the Senior Citizens' Recreation Center, he read the familiar sign over the building. Uncle Aaron would have been seventy-one now, if he had survived. Franz Heydrich. He had never known about Uncle Aaron.

Bewildered, he moved on and quickened his pace. Today was the twenty-seventh. The hearing was set for ten o'clock on the morning of the thirtieth. Berrey and Marks had urged the board to hold the hearing as soon as possible. There would be seven, maybe eight men on the board. And a lawyer presiding. The majority would come to it unprejudiced. He himself would sit with his lawyer in the front of the room. There would be witnesses in his favor. Stephen would be there.

At the top of the ramp leading down to the Santa Monica pier, Alan stopped to look at the twinkling lights of the merry-go-round, shooting galleries, and concessions, at the people coming towards him up the ramp. His eye rested on the spot a few yards down the ramp where he had seen the graffiti scrawled: *Kill faggots.* The vivid green paint was blurred now by the passage of feet. His shock and embarrassment were blurred, too. Time had done that. The shame was still there, though. It would be with him for a long time to come. He had been born two generations too early to be self-assured like the young nowadays.

Raus mit den Juden. Perhaps, as his father said, it was the same. With Uncle Aaron though, the Nazis succeeded. Uncle Aaron went down with nothing, not even the dignity of belief in himself, alone, in self-contempt.

Alan turned quickly towards the crosswalk and pressed the pedestrian button on the street light. At the hearing on Friday, he would try not to look as though he was apologizing for something awful that had happened to him in his childhood. Stephen had made that point on the telephone three days ago.

The light went green and the pedestrian sign went from "Wait" to "Walk." Halfway across the street, he felt the vibrator of his beeper throb in his suit coat pocket. He had forgotten about the beeper in the last two and a half hours, forgotten that he was on call in Donald's place. He saw an empty phone booth on the opposite corner and quickened his steps. More often than not, night calls were matters of simple medication.

He fished out a dime, closed the door, and dialed.

"Beverly Medical," the woman on his service answered.

"This is Doctor Stegman. I just had a beep from you."

"Yes, doctor. Dr. Sherman from the hospital is trying to reach you."

"Right. He's in the emergency section. Can you ring through over there and connect me please?"

"I'll try." She put him on hold. If Sherman was calling, it could be anything. "I've got Doctor Sherman on the line." The service operator came back on.

"Alan?" Sherman's voice sounded relieved.

"Yes, John."

"We had a patient brought in about thirty minutes ago. A forty-five-year-old male. He was involved in an automobile wreck. We examined him and found blunt trauma in the left lower side of his abdomen. There's also considerable gross hematuria with signs of blood in his peritoneum. We think he may need emergency surgery."

"Is he in shock, John?"

"No. He seems stable so far."

"Okay." He looked at his watch. "I'll be there within thirty min-

274

utes. I'm out in Santa Monica. I suggest, in the meantime, you do an IVP and try to locate the source of the bleeding."

"Right."

"Be there as soon as I can."

"Right." Sherman disconnected.

Alan returned the receiver to the hook, pushed open the booth door, and started down the sidewalk towards his car.

He would leave Banjo in the car at the hospital. From what Sherman said, it sounded like major surgery. With gross hematuria and blood in the peritoneum, there would be problems. If he got there in time, if there was to be surgery, he would get Johannson to assist. Johannson was good. Alan quickened his pace. He would be up late. Tomorrow, the movers were coming. He'd have to get up early, finish packing, and show them where things should go.

He took his car keys out to unlock the driver's door. The surgical procedure would most likely last until the early hours of the morning. He'd be a mess when the movers came. Tomorrow was Stephen's day off. He might call Stephen first thing in the morning. Ask him to come over and help. They could begin there.

Alan opened the door, stooped down, and pushed Banjo from the driver's seat. "Move over, boy," he said, fighting off a barrage of licks, "we've got places to go. *Fast.*" He started the motor and pulled out into the street. Friday was two days away. He would face that when it came. Now, he had a man on his hands with a bleeding gut. He would repair that, if he could. He would do what he knew *how* to do, save a human life. The rest he would tackle on Friday.